ANTHEM

SCHOLASTIC PRESS

DEBORAH WILES

ANT

HEM

**THE
SIXTIES
TRILOGY**

BOOK THREE

Library of Congress Cataloging-in-Publication Data available

ISBN 978-0-545-10609-2

10 9 8 7 6 5 4 3 2 1   19 20 21 22 23

Printed in the U.S.A.   23
First edition, October 2019

The text type was set in Futura
Book design by Phil Falco

for the music makers

TRY TO LOVE ONE ANOTHER RIGHT NOW

From "Get Together" by The Youngbloods

University of California, Berkeley student Mario Savio, a former SNCC volunteer during Freedom Summer in Mississippi, addresses his fellow students at a free speech rally at Berkeley in 1964.

"And you've got to put your bodies upon the gears and upon the wheels . . . upon the levers, upon all the apparatus, and you've got to make it **STOP!**"

Mario Savio, co-founder of the Berkeley Free Speech Movement

"We have a saying in the movement that we don't trust anybody over thirty."

Jack Weinberg, Berkeley Free Speech Movement, 1964

SIGNALS IMPLY A 'BIG BANG' UNIVERSE

The New York Times front page, May 21, 1965, announcing the May 20, 1965 discovery by scientists Arno Penzias and Robert Wilson

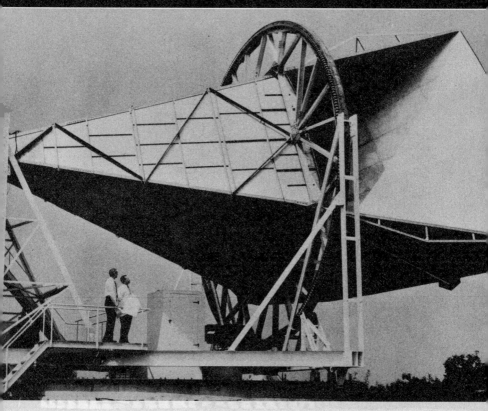

The Holmdel Horn Antenna was built in 1959 to make the first satellite phone call. Scientists at Bell Telephone Labs have observed with this telescope what may be remnants of an explosion that gave birth to the universe.

SO WE MUST BE READY TO FIGHT IN VIETNAM, BUT THE ULTIMATE VICTORY WILL DEPEND UPON THE HEARTS AND THE MINDS OF THE PEOPLE WHO ACTUALLY LIVE OUT THERE.

President Lyndon Baines Johnson, May 4, 1965

Women and children crouch in a muddy canal as they take cover from intense Vietcong fire at Bao Trai, about twenty miles west of Saigon, January 1, 1966. Paratroopers (background) of the U.S. 173rd Airborne Brigade escorted the South Vietnamese civilians through a series of firefights during the U.S. assault on a Vietcong stronghold.

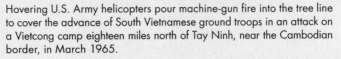

Hovering U.S. Army helicopters pour machine-gun fire into the tree line to cover the advance of South Vietnamese ground troops in an attack on a Vietcong camp eighteen miles north of Tay Ninh, near the Cambodian border, in March 1965.

A young boy walks with adult protesters during an anti–Vietnam War demonstration on Fifth Avenue, New York City, October 17, 1965.

THERE SEEMS TO BE MANY PARALLELS

that can be drawn between treatment of negroes and treatment of women. Women we've talked with often find themselves within a kind of common-law caste system that operates, sometimes subtly, placing them in a position of inequality to men in work and personal situations . . .

From "Sex and Caste, A Kind of Memo" by former SNCC Freedom workers Casey Hayden and Mary King, 1965

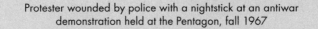

Protester wounded by police with a nightstick at an antiwar demonstration held at the Pentagon, fall 1967

"If a man like Malcolm X could change and repudiate racism, if I myself and other former Muslims can change, if young whites can change, then there is hope for America."

Eldridge Cleaver, *Soul on Ice,* **1968**

"I've had enough of someone else's propaganda . . . I'm for truth, no matter who tells it. I'm for justice, no matter who it is for or against. I'm a human being, first and foremost, and as such I'm for whoever and whatever benefits humanity as a whole."

The Autobiography of Malcolm X, **1965**

MALCOLM X MURDERED

A week after he was fire-bombed out of his Queen's home, Black Nationalist leader Malcolm X was shot to death shortly after 3 P.M. yesterday as he started to address a Washington Heights rally of some 400 of his devoted followers.

The New York Daily News, February 22, 1965

Ed White became the first American to walk in space, June 3, 1965, starting on the Gemini 4 mission's third orbit at 3:45 P.M. EDT over the Pacific Ocean near Hawaii, ending twenty-three minutes later over the Gulf of Mexico.

ON THE HEELS OF OPERATION PIERCE ARROW, A RESPONSE TO THE GULF OF TONKIN INCIDENT IN 1964, AND AT THE INSISTENCE OF A WIDER RESPONSE BY MILITARY CHIEFS, U.S. PRESIDENT LYNDON JOHNSON APPROVES OPERATION ROLLING THUNDER, THE FIRST SUSTAINED AERIAL BOMBING ASSAULT TARGETING NORTH VIETNAM AND A MAJOR EXPANSION OF THE U.S. INVOLVEMENT IN THE WAR IN VIETNAM.

CHINA

NORTH VIETNAM

Dien Bien Phu

Hanoi ⊛

Haiphong

Gulf of Tonkin

LAOS

HAINAN (CHINA)

Mekong River

Demilitarized Zone (DMZ)

Khe Sanh

Hue

Da Nang

South China Sea

THAILAND

SOUTH VIETNAM

Tonlé Sap

Nha Trang

CAMBODIA

Saigon ⊛

Gulf of Thailand

Can Tho

Mekong River Delta

100 MI
100 KM

ASIA

VIETNAM

U.S.

PACIFIC OCEAN

WATTS RIOTS 1965

A traffic stop escalated into six days of rioting in the Watts neighborhood of Los Angeles, leaving thirty-four dead, over one thousand injured, and four thousand under arrest.

After visiting the area of the recent riots and talking with hundreds of people of all walks of life, it is my opinion that these riots grew out of the depths of despair which afflict a people who see no way out of their economic dilemma. There are serious doubts that the white community is in any way concerned or willing to accommodate their needs. There is also a growing disillusionment and resentment toward the Negro middle class and the leadership which it has produced. This ever-widening breach is a serious factor which leads to the feeling that they are alone in their struggle and must resort to any method to gain attention to their plight. The nonviolent movement of the South has meant little to them since we have been fighting for rights which theoretically are already theirs.

Dr. Martin Luther King, Jr., about the Watts Riots, August 1965

National Guard on duty in Watts, Los Angeles, August 1965

Cesar Chavez, farm worker, labor organizer, and leader of the California grape pickers strike, speaks from his union office in 1965.

WHEN THE MAN WHO FEEDS THE WORLD BY TOILING IN THE FIELDS IS HIMSELF DEPRIVED OF THE BASIC RIGHTS OF FEEDING, SHELTERING, AND CARING FOR HIS OWN FAMILY, THE WHOLE COMMUNITY OF MAN IS SICK.

Cesar Chavez

The U.S. 173rd Airborne Brigade on a jungle "Search and Destroy" patrol in Phuoc Tuy Province, Vietnam, June 1966

Summer of Love 1967, Golden Gate Park, San Francisco, California

"We're more popular than Jesus now."

John Lennon, 1966

"The clothing and grooming of the student should reflect his serious attitude toward school and his own person. Two extremes are to be avoided: both a careless, untidy appearance, and a vain, effeminate use of extreme fashions. What the school seeks to promote in the student is a clean, neat, well-groomed, manly appearance."

from a California boy's high school dress code

"Tune In, Turn On, Drop Out."

Timothy Leary

Neither the Federal Executive Orders on fair employment, nor the Civil Rights Act which constitute the authority for this program for non-discrimination are relevant to the problems of homosexuals.

**June 9, 1965 letter from
U.S. Vice President Hubert Humphrey to
Frank Kameny, Mattachine Society**

A man gestures with his thumb down to an armed National Guardsman during a protest in the Newark Race Riots, Newark, New Jersey, July 14, 1967.

Newark Riots, July 1967

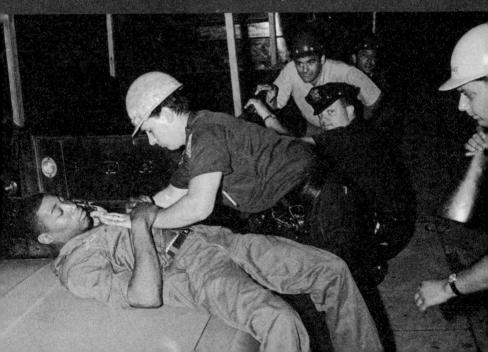

Two Newark, New Jersey, police officers arrested and beat a black cab driver on July 12, 1967, resulting in five days of rioting during which more than three thousand National Guardsmen and five hundred state troopers policed the city. Twenty-six people were killed, most of them African Americans, and hundreds were injured.

ON JULY 23, 1967, Detroit police officers raided a local establishment after hours where a party was going on to celebrate the return of two black servicemen from Vietnam. Rumors that the police were using excessive force and arresting all eighty-two partygoers resulted in five days of riots, during which thirty-three blacks and ten whites were killed, over one thousand were injured, and over seven thousand were arrested.

My solution to the problem would be to tell
[the North Vietnamese Communists] frankly that
they've got to draw in their horns and stop their
aggression or we're going to bomb them back into
the Stone Ages.

**General Curtis LeMay, Chief of Staff
of the United States Air Force, 1965**

This war has already stretched the generation gap so wide that it threatens to pull the country apart.

Senator Frank Church

1st Lt. Gary D. Jackson of Dayton, Ohio, carries a wounded South Vietnamese Ranger to an ambulance after a battle with the Vietcong during the *Tet* Offensive in the Cholon section of Saigon. Early on the morning of January 31, 1968, as Vietnamese celebrated the Lunar New Year, or *Tet* as it is known locally, Communist forces launched a wave of coordinated surprise attacks across South Vietnam. The campaign, one of the largest of the Vietnam War, led to intense fighting and heavy casualties in cities and towns across the South.

I THINK WE HAVE ALL UNDERESTIMATED THE SERIOUSNESS OF THIS SITUATION.

Deputy Secretary of State George Ball, 1965

As fellow troopers aid wounded comrades, the first sergeant of A Company, 101st Airborne Division, guides a medevac helicopter through the jungle foliage to pick up casualties suffered during a five-day patrol near Hue, April 1968.

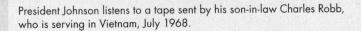
President Johnson listens to a tape sent by his son-in-law Charles Robb, who is serving in Vietnam, July 1968.

". . . I shall not seek, and I will not accept, the nomination of my party for another term as your president."

Lyndon Baines Johnson, U.S. president, March 31, 1968

U.S. National Guard troops block off Beale Street in Memphis, Tennessee, as civil rights marchers involved in a sanitation worker's strike pass by on March 29, 1968. It was the third consecutive march held by the group in as many days. Dr. Martin Luther King, Jr., who had left town after the first march, would soon return.

Like anybody, I would like to live a long life. Longevity has its place. But I'm not concerned about that now. I just want to do God's will. And He's allowed me to go up to the mountain. And I've looked over. And I've seen the Promised Land. I may not get there with you. But I want you to know tonight, that we, as a people, will get to the Promised Land!

Dr. Martin Luther King, Jr. speech delivered at the Mason Temple, Memphis, Tennessee, on April 3, 1968, one day before his assassination

"I think we can end
the divisions within
the United States.
What I think is quite
clear is that we can
work together . . . We
are a great country, a
selfless . . . and a
compassionate country . . .
So my thanks to all of
you and on to Chicago
and let's win there."

Robert F. Kennedy at the Ambassador Hotel after his
California presidential primary win and minutes
before his assassination, June 5, 1968

THE WHOLE WORLD WATC

Police and antiwar demonstrators in a melee near the Conrad Hilton Hotel on Chicago's Michigan Avenue, August 28, 1968, during the Democratic National Convention

E
D IS
HING!

Chant during antiwar protests at the Democratic National Convention, Chicago, Illinois, August 1968

It is easy to wax indignant over a bunch of clowns who try to disrupt operations of the guard in endeavoring to return peace to the streets in one of the city's most serious emergencies. These people know that President Johnson's bombing pause above the 20th parallel in Viet Nam has been productive of offers from Hanoi to engage in preliminary and conditional talks. The demonstrators must be working for communist North Viet Nam.

It is an outrage that this country has to deal with a second front at home against rioters and beatniks when its fighting men are risking death overseas.

Editorial in *The Chicago Tribune*, April 10, 1968

Truongan, South Vietnam, Nov. 16 — A group of South Vietnamese villagers reported today that a small American infantry unit killed 567 unarmed men, women and children as it swept through their hamlet on March 16, 1968.

They survived, they said, because they had been buried under the bodies of their neighbors.

Front page of *The New York Times*, November 17, 1969

IF YOU'RE NOT OUTRAGED, YOU'RE NOT PAYING ATTENTION!

"The Revolution Will Not Be Televised."
Gil Scott-Heron, composed in 1969

Peace-sign-flashing protesters in Grant Park, Chicago, during an antiwar demonstration at the Democratic National Convention, August 1968

A young army MP on duty during rioting at the Democratic
National Convention

An officer from the Chicago Police Department carries a young demonstrator, after he fainted in the lobby of the Conrad Hilton Hotel on Michigan Avenue during anti-Vietnam War protests outside the hotel, the site of the headquarters of the 1968 Democratic National Convention, August 26, 1968.

To be a Revolutionary is to be an Enemy of the State. To be arrested for this struggle is to be a Political Prisoner.

Bobby Seale, co-founder of the Black Panther Party, originally tried with the Chicago Seven (making the defendants the Chicago Eight), but so vocally opposed to his arrest while in court, the judge severed him from the case and tried him separately, 1968

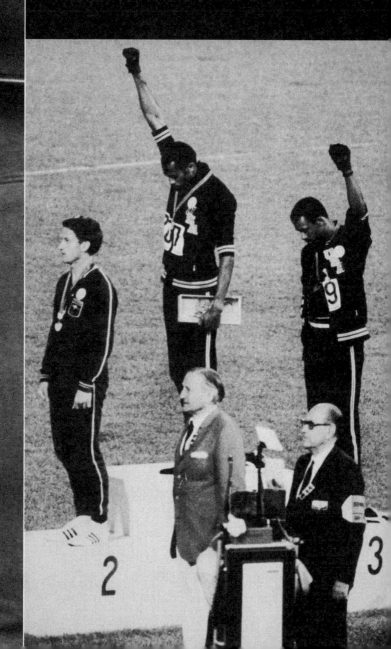

Gold medalist Tommie Smith and bronze medalist John Carlos in the 200-meter final raise black-gloved fists during the playing of the American national anthem at the medal ceremony on October 16 at the 1968 Summer Olympics in Mexico City.

RICHARD M. NIXON BECOMES PRESIDENT WITH 'SACRED COMMITMENT TO PEACE'

The Washington Post headline,
January 20, 1969

*Less than two hours later, however,
groups of militant and mostly youthful
demonstrators screamed anti-war slogans
and hurled rocks and beer cans at the closely
guarded Presidential limousine bearing Mr.
Nixon from the Capitol to the Inaugural
Parade reviewing stand at the White
House. A few small objects
hit the limousine.*

The Washington Post,
January 20, 1969

*From time to time, the shouts of anti-war
demonstrators gathered at Union Station,
three blocks away, could be faintly heard.
They repeatedly chanted verses and slogans,
such as 'Nixon, Agnew, you can't hide; we
charge you with genocide.' In all, opponents
of the President's Vietnam policies staged
three demonstrations, the largest of which
attracted more than 60,000 persons.*

The New York Times,
January 23, 1969

Protesting in front of the Federal Trade Commission headquarters during Richard Nixon's inauguration weekend, January 1969

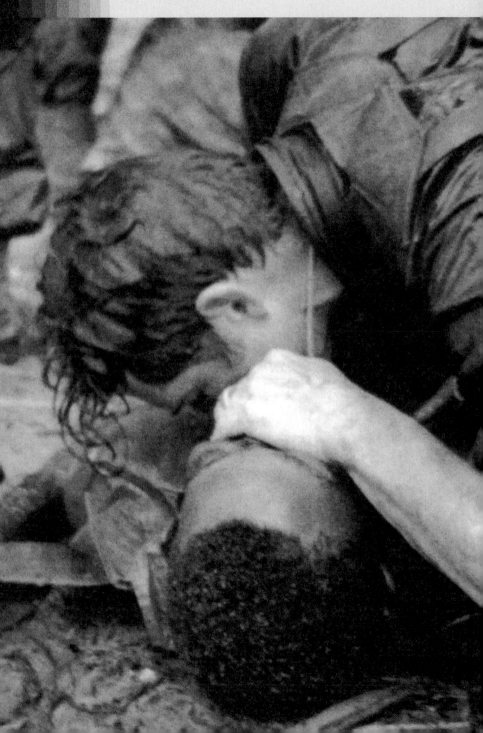

A medic of the 101st Airborne Division attempts to save the life of a buddy at Ap Bia Mountain, or Hamburger Hill, near South Vietnam's A Shau Valley on May 19, 1969.

For it seems now more certain than ever, that the
bloody experience of Vietnam is to end in a stalemate.
To say that we are closer to victory today is to believe
in the face of the evidence, the optimists who
have been wrong in the past.
Walter Cronkite "Report on Vietnam," CBS News, 1968

I'm not going to be the first American president to lose a war.
President Richard Nixon, 1969

"Since I have had a number of letters from people . . . asking me to warn readers, and, in the urbanely quaint words of one correspondent, 'Spell out what is happening on stage,' this I had better do. Well, almost, for spell it out I cannot, for this remains a family newspaper."
Clive Barnes reviewing the musical *Hair*
in *The New York Times*, April 30, 1968

The first Big Mac hamburger is sold by McDonald's in 1967 and costs forty-five cents.

"Let us begin the revolution and let us begin it with love: All of us, black, white, and gold, male and female, have it, within our power to create a world we could bear out of the desert we inhabit, for we hold our very fate in our hands."
Kate Millett, *Sexual Politics*, 1968

"What are the arguments against the draft? We hear it is unfair, immoral, discourages young men from studying, ruins their careers and their lives." [pause] "Picky, picky, picky."
Pat Paulsen on *The Smothers Brothers Comedy Hour*,
which was canceled by CBS in 1969 for being politically
controversial and critical of the U.S. involvement in Vietnam
and supportive of the emerging counterculture.

"Space . . . the final frontier."
Opening of *Star Trek*, which aired on
the NBC television network from 1966 to 1969

"In the future, everyone will be world famous for fifteen minutes."
Attributed to artist Andy Warhol, 1968

Dr. Christiaan Barnard performs the world's first human-to-human heart transplant on December 3, 1967, in Cape Town, South Africa.

Protesters for and against the draft resistance movement demonstrate outside the Arlington Street Church in Boston on January 29, 1968, as young men gather inside to turn in their draft cards. David Dellinger, chairman of the National Mobilization Committee to End the War in Vietnam, and a leader of the national draft resistance movement, accepted the cards along with others who counseled the young men in resisting the Selective Service System.

A young man sticks flowers into police gun barrels during an antiwar demonstration at the Pentagon, October 1967

*We deal with such things as the inner drama
of childhood . . . We deal with such things as getting
a haircut, or the feelings about brothers and sisters, and
the kind of anger that arises in simple family situations.
And we speak to it constructively.*

**Fred Rogers testifying before Congress, asking for funding
for *Mister Rogers' Neighborhood*, May 1, 1969**

*I grew up in the sixties watching B.B. King and
Tito Puente and Miles Davis and Coltrane, everybody, Marvin
Gaye, Jimi. And at the same time, with my left eye I was
watching Dolores Huerta, Cesar Chavez, Martin
Luther King, Malcolm X, Mother Teresa.*

Attributed to musician Carlos Santana

Sock it to me.

President Richard Nixon on *Laugh-In*, 1968

"NOW, YOU'RE EITHER ON THE BUS OR OFF THE BUS."

Author Ken Kesey

1

EVERYTHING THAT TOUCHES YOU

Written by Terry Kirkman
Performed by the Association
Recorded at Western Recorders, Hollywood, California, 1968
Drummer: Ted Bluechel, Jr. (concert)/Hal Blaine (studio)

Charleston, South Carolina
June 12, 1969

MOLLY

It's been so long since I've felt something.

You know how it is when your heart splits open. Blood spurts everywhere. You can slap your palms to your chest, you can clutch at your breast, but your heart won't be held. It struggles away from you, away from further damage. It won't be held, I tell you. It begins to dissolve, to disappear. Soon you will have no heart. Soon you will feel nothing.

This is how it is for me now. I survey the damage as I watch myself bleed to death. The mind can do that, you know.

Sometimes I try to talk myself out of it. "You're not bleeding to death, Molly."

But I am.

If Barry hadn't left, maybe I wouldn't feel this way. If the fight in our family hadn't been so awful, if we could have talked about it together . . . but yes, it was, and no, we couldn't have.

"He's eighteen. He can go where he wants, as long as it's not here," said Dad.

"He's your son!" sputtered Mom.

"My son will enlist in the army and do his patriotic duty, just as I did, or he will not live one more night under this roof!"

I just stood there. It was like watching television. Everything was happening right there in front of me, and there wasn't a thing I could do to change it.

"What is patriotic duty, Dad?" asked Barry. "Take a look at the news! You think what's happening in Vietnam is patriotic?"

My family is heartbreaking and the world is falling apart. I could make you a list.

Dad turns on Walter Cronkite every night after supper. The Battle of Hamburger Hill, the People's Army of Vietnam, the 101st Airborne, 72 Americans killed, 630 Vietcong, *and that's the way it is*, says Cronkite.

I want to leave the room, but the pictures on the television screen are so compelling. Angry people march in the streets, chanting, "Hey, Hey, LBJ! How Many Kids Did You Kill Today?" The police stand there like hulking monsters with gas masks and bayonets. Boys burn their draft cards. I can't look away.

"Traitors!" spits Dad. "I served with honor in Korea, for *this*?"

Dad runs his hands over his face like he's trying to scrub it clean of all the bad news. Then he goes to the kitchen to get his coffee before *Gunsmoke* comes on. Mom dumps a laundry basket full of clean towels onto the couch. They are still warm from the dryer. I tear May off the kitchen calendar and June stares at me. It's an anniversary month, a year since the argument. A year I haven't seen my brother.

When I was little, Barry would safety-pin a towel at my neck and let me jump off the coffee table into the pile of clean towels like Supergirl. "You're flying, Polka Dot!" And then he'd zoom me around the room on his shoulders.

But Barry is gone.

"The Communists are trying to take over the world!" Dad had yelled at Barry. "That's what they do! That's why we're in Vietnam!"

"*How* are the Communists going to take over the United States?" Barry yelled back.

"You never heard of the domino effect?" Dad's voice choked, he was so angry.

"Tell me about it!" I'd never heard Barry stand up to our dad like this, furious right back. "Tell me how the Communists are going to invade this country. Tell me we aren't killing innocent people. Tell me how it works, Dad. *Tell me!*"

Dad started for Barry, and Barry took a step back so quickly he stumbled. Dad stopped himself. Mom started up from the couch and then stopped *herself*. She put a hand on my shoulder like she was trying to protect Barry by protecting me.

I could still feel something then, and what I was feeling was terror. Terror that Dad would keep yelling, that Barry would keep yelling back, that a war was breaking out, right in our living room, that we were helpless against it, and hopeless against its outcome. I sat as still as a statue.

"The *Red Chinese* are right next door to Vietnam," said Dad, waving his arms. "There are a lot more of them than there are us. They're partners with the Russians — who now have the atomic bomb, may I remind you — and poof! No more Land of the Free, Home of the Brave, buddy boy. Don't you understand anything?"

"I understand *plenty*," said Barry. He shoved his hair out of his eyes. His hair that slicked back like a seal's when he swam all summer on the JCC swim team, the hair that got him suspended at school because it was longer than collar length, the hair that he'd defiantly stuffed under a wig in order to go to class — with all his buddies doing the same — so he could graduate.

"Then show some sense, or I'll show you the door!" said Dad.

"I can find the door by myself!" said Barry. He stalked away, away, away from us.

Wait! I wanted to call to him. *Come back!* But I couldn't move.

"And get a haircut!" Dad yelled after him.

Then there was silence. The clock over our couch that's shaped like a giant sun *tick-tick-ticked* in the silence.

No one believed Barry would leave us for good until he did.

His draft notice came in yesterday's mail. It was marked *Official Government Business*. It looked serious.

Mom hid it from Dad. "Not a word, missy!" she warned me. Then she turned up the volume on *Another World*, her favorite soap opera, and kept ironing. The iron hissed and steamed as she slammed it onto the collar of one of Dad's Sunday dress shirts.

"Mom," I ventured, hesitant. "I don't think you can hide something like this. It's an official government document."

Mom put the iron in its cradle, snapped off the television, and stared at the blank screen.

"Mom," I tried again. "You're scaring me. You could get in trouble. Barry could get in trouble. And maybe it isn't what we think it is."

Mom stiffened her shoulders, glanced at me, then stalked to the kitchen, where she fished the envelope out of the junk drawer. She coaxed it open using the steam from the iron. A minute later she pulled the letter out of its perfectly intact envelope and showed it to me. *Order to Report for Armed Forces Physical Exam.* On Monday, July 2, 1969, at 8:00 a.m., at the Federal Building in downtown Charleston.

She folded the letter and slipped it back inside its envelope. Then, very quietly, she said, "If it were an honorable war, I would be proud for him to go. But it's senseless. I know that now, even if your father doesn't. Amelia Daniels's son is missing. Naomi Reynolds's husband is dead. And for what? So many have died."

I held my breath.

"Even Walter Cronkite says we can't win," Mom continued, her voice rising. "He said it last summer, right on the *Evening News.*"

Then, a catch in her throat, my mother said, "I don't know where my son is. And now he will go to a senseless war halfway around the world in a little Asian country we never heard of before all this mess started, and he will be killed. For nothing."

My heart winced. What could I even say to this? I could only reply to her heartache with my own.

"I dream sometimes that I have found him," I finally said.

Mom gave me a long look. *"Do it."*

"Mom?"

In one swift movement, she dropped onto the couch, pulled me to her, and held my hands in hers. "He loves you best. Barry is your heart. That's why it's breaking."

Instinctively, I pulled my hands away and clutched at my heart, but it would not be held.

Mom spoke quickly, as if a plan was suddenly being born and bursting from her as the words tumbled out. "From the time you were old enough to toddle, you chased after him. You were his shadow, and he allowed it. He loved it. No one else can talk to him like you can."

"I can't talk to him at all now," I said. "We don't know where he is."

Mom stood up. A black sock from the laundry pile clung to her housedress.

She bit her bottom lip, then said, "Barry writes letters to Norman."

I blinked.

The rest came in another rush. "Your Aunt Pam told me,

months ago, which is why I've been able to bear his leaving. He's staying in touch. But Norman has sworn not to give Barry away, so we don't know where he is. We just know he's safe."

I rocketed from the couch. "I can't believe Norman didn't tell me! All this heartache! All this worry! I can't believe *you* didn't tell me! Mother!"

Truth? I couldn't believe Barry hadn't told me.

"I was sworn to secrecy by Aunt Pam," Mom said. "And you know I couldn't tell your father. He and your Uncle Lewis would have dragged it out of Norman, and he would have sent the entire U.S. Army for your brother with his draft notice in their hands."

My mother — I thought I knew her — was keeping secrets and hiding official government documents from my father.

The giant sun clock *tick-tick-tick*ed from its place on the wall over the couch, waiting for us to choose our next words.

Finally, I whispered: "What do you want me to do?"

Again clutching my heart. Foolish. *The heart will not be held.*

Mom dabbed her eyes with a clean pillowcase that was waiting to be starched and ironed. She looked at me like she was trying to memorize my freckled face, like she might see some of her son in it, like she was about to make the most important decision of her life.

She straightened her shoulders.

"Find him, Molly. Find your brother. Norman will help you. Bring him home, where he belongs. We'll figure something out. Maybe Dr. Kingsley will agree to declare him unfit and write us a note for the draft board — he's been Barry's doctor since he was a baby. Maybe my friend Sandra's husband — he's an attorney — can help us, or Barry can be a conscientious objector. Maybe on religious grounds."

"*Religious?*" Barry and Norman had a standing challenge to see who could get out of going to church the most.

Mom was pacing now, wearing a path on the shag carpet. "Your dad will listen to reason — I know he's upset that Barry is gone. Deep down he knows it's his fault. We'll figure it out as a family. All of us. Together. You just need to go get him and bring him home."

IN-A-GADDA-DA-VIDA

Written by Doug Ingle
Performed by Iron Butterfly
Recorded at Gold Star Studios Hollywood, California, and Ultrasonic Studios, Long Island, New York, 1968
Drummer: Ron Bushy

NORMAN

I'm a drummer. My name is Norman. I hate that name. My mother named me after Norman Vincent Peale and *The Power of Positive Thinking.* She's a positive person. She kills me.

So I'm going to change my name. Who has a name like Norman anymore?

"Norman Rockwell!" says my mother. "Look! He paints covers for *Boys' Life!*"

Who reads *Boys' Life* anymore? My mother wants me to be an Eagle Scout. It's a positive thing to do. I haven't been to a Scout meeting in three years.

Rock and roll drummers have names like Keith and Ron and Ringo. At school I get called Normal, especially by the hoodlums in PE. I'm going to change that.

I'm spending as much time as I can this summer grooving

on rock tunes and woodshedding in the garage, sharpening my chops, so I can start my own band.

Barry bought a Harley and sold me his school bus before he left, so I can carry my drum kit wherever my band plays. As soon as I get a band. As soon as I fix up the bus. It's a clunker from the Charleston school bus yard. It runs hot. In South Carolina, high school seniors drive the school buses — they don't need special licenses and they save the state money because the state only has to pay teenagers thirty dollars a week. They also give them first dibs when the clunkers are sold and replaced.

"It's not the one I drove," Barry said as he lifted the hood, "but it'll get you to gigs with those drums and you can tinker on it as you go. Keep a toolbox under the driver's seat."

That was last summer and I've been tinkering ever since.

"Groovy!" I said to Barry. "Thanks, man!"

"Nobody says 'groovy' anymore, Norm."

"I do."

Barry laughed and shot me that famous Barry grin. "Let me show you how to change the oil, man."

And just like that, the bus was mine. I practiced my turns and stops until I could do them in my sleep. CHARLESTON COUNTY SCHOOLS blazes across the sides in fat black lettering. I'm going to paint my band name over that when I get a band. And a band name.

Barry was going to be my guitar player — he has a brand-new Fender Stratocaster just like one that Jimi Hendrix smashed on stage — but now Barry is gone. He sent me postcards at first, then he switched to letters. Last month he wrote me about this guy Duane Allman over in Macon, Georgia, who Barry says is better than Hendrix. I'll believe it when I hear it.

Marching band practice starts in August at the high school. I'll be a senior and also section leader for percussion. I've talked Mr. McCauley into letting the band march into the football stadium this fall to the drum solo from "In-A-Gadda-Da-Vida." That means the toms, snares, bass drums, crash cymbals — they've all gotta know their percussion parts.

And I've got to write them. Mr. McCauley — who I like because he started a jazz band in school last year and introduced me to Buddy Rich and *Big Swing Face* — gave me the job. "They've all got to know the cadence, Norman."

People named Norman march in high school bands, so I gotta get out of band, but if I'm honest, I like band, and band's all I got right now: 22-1/2-inch steps on the field, 18 steps between the five-yard-line markers, pointed toes, crisp pivots, full roll-steps, sweeping flanks, sharp about-face, mark time, halt. Play in place. Play your crazy heart out.

I don't have anything else to do this summer except work my job at Biff Burger and get to Folly Beach as much as I can. I want to sit in with the beach bands, and I'm good enough now to do it. So: job, woodshedding, figuring out how to make the girls fall in love with me at my gigs, and trying not to be killed by my mother's positivity.

And, if I'm lucky, I can drive the bus to Macon or Atlanta. Barry said this Duane and his band play free concerts at the parks there. He sent me a copy of *The Great Speckled Bird* all about it. The band has two drummers! This I gotta see.

And Pam will let me go. She's cool that way, especially since she and Dad split last year. Now Dad — Lewis — lives in Mount Pleasant with *the floozie* and Pam has joined NOW — the National Organization for Women. She put a sign in our front window on Mother's Day, *Rights Not Roses!* I won't go with her to the grocery store anymore because she hands out pamphlets and tells all the checkers, "I'm liberated and you can be, too!"

Pam and my Aunt Janice are always cooking up some scheme that no ordinary mother would even think about. Hiking and camping for two weeks along the Appalachian Trail with me and Molly — one tent and no dads. Building a bomb shelter in the backyard with plans from *Life* magazine. Stuff like that.

Pam doesn't like it that I call her Pam.

"But you're liberated!" I tell her, and she sighs. "But I *like* being called Mom," she says. It's all very confusing. It's confusing, too, that Lewis doesn't come around much anymore. At least once a day, Pam brushes invisible lint off my shoulders and says, "*You* are a treasure. Don't feel abandoned by your father!" But I do.

When I listen to "In-A-Gadda-Da-Vida," I listen loud, with my head right next to the speaker, lying on the floor. The world is going down the crapper, but when I'm lost in the music — any music — I don't care. Sometimes I fall asleep to the song and I dream Barry and I are on a stage, and Barry is singing: *Oh, won't you come with me, and walk this land? Please take my hand!*

When I wake up, the song is over and all I hear is the record spinning on the turntable, that scratchy sound the needle makes while it waits for me to come rescue it.

WINDY

Written by Ruthann Friedman
Performed by the Association
Recorded at Western Recorders, Hollywood, California, 1967
Drummer: Ted Bluechel, Jr. (concert)/Hal Blaine (studio)

MOLLY

The first time I heard "Windy," I wanted to change my name. I *love* the Association. They are my favorite band. I love the way they harmonize and all the feeling they put into their songs.

Barry looks like their leader, Terry Kirkman, with the same blond hair, long sideburns, and crooked mouth with the gap between his two front teeth. And that smile! Just like Barry's.

I'm a charter member of the Association Fan Club, so I get a newsletter that's all about the band. Larry Ramos is from Hawaii and plays the guitar, like Barry. He's very cute. Ted is the drummer and he's maybe the cutest. Terry plays the recorder and the trumpet and the tambourine. And he wore a Nehru jacket, or something mod like that (it was lavender) on the Smothers Brothers' show with an orange silk tie — an ascot, that's what

Mom called it. Something Barry would never wear, but still, it was a very smart look.

I can even sing the harmony parts to "Windy," I've listened to that record so many times. Number one on the Weekly Top Forty four weeks in a row! And Windy is *me*. Tripping down the streets of the city, smiling at everybody she sees, reaching out to capture a moment — that's me.

Or it was. I'm not reaching out for *this* moment.

I want to ask Mom what planet we're from, if she thinks I can get away with leaving home to find Barry, that Dad would allow it, or that Barry would even come with me, if I could find him.

It will never happen.

But Mom thinks it will. She hangs up the phone in the kitchen, returns to the ironing board, and says, "Your Aunt Pam and I have it figured out. You're 'staying'" — she makes finger-quotation marks for *staying* — "with your Aunts Eleanor and Madeleine in Atlanta."

"They are my *great-great-aunts*," I remind her. "They are older than dirt and they can't hear. I don't think they even move."

"Exactly," says my mother. "Aunt Pam is calling them right now. Your dad and Uncle Lewis practically grew up with them every summer. They will be delighted to hear you are coming!"

"Does Uncle Lewis know the plan?"

"What he doesn't know won't hurt him. And what he doesn't know serves him right. What goes around comes around, after the way he has treated Pam and Norman."

"Dad will find out."

"Leave that to me. By the time you get back with Barry, I'll have a plan in place. It's only twenty-one days. Or less! You know how to travel. And camp. Plus, you'll have Norman."

"Great." As if Norman is the answer to anything.

Mom turns the television back on. The steam from the iron

hisses as she attacks one of Dad's pants legs with it. On *Another World*, Steve says to Rachel, "I happen to love Alice very much," and Rachel replies, "That is not true! You do not love Alice! You love me!"

"Look what I missed," murmurs Mom, like nothing is out of the ordinary and she hasn't gone bananas.

"Mom!" I stand between my mother and the television set.

She puts the iron down slowly and looks at me, her jaw set. "I would do it myself if I could." Her voice is steely and flat. "And I know you can."

I stare back at my mother for a long, lonely moment.

And that's when I realize, when it comes to Barry, what's true for me is also true for her:

The heart cannot be held.

BAD MOON RISING

Written by John Fogerty
Performed by Creedence Clearwater Revival
Recorded at Wally Heider/Hyde Street, San Francisco, California, 1969
Drummer: Doug Clifford

NORMAN

Molly throws her tote bag into the booth and flounces onto the seat after it. Her ponytail swishes wildly left, then right, as she faces off with me at Shakey's Pizza on Highway 17. She's wearing a yellow-and-orange paisley skirt, a solid orange top, and a whole lot of rage. She does that. She can wear rage because she's an emotion machine. I raise my eyebrows but keep playing the drum solo to "In-A-Gadda-Da-Vida" on the tabletop with two wrapped straws.

"Stop that!" She snatches a straw from me, unwraps it, and plunges it into the Coke I've bought her. She doesn't even say thank you.

"I could have used *knives*." I try to snarl, but I don't have it in me. Probably because my name is *Norman*.

Instead, I say, "Keep your voice down, will ya? I'm trying to get a gig here!" I came from work. I've been trying to get the manager's attention for an hour.

"I have a bone to pick with you, mister," she hisses. "A whole skeleton!"

Then she takes a long suck on her straw, as if to prepare herself.

"Dish," I say. She can't scare me. She's just a cousin, not a real girl. Real girls scare me plenty.

"You know where Barry is, and you didn't tell me!" she explodes. "You let me worry myself *sick* over him!"

My shoulders slump. Busted.

"I was following orders. You know how Barry is about orders."

"I could wring your scrawny neck, Norman. Where is he?"

"He's safe."

"No, he's not. Have a look."

She thrusts a piece of paper at me, like it's a missile. *Order to Report for Armed Forces Physical Examination.*

"Oh, no." That's all I can say. I know what this is. My friend Max's brother got one a few months ago, and he's already gone. Off to Vietnam. "Oh, no."

"Oh, *yes*," Molly snaps. "Where is my brother, Norman?"

I scratch behind my ear, open my straw, stick it into my Coca-Cola, and take a long drag. Molly crosses her arms and says, "I hope you ordered pizza, because we're going to be here a while. We've got a trip to plan."

I choke. "What trip?"

"We've got to get Barry, Norman. We've got twenty-one days. He won't know about this. He'll be arrested when he doesn't report. They'll be looking for him as a draft dodger."

"Do you think you're going to get him to come back here and be inducted into the army in three weeks?"

"No, Mr. Smarty-Pants. I have other plans."

I open my mouth to ask *what plans?* just as the pizza arrives along with the manager, Mr. Harter. He is tall and skinny and wears a red-and-white-striped shirt, a tiny black bow tie, and a straw hat — the Shakey's uniform. He puts the pizza on the table and says, "Norman, we'll try out your band this Friday night, how's that? About eight o'clock? The families with young'uns will be gone by then."

I can't believe my dumb luck! I've been coming in here for weeks, trying to convince Mr. Harter to let me play on a weekend. Shakey's is the only good hangout that's not at the beach.

"No hard stuff, son," he says.

"Yessir!" I manage. "Thank you, sir!"

"It's just a tryout," he goes on to explain. "Sherman McCauley and I were in a band together, too, back in the dark ages — and he says you're worth the risk."

"I understand completely," I assure him. "We'll be here and we'll be ready to go — thanks again!"

As Mr. Harter evaporates, Molly almost stabs me in the eye with a slice of cheese pizza.

"You don't have time for a band gig! We have twenty-one days, wise guy. And you don't have a band."

"I'll get a band." I sound desperate, I know, so I change the subject. "And you are out of your tree, Molly, if you think we're going to drive all the way across the country to find your brother — who's my cousin and my best friend, by the way, so it's not like I don't care about him, too. Waving a draft notice in front of his face isn't going to make any difference to him."

"You said 'across the country.' Where?"

She's got me. I sigh a big one. "San Francisco."

Molly doesn't even blink. "We leave tomorrow," she says.

"We can use the school bus." She pulls a black-and-white composition book from her tote bag, a mechanical pencil, a Hi-Lighter, and a 1969 Rand McNally Road Atlas.

Then she gives me the Stare of Death and says, "Now help me figure it out."

COME TOGETHER

Written by John Lennon and Paul McCartney
Performed by the Beatles
Recorded at Abbey Road Studios, London, England, 1969
Drummer: Ringo Starr

They hashed it out at Shakey's.

"It's not a draft notice," Molly said. "It's the order to appear for a physical."

"That's just a formality before the induction notice comes," Norman replied. "Barry's a champion swimmer. He rode a Harley-Davidson to California last year. No way he will fail the physical."

"All the more reason to go get him," Molly sniffed.

"Why?"

"Because! If he goes to Canada, I'll never see him again!"

"Why would he go to Canada?"

"Because I'm going to tell him to run! That's why. I saw it on the news — a whole lot of boys being drafted are heading to Canada so they won't have to go to Vietnam."

Silence.

"Really?"

"Really. I've thought about it. It's the only way to keep him safe and out of jail."

"Really?"

"Stop that."

"I thought you were going to bring him home."

"I'm not gonna do that," said Molly. "He doesn't want to go in the army and that's all my dad will care about. Mom just can't see it."

"Your mom will kill you."

"No, she won't."

"And what if he doesn't run? What if he decides to enlist, out there in California?"

Molly's eyes filled with tears. "I'll go without you if you won't go. By rights, that bus is mine. It was Barry's first, so I can take it back on his behalf."

"You can't drive," Norman said in his flattest voice. "You're thirteen."

"Fourteen!"

"Barely! You can't drive!"

"I'll find someone who will!"

Norman stood up. Sat down. Stood up again and walked outside. He stood in the Shakey's parking lot and yelled to the heavens. "Gaaaaaaaa!"

Mr. Harter stopped by their table and looked out at Norman, then at Molly.

"He does that," she said. "It opens the lungs. Helps his singing."

Mr. Harter left the check and moved on without a word.

Molly gathered her things and scooted out to her cousin.

"We're gonna need money," she continued, as if nothing had interrupted their conversation. "For the pizza, and for the road. I've got some. And Mom will help me. Remember, it's her idea for me to go."

Norman sighed to the same heavens and rubbed his face with his flat palms. "That means my mom knows about this plan, too."

"They were talking on the phone when I left."

"Great." Positive Pam would be waiting for him when he stepped across the threshold at home. She'd be smiling. She'd be packing his things. She'd be making them sandwiches.

And she'd be relieved. She had witnessed Norman's devastation after Barry had left. The funk had been bad, he knew. The pressure to hold on to Barry's secrets had been immense, especially after Pam had intercepted a letter in the mailbox, no return address. Norman couldn't write him back if he wanted to.

He kept the letters in a metal box from his Boy Scout days. He kept the box under the driver's seat of the school bus. The anxiety the letters caused him was tremendous, not to mention the idea that he might never see Barry again. Mostly, he just didn't talk about it.

Norman paid for the pizza, and the cousins walked home past Sullivan's Shoe Shop, where Norman's Uncle Bruce resoled half the shoes in Charleston. Norman's grandparents had worked in the front of the store selling shoes for years while Bruce cobbled in the back and Pam brought Norman over to give Bruce — and herself — a break. Bruce would take Norman to the drugstore across the street for lime sherbet while Pam answered the phone for her parents. *Do you have Buster Browns in Girls size 12? Do you have Mary Janes? The Florsheims you sold me are too tight!*

Now Mommy-Ann and Pop were gone, and Bruce had other help in the shop, but it wasn't the same. Lime sherbet wasn't the same, either.

It was after five, and the shop was closed up tight. Molly and Norman turned into the neighborhood behind the row of shops on Highway 17. Norman was only two and a half years older than Molly, but he towered a foot above her. His size 14 Florsheim wing tip shoes clacked smartly on the sidewalk, next to

Molly's Keds. He would drop Molly off at her door and walk the three extra blocks to his.

It was June and it was hot in South Carolina. The water temperature in the Atlantic Ocean was already close to its summer perfection. Charleston kids were crowding the beaches and making themselves a nuisance for the summer visitors to Folly Beach, Sullivan's Island, and Isle of Palms.

Norman longed to be with them. The Shakey's gig would be a way for him to tell the beach bands that, yes, he had real band experience.

Once he got a band.

"I need a day," he finally told Molly. "I need to talk to Mr. Harter about the gig, and to Mr. McCauley about marching band. I need to look up some stuff. I don't even know how long it takes to drive to San Francisco from here."

"It's all in the atlas," said Molly.

Norman shoved his hands into the pockets of his khaki slacks. Maybe Mr. Harter would reschedule. Maybe Mr. McCauley would understand. He could work on the drum notation on the road. Biff Burger would not hold his job, but he didn't care about that. He hated that place, and he could get another job when he got back.

"I want to salvage some of my summer," he finally said.

"You will," said Molly. "I promise."

I'M A BELIEVER

Written by Neil Diamond
Performed by the Monkees
Recorded at unattributed studio, New York, New York, 1966
Drummer: Mickey Dolenz (concert)/Buddy Saltzman (studio)

MOLLY

It turns out there is plenty to arrange if you're going to take a cross-country trip to rescue your brother.

Norman opens the wide back door of the bus and yanks out three rows of seats — six seats — at the back of the school bus and puts down plywood to create a smooth surface to house his drum kit. Aunt Pam finds us some foam rubber to put under our sleeping bags.

"Why do I have to sleep next to the cymbals!" I yell at Norman, who's now at the front of the bus pumping pedals and turning the ignition on and off, his toolbox open and spilling tools near the stepwell.

"They'll be in cases!" he yells back. "Don't be a baby!"

"I'm not a baby!" I swing myself around the shiny metal pole beside the stepwell so I can avoid Norman's tools.

"Don't play on the stanchion," he says. "It's a grab bar, not a jungle gym."

I land deftly in the stepwell. "I'm going home to pack," I sniff. "And to call my friend Diane, to tell her I can't go to her pool party this weekend. See? I'm making sacrifices, too, Norman."

In my suitcase I've got seven pairs of underwear, seven pairs of shorts, seven tops, seven pairs of socks, a jacket, a sweatshirt, one pair of slacks, and a pair of pajamas. I'm wearing my Keds and the eighth pair of everything else. I've got my comb, brush, rubber bands for my ponytail, Jergens lotion, toothbrush, toothpaste. And my transistor radio so I can keep up with the Weekly Top Forty.

"You'll find a laundromat along the way," says Mom as I'm clicking shut my suitcase. "In any small town, just ask. Here's my coffee can of change. Call me every day from a pay phone so I know you're tucked in for the night."

"But that money's for your bowling league."

"It's for when I host bridge," Mom corrects me. "Doesn't matter. We'll do pot luck. I want to know you're all right, and you need clean underwear. What if you're in an accident?"

"We won't be."

She pats on her helmet of hair, touches her single string of pearls, sighs as if she's almost second-guessing herself, then plunges ahead. "Norman is a good driver. Not as good as Barry, but good. You keep him awake on the road. Stop at KOA campgrounds — Aunt Pam has a brochure with locations. They won't care that you're in a school bus. And they have washers and dryers. Aunt Pam will give you the tent we used on the Appalachian Trail last summer. Take a rope to hang your clothes on to dry. Take towels. Washcloths." She starts folding some of both from the ever-present pile on the couch.

Dad comes in from the garage and heads for the coffeepot. He grumbles about me leaving and says, "That Norman doesn't have the sense God gave a gnat."

"Let them go," my mother says, her voice more pleading than commanding. "Atlanta's a big city. It's only a few hours away and The Aunts can use the company."

"Madeleine and Eleanor have got to be pushing eighty," insists my father. "They can't do like they used to do when Lewis and I spent summers there, you know."

"Mitch." My mother sets her jaw. My father yanks the milk out of the fridge and slams the refrigerator door. I walk out the kitchen door and into the garage, where I don't have to hear their argument. I'm anxious enough already. I walk the three blocks to Norman's house.

Aunt Pam is orchestrating our departure like we're the Marines getting ready to take Hamburger Hill. She has stuffed an ice chest with tuna fish sandwiches and boiled eggs. She's got top-less cardboard boxes filled with folded blankets and cans of food and batteries and flashlights and matches and a sewing kit.

"You never know when the seat of your pants will split!" she says. "You're going to see this beautiful country! And meet such wonderful people! It's *very* exciting!"

"That's what you said about the Appalachian Trail," Norman says. "And it was *not* exciting."

"We should have had a bus! Want me to come?"

"No!" Norman and I say it together. Aunt Pam laughs and heads back inside.

Norman stands at the front of the bus and looks up to the darkening sky. The first fireflies blink on and off.

"We don't even know where to find Barry, Molly. He doesn't give me a return address. All we have is a postmark."

"We just need to get there, Norman," I explain for the hundredth time. "More will be revealed."

"How do you figure that? San Francisco is a big city! Are we just going to hang around the post office and hope he shows up?"

"We'll figure it out. You don't want him to end up in jail, do you? While you happily drive his bus all over Charleston?"

"Stop trying to make me feel guilty," Norman says. "And you know what, Molly? Barry can take care of himself. He always has." But he sounds resigned, finally.

We load the bus and fight over territory. Norman is cramming his entire life inside, including his record player and records, a case of engine oil, a huge jug of water for when the engine overheats, a toolbox, jumper cables, and Barry's guitar, along with an amp full of dials that has *Gibson* sprayed across the top corner, and extension cords. Other cords. Wires. So many cords and wires.

"There are six thousand four hundred thirty-five extension cords in here!" I yell.

"Six thousand four hundred thirty-*four*!" he hollers back.

There are more Aunt Pam boxes — a tablecloth and a can opener, loaves of bread, paper plates and plastic utensils, and even a Mason jar full of last summer's peaches. I stumble over the grate that usually lives on the charcoal grill on the patio and fall into a jumble of camping supplies, crushing the box they're in and bruising my hip.

"Can you bring me Barry's guitar?" Norman asks.

"Can't you take out any more of these seats?"

"That's plenty," Norman says. "We just need to take out enough for sleeping bags and the drum set."

"Why do we need your drums? Are you planning to set up in campgrounds and entertain the masses?"

Norman ignores me. "The rest of your stuff can go on or under the seats, like mine. There are still nine rows of seats — that's eighteen seats, for the math challenged — and I don't have anywhere to put any more of them."

"Fine," I huff as I strap the first aid kit to the bus console and throw my pillows onto the front seat behind the driver. "I'm good at math," I inform him. "And I'm navigating."

"You can navigate," he agrees. "But *I* am picking the route."

"Why?"

"Because if I'm going to give up my summer to drive you on a wild-goose chase against my will, I'm going to get something out of it, too."

"Like what?"

"Like music."

"The bus has no radio," I say in my most smug voice.

Norman points to a box on one of the seats. "It has a radio. I just need to install it." He throws his suitcase down the middle of the aisle, where it pops open and out spills his freshly pressed white shirts and khaki pants.

"Norman! Your mom will have a cow."

"No, she won't. She's positive." He heaps the clothes back into the suitcase. "Geez, she packed my Boy Scout shirt! And sash! What does she think we're gonna do, go to a jamboree?"

From his back pocket he pulls a pair of drumsticks and a rolled-up copy of a magazine. "Live music. That's what I want." He hands me the magazine and I unroll it. *The Great Speckled Bird*.

"What's this?" I pick my way over the spilled tools and follow him out of the bus and around to its open hood.

"It's an underground newspaper. Printed in Atlanta. Barry hooked me up with it."

"What's it for?"

"What it's *against* is more like it. It's anti-establishment."

"What?"

"Never mind," he says. He begins jimmying the hood. "Live music. That's what it's for."

"Where?" This could be bad.

Norman lets the hood fall and then slams it shut with a bang. He looks me straight in the eye.

"Everywhere, cuz. *Everywhere.*"

7

GOOD MORNING, STARSHINE

From the musical *Hair*
Written by James Rado, Gerome Ragni, and Galt MacDermot
Performed by Oliver
Recorded at unattributed studio, May 1969
Studio percussion

Uncle Bruce was there to see them off the next morning. He always smelled of leather, glue, and shoe polish. He pressed an envelope full of ten-dollar bills into his nephew's hands. "Lots of luck," he said. "Take your good shoes."

Norman laughed. "I've got 'em!" He hugged his uncle. "Thank you so much!"

Uncle Bruce, who wasn't much taller than Molly, reached up and patted Norman affectionately on the cheek three times with a strong and callused hand. Then he hugged Molly. "Take care of each other out there," he said.

"We will!" Molly replied with more enthusiasm than she felt. She climbed on board the bus.

"Showtime!" Aunt Pam sashayed out the kitchen door with a box in one hand and a thermos of hot coffee — *already sugared and creamed!* — in the other. She smiled herself past Uncle Bruce and Norman, followed Molly onto the bus, and gave her the box. It was labeled *AAA Maps and Useful Things*.

"Keep this in a safe place," she said. "I called Triple A and ran down to get these. Road maps for each state, recommendations for lodgings and restaurants, lists of campgrounds and motor vehicle laws in each state, and a copy of *Sportsmanlike Driving*. Plus, I made sure the bus is on our Triple A policy. Whatever you do, don't lose the membership card!"

"I won't." Molly put the box on her seat behind the driver, while Aunt Pam put her hands on her hips and surveyed the work they'd taken two of their precious twenty-one days to do. "You're going to be just *fine*," she said. She hugged Molly and said, "One more thing," then gave her a copy of *An Adventurer's Guide to Travel across America* that she had stashed on the driver's seat the night before, so as not to forget it. "Lots of tips!"

"Thanks, Aunt Pam."

Norman stood on the driveway about to board the bus and saluted his mother from the doorway. She returned his salute and stepped into the aisle for him. Norman climbed on board and flopped into the driver's seat. "Where's your mom?" he asked Molly.

"I told her not to come. She's overwrought about everything. And she doesn't want Dad to come with her. Obviously."

"Don't worry about Janice," said Aunt Pam as she left the bus. "Don't worry about anything. We are strong women here, and we'll hold down the fort. We're a team — a four-person team. Now you two better get going — the day's wasting!"

And that was how they got under way. The bus roared to life. Molly took up her position on the seat behind the driver. Norman reached over and pulled the long-handled metal lever toward him, locked it into place, and the folding bus door was closed.

He waved, like royalty, out the driver's-side window to no

one, because no one was on that side of the bus. Aunt Pam blew kisses. Molly waved back. The gears and the pedals began their grumbling and grinding. Norman danced in the seat as he tried to keep up with a clutch, gearshift, and steering wheel, trying to remember all that Barry had taught him when they'd practiced in the high school lot.

"Can you even drive this thing?" were Molly's first encouraging words.

"We're gonna find out," Norman replied. Then he cursed under his breath.

Molly crossed herself, even though she wasn't Catholic.

"Hail Mary full of grace!"

"Shut up!" Norman shouted. He reached for the gearshift with one hand and turned the giant steering wheel with the other. His body bounced on the seat and his legs pumped as he released the clutch and the brake and pressed on the gas. He was a marionette suddenly free of his strings. The bus jumped forward three times and then smoothed into a roll that took them out the driveway and into the wide world.

The bright summer sun washed the world white. The usual morning mist hung over the salt marshes and under the river bridges. It was low tide. The air was damp and laden with the pungent smell of pluff mud — the natural decay of the marsh grasses and marine life in the slippery Lowcountry muck. It reached their noses as it sifted through twenty-four open bus windows. Charleston, South Carolina, disappeared behind them.

"Barry," whispered Molly, although Norman wouldn't have heard her unless she'd shouted it. "Here we come, brother. Please be there. Here we come."

GOOD GOLLY, MISS MOLLY

Written by John Marascalco and Robert "Bumps" Blackwell
Performed by Little Richard
Recorded at J&M Studio, New Orleans, Louisiana, 1956
Drummer: Earl Palmer

The arguing started early.

"We are *not* going to Macon! It's miles and miles out of our way!"

Norman kept driving, kept silent. Molly tried listening to Saturday's Top Forty on her transistor with her earphone, but the bus engine was too loud, so she gave it up. Five hours later, after they'd driven to Macon, Georgia, and found no Allman Brothers in City Park or anywhere else, they stopped at the H&H Restaurant for an early lunch.

Norman maneuvered the bus into five perpendicular spaces at the edge of the too-small parking lot, killed the engine, and opened the folding door for his cousin. "I'll buy."

Molly wanted to protest, but Aunt Pam's coffee had gone right through her and she needed the bathroom more than she needed to complain about the route once again, so she fled down the bus steps without speaking and ran into the restaurant.

"Hold on there, baby girl!" a voice called after her as she weaved past red-checked tablecloths to the back of the restaurant. "You gon' eat sumthin?"

Molly's sense of politeness was extinguished by her need to relieve her bladder. She kept moving, found the bathroom, and shut herself inside with a slam.

Norman appeared in the doorway next. The voice, which belonged to a black woman wearing a full-length bib apron, offered up a question next. "You with that white girl just road-runnered herself through here?"

Norman nodded. "Yes'm, I'm sorry." He looked around at the faces ignoring him in the restaurant. They were black and white, sometimes at the same table, talking and eating together. And this black woman was definitely in charge. He swallowed.

The woman gave Norman a measured look. "Bathrooms are for paying customers, baby."

"We're gonna eat," said Norman. "Do you have hamburgers?"

The woman nodded. "Here's you a menu, baby. Sit yourself down right here and I'll bring you a drink. You like Co-Cola?"

"Yes'm."

"Two Co-Colas, comin' up. And two burgers. French fries."

The woman took the menu from Norman and disappeared.

Molly returned from the bathroom to apologize for her temporary bad behavior. *You treat everyone with respect*, her mother had taught her. *That's the right way to be.*

If nothing else, I have impeccable manners, Molly told herself. But the woman who'd called after her was deep in the kitchen.

Molly sat down, snatched the two sets of napkin-encased silverware from Norman's drumming hands, and resumed her sniping, now that she didn't have to shout over the engine and the traffic. "We've got sandwiches on the bus. This is wasteful!"

"We can eat them for dinner," Norman pointed out. "I got us hamburgers. I need a hot meal."

"We need to get to Atlanta before dark. The Aunts are waiting for us, and my mom is calling after the news, to make sure we got there, so I'll have to talk to my dad."

A black man in an apron brought them two Cokes with straws. "Mama Louise be out directly," he said. "Lurleen burned the biscuits. How y'all doing?"

"We're fine!" Molly answered with a wide, false smile and a *please-go-away!* voice, as she pulled a Georgia state map from her tote bag and began to unfold it on the table as the man turned his attentions to the table next to them.

"We have no time for this," she stated flatly. With her Hi-Lighter she began to mark the route they'd taken instead of the one she'd so carefully constructed. Norman thrummed on the table with his hands, playing the drums to "Grazing in the Grass," which was spinning on the jukebox.

"The Friends of Distinction!" he said. "Listen to those congas!"

The in-charge woman appeared at their table, her arms laden with their dinner plates. "Folks call me Mama Louise," she said, setting the food on the table. "I brought you a side of collards, like I do my musician boys. They love 'em. I cooked 'em myself today."

"I'm so sorry for running through earlier," said Molly in her most polite voice.

"That's okay, baby," said Mama Louise with a confident smile. "A body's gotta do what a body's gotta do."

"What musicians?" asked Norman, his hamburger halfway to his mouth.

"My boys!" said Mama Louise, hands on her hips now. "You a musician, too?"

"Yes'm," said Norman as his face reddened. Was he? He wanted to think of himself that way. But a musician had a real job, playing music.

"Do you have names?"

Molly and Norman exchanged a look and introduced themselves to Mama Louise.

"Well, good" was all she replied. "I'll leave you to your dinner."

The hamburger was the best Norman had ever eaten. A hundred times better than anything at Biff Burger. Molly nibbled on the French fries that Norman drowned in ketchup. She drank her Co-Cola and noticed the people around the room, deep into their fried chicken and butter beans and conversations.

Restaurants in Charleston were not integrated, and at school this year, when black students enrolled because the Supreme Court said Senator Thurmond could no longer keep South Carolina schools segregated, Mayor Gaillard had to send in the police to keep the peace. They'd been on campus for weeks, while white kids threw over black students' tables in the lunchroom and fistfights broke out.

At the H&H, folks were eating together like they did it every day. Molly began to wonder about Mama Louise — she acted like she owned this place — just when she came back to their table with the check and to see if they needed anything else.

"Where you children headed?"

Molly opened her mouth to speak, but Norman shoehorned ahead of her.

"We're on the way to Atlanta," he said in a rush, preventing Molly from giving a longer explanation. She made a face at him.

"Atlanta!" said Mama Louise. "That's where my boys are headed! They're in a beat-up old E-con-o-line van that looks like to break down any minute. If you pass 'em on the road, stop and pick 'em up."

"Yes'm," said Norman for the fourth time. "We sure will."

"They's a passel of 'em," said Mama Louise.

"We've got a —" started Molly.

"Big car," finished Norman.

"They'll be thankful for the ride," said Mama Louise. "Maybe let you play with 'em, if you want. What you play?"

"I'm a drummer," said Norman. He *could* say that much.

"Oh," said Mama Louise with a hint of disappointment. "They've already got 'em a drummer. They got two, matter of fact."

Norman's pulse quickened. "What?" He sat up straight. "Is it a rock and roll band?"

"It sure is," said Mama Louise. "And I feed those boys same as I just fed you. You play that rockin' roll?"

Norman stood up, lightheaded. "Is it . . . ?" He couldn't form the words; they'd left his head.

"Is it what?" asked Mama Louise. "You okay, baby?"

Molly blinked at her cousin and stood up because he had. "Are we ready to go?"

Norman's mind came back to him. "Are they the Allmans?" he squeaked.

Mama Louise smiled. "Some of 'em is," she said. "Duane and his baby brother, Gregg. But there's more. You know 'em?"

"We-have-got-to-go," Norman said in a commanding tone Molly had never heard. "Now." He reached into his pocket for money to pay the bill. "Thank you, Mama Louise!"

Mama Louise, a perplexed look on her face — or as perplexed as look as Mama Louise allowed herself — walked the few feet to the cash register. "You young'uns travel safe out there," she said. "They's good people in Atlanta. Got me a grown-up boy there, too. He's tall and strong, a mighty fine young man."

"Yes'm," said Norman as he shoved bills across the cash register counter. "We'll be on the lookout."

"What's going on with you?" asked Molly when they got to the bus.

"Nothing," Norman lied. "Nothing. You're right. We need to get to Atlanta, pronto."

"I'm always right," said Molly with a sniff as they climbed onto the bus. "You'll see. Let's go."

LUCY IN THE SKY WITH DIAMONDS

Written by John Lennon and Paul McCartney
Performed by the Beatles
Recorded at EMI/Abbey Road Studios, London, England, 1967
Drummer: Ringo Starr

At least they were now headed in the right direction.

Molly took the rubber band out of her hair, brushed it so she could capture the loose strands around her face, and snared her hair once again in a ponytail.

"Doesn't that hurt, when you pull your hair so tight?" asked Norman.

"It's my signature look," said Molly. She opened the road atlas across her lap. "It will take us two hours to get to the house with all this highway construction. I'm doing *math*, Norman."

It took three. The bus bumped and rocked as they headed straight up the new section of interstate highway, past construction crews, to where the road closed and Molly directed Norman onto alternate routes.

Norman had to listen intently to Molly's directions while keeping the bus in his lane — something he'd practiced to perfection on the desolate road all the way to Macon. There had been little traffic or construction on that route . . . so little he'd gotten sleepy and was glad he'd stopped for the Coca-Cola at lunch instead of making the Kool-Aid Pam had packed. Now, as rain started, Molly walked through the bus snapping the windows closed while Norman switched on the giant windshield wiper and stole looks onto the shoulder of the road, looking for a stalled vehicle or hitchhikers with long hair and guitars.

The Atlanta skyline appeared as they rounded a curve on Interstate 75 and, as if on cue, the rain stopped and the sun came through the clouds. According to *An Adventurer's Guide to Travel across America*, Sherman had laid waste to Atlanta during the Civil War and the city had been busy pouring concrete and raising buildings ever since, as the self-proclaimed "Capital of the New South." It took Molly's breath away to see it rise up like Oz, the Emerald City. She'd forgotten.

They used Janice's handwritten directions to exit the freeway and maneuver the school bus through downtown traffic, into Midtown and along Piedmont Park, to find The Aunts' house on Fourteenth Street in a neighborhood of stately old homes that had been built just before the Depression. The house had belonged to The Aunts' brother, Uncle Watkins, who had died before Molly and Norman were born. The Aunts, two sisters who never married, had lived there together on their own ever since.

Norman parked the bus on the street and turned off the engine. Then he banged his head against the steering wheel. Repeatedly.

"What are you doing?" Molly asked.

Norman turned to her. "Are you kidding? That was horrible! I almost hit twelve cars, trying to drive in this city! I counted!"

"You went over the curb twice," Molly intoned.

"Gaaa! You try this!" Norman shouted. "And I get no thanks!"

"Thanks for not killing me, Norman!"

091

They sat in silence for a long moment. It had been a full day capped by a harrowing ride on narrow city streets.

Molly finally spoke. "You're doing a good job."

Norman took his hands off the giant steering wheel and sighed. "I want off this bus."

The house was wide and inviting, with a deep porch supported by four white columns across the front. No one answered the door when they knocked. They tried the doorbell. "Maybe it's broken," said Molly.

"Maybe they're just so ancient they can't hear it," returned Norman. "When's the last time we were here, anyway?"

Molly shrugged. She had probably been in elementary school. Her dad and Norman's were not The Aunts' favorite nephews. They had pushed to sell the house and move The Aunts to a small place in Charleston after Uncle Watkins died. "Mother's silver won't even fit in that house!" Aunt Eleanor had argued. "I am not leaving the family home!" Then she'd shut the door on her nephews.

"Let me try," said Molly, just as the front door opened. Slowly. A boy in jeans, with a head full of disheveled brown curls and no shirt or shoes, stood in the doorway rubbing his eyes as if he'd been asleep.

"It's unlocked, man."

Norman stared in surprise. Did they have the wrong house?

"Who are you?" he asked.

But the boy had disappeared and left the door open. Norman stood like a statue staring after him. Molly knew they had the right house. *Intruders!* was her first thought, then, *I should panic!* But this was a kid, like her, and he was mostly asleep.

She tugged on Norman's sleeve. "Don't just stand there with your mouth open, Norman! Come on!" She stomped after the boy, leaving Norman on the porch as she called into the house, "Where are my aunts? What have you done with them?"

A girl's voice carried from the direction of the kitchen. "Who is it?"

Norman plucked Aunt Janice's directions from the pocket of his white oxford button-down shirt — this was the right place, the number was on the house next to the front door. He followed his cousin inside.

A rich, robust smell — roast beef? — met his nose as he found himself in the kitchen with Molly and a girl with dangling earrings and long black hair who looked to be Norman's age. She was stirring the contents of a pot on the back of the stove. She wore a bandana and had a ring on every one of her fingers.

"They're upstairs getting dressed for dinner," she was saying casually to Molly. "We're having beef stew. Did they invite you for supper?" When Norman appeared in the doorway, she cooed, "Hi, handsome." Suddenly, Norman felt his pulse beating in his ears. It drowned out all other noises.

"Yes, we were invited," Molly said. "We're *family*. Who are you?"

The girl rapped her wooden spoon on the top of the pot, laid it across the lip, and looked Molly square in the face. She had brilliant blue eyes. Norman stared at her and swallowed.

"My name is Lucy," she announced.

"Lucy who?"

"Lucy Inthesky."

"*Inthesky?*" Molly sounded out this strange last name in her head, *Inthesky.*

"With Diamonds," the girl finished.

Molly's eyebrows arched in astonishment, then sank to murderous levels. "Are you kidding me?" She put her hands on her hips and leaned in. "Listen, sister . . ."

"Oh, brother," said Norman. He gave his head a brisk shake to break the spell he'd been under. "I'll go check on them."

A warble came from the top of the wide staircase by the front door.

"Norman! Is that you, dear?"

Suddenly, Jean-boy was at the bottom of the stairs looking up and buttoning his shirt. He and Norman nearly collided as they called at the same time, "Yes, ma'am!"

"Oh, good!" Aunt Eleanor called. Or was it Aunt Madeleine?

Aunt Madeleine came to stand next to Aunt Eleanor. Or was it the other way 'round? Aunt Eleanor declared, "We've got a guest for supper!"

The sounds of arguing came from the kitchen.

"Two guests!" said Aunt Most Probably Eleanor. She was doing all the talking. She cocked her arm and hung her pocketbook on the inside of her elbow.

Aunt Surely It's Madeleine smiled and smoothed the front of her dress with both hands. She wore stockings and sensible shoes.

Jean-boy was already halfway up the stairs. At the top he dutifully gave Aunt Madeleine his arm. She clutched it, held the banister with her free hand, and slowly came down to dinner, one step at a time, without saying a word. Jean-boy seated Aunt Madeleine in an armchair in the foyer, where she folded her hands and closed her eyes, waiting with a soft smile on her face. Jean-boy went back for Aunt Eleanor.

"Thank you, sweet boy," said Aunt Eleanor, fresh from her afternoon bath and liberally dusted with Cashmere Bouquet powder. She wore cat's-eye glasses on a beaded chain around her neck. "I always told your father that you were the best-mannered child I'd ever met!"

By this time a fuming Molly had joined Norman to watch the parade into dinner. The cousins exchanged looks and followed the procession into the dining room, where Lucy In The Sky With Diamonds, wearing hot mitts over her ringed fingers, was busy setting steaming hot bowls of beef stew onto china plates. She swished around to each place setting in a skirt of many colors that almost covered her bare feet. She avoided Molly and smiled wide at Norman. Red heat raced up his pale white face.

Jean-boy seated Aunt Madeleine at one end of the table, pulling out her chair for her. Molly nudged Norman with her elbow, and he swiftly did the same for Aunt Eleanor at the other end. As she was seated, Aunt Eleanor placed her pocketbook on the table, where it sat for the entire meal.

"I followed your recipe exactly," Lucy said to Aunt Eleanor. "I hope you like it!" She cast a hesitant and hopeful look at Molly.

Molly addressed her aunt directly. "Aunt Eleanor?"

"Yes, dear?" said Aunt Eleanor as she settled herself in her chair.

"It's Molly!"

"I know, dear," said Aunt Eleanor. But she didn't.

"From Charleston!" said Molly.

"Yes, of course, dear!" said Aunt Eleanor.

"And Norman!" said Molly. She had a wild thought and added, "Norman, your numbskull nephew!"

"Hey!" Norman protested. Then he added, "Hi, Aunt Eleanor."

"I'm so glad you children could join us," said Aunt Eleanor. "Molly and Norman have been visiting from Charleston! Mitch and Lewis's children! It's been too long! We saw Barry not a month ago here, didn't we, sister? My, how he is all grown up!"

Molly was quite sure they hadn't. "Aunt Eleanor!" she said, desperation in her voice.

"Yes, dear?"

Molly looked at Norman with *do something* eyes, and Norman shrugged. She sat on the chair that Jean-boy indicated was hers, since The Aunts' eyes were now on her. "Never mind," she said. She put her napkin in her lap.

Crystal water glasses were half-full and silver spoons rested daintily on cloth napkins beside each bowl of stew. Two extra places had been hastily set.

095

Norman retreated to the kitchen to help Lucy bring out stew.

Jean-boy settled himself across the table from Molly. He picked up Madeleine's napkin and fluffed it, then placed it in her lap. Madeleine smiled sweetly at Jean-boy. She patted his smooth hand with her wrinkled one. Jean-boy lifted his free hand and captured Madeleine's old hand between his two young ones.

Molly gestured at Norman as he returned from the kitchen, but Norman only had eyes for Lucy. Molly cleared her throat, but Norman didn't notice. She felt a moment of panic. And then resolve. She would fix this. Yes, she would.

Eleanor lifted both her hands, palms up, to signal the grace. They held hands around the table like it was the most natural thing in the world to do. Heads bowed, even Molly's.

"Now thank we all our God, with hearts and hands and voices," said Aunt Eleanor, her voice strong and sure, even with its warble. "Who wondrous things has done, in whom this world rejoices. Who from our mothers' arms, has blessed us on our way."

Molly looked up to see Norman staring at Aunt Eleanor, whose eyes were scrinched shut and whose hands clasped Molly's and Lucy's. "With countless gifts of love, and still is ours today. Amen."

A chorus of *amens* rounded the table. Molly screwed up her courage and once again cleared her throat.

"And now!" chirped Aunt Eleanor. She smiled warmly at Molly while she tucked her napkin into her lap. Molly returned her smile. *Finally!* Then Aunt Eleanor turned her gaze to Lucy and said, "Introduce us to your friends, Molly dear!"

Norman opened his mouth, shut it, then pinched the end of his nose with the back of his thumb and a curled forefinger as he raised his eyebrows and looked at Molly. Molly wasn't sure how to tell her aunts that they were living with imposters. A tiny yellow bird popped out of a cuckoo clock on the dining room wall and began to sing the hour, which gave Molly a chance to gather her wits. As the bird finished and disappeared into the clock, Molly had a plan. She'd let Lucy do it. Her steely gaze fell on Lucy as she said in a quiet voice, "Yes, Molly . . . please introduce us."

Lucy pursed her lips and returned Molly's gaze. Jean-boy spoke up and waved an arm across the table toward Molly and Norman. "This is Eleanor Rigby and Father McKenzie."

Norman began to cough. He covered his mouth.

Aunt Eleanor beamed at Molly. "Eleanor! Such an old-fashioned name and such a good one, don't you agree!" she proclaimed with a small clapping of her hands. "It's mine as well, and this is my sister, Madeleine."

Aunt Madeleine smiled in silence and tilted her head to one side like a puppy. *Nice to meet you*, she seemed to say.

Molly blinked, unsure what to do next. Her aunts looked so pleased and so . . . satisfied. And she was Eleanor Rigby. "Ah," she said. "Look at all the lovely people."

"Lonely," corrected Norman. He drank some water.

"Oh, no need to be lonely here," said Aunt Eleanor. "We have plenty for you to do, don't we, Madeleine?"

Aunt Madeleine nodded sweetly.

"What do you *like* to do?" Aunt Eleanor inquired. She smiled broadly at Father McKenzie.

Norman could feel Molly's stare boring into the side of his face. He shook it off and said, "I darn my socks in the night when nobody's there."

Lucy burst out laughing, covered her mouth, looked apologetically from person to person, recovered herself, and said solemnly, "Look at him . . . working!" She snorted a laugh, which made her laugh harder.

Norman blushed. He was so pleased with himself. He had made Lucy laugh.

Molly side-kicked Norman under the table.

"Heavens!" said Aunt Eleanor. "We still have Brother's socks upstairs in a dresser drawer. You are welcome to them, child."

Then, as if she'd just noticed no one had touched the stew, she said, "Eat! Eat! Before supper is cold!"

Aunt Madeleine took a sip of the broth in her bowl. Her eyes crinkled and she smiled at Lucy with pleasure.

"I so hoped you'd like it!" said Lucy, the delight obvious in her voice.

Molly picked up her spoon while she tried to figure out what to do next.

"It's *just* as I remember it in my childhood, dear," said Aunt Eleanor to Lucy. "Mashula's recipe passed down the generations. You know, your mother mastered the recipe as well."

"Thank you, Aunt Eleanor," said Lucy.

Molly let the handle of her spoon clink decisively on the side of the bowl. She stared at Lucy, who would not look at her. The dilemma was clear. The answer was not.

"Excuse me, please," said Molly. "Father McKenzie? Can I see you in the kitchen?"

Molly would have hauled him in if he hadn't popped up himself and almost beat her there.

"Bring the salt!" called Aunt Eleanor after them.

"We should call the police!" whispered Molly at the stove.

"No!" said Norman, his voice a hiss.

"Why not?"

"Because right now everything is *working* here, don't you see?"

"No, I don't! These are intruders! Explain!"

"The Aunts are happy. They are cared for. So what if they're dotty and can't remember what you just told them?"

Molly sputtered a reply. "Norman, this is a problem! You just want to hang out with Lucy!"

Norman took stock. Here was his chance to call the whole thing off and go home, but he was about to push for them to go on. He was crazy, but it was too late to turn back now. The Allman Brothers might be here.

"We're going to California, have you forgotten? If you call the police, our dads get involved and it's all over. Is that what you want?"

Molly considered this. They'd never get to Barry if they called the police.

"Good point," she conceded. "But I'm telling Mom. A grown-up needs to know. Mom got us into this. She'll know what to do."

"Fine," Norman answered. "That's responsible." He knew it was. He should have thought of it himself. His mind was trapped in visions of Lucy's smile and the promise of music maybe all the way to San Francisco.

"I know," said Molly, "someone has to be." She was smug in her victory, right as usual. She left Norman in the kitchen, then turned back to him and said, "Bring the salt."

10

ELEANOR RIGBY

Written by John Lennon and Paul McCartney
Recorded at EMI/Abbey Road Studios, London, England, 1966
No percussion
Performed by the Beatles

The phone call was the easy part. Molly's father talked with Aunt Eleanor, and with Molly, and seemed satisfied. When Molly explained the actual situation to her mother, Janice spoke in hushed tones from a corner in the kitchen while Molly's dad watched whatever came on after the news. "They didn't recognize you out of context, of course, without your parents, and it's been so long!" Then she said, "Eleanor tried to tell me when we called that you were already there, but I thought that was just her ditzy nature! They've always been ditzy, you know. Are they okay? Are these kids good to them?"

Yes they were, and yes they were.

"Still," said Janice, "Aunt Pam and I will come tomorrow. I'll let your dad know she and I are taking a little jaunt just to check on you all in Atlanta — he'll be glad of that. You go on your trip. We're right behind you."

Molly hung the phone back in its cradle on the kitchen wall.

"My mother is coming tomorrow," she told Lucy, who had been listening intently to Molly's half of the conversation as she washed dishes.

"I never meant to be you," Lucy replied. "I just wanted a place to crash for the night, and they invited me in. Eleanor called me Molly, and I just went with it. She kept asking me where Norman was, and then suddenly, there he was." She gestured to Jean-boy, who was helping Norman settle The Aunts in their recliners in front of the television set in the next room. "He asked if he could cut the grass or wash their car in return for a meal. He needed a bath as much as something to eat. Your Aunt Eleanor didn't see his tangled hair. She saw Norman and hauled him inside and fed him coconut cake and a glass of milk. And that was that. He was Norman."

"He's homeless, then," said Molly.

"He's a traveler," Lucy corrected. "Like I am. Looking for something we can't even name right now. Family maybe. A different kind of family."

Molly stood in the kitchen and watched Jean-boy, the imposter Norman, tuck a blanket around Aunt Madeleine's lap. "It's got to be ninety degrees in here, Aunt Madeleine," he said. Aunt Madeleine patted him on the cheek and smiled a thank-you.

"What's his name?" Molly asked.

"He calls himself Marvin."

Molly tried it on her tongue. "Marvin." She watched as Norman and Marvin set up The Aunts for their after-dinner television watching. Norman fiddled with the antennae on top of the TV. He gave the set a bang. "There. That's better. You know they have color television now, Aunt Eleanor."

Lucy wiped down the kitchen counters, and Molly hung the wet dish towels to dry.

101

"Where are you from?" Molly asked Lucy.

"Up north a ways," Lucy replied, as vaguely as possible.

"So neither of you has a home?" asked Molly, then remembered her manners. "I don't mean to pry, but . . . you're here in my aunts' house. Why?"

Lucy began to make coffee. "I left home," she said. She put two cups onto two saucers on the counter. "I haven't found my new home yet."

"What about Marvin?"

"You'll have to ask him," said Lucy. "There are lots of us out there now, young people who don't want what our parents have, don't want a world full of hate and war. Is that what *you* want? This is the dawning of the Age of Aquarius — haven't you heard?"

It made no sense to Molly. "Aquarius" was just a song. You grew up, you went to college — or not — you got married — or not, but most likely you did — and you had kids — or not, but most likely you did — and you lived in a house where you had your own dishes and your own neighbors and your own backyard and friends and cookouts and parties and birthdays and years and years of things you did in that house, with your family, until you grew old, and you were happy — or not — and that was how it worked. Right?

Lucy poured the coffee into The Aunts' china cups.

"They'll be up all night with that coffee," said Molly, even as she realized a moment later that it was what her mother always said to her father when he made his nightly coffee.

"They read into the night," said Lucy. "And they sleep late, which is good, because so do we, after we've been on the Strip half the night."

"What's the Strip?"

"We'll show you later," said Lucy. "Here. Help me with these."

They all watched *The Dating Game* and half of *The Newlywed Game* together, after which the television was snapped off and The Aunts were escorted back upstairs.

102

"They've got their own bedrooms," Molly observed.

"And their own televisions," marveled Norman.

"And they'll get breakfast in bed tomorrow," said Lucy.

"Served on trays that belonged to their mother," said Marvin.

Trays that would have belonged to my great-great-great-aunt, thought Molly. "You're good to them . . ." she said to both Marvin and Lucy, her sentence trailing off.

"They're good to us," said Lucy. "It's the least we can do for the room and board."

They made their peace with one another in the kitchen. Marvin seemed unfazed that Janice and Pam were arriving the next day. "Doesn't matter where I lay my head," he said. "Everything's temporary. But I like your aunts. They are sweet old ladies."

"They do all right on their own," said Lucy. "They've just been lonesome and they enjoy the company. And you should see the freezer! There are enough TV dinners in there to last two lifetimes."

"When are you leaving?" asked Marvin. He made himself a sandwich.

"Tomorrow morning," said Molly.

"Too bad," said Marvin. "There's free music in the park on Sundays, bunches of local bands, and this great new band from Macon, the Allman Brothers, show up most Sundays."

"I knew it!" said Norman. He spun in a complete circle and drummed his fingers on the countertop. "I knew it!"

"We don't have time for lollygagging in any park tomorrow, Norman," snapped Molly. "Or have you forgotten?"

Norman pointed at his cousin, his index finger as straight as a knife. "Maybe *you* have forgotten our deal, cuz. Music." He pulled *The Great Speckled Bird* from his back pocket and flapped it on the kitchen counter, where it unrolled itself.

"The *Bird*!" said Marvin, his mouth full. "I sell that on the Strip. Half the hippies in town sell the *Bird* for some dough. Come on.

I'll show you where. It's happenin', man. It's the scene. Music, madness, and a little mayhem."

"All peacefully parceled out," added Lucy.

"No!" said Molly. There had been enough mayhem in this day. She couldn't imagine more. No matter how peaceful Lucy promised it would be, it made her anxious.

"Yes!" said Norman, his eyes shining with anticipation.

"No!" Molly stamped her foot and at the same time wondered how she would get across the country and all of the unknowns she couldn't imagine if she couldn't even walk downtown in the city of Atlanta.

As she began to flounce away, Norman stepped in front of her. "Yes," he said, his face suddenly serious. "You were right about the phone call, but you're wrong about this." Molly frowned and took a step back. Norman felt strong and sure of himself for once. "I'll go without you," he said.

Molly looked her cousin full in the face but remained silent. Then she turned and left the room. She was getting very good at leaving a room when it suited her. She sat in a Queen Anne chair in the living room and considered her options. As she did, something in her relaxed and she felt a tingle across her shoulders, a dusting of possibility, as well as a dread of being left alone with her aunts in this mausoleum of a house.

Back in the kitchen, long-haired Lucy-in-the-sky, with her rings and her twinkling diamond-blue eyes, entwined her arm with Norman's. She clasped his hand. Norman felt the hair on his neck stand at attention.

"She'll come," Lucy said in a magically soothing, musical voice. "She's been issued a cosmic invitation. The vibes are pulling her there already."

11

WITHIN YOU, WITHOUT YOU

Written by George Harrison
Performed by George Harrison and the Asian Music Circle
Recorded at EMI/Abbey Road Studios, London, England, 1967
Tabla/percussion: Natwar Soni

By the time they left The Aunts' house, all four of them together, it was close to summer-dark, almost 9:00 p.m. Fourteenth Street was littered with young people wandering from Piedmont Park on one end to the Strip on the other. Marvin pointed out landmarks on the way.

"That's the Twin Mansions," he said. "The French Consulate was there, but they moved out so freaks crash there now, or at the Columns. And that," he said, pointing, "that is the Black Panther headquarters."

"Really?" said Norman.

"I think he is misinformed," said Lucy.

"I thought these houses were castles when I was a kid," said Molly, the first words she had spoken since leaving the kitchen. "Now they all look like they're falling apart." She had wordlessly vacated her Queen Anne chair and followed them out the door. It had been that simple.

"The neighborhood's changing," Lucy explained. "That's why we're all camped out here. Cheap rent."

Lucy now tinkled when she walked. She had tiny bells on her lace-up sandals, and bracelets on each arm. She walked way too close to Norman for Molly's comfort, so Molly parted them, silently, with her arms, like a chaperone at a school dance. Then she stepped between them and walked ahead of them, her point made.

Lucy sidled back to Norman, who shoved his hands in his pockets, pursed his lips, and stared at the motorcycles and bikers at the Catacombs. "That's a great pad to crash later," said Lucy. "By then, most of the bikers are down on Tenth Street."

They rounded the corner at Fourteenth and were officially on the Strip, the blocks of Peachtree Street between Eighth and Sixteenth Streets. It was dusk. The river of humanity that flowed along the sidewalks on Peachtree crested over Norman and Molly. Norman, senses already on overload, instinctively grabbed Molly's hand so they wouldn't get separated. Molly grabbed back and took a deep breath as they entered another world.

"This way!" sang Lucy as Marvin grabbed her hand and she grabbed Norman's other hand and the four of them snaked around bodies wearing beads and bracelets and braids; bodies in bell-bottoms, bandanas, and flowered shirts and skirts. Bodies nodding, laughing, smoking, singing, selling all manner of goods including *The Great Speckled Bird*. Norman shouted that he wanted to buy a new copy, but Marvin yelled, "Let it go, man! They'll be in the park tomorrow! Come on! Ziggy!" Marvin was a different person on the Strip. He was open and light-filled, waving his free arm in front of them like he was leading them off to Oz to see the Wizard.

Molly swallowed, took a deep breath, and opened her eyes wide to take it all in. *I've gone down Alice's rabbit hole*, she thought. She wouldn't have been surprised to see Alice herself, the dormouse, the caterpillar and his pipe sitting on his toadstool, the Mad Hatter and the Cheshire Cat. It felt so utterly . . . unreal? Yes, she thought. Unreal. Not like real life at all. Unreal.

Norman hauled her past the Hare Krishnas dancing and shaking their tambourines and selling incense for ten cents a stick, next to the boys with hair to their waists who played bongos on the curb, and a harmonium player — or was it a sitar? Molly didn't know either instrument — who sat with the Krishnas and played the same six notes over and over again, their heads bobbing and warbling to some invisible scene within them.

The last wash of daylight created warm golden shadows that blanketed the beat. The air surrounding them was flowery and sweet, laced with the smell of sweat and sun-singed leaves.

Beards and bare feet; sandals and suspenders; headbands and felt hats. Bodies — including theirs — weaved and waved in time to some kind of different rhythm, a rhythm that enveloped them and lifted them into a place not of this world, a rhythm pulsating, undulating, within them and without them, everywhere.

I should hate this, Molly thought, but she didn't. *I should be afraid*. But she wasn't. She couldn't resist the energy. She felt pulled along like a thread in a tapestry. And now, suddenly and surprisingly, she was *in it*, right in the middle of *it*, whatever *it* was. She was *here*. *Now*. There was a great vitality here that propelled her along on its own dedicated highway.

Molly's carefully cinched heart began to open, like the softest, loveliest lotus flower. She could feel its insistent beat within her fourteen-year-old chest. *It's been so long since I've felt something.*

She forgot about her old trip and began a new one. She closed her eyes and bumped shoulders, hips, arms, with the great wash, as her guides pulled her past a leather shop with its heady smells, past a record shop plastered with posters announcing local bands and concerts, and into a shop decorated in wind chimes and pendants, peace signs and paper flowers.

As she opened her eyes, posters told Molly to

Let Your Freak Flag Fly!
Be Peculiar.
Don't Trust Anyone over Thirty.
Make Love, Not War.

"You need this," said Lucy. She pulled a long, gauzy fabric in swirls of peacock blue, ocean green, and deep purple from an open dresser drawer full of similar goods. Molly shook her head, as if to wake herself from her dream. "I'm fine," she said. She wore her third outfit of the trip: shirt, shorts, socks, and Keds, all of them in solid cotton colors.

"Trust me," said Lucy, her bracelets singing a tinny little song. "You *need* this." She laughed in an affectionate tone and paid for the skirt before Molly could resist further. So Molly quit resisting.

"It's perfect!" said Lucy. She wrapped it around Molly twice, right over her shorts, looped the strings through soft fabric hooks, and tied them in a bow at Molly's hip. "There! We're twins!" she said. The bottom of the skirt brushed the tops of Molly's Keds.

Lucy took the green rubber band out of Molly's hair and snapped it onto Molly's wrist. "Jewelry!" Then she fluffed Molly's long brown tresses around her shoulders and wheeled her around to look in an old dresser mirror. Scarves peeked from another dresser drawer and Lucy pulled out an orange one and tied it around Molly's forehead.

Molly laughed with the kind of belly laughter that signals delight, a natural high. "I don't recognize myself!" she said with a wide smile. But she didn't mind. It made her happy.

Norman bought a pair of sandals. They were two sizes too small, but the largest size they had. Marvin talked him into them. "You can't wear *church shoes* on the Strip, man. Or anywhere! It's not cool. So your heels hit the pavement? No biggie."

Norman looked at his gigantic feet. They were very white. "Groovy" was all he could think to say.

Marvin laughed. "Nobody says 'groovy' anymore, Norman."

Norman tucked his wing tips under his arm, and Marvin cast a thoughtful look at Norman's long feet. "Really, man. You should just go barefoot."

"Groovy," Norman repeated. He wiggled his toes in his short shoes.

At Tenth Street, they waded past a gaggle of Atlanta City Police who were using bullhorns to remind the crowds of the 11:00 p.m. curfew. Bikers congregated at the parking lot on the corner, revving their motorcycle engines and creeping closer to the police. It looked like a confrontation was brewing.

"They hate us," said Lucy. Molly wasn't sure if she referred to the bikers or the police, or both.

"Turn right," said Marvin. The crowd thinned as they got onto a side street. "I know this neighborhood. I used to crash here sometimes, before I met your aunts."

Just then a tall, barefoot boy with an enormous Afro, striped pajama bottoms, and no shirt or shoes came toward them on the sidewalk.

"Hey! What's happenin', Superman," said Marvin.

"Hey! Marvin Gardens! Hey, man!"

"Marvin *Gardens*?" said an incredulous Norman. "Your name is Marvin *Gardens*?"

Marvin laughed as he embraced Superman. Then he grinned at Norman. "You don't think anybody here goes by his real name, do you, man?"

"But Marvin *Gardens*? That's a property in Monopoly!"

"That's my name!" said Marvin. Then, addressing Superman, he asked, "What happened to your cape, man?"

"My old lady took it," said Superman. "She saw me lookin' . . . at Frida Kahlo and she took away my superpowers."

109

"Bummer, man."

"No sweat," said Superman. "I'll get 'em back. Lois Lane can't resist Superman." He wore an enormous cross on a long silver chain around his neck. He nodded in recognition at Lucy and called her Miz Diamond Skies. She returned his nod with a demure smile. Then Superman's gaze fell on Norman. "Who's the cat with the walkin' shoes?"

"This here," said Marvin Gardens as he gave Norman his Strip name, "is Normal."

Norman groaned. Suddenly, he was wearing gym clothes that showed off his alabaster-white legs, and he was trying to do a pull-up to the jeers of the degenerates in PE.

But then Lucy's hand found his. "He's anything but," she said.

Norman's breath caught in his throat. He stood taller and looked Superman in the eye as if to say, *That's right, I'm anything but normal*, even though in his heart he knew he was.

"I'm not Normal," he croaked, meaning that wasn't his name, but it came out all wrong and Molly winced for her tongue-tied cousin whose hand was still wrapped around Lucy's.

Lucy laughed and kissed Norman on the cheek . . . which Molly observed almost made Norman's knees buckle. She looked at the skirt Lucy had given her and wondered what had possessed her to say yes to any of this.

"We've got to go," she said. She felt far away from the flow of the Strip; its effects were evaporating.

"And this is his sister —" said Marvin Gardens, as if he'd just noticed Molly.

"Cousin," interrupted Molly. "I'm Eleanor Rigby. Nice to meet you. We've got to go." She tugged on the dumbstruck Norman and turned to leave.

"Not that way, Eleanor Rigby," said Superman. "Cops and bikers are about to start a rumble to clear the freaks off the street. Come this way." He held a brown hand out to Molly and she stared at it. *What does he want?* went through her head along with a tiny panic at not knowing what to do or how to respond to this offering from a stranger. She could just turn and walk away. She'd perfected that move since they'd arrived in Atlanta.

She settled for a prim "Thank you." Superman stared at her with dark eyes that held a kindness that seemed to sense her lifeless heart trying to stay open, trying to find a beat. He smiled a sloppy, warmhearted smile. Molly smiled back.

"Got something to show you," Superman said.

The streetlights clicked on along Peachtree Street. The little band of five now walked up Tenth Street and into the shadows. They left the great wash behind them and ventured into the soft night, children following a skinny Pied Piper in striped bell-bottomed pajama pants.

MERCY, MERCY, MERCY

Music written by Joe Zawinul
Performed by Cannonball Adderley
Recorded at Capitol Records, Hollywood, California, 1966
Drummer: Roy McCurdy

Lyrics by Johnny "Guitar" Watson and Larry Williams
Performed by the Buckinghams
Recorded at Columbia Studios, Chicago, Illinois, 1967
Drummer: John Poulos (concert)/John Guerin (studio)

The house was an old green Victorian with trim painted the colors in Molly's skirt. A sign posted at the door said BE-IN BY THE LAKE AT PIEDMONT PARK SUNDAYS! MEET HERE AT 12:30 P.M.

"This is the Twelfth Gate," said Superman. "My friend Robin started it as a coffeehouse. We usually have folk singers and poetry, but there's *jazz* tonight. Very special."

"I'm in!" said the very *not-in* Norman. He'd never heard a live professional jazz band play. His heart beat faster thinking about what waited for him just through the door.

"You're hip to the scene?" said Superman with another smile. "Got any bread?"

"I do," said Lucy.

"How do you always have money?" asked Molly.

"I came into this world with money," said Lucy with a sigh.

"Then what are you doing here, living with my aunts?"

Lucy fished in her fringed shoulder bag. "Money isn't everything." She began pulling bills from the inside of the tiny beaded bag. "Just be my friend for a night, will you?"

Superman ushered them into the foyer, where a heavily tattooed man named Pete wore a jean jacket with no sleeves, a handlebar mustache, and a ponytail to rival Molly's. He repeated a litany in a gravelly monotone:

"Welcome to the Twelfth Gate. The cover charge is one dollar tonight. You don't have to buy anything to eat or drink, but we appreciate it if you do. We brew Georgia sassafras tea. Also Darjeeling. No drugs allowed. No alcohol. This is not a crash pad. It's a coffeehouse sponsored by the Methodist church. Are you in or out?" He held out a lined hand.

Lucy handed him four dollars.

"Enter," said tattooed Pete. Superman offered his hand to Molly once more. Surprising herself, Molly gave it to him this time. Superman kissed it, bowed, and disappeared back to the street. Molly blushed and watched him go.

Lucy waltzed inside, pulling Norman behind her.

Molly hesitated.

"It's cool," said Marvin Gardens, guiding Molly inside. "I've been here before. Don't worry."

A thick haze of cigarette smoke surrounded them as they went through a second set of double doors and into a candle-lighted, cozy living room with red walls, a fireplace, a long wooden table in front of old church pews against the wall, and a busy kitchen in the back. A second room was set up with ticky-tacky tables topped with small candles in glass jars. Two bearded young men played chess at a table and one poured tea from a fat white teapot.

The stage was in the living room by the fireplace. The wall behind the stage was plastered with gray egg cartons.

"For the acoustics," said Marvin Gardens. "Sounds better."

113

On the stage, a record player on a stool played a song about finding a new world somewhere, as Norman scooted behind a long table and into a pew already half-full. He was followed by Molly, who had once again insinuated herself between Norman and Lucy, which left Lucy to follow Molly onto the bench, with Marvin Gardens the caboose of their little train.

"That song is by the Seekers!" said Molly as she situated herself. She took the rubber band from her wrist and began to gather her hair together. It was hot. Her orange scarf fell off her forehead and Lucy caught it.

"I have that record!" crowed Molly. "It was number two on the Weekly Top Forty!"

"How do you remember that?" asked Lucy. "That song is old. I was just starting high school when it came out, so you must have been ten."

Molly's face colored at the realization that Lucy was so much older than she was, but she recovered quickly. "I write the Top Forty numbers on all my records," she said with a superior sniff. "And I don't listen to boring old jazz."

"Jazz isn't boring," stated Norman.

"Nossir, it isn't," said a voice on the other side of Norman.

The man wore round granny sunglasses, a short-cropped Afro, several earrings along his right ear, and just as many necklaces that tumbled together along his chest. His skin was the color of the wing tip shoes Norman carried under his arm. Now the man pointed at the shoes. "You like jazz, Florsheim?"

Norman put the shoes on the floor at his feet. "Yeah," he said. Then, flustered, "Yessir." He had never sat so close to a black man. And this one was immediately fascinating. There was a smoothness in his voice, like Superman's, and also an authority. His question was almost a challenge, but at the same time, it was mellow. And he seemed much older than anyone else in the room.

"What do you know about jazz?"

Norman blushed. "Well, I'm in band." He cringed. *Don't be a moron, Norman.* "Marching band." *Even worse, Norman!* "My band director . . ." *Just stop, Norman!* "Big Swing Face — Buddy Rich . . ."

"You got a jazz band in your school?"

"Yessir," said Norman. "Just started."

The man nodded. "Good." Someone removed the record player from the stool and a band shambled onto the stage with their equipment, to polite applause. Norman drank in the setup and the instruments — especially the drum kit. It was a small setup, the kind Mr. McCauley had for jazz band practice. Norman detailed it out loud like any good jazzhead would do. "A black pearl jazz set with a twenty-inch bass drum, two tom-toms, and a snare."

The man nodded again and added, "That's an eight-by-twelve tom, a fourteen-by-fourteen floor tom, and a fourteen-by-five snare. Probably Zildjian cymbals: a crash, a ride, and a pair of hi-hats."

As if they'd known each other for years, Norman returned the man's volley with "Probably an eighteen-, a twenty-two-, and a fourteen-inch," which made the man laugh.

The band tuned up. Every one of them was wearing a suit.

"Buddy's good," the man said. "These guys are good, too." He joined in the applause. "My name's Jay," he added. He stuck out a hand and Norman shook it. "Nice to meet you, Florsheim. You from around here?"

"No," said Norman. "We're just passing through."

"Through to where?"

Norman rubbed two fingers on his forehead. "California."

"You got wheels?"

Norman nodded.

"What kind?"

Norman blinked. "Well . . . a school bus," he said.

Jay laughed. "Perfect! A school bus!"

"Is that bad?" Norman could feel Molly staring at him, boring her usual hole into the side of his face.

"No, man," said Jay. "Whatever floats your boat. Just wondered if you were hitchin'. Lots of kids out on the road, hitchin' these days; I've done a good bit myself, but California is a long way away."

Norman tried to think of a way to make conversation. He didn't want Jay to ask him why he was going to California in a school bus.

"Are you from here?" Norman asked.

"For heaven's sake!" Molly tugged on Norman's shirt. She clenched her teeth and said, under her breath, "Leave the nice man alone."

Jay smiled at Molly but said nothing.

Norman knew that anything he said in rebuttal would seem childish, so he sat in silence, blushing with secondhand embarrassment, and was glad it was too dark for anyone to clearly see his face in the candlelight.

A bushy-bearded emcee wearing red suspenders stepped gingerly on stage with the band, trying to find a bit of room. He held up two fingers in a peace sign.

"We're trying something special tonight, Twelfth Gaters," he said. "Please welcome, on his way to play Paris and stopping here as a favor to the Twelfth Gate . . . Cannonball Adderley!"

More polite applause from the folkie crowd filtered to the stage.

"Who?" asked Molly.

Cannonball held his sax in both hands and wasted no time. "That's right," he said. "We've got some of the band here tonight with a layover in Atlanta, meetin' up with the rest of us tomorrow, on our way to play in Par-ee!"

116

"Take me with you!" came a shout from the corner, followed by laughter.

"We 'preciate the opportunity to jam with you good people tonight! Thank you to Robin and Ursula and the Twelfth Gate!"

"That's Cannonball," said Jay. "He used to be a high school band director."

"No kidding!" said Norman.

"Then he worked with Miles," said Jay. "You know Miles?"

Norman nodded. Not well.

"Learn Miles," said Jay, "and you'll learn how to listen. Who you listening to tonight?"

"Shhh!" hissed Molly, who was not enjoying herself in spite of the fact that Lucy had ordered them tea and a pastrami sandwich from the kitchen.

"The drummer, I guess," said Norman, ignoring his cousin. "I'm a drummer."

"Me, too," said Jay. "And I came to hear this one — Roy McCurdy. He's played with Sonny Rollins. You know Sonny?"

Norman shook his head.

"You will," said Jay. "Just listen tonight. Your lady is right."

"She's my cousin."

"Stop. Making. Friends," said Molly. She looked hesitantly at Jay to see what he might say, and when he said nothing, she added with as much authority as she could muster, "We should go. We have a long way to travel tomorrow."

Norman sat between the needle-scratch voice of his cousin and the smooth tones of this man Jay and wondered what to do as he watched the band tune up. The promise of hearing live jazz for the first time in his life was thrilling. He did not want to miss it.

"Chill, little lady," said Jay, and Molly, sandwiched between her cousin and his paramour, Lucy, sighed and slumped back against the church pew. Lucy quietly tied Molly's orange scarf around Molly's wrist while Marvin Gardens poured tea.

Jay smiled, sat back, and closed his eyes. "I love the beat."

Molly lasted the length of two jazzy tunes. Then, as Cannonball began to introduce his band, she said, "Norman, let's go."

But Norman was floating and feeling the groove. This band was tight, clean, and precise. They could swing hard and stay in the pocket, something the newly formed St. Andrews Parish High School Jazz Band couldn't begin to touch. *Technique* was a word Mr. McCauley used a lot, and now Norman understood what it meant. A recording couldn't capture the energy, the push, and the drive — not to mention the physicality — of the players, their delight, and the jazz faces they made. Norman wanted to stay on his cloud.

"We're not leaving," he told Molly. "Not a chance."

"Now, sometimes," said Cannonball from the stage, "we find ourselves faced with adversity!"

"Yeah!" said the small crowd. Suddenly they were all jazz converts. The piano player started noodling behind Cannonball, with the beginnings of a new song hinted in snippets on the Fender Rhodes.

"The fuzz may be after us —"

"Yeah!"

"Or we might not have a pad to crash in for the night —"

"Yeah!" The drums kicked in. Norman sat up straight.

"Or we don't have enough coin for our next meal —"

"Yeah!"

"Or our old ladies have left us —"

Groans from the boys, laughter from the girls.

"And we don't know just what to do!" said Cannonball.

Molly knew just what to do. She grabbed Norman by the sleeve of his white oxford shirt. "It's late!"

Norman shook her off.

"And it's times like these," said Cannonball, his voice escalating and the crowd with him, "that we ask for Mercy, Mercy, Mercy!"

"This'll be good," said Jay. "Sit back, man. Don't think it. Feel it. Listen to that slow, bluesy drag."

The first line of the melody began to slide off the Fender Rhodes keys, and the trumpet joined in. It took only four measures for Molly to recognize the tune.

"I know it!" she said in wonder. "The Buckinghams sing it! It was number five on the Weekly Top Forty. It's got words!"

Jay laughed. "It was jazz first, my lady. And this one's oozing soul, can you dig it?"

Lucy knew the song, too. She began to sing it softly and bob her head from side to side. "C'mon, Molly. Sing it with me! 'There is no girl . . .'"

And, much to her own surprise, with a live band to inspire her, Molly sang along with Lucy. She loved this song.

"Sing it like a moan," instructed Jay, "not like a pop tune. *Feel* the music. Space out your notes, like Cannonball's sax. Put some longing in there!"

Lucy closed her eyes, tilted her head, and sang louder. Molly was immediately self-conscious and stopped, but when other kids in the room started to sing, too, she tried again. She closed her eyes, which allowed her to pretend no one could see her. She grabbed a hunk of her skirt in her fists on either side of her legs, as if she needed the ballast. She hummed at first, then she whispered the words, and then she sang them. As the singers got louder, so did she. Against her will, her head began to bob from side to side. She tightened her grip on her skirt and sang louder. She heard Lucy singing louder next to her, and she began to compete with her, still with her eyes closed, her head tilting in time and her fists letting go of her brightly colored new skirt, her

119

hands then weaving back and forth, back and forth as, without realizing it, she began to sway with Lucy and the music that filled the room.

Jay nodded his head to the draggy beat and began to drum the tabletop with his palms, like he was playing bongos. Norman longed to pull his drumsticks out of his back pocket and play on the tabletop along with Jay and Roy McCurdy, but he didn't have his sticks with him, and he was too shy. Instead, he put his elbows on the table and his hands firmly on the sides of his face, as if he was keeping his head attached to his body while he watched the amazement before him and kept his hands still. He wasn't sure what sight was more amazing: his cousin swaying next to him in a dream state or the live band playing the groove right in front of him.

"Come on, Florsheim!" said Jay, more animated as the music reached a crescendo. "Beat it! This is how you learn!"

Norman didn't need a second invitation. The rhythm carried him into his own emotional stratosphere as he opened his palms and began to match Jay, beat for beat, the table becoming their own personal drum kit as they traded off licks, then went back to playing in time together.

"Yeah!" said Jay, and Norman laughed.

The band was buoyed by the audience's delight and their part in creating it. The trumpet wailed, the sax moaned, the Fender Rhodes swayed. The cymbals crashed and the snare filled in all the empty spaces. The drummer's sticks flew. A live music jazz-pop moment carried them to the crescendo at the end.

"Mercy, mercy, mercy!" said Cannonball. "A big thank-you to all the freaky people! All the beautiful people. Thank you!"

"We're the beautiful people," cooed Lucy. Molly immediately crash-landed.

"Did you hear it?" asked Jay.

"Oh, yeah," said Norman over the applause. The rhythm had

informed the beat of his heart. The melody had rushed into his blood. The soul had got under his skin.

"Groovy," said Jay, and Norman laughed. He longed to rush the stage and talk to Roy McCurdy about his drums, ask him how he was getting that sound, what he did to make that magic, but the band was already disappearing through the kitchen.

"Bring your girl to the park tomorrow," Jay said.

"She's my cousin," repeated Norman. Then, as if he had magic news to impart, he said, "I heard the Allman Brothers will be there!"

"Band," said Jay. "The Allman Brothers Band. I heard that, too. Maybe I'll catch you there, Florsheim. Stay cool."

13

SPINNING WHEEL

Written by David Clayton-Thomas
Performed by Blood, Sweat & Tears
Recorded at Columbia Recording Studios, New York, New York, 1968
Drummer: Bobby Colomby

MOLLY

I don't know what possessed me. I know I say that a lot now, at least to myself, but honestly, I don't know what possessed me, running all over Atlanta city streets with strangers, pretending to feel something — singing in public! — not me at all, not me to behave in such an unladylike fashion.

I'm a careful girl, but then I'm not, because if I were truly careful, I wouldn't be here in Atlanta by myself, now, would I? Yes, Norman's here, but Norman doesn't count. He wants to be here. Suddenly, the boy who didn't want to leave home is having the time of his life. He's probably forgotten all about Barry, but I haven't. When I opened my suitcase this morning, out fluttered Barry's letter, *Order to Report*.

It's Sunday morning and I can smell bacon frying downstairs in the kitchen. No sign of The Aunts. I climb out of this enormous bed in one of the endless bedrooms in this cavernous house, get dressed, brush my teeth so hard my gums hurt. Then I pull my ponytail so tight my eyebrows smile at me. I don't care. My heart has closed up shop and hung a sign on the door: GONE OUT OF BUSINESS.

I have no business acting like a hippie in this crazy city and traipsing around in a long flowy skirt with my hair flying every which way, pretending we don't have somewhere else to go. And furthermore, I'm out here against my will.

Or am I? It's complicated. The phone rings.

"We are having the car serviced," Mom says. "We'll be there for lunch tomorrow. But you go on, Molly — don't waste another night in Atlanta. We'll leave bright and early in the morning."

I bang out the front door with my suitcase and the sunshine nearly blinds me. In the bus, Norman has all the windows down and the toolbox open, spilling wrenches and screws and screwdrivers.

"What are you doing?" I don't have time for good morning.

"Installing the radio," he says. "What's it look like?"

"How long is this going to take?" I snap. "It's already ten o'clock!"

"Keep your pants on," returns Norman. "I'm almost done."

"Well, hurry!"

"Where've *you* been? I got up hours ago. I had to chase away fifteen kids who slept on the bus last night!"

"What? How did they get on?"

"I must've forgot to lock the door."

"Are you sure the lock works?"

"Yep."

"Did they take anything?"

"Nope."

"Did you check?"

"Yep."

123

I am out of patience. "You really can't forget to lock the doors, Norman. We're traveling across the country, you know. We have to stay safe at night."

"Yep."

"Did you get gas?"

"Yep."

"Say something else."

"Hand me that Phillips head screwdriver," Norman says. "And go eat a hot breakfast."

"No time," I tell him.

"Yes, time," my cousin replies. "I need to check the engine before we leave, add oil, probably — water, too — and I'm not going to rush it. I don't want to break down in the middle of nowhere with you."

I hand him the screwdriver, step gingerly over the spilled toolbox, put my suitcase in the third row behind my navigating seat, and sit with a thump next to it.

I make a declaration. "It stinks in here." No response. I open the road atlas, using the suitcase as a desk. "You just want to stall so you can listen to that band in the park."

"Yep," Norman says. "I do want to listen to that band in the park, and I'm gonna do that. You want to drive off without me, be my guest."

I slap shut the atlas. I have a headache. I'm having strangulation fantasies. We need to get going! "You are impossible!" I say.

"Yep."

"Stop saying that!"

"Nope."

And now I lose my temper. Barry would have listened to me. Barry would have understood how anxious I am, would have said something comforting. But Norman is a lunkhead.

"You just want to be with that girl! You never had a girlfriend and now somebody likes you and it's gone to your head! That girl likes everybody, Norman. You're not special! Have you forgotten why we're here in the first place?"

Norman ignores me. He thumps into the driver's seat and turns on the radio. Static plays. He tweaks the right-hand dial until he finds a crackly station. "It'll come in clearer when I install the antenna," he says. "I'll do that after breakfast."

"Norman!" I am on my feet. "I want to talk to you!"

In one furious move, Norman jumps from his seat and wheels to face me. I take a step backward in shock. "I *don't* want to talk to *you!*" he shouts. "And I am *not* going to argue with you, so just *shut up* and try listening for a change."

I feel as if I've been slapped. I grip the top bar of the seat in front of me and slowly sit down. Norman never shouts. Norman is milquetoast in wing tip shoes. But I don't know this Norman. He sounds vicious. And he is not finished.

"*You*, in your self-righteous ponytail, acting holier-than-thou and like you're the only one who cares about anything — just stop it! We had a deal. I said I'd do this if I could listen to music. I'm going to this park, and then, if you want, I'll drive all night to the next stop — wherever it is, I'm sure you have it all mapped out —"

I am quivering, trying not to show it, trying to look like I don't care, but I know it's not working,

Norman sucks in a jagged breath and barrels ahead. He seems thrilled at his anger — look who's self-righteous now! — and points his finger at me —

"Look. I'm just as anxious to find Barry as you are, but it's not going to take us three weeks to drive to San Francisco. And back! I'm going to listen to this band! I only know about them because of Barry, and when we get to San Francisco — and if we even can *find* Barry — I'm not about to tell him I had a chance to listen to these guys and I didn't take it. How will *you*

125

feel when I tell Barry I didn't go see his hero, the greatest guitar player of all time, because *you* wouldn't let me!"

I'm not going to answer that. I can't even hear it. I blink back tears and try not to look at Norman, try not to move.

"And don't call me Norman," he finishes. "My name is Florsheim." He jumps over the bus stepwell and onto the grass by the sidewalk. Then he takes giant strides to the front door — in his Florsheim wing tip shoes — and disappears into the house.

Birdsong comes through the open windows. A horn honks in the distance. I rest my forehead between my hands, on the bar of the seat in front of me. The inside of my nose begins to sting, and I know what's coming. One tear falls onto the floor of the bus, then another.

I am *not* holier-than-thou. I am the responsible one. I am the one who planned the route and navigated us this far and tried to keep us on track. I'm the one who wanted to call the police. I'm the one who told Mom what was happening. I'm the one who said no to the Strip. I'm not falling all over Marvin the way Norman is falling all over Lucy — he is *out of control.* I'm the one Mom depends on, and even Barry depends on me now. I'm the one who can save him! I'm the one.

The sting in my nose becomes an upheaval in my chest, like water straining at a dam and surging over it, into my throat, into my eyes, until I can't see the floor at my feet, the floor I've been staring at so I can hold myself together.

And there it is then, my old friend, my heart. My poor, poor broken heart begins to sob. Sobs of grief and loss and over-whelming sadness.

I want to scream, *Mom! This is too hard! Who's the grown-up here, anyway? This is a crazy idea, just like I told you in Charleston! I should walk into this house right now and tell The Aunts who we are — insist on it, no matter how confused they'll* be — they're already so confused, what does a little more confusion matter? And we'll all sit on the couch and wait for you and Aunt Pam to show up, and then we'll put you on a bus to San Francisco! And we'll go home!

My nose runs and my tears fall and I wipe at them with my hands, which means I have tears and snot all over my hands and face. "Who does something like this?" I say in a whisper. "Who puts this kind of responsibility on their *children*? Mom, you and Aunt Pam are crazy!"

I have proof of this. Last summer, after Dad made Barry leave and after Uncle Lewis left Aunt Pam and Norman for the floozie, that's when Janice and Pam decided on the Appalachian Trail trip — *Without men! Come on, you'll love it!*

They were so mad at the men. At *all the men.* So the four of us went, and we got so lost more than once and I, Molly, figured out the route with my trail maps every time. *Math, Norman.*

And Norman — almost an Eagle Scout, never an Eagle Scout — knew how to make our fires and how to extinguish them safely. Norman hiked out for food and supplies and discovered showers and came back and brought everyone with him and we got clean and ate chicken pot pie and cherry cobbler at a trail kitchen in a tiny town surrounded by mountains and laughed like we had just discovered civilization and were so relieved to be alive.

I, Molly, figured out how to hang our food high in a tree so critters couldn't get it. "We're survivalists!" chorused Aunt Pam and Mom, while they played canasta by the fire. We were all so unprepared.

The trip had been boot camp for the heartbroken.

"We could have just gone to the beach!" Norman had said as we started out. "This is too hard!" But we did it, and we did well. When we were eaten by mosquitoes or hungry from a day

127

without food, or soaked to the bone from two days of rain, or when there were seventeen problems to solve, Norman and I took to saying to each other, *You okay? I'm okay. You?* Then, *One thing at a time. What's next?*

Mom and Aunt Pam wouldn't have survived without us. I sigh at the memory. And then it hits me: This trip, right now? This is the same trip. Norman isn't angry at *me*, he is furious with *them*. And so am I.

We are in this crazy scheme together, all four of us — that's what Aunt Pam said when we left yesterday, too. Only this time, Mom and Aunt Pam are in Charleston playing canasta, sure in their children's abilities to drive a few miles — oh, just across the country and back!

But Norman and I, we're right in the thick of it.

"Ugh!" I can't believe it. But I get it now and I know what to do. I open the ice chest and stick my entire face into the cold water it offers up. Water drips from my face, down my neck, arms, and elbows, and onto my chest, under my white Brooks Brothers blouse. It feels good on a day that is already hot. I fan my hands across my face and flick away the water along with snot and tears.

Then I take a deep breath and laugh. *My name is Florsheim.* Ha! This is all so crazy it might just work.

If the music is all Norman wants, I can give it to him. I've done all the math necessary to figure out the mileage between Atlanta and San Francisco, and I know how long it will take us. We have time to get there, plenty of it. What we don't know is how long it will take to find Barry and what will happen after that.

I sigh out the burden of being fourteen and doing this impossible thing. I still don't know what's possessing me. Love? A broken heart? A crazy scheme? All of these things. And maybe, if I'm honest, there is something else. Maybe I want to know what's out there. How many kids get a chance to go see it for themselves like this?

We do.

I hop off the bus. "Norman!" I shout. We're in it together, I see it now. And I know what to say to my cousin.

Okay. One thing at a time. What's next?

14

STATESBORO BLUES

Written by Blind Willie McTell
Performed by the Allman Brothers Band
Live at Piedmont Park, Atlanta, Georgia, 1969
Recorded at Fillmore East, New York, New York, 1971
Drummers: Butch Trucks and Jai Johany Johanson (Jaimoe)

Marvin Gardens helped Norman tinker under the hood of the bus. He knew more about engines than Norman did, it turned out, and Norman was glad for the help. By the time the sun was directly overhead at noon, they closed the hood, killed the engine, and heard music.

"It's a local band," Marvin said. "No sweat. Some of them are pretty good, and they'll play until the Allman Brothers show up."

The Allman Brothers *Band*, thought Norman, as he and Marvin Gardens closed the bus windows. "Leave a couple of them down," instructed Norman, "or the heat'll cook everything in here." He wore a white T-shirt, khaki slacks, and his too-short sandals.

A stream of young people flowed past them and into Piedmont Park. Molly sat on the curb and watched them. She was certain some were younger than she was. And none of them seemed to care that they looked homeless. Maybe they were.

She retied her Keds and tightened her ponytail. These kids didn't seem like the same ones she'd seen the night before on the Strip, but of course they were. Now she saw their matted hair and dirty feet and wrinkled clothes, and watched how they slumped, shuffled, or stumbled along like they were half in a dream.

Their beads were tacky and their bracelets were cheap. Their pants were too long and worn-out at the cuffs and knees, and the boys were often shirtless, like Marvin Gardens was once again. They smoked and shared their cigarettes, but they hardly spoke.

They're zombies. Molly could not imagine that Barry had been in this place, with these people, writing to Norman, telling him to come hear this band.

The screen door banged behind her and Lucy twinkled to the bus. She wore yesterday's colorful skirt as a short dress today. She had wrapped it around herself twice and tied it under her arms. The sheer fabric made it obvious she was wearing nothing underneath. She sported the sandals with the tinkling bells and rings on every finger, as usual, but no bracelets or earrings. Her long brown hair swept across her bare shoulders.

"Ready!" she said. "Where's your pretty skirt, Molly?"

"I left it on a hook in the bathroom," Molly replied. "You bought it, it's yours."

Lucy pouted. "It's a gift. Take it. I want you to have it."

Molly stood up and dusted off the seat of her shorts. "Nah," she said. "It's not my style. Thanks anyway."

Norman reached for his white oxford shirt that hung on the door of the bus. Marvin stopped him. "T-shirt's enough, man," he said with a half smile. "Gonna be hot out there."

Norman stopped himself from saying, *But I'll feel undressed.* Instead, he nodded, tossed the shirt onto the driver's seat, and they were off.

131

*   *   *

Piedmont Park was many times larger than Charleston's prim Marion Square and more majestic than the Battery, the elegant promenade that meandered along the Ashley and Cooper Rivers at Charleston Harbor. It swallowed them into its belly as they walked through the Fourteenth Street gates and onto winding pathways, under a green canopy of trees and around benches and bends and curving stone balustrades, remnants of old buildings that had once stood in the park.

BE-IN BY THE LAKE AT PIEDMONT PARK SUNDAYS! the sign outside the Twelfth Gate had proclaimed last night. Molly wondered where the lake was. She wondered what a *Be-In* was. As far as she could see, there were people picnicking or playing ball or walking dogs or sleeping on blankets in the shade.

The music carried Molly, Norman, Lucy, and Marvin Gardens into the same stream as the young freaky people of all shapes and colors flowing toward the same source. It got louder as they went up the hill to a stone stage. Young people stood on the flat tops of the low pillars and sat along the stone walls and on the first set of stairs, sprawled all over the grass in front of and behind the natural stage where a band was tearing down or setting up, plugging equipment into the electrical outlets built into the balustrades. Girls sold beads in the crowd, couples kissed or sunbathed, and a little dog ran through the crowd yapping. A young man stood at one of the microphones and announced, "This is by a cat styles himself E. E. Cummings. Y'all know it — it's called 'I Sing of Olaf.' Let's go!"

He unfolded a piece of paper and began to shout about a man named Olaf, "whose warmest heart recoiled at war / a conscientious object-or."

Cheers rose from the crowd — "Yeah!" — as the reader continued. "Right on!" Some, including Lucy and Marvin Gardens, chanted favorite lines along with the reader.

Norman had never heard anything so radical spoken aloud in

a public place. He had never heard anything so radical, period. "Did you hear that?" he said to no one in particular.

Molly had been about to ask the same thing. She stood on tiptoe to see through the crowd and get a glimpse of who was speaking.

As Norman handed over fifteen cents for a new copy of *The Great Speckled Bird*, a guitar screamed its first sliding notes across the crowd.

"It's them!" Marvin Gardens cried out just as a second guitar's riffs spun out to meet the first wild cheers rising from the crowd.

Norman slapped *The Bird* at Molly and she caught it in her arms just as Norman and Marvin Gardens disappeared in the throng.

Lucy sighed. "Oh, well," she said. "It's the rock and roll that always takes them. It's as powerful as first love, you know. Now, let me see . . ." She looked toward a group of young men standing around a metal coffee can fire. A poster read DRAFT CARD BURNING HERE! Two policemen stood nearby, ready to arrest the first taker. Icy shivers flew across Molly's shoulders.

"Wanna come with?" asked Lucy.

Molly shuddered. "No, thanks." She wondered if Barry still had his draft card.

"Hello, Hotlanta!" came a mumbly, slurry voice at the mic. "We're the Allman Brothers Band, glad to be here."

"We love you!" shouted a group of girls in front of the steps.

"We love you, too," returned the man at the microphone. He wore a T-shirt with a motorcycle on it and had long, golden-red hair. Molly walked closer. The way he held himself seemed shy. *Closer*, she told herself.

"We've been working up this one," the man said, "a number by Blind Willie McTell called 'Statesboro Blues.' Anybody here from Statesboro, Georgia?"

"Yeah!"

133

The guitar player smiled as someone counted in the band, and suddenly the red-haired man was all intensity, all business. *Da-da-da-da-DUN* snapped the organ-drums-bass together as one, and they were off, the guitar squealing on and on like a little girl with her pigtail relentlessly pulled. Then the organ player began to sing in a gravelly growl, "Wake up, Mama!"

It was loud. It was straight-ahead. *It's noisy*, thought Molly. *Why can't they just sing a song with a melody and a harmony and nice words with lots of feeling?* Molly covered her ears, uncovered them, and remembered how Barry used to play Jimi Hendrix at a shattering volume on his record player over and over again after school, "Purple Haze" and "All Along the Watchtower," Barry with his guitar in his hands, trying to replicate what he heard.

When she'd complained, Barry had said, "Listen to how he bends those notes, Polka Dot! It's amazing! Here, like this."

"It's not even music, Barry!" Molly had protested.

"It's more than music," Barry had replied.

"You should listen to the Association," Molly had implored. "You could learn a lot about real songs, and they have *three* guitar players."

Barry had mussed her hair and said, "You're sweet." The conversation over, Molly had left the room, shutting Barry's door behind her.

But wait. This, on stage right now, suddenly had a melody. Sort of. Where was Norman? Molly began to thread through the crowd in earnest, coming closer to the stage until she could see the six musicians at the top of the stairs, their fingers flying over their guitars, over the organ keys, and two drummers, their arms and legs, hands and feet, working hard, rocking out behind and over their drum kits. They were already drenched with sweat in the afternoon sun, each drummer with his own vocabulary but both keeping the beat in tandem with the bass player, all of them concentrating together on an intricate blues-jazz-rock ballet.

Molly weaved to the left of the stage and up the rise for a better view. That drummer on the left looked suddenly familiar. His bass drum was painted black and in big white letters was printed JAI JOHANY JOHANSON.

Jai. Jai. *Jay.*

"Norman!" she called out, her head snapping around as she wheeled to find her cousin. "Norman!"

The music was deafening and the crowd was in the groove. No one heard her.

MOUNTAIN JAM

Performed by the Allman Brothers Band
Live at Piedmont Park, Atlanta, Georgia, 1969
Recorded at Fillmore East, New York, New York, 1971
Drummers: Butch Trucks and Jai Johany Johanson (Jaimoe)

NORMAN

I see him first. He's sitting up there behind his drum kit with no shirt and a necklace made out of shark's teeth, those granny sunglasses, and a slouchy hat. And I know it's him. Jay. Jai. There he is. *Maybe I'll catch you there, Florsheim.*

It's more than Barry could have described, and he had tried. He was right about Duane Allman, the guitar player — he's unbelievable. He wears a glass bottle, like a pill bottle, on the ring finger of his left hand, and he uses it to make those notes bend, wail, cry, and beg for mercy.

There are two guitar players, a bass player, an organ player who sings — Duane's brother — and two drummers, just as Barry said there were. The pictures in *The Great Speckled Bird* were distant and grainy and I never would have recognized Jai Johany Johanson, but I know the band calls him Jaimoe. I know all their names.

136

They play for hours, for days, for an eternity — I don't know how long they play, but I am *in it*, I am part of it, I am. The beginning and the end, every color, every pulse, every body on this planet and every other, stardust. Every hair on every head, counted. Every note ever played, every song ever sung. I swim in it until there is no "I" anymore, there is just us. And when I think it will get no better than this, they kill me with a last jam.

The percussion starts it off, Butch on the kettle drum, a steady beat, then Duane and Dickey noodling on their guitars, playing back and forth, call and response, like preachers do with hymns. Berry joins in with his bass guitar, Gregg layers in the organ, and then Butch and Jaimoe tap the edge of the snare or the hi-hat, stating the time, keeping it, daring the crowd to guess what they're about to play. Some already know and are cheering them on — *get going* — but they tease us while kids catcall and whistle and jump up and down. *Play it!*

When they've hinted at the melody just enough, the fans start screaming for it — screaming like they're on fire. They clap in time, *one-one-one-one*, every single note, until Duane breaks into the full melody and the whole band follows. A cheer rises up like Moses has just parted the Red Sea. The organ wails and the Allman Brothers Band takes us to the Promised Land.

It's Donovan's song "There Is a Mountain" — I recognize it. But it's theirs, too, their own interpretation, a mountain jam. It's tight. It's in the pocket. They are locked into one another like they share one nervous system, communicating like they're all a part of the same body, like nothing I've ever imagined was possible.

"It's all about listening," Mr. McCauley always tells us in band. "You can't jam if you can't listen."

Last night, Jai — Jaimoe — added, *Don't think it, feel it.*

Seems to me, everyone feels it. The crowd is part of the band, the band is part of the crowd, everyone moving in time, together.

137

The drums become my heartbeat, and now I understand how to play them — like a life force.

Well into the groove, after everyone in the band has played smoking solos that ride the top of the beat, the song "Shenandoah" creeps into the jam and runs through it. Then, seamlessly, "May the Circle Be Unbroken" plays to the cheers of the crowd, until, quietly, Donovan's mountain creeps back in to make a real circle of the song.

Everyone is moving, dancing, arms flying above them or entwined with the person next to them. With an incredible crescendo, the guitars scream, the organ wails, the bass roars, and the drums propel all of us to the finish. *Amen. Amen. Amen.*

"Amen!" shouts Marvin Gardens. I had forgotten he was there. I had forgotten anyone else was there, or maybe it was just that, for a timeless moment, there had been no separation between any of us.

"Thank you!" calls Duane, his guitar slung around his neck, and his hand gripping the microphone. "We're the Allman Brothers Band. Berry Oakley, Dickey Betts, Butch Trucks, Jai Johany Johanson, Gregg Allman, and I'm Duane Allman. Thank you!"

16

THERE IS A MOUNTAIN

Written by Donovan Leitch
Performed by Donovan
Recorded at CBS Studios, London, England, 1967
Percussion: Tony Carr

MOLLY

What a lot of noise. They are completely ruining Donovan's song. They're not even singing the words!

Then there is this kid with a flute who is playing the melody in the crowd and gets all these other kids to trail after him like he's Pan, the Greek god of shepherds, and he's leading his sheep to the meadow. It's such a long train I can't get past it to find Norman, and when I finally do, I discover him in a gaggle of kids behind the band. He's lying under a tree on the grass near the drummer, Jai — so obviously he found him first, but he's lying there with his eyes shut and his arms out like he's Jesus blessing the lambs. Or maybe like he's been knocked out. I notice he's barefoot.

I shake him and call out, "Norman!" but he doesn't budge. The band is so loud and the guitars are screaming at each other and the drummers are trying to see who can be the loudest and there is no song!

"He's okay!" shouts Marvin Gardens, who is standing there weaving and bopping over Norman like a lunatic. "He's diggin' it. He'll be back."

"Where are his shoes?"

Marvin Gardens shrugs. "Somewhere."

I cover my ears. "I'm going to the house!" I shout. Marvin Gardens waves a loopy hand in acknowledgment and I pick my way around all the hippies and find my way out of there. I see a short kid in blue jeans wearing Norman's shoes. Or at least I think they're Norman's shoes — they are way too big for this kid. But I keep walking. I am not the keeper of my cousin's shoes.

If I live to be a hundred, I will never understand this music.

NORMAN

I'm slammed instantly back to earth and rush the stage as soon as Duane announces the end. There's no room to move, with all the equipment, but I thread my way to the front of Jaimoe's kit anyway and . . . I just stand there, mute. I don't even know what to say. *I have my drums in the bus — wanna jam? How can I learn to play like that? Take me with you!*

Jaimoe is mopping his face with a rag. "Florsheim," he says. He points a drumstick at my feet. "You lost your shoes."

I have also lost the power to speak.

There are other kids then, eager to meet the band, and I get bumped aside by them, and by those who are helping move the band's equipment off the stage because another band is up next, and a couple with flowers in their hair is getting married on the steps by a tall man in a black top hat, and I don't see the Allman Brothers Band suddenly, not even Jaimoe, and I start to run, grabbing a tree as I spin around it, and suddenly Jaimoe is there by my elbow. He says, "You want to keep your jazz. Play your rock and roll, but keep your jazz."

Yessir, I start to say, but I catch myself. "Right on," I say instead. My voice is a croak.

Jaimoe's whole face smiles at me, a kid whose life has just been changed forever. He says, "Jazz is American music. Everything else builds on it — country, soul, blues, rock and roll. Jazz is music to feel by. Listen to it, practice it, and use it to add texture and mystery to whatever you play. You take what is, and you improvise. That's what you heard today."

"And blues," says another voice, more to Jaimoe than to me. "You heard a whole lot of blues." Then he points to me. "Is this the kid you were talking about last night?"

"That's him," says Jaimoe.

I say nothing. I try to smile. *How do you do, Duane Allman? My cousin Barry is missing, but I'm here to see you in his place, and I can't wait to tell him I met you, that your band is amazing.*

"Where's your bus?" asks Duane.

I gesture in the direction of Fourteenth Street.

Jaimoe laughs. "Skydog here is a blues man. I jammed with him in Muscle Shoals. You know Muscle Shoals?"

I shake my head.

"You should know it," says Jaimoe. "Lots of good music getting put together there. And they've got a great studio drummer, Roger Hawkins. He'd be worth listening to. He's on your way to California."

Finally, my voice comes back. "Where?" I ask.

"Muscle Shoals, Alabama," says Jaimoe. "FAME Studios. Rick Hall's place. Tell him Jaimoe and Duane sent you."

"Okay," I say, just to have something to say.

"Okay?" asks Jaimoe. "You'll go?"

"I'll go," I promise.

"Good man," says Jaimoe. Duane smiles with a tiny nod and Jaimoe says, "I can tell, man, you're gonna learn to feel it."

"How do you do it?" I ask.

"Do what?"

"How you play . . . it's jazz and it's blues and it's rock and roll."

"I told you, man. Learn to listen. And practice until your fingers fall off."

"You know R&B?" asks Duane.

"Rhythm and blues?"

"Go to the Shoals," says Duane. "And listen to WLAC. It's 1510 on the AM dial, Nashville. At night they boost the signal and you can tune it in most anywhere. They play R&B all night — I love that stuff. Grew up listening to it."

I have no answers to this but *okay*. Which I say. I don't say, *Can I come live with you? Can you teach me?*

"You're a southern boy," finishes Duane. "Know your musical roots."

"Fourteenth Street," I say. "That's where the bus is. Do you need a ride?"

Now Duane laughs. "Sometimes we do, man. But not today."

Kids have collected around us, listening, waiting their turn to connect but pushing in on us with impatience. Kids are clustered around Butch and his drum kit, Berry and his bass, Dickie and his guitar, Gregg and his organ. Equipment cases on the grass are snapped open and some kids are rolling up wires and unplugging cords, disconnecting pedals and taking the cymbals off their stands while they wait for the musicians to fill the cases with their instruments.

"I . . . I gotta go," I say. I know I do, but it's killing me.

142

"Peace, brother," says Jaimoe. He holds up two fingers. So does Duane. And just like that, the spell that held the three of us in a private bubble is broken and the waiting gaggle swarms in.

MOLLY

The sun has slipped behind the tops of the tall buildings surrounding the park. The shadows are long and cool. It's going to be a good night for a long drive. I hope I don't have to stay awake for Norman. I am beyond pooped.

I call Mom from the house phone just to check — because I am responsible — and she says her car is ready, they'll be here, don't wait for them, they're on the way tomorrow, get a good night's sleep and leave early. But we are leaving now.

I help turn on all the lamps inside the house. They make the rooms look like they're bathed in butter. Lucy prepares TV dinners while we wait for The Aunts to make their appearance at the top of the stairs.

"How do you always have money?" I ask her again.

Her hair is clipped to the top of her head — it's hot in the kitchen. "I knocked over a bank last Saturday."

"Really," I return. "Are you rich?"

Lucy turns on the window fan and sighs. "My father's a heart surgeon," she says. "And he doesn't understand that a heart needs more than money."

"Oh," I say, wishing I hadn't asked. "I'm sorry."

"It's okay," she says. "I'm glad your mom and your aunt are coming tomorrow. I'm making Mashula's fried chicken and potato salad. I hope they let me stay."

"I do, too," I say, and I'm surprised to realize I mean it. "Do you like Norman?" I ask.

"He's cute." Lucy pulls on her hot mitts as the oven timer goes off. "He needs to loosen up. I was just trying to help."

"I see," I say in my most sarcastic tone of voice.

"Do you like Marvin?" she asks me in counterpoint.

"I hadn't thought about it," I say honestly. "I'm a girl on a mission. No time to think about cuteness."

143

"He lived under a bridge in Piedmont Park before I met him," Lucy says, not one bit interested in asking me about my mission. "Now he's escorting your aunts to dinner every night and taking up their breakfast trays in the morning. He's watching *The Newlywed Game!*"

Lucy laughs at this, but I shudder to think of anybody living under a bridge. I shudder to think it could be Barry.

We all eat Swanson TV dinners together in the dining room and wait until Aunt Madeleine and Aunt Eleanor are settled in front of the television before Norman and I make our good-byes.

"Good-bye, good-bye!" we call to them. They wave us away during a commercial and tell us they love us. I think they mean it.

Marvin Gardens fills the ice chest with ice and sticks a few bottles of soda deep into the coldness.

"Happy trails," he says.

Impulsively, I hug him.

"Heeyyy!" he says. Then, "Far out!"

"Take care of yourself," I say.

"Yeah," says Norman. "And thanks for all the help."

Marvin salutes us and watches us pull slowly away from the curb, the engine coughing to life and Norman doing his usual jumpin'-jack-flash in the driver's seat.

Kids are milling around us, walking in the street, waving a hand as we pass them. The sifty dark is full of shadows as we drive along the Strip out of town. Traffic moves slowly because, as Lucy told us, so many cars are full of people from the suburbs who come to stare at the hippies. We creep the four blocks from Fourteenth to Tenth and finally roll out of the city of Atlanta.

"You okay?" Norman asks me. He's craning his neck, looking at me in the wide student mirror at the front of the bus. I see his face turned up, questioning.

I smile at him from my seat behind the driver. "I'm okay. You?"

I reach over the silver half-high partition between our seats and pat him on the shoulder. He turns on the radio . . . and wouldn't you know, the song playing is actually "Jumpin' Jack Flash" by the Rolling Stones. Number three on the Weekly Top Forty last year.

Norman turns up the volume.

We are driving west. We are on our way.

IT AIN'T ME

**From "Fortunate Son"
by Creedence
Clearwater Revival**

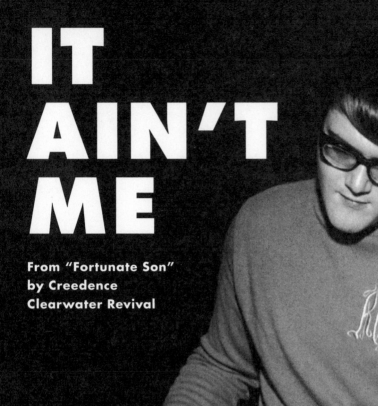

Session drummer Roger Hawkins, a member of the Muscle Shoals Rhythm Section also known as the Swampers, rehearses at FAME Studios in 1968 in Muscle Shoals, Alabama.

I'm not kidding myself. My voice alone is just an ordinary voice. What people come to see is how I use it. If I stand still while I'm singing, I'm dead, man. I might as well go back to driving a truck.

Elvis Presley

As for those deserters, malcontents, radicals, incendiaries, the civil and uncivil disobedients among the young, SDS, PLP, Weathermen I and Weathermen II, the revolutionary action movement, the Black United Front, Yippies, Hippies, Yahoos, Black Panthers, lions and tigers alike—I would swap the whole damn zoo for a single platoon of the kind of young Americans I saw in Vietnam.

Spiro T. Agnew, vice president of the United States, 1969–1973

'SALVAGE' OF REJECTS TO BE ROLE OF DRAFT

NEW YORK (UPI) — Defense Secretary Robert S. McNamara, in a dramatic major policy shift, today announced that 100,000 draft rejects would be taken into military service annually in the future to 'salvage' them for society.

The Desert Sun, August 23, 1966

A Titan II ICBM (intercontinental ballistic missile) in its silo underground, ready for launch in case of nuclear attack by a foreign power on U.S. soil

THE UNLEASHED POWER OF THE ATOM HAS CHANGED EVERYTHING SAVE OUR MODES OF THINKING, AND WE THUS DRIFT TOWARD UNPARALLELED CATASTROPHE.

Albert Einstein

In my view it is a national disgrace that the term 'egghead' as a synonym for intellectual excellence has become a derogatory expression. Let me tell you that it is the 'eggheads' who are saving us — just as it was the 'eggheads' who wrote the Constitution of the United States. It is the 'eggheads' in the realm of science and technology, in industry, in statecraft, as well as in other fields who form the first line of freedom's defense.

Bernard Schriever, architect of the U.S. Air Force space and missile programs

Miles Hinton at New Buffalo Commune,
Arroyo Hondo, New Mexico, 1967

Building the communal house at New Buffalo Commune,
Arroyo Hondo, New Mexico, 1968

"Fifteen of us lived together, one room per family, and a kitchen and a communal room. I can't say that I enjoyed that kind of living. It always seemed that women ended up doing a lot more chores than the men. The men played music, smoked the herb, chopped wood, and repaired vehicles. The lack of privacy was a test."

Lisa Law, New Buffalo resident and photographer

Map of New Mexico communes above Santa Fe, New Mexico in 1969

The Jaggers, house band of the Institute of American Indian Arts in Santa Fe, in LIFE magazine, December 1, 1967

From left to right: John Gritts (a Cherokee) on bass, Rosemary Peso (an Apache) on vocals, Loren Moore (an Oneida) on drums, Dennis Stover (an Athabascan) on lead guitar, and Alfred Young Man (a Cree) on rhythm guitar.

"A real woman's movement is dangerous. From the beginning it exposed the white male power structure in all its hypocrisy. Its very existence and long duration were proof of massive large-scale inequality in a system that pretended to be democracy."
Shulamith Firestone, founding member of New York Radical Women, Redstockings, and New York Radical Feminists, 1968

"This is to respectfully request a city permit for a demonstration in Atlantic City on Saturday, September 7, 1968 . . . The purpose of the demonstration is to protest the Miss America Pageant, which projects an image of women that many American women find unfortunate; the emphasis being on body rather than brains, on youth rather than maturity, and on commercialism rather than humanity."
August 1968 letter from Robin Morgan of the women's liberation movement to Richard Jackson, the mayor of Atlantic City, New Jersey

"We know, because we have been there, that the American public has not been told the truth about the war, or about Viet-Nam . . . we believe that true support for our buddies still in Viet-Nam is to demand that they be brought home (through whatever negotiation is necessary) before anyone else dies in a war that the American people did not vote for and do not want."
Vietnam Veterans against the War, 1967

17

COLD SWEAT

Written by James Brown and Alfred "Pee Wee" Ellis
Performed by James Brown and the James Brown Orchestra
Recorded at King Studios, Cincinnati, Ohio, 1967
Drummer: Clyde Stubblefield

"'A night drive through the North Alabama mountains is inadvisable.'" Molly used a flashlight to read the warning in *An Adventurer's Guide to Travel across America.*

"They're just hills," said Norman, although he was already white-knuckling the steering wheel in the dark. He was wearing the same khaki slacks and had put on his white oxford shirt over his T-shirt but had discarded his wing tips for the only other pair of shoes he'd brought with him, a pair of black Converse Chuck Taylor All Stars high-top sneakers, size 14. They looked better with his slacks than they did with his gym suit at school. And they were more comfortable for driving than the wing tips. He did not mourn the loss of his sandals.

"I routed us through Birmingham," Molly said as they pulled onto the highway out of Atlanta.

"Can you figure it out through Muscle Shoals, Alabama?

Here's the address I got from the long-distance operator. You'll need the street map to find it."

"Why?" It was a curious question, not an accusation.

"Music" was all Norman would tell her. He couldn't begin to relate the head-rattling astonishment of the past twenty-four hours, from the moment they walked the Strip to the moment they drove it, leaving Atlanta.

Molly consulted her maps. "Okay. I can do that."

She scribbled the route to Muscle Shoals on a piece of note paper from a pad Pam had given them. It had poodles across the top of it. Then she yawned. "Aren't you tired? Do you want to stop?"

Norman shook his head. "Nah. I can get us to Muscle Shoals. And there won't be traffic. You sleep. I've got the radio. Will it bother you?"

"No, it's fine. I could sleep for a week." Molly held on to the bars across the tops of the seats, weave-walked the aisle in the dark, dug her transistor radio and earphone out of her bag, and dove into her bed at the back of the bus.

Norman drove into the deepening night, sitting on Molly's directions to make sure they were close at hand. He turned the radio dial to 1510 AM, WLAC Nashville. It came in clear and crisp over the night airwaves. A thrill shot through Norman's chest. Just as Duane had said, there it was. John R the disc jockey was selling chickens.

How'd you like to have fried chicken on your table just about any time you wanted it, right? Well, look here, baby, you can!

Norman laughed. For the next three hours, he drove through the night and listened to "The Nighttime Station for Half the Nation!" The WLAC disc jockeys played Sonny Boy Williamson and Aretha and Little Richard. Between songs they sold everything from Bibles to Royal Crown Hair Pomade.

B.B. King played his guitar, Lucille — or maybe Lucille played B.B. Then Louis Jordan and his band sang "Caldonia!" *That's*

158

some jump blues for you jazz cats out there! I might even call it rock and roll! Ain't that a mess! Sister Rosetta Tharpe sang "Didn't It Rain?" *Listen to that guitar wail! An oldie but a goodie for all you gospel lovers out there! Comin' up, a little boogie-woogie, and a little Muddy Waters, right after we sell you some records. Don't go nowhere, ya hear?*

There was something magical about night driving that lent itself to listening. Norman got so wrapped up in driving and listening, he didn't think to look at the gas gauge. When John R played "Cold Sweat" by James Brown, Norman pulled off the highway at a sign that said PICNIC AREA, onto a sandy lane lined with pines, and got as still as he could.

It was the beat, he told himself. What was that beat? He tried to tap it out on the steering wheel. The drummer was hitting the snare on the two and four but missing that fourth beat by an eighth note and playing between the beats — or was it instead of the beat?

Every instrument — the guitars, the horns, the drums — acted as percussion, too. And the energy! James Brown screamed and moaned and sang and called out, *Excuse me while I boogaloo!* And then — *Let's give the drummer some!* A drum solo!

Suddenly, "In-A-Gadda-Da-Vida" was something Norman left behind, in childhood.

"Cold Sweat" ended and John R came back to preach. *Now look here, baby, you got your jazz, you got your soul, you got your rock and roll. And when you put 'em all together, what you got? You got funk!*

Norman rested his forehead between his hands on the giant steering wheel. He was tired. And he finally noticed the gas gauge. John R was signing off and giving the turntable to Gene Nobles for his *Midnight Special* program.

"Have a little mercy there, honey," John R said in a gravelly-voiced growl. "I'm here, way down south in the middle of Dixie."

*　　*　　*

A Texaco station was open in Anniston, Alabama, its big bright star beaming like a beacon guiding him forward.

Norman carefully pulled close to the pump, turned off the radio, and cut the engine. An attendant wearing a Texaco shirt appeared and pumped his gas while Norman sat in the driver's seat and counted the bills Uncle Bruce had given him. It was a lot of money. Enough to pay for gas all the way across the country and back, at least, depending on what happened to them. Between this and what Pam and Janice had given him, what Molly had, and what he had saved himself, they were so far, so good with money.

Norman tucked Uncle Bruce's envelope under the seat, inside the box of letters from Barry. He left the bus.

"That's fourteen dollars and seventy-two cents," said the attendant. The badge sewed into his shirt said Buddy was his name. "You must have been driving on fumes."

"It's got a sixty-gallon tank," said Norman.

"Well, you just put upwards of forty-five gallons of gas in her. That's fumes, for a sixty-gallon tank. You want to fill up before you get too low. You get a burp of air in the tank, that kills the engine. Maybe you should take some extra gas in the vehicle."

He pronounced it *vee-hickle*, then spit on the concrete beneath their feet. His spittle was the color of stained teeth.

"Yessir," said Norman. The glare from the fluorescent lights was fierce and the night bugs flew into the brightness, buzzing and biting.

Buddy was sizing him up, Norman could tell. He watched him glance at the South Carolina license plate and the CHARLESTON COUNTY SCHOOLS on the side of the bus. "You got a gas can?"

"Nossir." How could he have forgotten a gas can? He had everything else.

160

"Come on," Buddy said, and Norman followed him inside the station to the garage bays, where Buddy picked around and found two banged-up but serviceable five-gallon gas cans.

It took him so long to find them, Norman got nervous. "That's okay . . ." he began.

But the man hefted the cans at his ears and said, "Yep, empty. Won't charge you for the cans, but you gotta pay to fill 'em up."

"Sure," said Norman. "Thanks. Can I use your bathroom, too?"

Five minutes later, Norman's bladder was empty and the gas cans were full. He paid Buddy and opened the back door of the bus. The light from the overhang cast a ghoulish glow on his drums. They peeked out of cardboard boxes with no tops, like colorful rounded mountains rising from the brown earth.

"You got drums," said Buddy.

"I'm a drummer," Norman replied.

He shoved the bass drum over to make room for the gas cans, and Buddy helped him lift them into the bus. Molly was completely hidden in the shadows, inside her sleeping bag. He hoped she'd stay that way. He did not want to have a conversation with Buddy about why he had a girl hidden in the back of the bus.

"Thanks a lot," he said as he began to swing the back door closed. Molly moaned softly and turned over. *Don't panic*, he told himself. He latched the back door, double-timed it to the front of the bus, and climbed on board.

Buddy watched him and followed him around front to the folding door. He put his hands on the body of the bus, on either side of the door opening, and looked up at Norman with raised eyebrows. "You gonna be okay out there?"

"Yessir," said Norman, too quickly. "I'm almost there. Thanks a lot for the gas cans."

"That's a lot of gas for *almost there*," said Buddy. His face was very white under the fluorescent lights, his skin very tight over his cheekbones.

"Yessir," said Norman as he settled into the driver's seat, depressed the clutch, and turned the key in the ignition.

Buddy stood where he was. "Your folks know you're out here this time of night?"

"Yessir." Norman began to sweat.

"What's your destination?" Buddy placed one black, shiny-shoed foot on the bottom step but did not board. *Des-tee-nation*, he'd said.

"Birmingham," Norman lied, as he put his right foot on the brake and his hand on the long gearshift lever. "My aunts live there. They're expecting me."

But Norman could not shut the folding door and drive off while Buddy held it open with his foot.

Buddy rapped his fingertips, *one-two-three-four, one-two-three-four*, on the yellow body of the bus. Norman's pulse raced as he revved the engine. "I . . . gotta go." His nerves made his voice shake.

Buddy pursed his lips and finally said, "Who you got back there, son? Huh?"

"Nobody!" Norman said, but he knew Buddy wouldn't believe his lie.

"Then you won't mind me having a look, now, will you?"

"Wait —" Norman started.

"Graaaahhhhhhh!"

Before Buddy could take a step onto the bus, a figure leaped, hollering a night-of-the-living-dead scream, from where he'd been hiding, four seats back. *"Graaaahhhhhhh!"*

Every muscle in Norman's body froze. Buddy jerked his foot off the step like it was on fire.

The figure rushed to the front of the bus, grabbed the shiny metal door handle with both hands, and yanked it to the left with such a mighty force that the door flattened into Buddy and slammed him in the face. Buddy stumbled backward and fell hard into a gas pump, hitting his head on the glass and sliding to the concrete. He brought a hand up to his head and sat there, dazed.

"Go!" shouted the figure next to Norman. He was a young black man. He wore stiff green pants, a white T-shirt, and silver dog tags on a chain around his neck. He looped one arm around the stanchion at the top of the stepwell while the other hand held fast to the door handle.

Norman's panic propelled him as he shoved the engine into gear and jumped his body into action, pumping, jerking, lurching, squealing, turning the bus so tightly he thought for one terrifying moment it might tip over, then racing it down the vacant street and into the black night.

The figure held on to the stanchion and swung fully into the stepwell as the bus careened away. He slammed into the half-high barrier wall on the front passenger side, and scrabbled to find his balance, all the while yelling:

"GO GO GO!"

18

AIN'T NO MOUNTAIN HIGH ENOUGH

Written by Nikolas Ashford and Valerie Simpson
Performed by Marvin Gaye and Tammi Terrell
Recorded at Motown Studios, Detroit, Michigan, 1967
Drummer: Benny "Papa Zita" Benjamin and Uriel Jones

Performed by Diana Ross & the Supremes
Recorded at Motown Studios, Detroit, Michigan, 1969
Drummers: Uriel Jones and Richard "Pistol" Allen, of the Funk Brothers

"Norman!" Molly shrieked from the back of the bus as she struggled to get up. They must have had an accident, she had to wake up, had to get to her cousin. "Normaaaaan!"

"Stay there!" screamed Norman as he tried to stop the bus from swinging wildly back and forth and skidding off the road into a ditch. He was horrified to realize they could smash into a telephone pole and burst into a fiery furnace with a full tank of gas.

"Go!" the stranger urged once again. "Get away before he can come after you!"

Norman yelled at the stranger. "Who are you?"

"Norman!" Molly wailed. She had grabbed on to a bus seat and was finding her footing. "Turn on the lights!"

"Everything's fine! Go back to sleep!" The bus was dark, with only the instrument panel lighted.

Molly got halfway up and fell back on her bottom. "What are you doing?" *A night drive through the North Alabama mountains is inadvisable.* Were they there already? "What's happening?" She got on her hands and knees.

Norman was half standing in a crouch over his seat, his legs shaking with the effort, looking ahead, looking in all the mirrors, looking to the right and left, his right foot riding the accelerator.

It was like saddling a bucking bronco that got tired of fighting. Finally, the bus began to behave and calm itself under Norman's ministrations. Molly got to her feet and began making her way to the front in the dark. "Are you okay?"

"Fine! Fine!" called Norman. "Everything's fine now!"

He did not turn on the interior lights. All he needed at this point was Molly to rev up her emotion machine.

"Please go back to sleep!"

Molly kept coming up the aisle. Norman cast a glance to his right. The black man in army fatigues squatted in the stepwell where the silver partition wall hid him from view. He stared at Norman but did not look scared.

Molly had almost reached her usual seat behind the driver. Norman swung the steering wheel left a half jag, which threw Molly off balance. She landed in a seat on the right side of the aisle with a thump.

"I need a bathroom, Norman! Why are you driving like a crazy person?"

"Deer," said Norman. "You don't want me to hit a deer, do you?" *Think, Norman, think.*

Molly rubbed her eyes. "Bathroom" was all she said.

The bus once again purred and growled its usual straight-ahead noises, so Norman sat fully on the driver's seat, but he did not slow down. He was not about to stop yet — what if Buddy

165

was hot on his tail? He was not about to carry this stranger with them through the night, either. Ahead he could see no stores or towns, just lonely road with the occasional car or lumber truck coming the opposite direction, headlights glaring into theirs.

"I don't see a place," he said.

They came to a junction and Norman turned right, as much to hide from the possibility of Buddy as anything else.

Two miles up the road, Molly pointed to a driveway with an ornate arched metal sign that gleamed in the headlights. She ordered Norman to stop.

"That's a cemetery!"

"I can't wait."

He didn't have a better idea. It would be a perfect spot to hide the bus until Buddy went home for the night. He hoped they hadn't hurt him. Norman turned into the pebbled driveway. The bus rumbled and weaved on a rutted dirt road past white obelisks and gray crypts and engraved stones, past trees with low branches covering stone benches and hovering over angels with wings and archangels with trumpets.

"Far enough!" said Molly. "Stop! I have to get off."

As soon as Norman stopped the bus, Molly popped up to the front.

"Wait!" Norman said, but there would be no waiting from Molly.

Norman jumped from his seat to block Molly, grabbed the door handle, and hoped the stranger would jump out as soon as he opened it. He forgot that opening the folding door would turn on the stepwell light, which was very bright. It illuminated the stranger like a sudden spotlight just as Molly pushed past Norman, grabbed the stanchion, and swung herself around it to take the steps.

"Holy —" Norman began, but he was drowned out by the screaming. Molly screamed and so did the stranger, which made

Norman scream, and then the three of them stood there at the front of the bus, screaming as loud as they could at one another. Loud enough to wake the dead.

"Don't hurt us!" Norman yelled. He grabbed Molly and pulled her to him.

"I'm not hurtin' nobody," said the stranger, his hands up like he was under arrest. "I just want a ride."

"How did you get in here!" Molly's breath was shallow and short. "Have you been hiding in here since we left Atlanta?"

"I got on when you stopped for gas. I didn't know you were in the back asleep. I just need a ride. I was gonna ask, but then I saw —"

"The deer?" asked Norman, pointedly.

The stranger stared at Norman, and Norman returned his gaze.

"Yeah," said the stranger. He put his hands down.

A cicada flew in through the open door and found the dome light above the stepwell. Molly swatted at it and retreated to her seat behind the driver. *Now what?*

"What you did back there . . ." began Norman.

"Yeah," said the stranger.

"What did he do?" asked Molly.

Norman thought for a moment and answered, "He helped."

"Can you give me a ride?" the stranger asked.

"Where are you headed?"

"Wherever you're goin'."

Norman pulled at his earlobe. "Molly?"

Molly started for the back of the bus. "Please turn on the dome lights," she said in a snippy voice. "I need my bag of essentials."

Norman obliged.

The seconds ticked by in a quiet eternity as Molly got her bag in the back and walked to the front, where she waited for the stranger to get off the bus so she could make her way out. The night air was cool, and there was no moon. Sparkling stars covered the night sky like a diamond blanket over the "Rest in Heaven" section of the cemetery.

Molly shouldered her bag. "Don't come over by the Angel Gabriel. I need some privacy."

"You got it," said Norman.

"And after that, some supper."

"It's after midnight!"

"I *know.*"

An hour later, the three of them had introduced themselves ("like civilized people do," insisted Molly) and had consumed the sodas Marvin Gardens had put in the ice chest, along with the peanut butter sandwiches and cookies that Pam had packed for them. They ate them on a long granite ledger stone the length of a dining room table — or a person — marking the grave of Simon Tallow, age nineteen, who had died in 1864, fighting for the Confederate States of America.

Darling, we miss thee was etched in the stone.

It was the first time Molly had ever eaten at the same table as a black person. No white kids at school would do it, but everyone at the H&H in Macon did it, and Superman had kissed her hand.

His name was Ray, the stranger told them.

"What's with the army pants?" Norman finally asked.

"Fort McClellan," answered Ray. "It's near here."

"You stationed there?"

"Not anymore."

Silence.

Are you discharged? Are you a deserter? Molly dearly wanted to ask the questions but settled for "Where are you from?"

"Mississippi," Ray said. "If you're goin' that way, that's the way I wanna go, too."

"We're going to Muscle Shoals, Alabama," said Norman.

"But we're also going to Memphis, Tennessee," said Molly, "and that's right above Mississippi."

"Molly . . ." began Norman as Molly's face reddened. She had impulsively showed off her map knowledge.

"Can I come with you?" Ray asked. "I can drive. I got my license. I drive a stake-bed truck on our farm; it's bigger than your bus."

When neither Molly nor Norman replied, Ray tried again.

"I've been driving longer than you have."

"How old are you?" Norman asked.

"Nineteen."

"I just turned seventeen."

"Me, too," said Molly.

"You're fourteen," said Norman.

They fell silent while the night creatures sang around them. They were unpracticed at conversation.

Ray pointed at Norman's shoes. "I used to have a pair of those," he said. "Mine were white." He wiped sandwich crumbs from his face with his hand.

Another awkward silence. Then Norman said, "Can you drive for a while, then, Ray?"

"I sure can."

"Norman," said Molly. She looked at Ray apologetically and he returned her gaze with a fiery look. He wasn't afraid of her. She set her jaw and made herself glare back, although it made her nervous. He tugged on his ear and looked away.

"It's either that, or we sleep in the cemetery tonight," said Norman.

They climbed on board the bus, and Norman handed Ray the directions. "It's pretty simple."

169

"I know the way," said Ray.

"Okay if I sleep?" asked Norman.

"I'll stay up," said Molly. "I've slept."

"We'll trade off," said Norman. He tossed his pillow and blanket on one of the seats. Ray nodded.

Six hours later, as the sun crept between the pines and swelled into the summer sky, a school bus with South Carolina tags pulled into the parking lot at FAME Studios in Muscle Shoals, Alabama. It parked out of sight of the main road. By the time someone arrived to unlock the studio and start the day's sessions, three teenagers were sleeping soundly on a bus in the shade of some longleaf pines.

19

THE ROAD OF LOVE

Written by Clarence Carter
Performed by Clarence Carter with Duane "Skydog" Allman
Recorded at FAME Studios, Muscle Shoals, Alabama, 1969
Drummer: Roger Hawkins

They woke up roasting. It had been so cool in the night, they had closed most of the bus windows. Now it was noon and the heat inside the bus had them broiling.

"We need a fan!" was the first thing Norman heard from the back of the bus — *Molly* — combined with a rapping on the bus door.

"Anybody in there? Open up!"

Ray dove under the seat he'd been sleeping on. Molly shut her mouth and made herself small next to the drums. Norman ran in his stocking feet to the folding door and opened it. "Sorry!" *It must be the police.* "I can explain!"

It wasn't the police. The man at the door had long hair shaped like a bowl on his head and sideburns to his chin. He wore brown slacks with cowboy boots, a brown patterned shirt open at the collar, and a black leather jacket.

"Peace, man," he said, holding up two fingers in salutation.

"I was starting to get worried I had the wrong bus. We didn't expect you so soon."

"Uh?" Norman was confused.

"Come on in," said the man with a wave. "Wash up! We'll feed you. I'm Rick Hall — welcome to FAME."

"Uh . . . yessir," Norman answered. "Thank you, sir."

He cast a look at the seat where Ray had been. It was empty. He couldn't see Molly, either. "We'll be right there," he said.

"Suit yourself," said the man. "Bring the cymbals with you." He walked back to the building that proclaimed itself to be:

F A M E

RECORDING STUDIOS INC.

PUBLISHING CO. INC.

PRODUCTIONS INC.

603

"No commas," said Molly. Suddenly, she was at Norman's elbow.

"What?"

"The sign. No commas."

"Oh."

"S'cuse me," said Ray, who had now appeared as well. Norman and Molly parted to let him off the bus, and he made for the scrub pines behind the studio.

"Where's he going?" said Molly. "Not even a *good morning* or *thanks for the ride*."

"He'll be back," said Norman. "Do we have cymbals that don't belong to me?" He was already threading his way over a castaway pillow and blanket to the back of the bus. Molly began opening windows. Norman moved boxes and looked under seats and buckled to one knee when he stepped on the foam rubber. "We need to get rid of more seats!"

"Told ya!"

He found his footing and a black case he hadn't noticed yesterday. He laid it on top of Molly's sleeping bag and opened it. Cymbals. And a note, written in tiny, neat print, around the blank edges of a copy of *The Great Speckled Bird*:

> *Florsheim: These belong to Roger Hawkins. I borrowed 'em and said I'd get 'em back, but I'm late on the return. Thanks for toting them to the Shoals for me. I'll let them know you're coming. Wasn't sure which house on 14th was yours, so we just snuck 'em on the bus. Keep your doors locked, traveling to California. Learn to listen. Peace. Jaimoe*

"Hey! Come in, come in, all of you, come in!" said Rick Hall as Norman, Molly, and Ray stepped into the lobby. "We got collards and sweet potatoes, sliced tomatoes, and fried chicken. You hungry?"

They were. Introductions were made all around. "These gentlemen are my house band, the Swampers," said Rick. "Roger Hawkins on drums, Jimmy Johnson on gee-tar, Barry Beckett on keyboards, and David Hood on bass. Say hey, boys. And Spooner! Get in here, Spooner!"

The band was already eating. They wiped hands and shook with Norman and Ray, but they just nodded at Molly, who was fine not shaking hands with a bunch of guys eating their lunch. Ray was hesitant to offer a hand at first, but the band members — all of them white — were not. Molly noticed Ray was no longer wearing his dog tags.

"And this," said Rick, referring to a group of musicians just joining them, some black, some white, "is my horn section today. Andrew Love, Charlie Chalmers, Wayne Jackson, Floyd Newman.

173

The Memphis Horns on loan from Stax. Best you'll ever hear, mark my words."

Rick gestured at the table. "Join us," he said, to both the horn section and the hungry travelers. "We get lunch brought in when it's this many of us. It's easier than all of us going to a restaurant where we still get the side-eye. You know what Governor Wallace said about 'segregation now, segregation forever.' We don't hold with that here. We make music. Music is colorblind. Sit. Here, let me take those."

Rick took the cymbal case from Norman and passed it to Roger Hawkins. "Thanks" was all Roger said, and he went back to his chicken.

"Duane called me in the middle of the night!" said Rick as he pulled sodas from the machine without putting any money in. "Said to watch for you kids tonight, and here you are already. You ever been in a recording studio before?"

All three teenagers shook their heads. Rick roared with laughter. "Well! We'll show you around, won't we, boys? I hear you're a drummer, Florsheim. We're always looking for new talent. Duane put up a pup tent in my parking lot and camped out there, trying to get a gig last year. I gave him his chance! So a drummer in a school bus is no surprise to me. Maybe you'll stay! Duane liked it so much here, he bought a cabin over on the Tennessee River, didn't he, boys?"

"The boys" lit cigarettes and sat back as Molly and Ray ate and Norman tried to tell Rick he wasn't *that* good a drummer, he just had a starter kit. Roger Hawkins said quietly, "That's all you need." He stubbed out his cigarette in his plate and said, "Son, I used to play on cans."

Norman smiled even as his face colored red. "Me, too."

Roger stood up and wiped his fingers with a napkin, tossed it in his paper plate. "Come on, I'll show you. We got a few minutes, Rick?"

Molly and Ray followed Norman down the hallway to the studio. Norman stopped at the door so quickly they nearly ran into him. Above the door was a sign Norman read out loud:

THROUGH THESE DOORS WALK THE FINEST MUSICIANS, SONGWRITERS, ARTISTS AND PRODUCERS IN THE WORLD

Rick threaded himself between Molly and Ray. "Aretha recorded here," he said, slapping Norman on the back and guiding him into the studio. To Molly and Ray he said, "Not you two. You two come with me in the control booth." Ray gave Molly his fiery look. She returned it with a steadiness that surprised her.

The drum set was a Ludwig, with a burgundy 22" bass, a 16"x16" blue glitter floor tom, and a 13"x9" sky-blue pearl mounted tom, a 5 ½"x14" chrome snare, two sets of cymbals, and a pair of hi-hats.

"It's a mix-and-match set," said Roger. "It's all you need. You just want to sound good. And every song needs something different, as you can imagine."

Norman nodded. He could not imagine. Not at all.

"Have a seat."

Norman sat behind the drums in the studio where Aretha Franklin had recorded. "And Otis Redding! And Clarence Carter! And Duane — don't forget Duane!" called Rick over the playback speakers as he and Molly and Ray watched through the control booth window that spanned the wall. Norman picked up the drumsticks from where they rested in their holder. They were sleek, like racehorses, compared to the thick marching band sticks he used.

Roger sat at a second set, a blue Ludwig silver sparkle matching set with FAME splashed across the bass drum. "Single stroke roll," he said, and began to play. Norman followed him. *Warm-ups*, he thought. *Just like in band.*

"Double strokes," said Roger. The two of them played together. "Watch your time. Follow me. Now, a few flams. Some paradiddles. Add a little hi-hat, mind your feet. Work on control, not speed."

Norman kept up — he was surprised. Triplets. Rolls. Fills. Every nerve in his body was alive and vibrating to the tempo and this unexpected opportunity.

"Good," said Roger.

Rick's voice came over the playback speakers, loud and insistent.

"We got two minutes for you to play around, son, and then it's back to work for the band. Here ya go. You know Wilson Pickett's 'Land of 1000 Dances'?"

"Yessir," said Norman. He'd played his drums to it at home. It was a great song.

"Number six on the Weekly Top Forty," said Molly.

"Yessiree, little lady," said Rick. He beamed. "We recorded it right here — my band with Roger on the drums. Added the Memphis Horns. You ready, Florsheim? Go!" He pushed a button on the console and a school bell blasted from the speakers as "Land of 1000 Dances" began with Wilson counting them in, screaming "One two three! One two three! Ow!" And then Roger's *snap* on the snare drum.

"Cymbals!" shouted Roger. Norman jumped in his chair but hit the crash cymbals. "Now straight-ahead," hollered Roger as he played along with himself on the recording and with Norman in the studio. "It don't get much simpler than this! Fours on the snare, a little help from the cymbals, don't forget the kick drum."

A red light glowed in the control booth and colored dials on the sound board twinkled.

"Recording!" Rick announced. "Take one, rolling."

"What?" Norman panicked.

"Keep playing," said Roger. "You're doing fine."

Norman began to sweat, even though the room was so earnestly air-conditioned it felt like a Popsicle. But he didn't stop. Molly stood at the glass, watching and singing under her breath. "Na na na na na . . ."

"He's not bad," murmured Rick. "He's not good, neither." The band had gathered in the control booth now and was watching the scene, Wilson Pickett screaming, "Ahhh . . . help me!" and Roger yelling, "Fills! Fills to the end!"

When it was over, Norman started to laugh with delight, which made Roger laugh, jump from his seat, and high-five Norman.

"Great!" said Roger. "Great fun. Could you feel it?"

Norman nodded. He would feel it for a very, very long time.

From the control booth, Rick boomed, "Back to work! Playtime's up! Get the drums back in the drum booth! You kids can stay and watch if you want to, but you gotta keep out of the way."

"Where you headed?" asked Roger. He began to take apart his drum set.

"California," said Norman.

The band filtered into the studio and began tuning up. Roger hefted the cymbal case and handed it to Norman. "Not mine, Florsheim," he said. "These belong to Al Jackson, the session drummer at Stax Records in Memphis."

"What?!" Rick exploded. "Not even ours? After all that?"

"Nope," said Roger. "I promised them back to Al, and you lent them to Jaimoe when he came to visit Duane."

Rick let loose a string of expletives that made Molly quail. Were they in trouble now?

She took a breath. "Well . . . we're going to Memphis."

177

Ray pulled on his ear and watched the conversation with raised eyebrows.

"Oh," said Norman from the studio. "Right. We're going to Memphis."

"Then take 'em to Memphis!" shouted Rick. "We have work to do!"

"Can you drop them by Stax?" asked Roger. "Don't mind Rick. He's all bark, no bite."

"I bite plenty!" said Rick from the booth. The playback speakers rang with more expletives.

Norman and Molly exchanged a look, with the glass between them. Ray edged toward the door of the booth.

"Will you tell them we're coming?" asked Norman.

"Yes, yes, fine, fine!" said Rick from the control booth. "I'll call Estelle. Or is it Al Bell now?"

"They're both still there," said Andrew Love, saxophone in hand.

"I'd call Jim," said Wayne Jackson. He was unpacking his trumpet.

More expletives. Rick ran a hand through his long hair and then put both hands on his hips and sighed.

"It's not your fault," he said to Norman. "Stay. Watch the band at work if you want. You won't hear any finer."

The edge in the room evaporated.

Around them, the musicians tuned horns, guitars, a bass, and riffed on the piano.

"All right!" hollered Rick from behind the glass, so loudly Molly and Ray jumped. "All right, all you sons-a-guns! Let's do it one more time. I got guys out in the hallway that play better than you! Let's get it right this time! Take fifty-two!"

20

IN THE MIDNIGHT HOUR

Written by Wilson Pickett and Steve Cropper
Performed by Wilson Pickett
Recorded at Stax Records, Memphis, Tennessee, 1966
Drummer: Al Jackson, Jr.

They left two hours later with the cymbals and Wilson Pickett's "Hey, Jude" single featuring Duane and Roger and the rest of the Swampers and the Memphis Horns, as well as a small reel-to-reel tape of Norman playing with Roger. Norman put his treasure in the box of letters under his seat.

They also left with the key to Duane's cabin. When Norman had said they needed to check the oil and engine before they left, Roger had told them, "Stax'll be closed up tight by the time you get there. Get a fresh start in the morning." Molly had rolled her eyes but didn't argue. She'd asked to use the phone to make their daily call.

As they boarded the bus, Ray held back and said, "Got to get home, so I might head out. Thanks anyway."

"Stay, man," said Norman. "I promise we'll leave first light. You can be home for breakfast."

Ray looked around the almost empty parking lot, in the almost empty town of Muscle Shoals. "First thing," he agreed.

The cabin boasted a wall of windows overlooking the lake. It was rustic, but it was enough. Pecan trees grew in the yard and cicadas called insistently from the trees.

While Norman idled the engine and checked the bus gauges, Molly and Ray busied themselves pulling fallen branches from the surrounding woods and sawing them into serviceable firewood. Norman started a fire and Ray kept it fed while Molly foraged for supper by unpacking one of Aunt Pam's boxes. Ray and Norman took out two more bus seats and carried them to the cabin porch. They sat on them with heavy thuds, tired.

The aroma of baking potatoes and bubbling beans reached their noses.

"And there's Kool-Aid!" called Molly, stirring the contents of a metal pitcher with a wooden spoon.

Our second supper together, thought Molly. She had found a can of beef stew in the box and they'd added it to their feast, splitting it three ways after warming it on the grate over the fire.

"Bus didn't sound too good over those hills last night," said Ray.

"I know," said Norman. "It struggles with hills."

"Are we all right?" asked Molly.

Norman shrugged. "We've got to be."

The setting sun painted the sky with its oranges, yellows, pinks, and reds.

Ray swabbed at the dregs of his beans with a piece of bread. "You got a band?"

Molly answered before Norman could. "He wishes he did."

"I will one day," said Norman. "I can't wait to tell Barry about all this. He won't believe it. I can't believe it myself! I played drums in a real studio, with a real drummer! And I was good! Wasn't I good, Molly?"

Molly sighed as she opened a bag of cookies and passed them around. "I can't tell if you're good or not, Norman. Drumming is a lot of noise to me."

"You don't know how to listen," said Norman. "When I'm a famous drummer, you'll regret those words."

Ray ate a cookie and said, "You gotta change your name to be a famous drummer." He smiled as he said it, maybe the first time he'd smiled since Molly and Norman had met him.

"I know!" Norman emptied the last of the beans out of the can. "They called you Florsheim back there."

"That's a brand of shoe," said Norman, who was wearing his high-tops.

"You need a name like King Curtis," said Ray. "You know him?" Norman shook his head.

"You think these cats today good? You ain't heard nothin'. You listen to 'Memphis Soul Stew,' and then tell me about good players."

The fire popped and cracked as the cicadas went to sleep and the crickets and tree frogs began their choruses.

"You play?" asked Norman. He took a cookie.

"Not music," answered Ray. "I play ball. Or . . . I did."

They fell into an uncomfortable silence. Norman stood up abruptly. "I'm going to get more wood before it's full dark."

Ray stared at the fire and spoke, as if mesmerized by the flames. After a quiet minute, he spoke. "I got shot five years ago. I thought they wouldn't take me, wouldn't draft me, but now they taking just about anybody. Especially if they're black. They already took my friends."

Molly blanched. *"Shot?* Like with a gun?"

"Yeah. Rifle."

"Where?" *Can I ask that?* "Oh. Sorry."

"In the head."

"Really?"

"Yeah." Ray turned to Molly and touched a scar on his cheek just below the cheekbone.

Molly reached out a hand to touch it, but stopped herself.

"Got it registerin' to vote," said Ray. Then he corrected himself. "Helping the Freedom Fighters register black folks to vote. In Mississippi. In my hometown."

Molly had no words. So she folded her hands in her lap and made sure she looked Ray in the eyes.

Really? Her throat tightened. She opened her mouth to breathe.

"I'm registered now, too," Ray said with pride.

The fire shifted as Norman returned, his arms full of firewood. "There's a whole bunch of it stacked on the side of the house!" He dropped the wood onto the ground by the firepit and swiped at the wood chips on his clothes.

Ray changed the subject. "Why are you goin' to California?"

"My brother is there," Molly answered, not sure how much to tell.

Norman tossed a log onto the fire and completed Molly's sentence. "And he's being drafted."

"Like me," said Ray.

Molly saw her chance to ask. "Are you . . . are you AWOL? Did you desert?"

Ray shook his head. "No. I got a two-week furlough. I'm goin' home to see my mam and pap. And my sis. Then they ship us out, after jungle warfare school. In Panama."

Ray looked away.

"You live in Memphis?" Norman asked.

"Mississippi. Greenwood. You don't have to take me there. I'll ride to Memphis and get myself home from there."

"You're going to Vietnam," said Molly, like she'd just discovered a secret.

Ray wiped his hands over his face and said, "My friends are already there. One come back in a box. He was a hero. I ain't no hero. But I don't want to be a coward, neither."

Molly found some words. "Nobody who gets shot in the head helping people register to vote is a coward."

"What?" Norman stopped poking the fire with a stick.

"Long story," sniffed Molly. "You weren't here." Her ponytail was sloppy. Her Keds were dirty. She scooted closer to the fire in her folding chair.

Norman flopped his tall frame into his chair, lost his balance, and tried not to topple over. Ray reached for the chair and held it until Norman righted himself. Norman looked at Ray in all seriousness. "Tell me."

"Nothin' more to tell," said Ray. The companionable moment had evaporated.

Molly hesitated and then asked, "Who shot you, Ray?"

"White man," Ray answered tightly. "White folks don't want black folks to vote in Mississippi, maybe not anywhere. But we vote now. That's a change come about because folks worked together and changed the system."

Norman shifted in his chair. What could he offer to this? "The police are always at our school now," he finally said, "ever since it was integrated this year. There are fights every day in the lunchroom. I just stay out of there."

A log settled on the fire with a *chunk*.

"Where I live, there are only black kids now at what used to be the white kids' school," answered Ray. "All the white folks started their own school. Private school. They ain't goin' to school with us. Stayin' away — that ain't gonna help nuthin'. That just means you hold on to the power and keep it to yourself." His tone was defiant.

The silence that enveloped them was suddenly ragged. Molly tried to think of what to say. "I would go to school with you," she said quietly.

183

"Would you go to Vietnam with me?" asked Ray, a challenge in his voice.

The color drained from Molly's face.

"What do you mean?" asked Norman. "Plenty of boys — black and white — are going to Vietnam."

"I mean the government's sending more blacks than ever to Vietnam now. They say it's so we can have a trade. So we can have a job, a steady paycheck. But that's not true. They need bodies to fight their war. And it's okay with them if we get killed. So they lower the requirements. If you're poor and black, got two arms and two legs, and got a brain in your head, you're going to Vietnam," Ray finished. "Even if somebody shot you when you were just a kid, just fourteen years old."

"I'm fourteen," said Molly to no one. She was shaking, even though they were just talking.

"Nobody's gonna shoot you, white girl," said Ray. "You ain't who they trying to get rid of."

Molly was breathless. A breeze tugged at the fire. The night surrounded them.

"What are you saying?" asked Norman.

"I'm saying it's not enough to say you'd go to school with me," said Ray. "It's not enough to stay away from the lunchroom. It's not enough to say *Too bad* or *Who shot you, Ray?* It's not enough to feel sorry for me, if that's what you feel. Because you can't help me right now. But you white people hold the power, and you can help others."

"How?" It was a whisper from Molly.

"We had some white folks come to our town five years ago," said Ray, softer now that he was telling a story. "One of 'em stayed in our house. They didn't just talk. They helped change things and so did we. Some of us died. I almost died. Lots of us went to jail. But we didn't run away. We stood up to the bullies."

He looked at Norman and continued. "Sometimes the bully is a gas station man. And sometimes the bully is the U.S. government. Things need to change in this country. And change ain't comfortable. It's easier to stay comfortable, especially if you hold the power. But that doesn't help everybody else who's suffering because of the bullies. You got to go after the bullies. I would do it again. I would go after the bullies."

There was a long silence between them. Norman broke it when he said, softly, "I don't know how to go after bullies."

Ray turned his head and locked eyes with Norman. "It's not my job to teach you," he said. "You got to learn for yourself."

Ray got up, added a log to the fire while Norman and Molly watched, poked it with a stick, and walked into the woods. "Be back directly."

An owl hooted from a tall tree somewhere. Molly felt teary. "I don't understand," she said in a low voice.

Norman exhaled through closed lips and puffed cheeks. Clearly he was in over his head, out here in the middle of nowhere, Alabama, on the road with a boy who was braver than he'd ever be, a boy who knew things he needed to know. He wanted to go home to his comfortable life. But was it comfortable, really?

"It's late," he finally said. "We have a long way to go tomorrow." There was no way to articulate what he was feeling. He hardly knew, himself.

Molly wiped at her eyes. "Okay," she said. She didn't want to go home. She didn't want to keep going. She wanted to turn back the clock, to a time when she was innocent and her life was easier. But somewhere inside herself, in a place she could not yet touch, she knew that easier wasn't the answer.

BROTHER LOVE'S
TRAVELING SALVATION SHOW

Written by Neil Diamond
Performed by Neil Diamond
Recorded at American Sound Studio, Memphis, Tennessee, 1969
Drummer: Gene Chrisman

They were quiet with one another as they crossed into Mississippi the next morning just as the sun burst into a bright yellow lemon behind them. The sunshine lightened their mood.

"More hills," remarked Ray. "Bus don't sound too good." He was eating an apple.

Norman grimaced as he drove. "It'll get us there. Don't worry."

"I'm worried," said Molly. Her hair was tidy in its ponytail once again. She tuned the radio as they drove, looking for AM stations playing the Weekly Top Forty records.

They stopped for gas in Southaven. Norman once again checked the oil and added a quart. Ray and Molly wordlessly watched a brown-skinned girl with hair that glistened in the morning sun walk down the road past the service station. She carried a baby on her hip. As they pulled out of the gas station and began to pass her, Molly spoke up.

"Maybe she needs a ride, Norman."

"Who?"

"That girl!" The girl watched the bus drive by. Her baby, black curls bouncing, waved at the bus.

"She probably lives here," said Norman.

"That doesn't mean she doesn't need a ride," said Molly. "She might have a long way to walk."

Norman kept driving. Molly watched the girl and her baby recede as the bus windows clicked past her like movie frames.

"Now we'll never know what happened to her! Just turn around, Norman!"

"No! She's none of our business! She's just walking down the road!"

Ray tossed the core of his third apple out the window and said, "You mean you're not gonna offer her a ride? She's a girl with a baby."

"Because I said I'd get you to Memphis for breakfast!"

"I don't live in Memphis," said Ray. "I live in Mississippi. You can drop me right here, right now."

When Norman didn't answer immediately, Ray said, "Stop the bus, man. I'm off."

"Gaaaaa!" Norman beat on the steering wheel. "Fine. We'll pick her up."

He turned around in the Farm Bureau parking lot. They headed back toward the service station. The girl was gone.

Norman pulled into two spaces at the far end of the Winn-Dixie parking lot and put the bus in park. Ray stood in the aisle and hoisted his knapsack. Molly started to cry.

"What?" Norman stood up and faced them both.

"I don't like good-byes," Molly said.

"Look, man," said Norman. There was nothing he could do about Molly. It was hot. He was frustrated. He began unbuttoning his white oxford shirt. His white T-shirt gleamed underneath it. "You don't have to get off. You said yourself last night it would be easier to find a ride south from Memphis."

"Don't want to ride with nobody who won't pick up a body in need. Two bodies."

Norman draped his shirt over the back of the driver's seat. He wiped his palm across his forehead. Sweaty.

"I will," he said flatly. "From now on I'll pick up every hitch-hiker I see. But I would like to point out that she wasn't thumbing a ride, and she's gone now, so she probably walked from the service station to her house." He gestured at the shotgun houses lining this stretch of road.

Ray looked at the houses and then at the Winn-Dixie. Molly blew her nose into an Aunt Pam napkin. Ray turned his attention to her.

"You sure do . . ." started Ray, trying to find a word that wasn't *cry*.

"Emote," finished Norman.

"Yeah," said Ray.

"You can leave if you want," said Norman. "I'll pick up the 'bodies in need,' whether you stay or not."

"Promise you'll do it," said Ray. "It's important."

"I promise."

Molly stood up from her seat behind the driver. "Look! There she is!"

The girl came out of the Winn-Dixie with her baby and a paper sack.

Ray gave Norman his fiery stare. *Well?*

Norman sighed and opened the bus door, clambered down the steps, and waved at the girl, who was still far away. "How far you going?" he shouted.

The girl looked behind her, then back at Norman, stunned then scared.

Ray hopped off the bus. "That's not how you do it! You all lily white and tall and got a bus and calling to this girl. You're in Mississippi, man!"

He strutted to the girl and had words with her that Norman couldn't hear. He pointed to the bus. They talked and the baby played with his hands. The girl smiled. Molly stood on the bottom step of the stepwell, at the folding door, and watched.

Soon the three of them — Ray, the girl, and the baby — approached the bus.

"This here is Emily," said Ray. "And her baby, Christian. Emily, this is Florsheim and Molly."

Norman winced at the name.

"Pleased to meet you," said Emily. Baby Christian gurgled and hid his face in Emily's neck.

"She ain't going far, and I told her we can tote her."

"Happy to," said Norman. "*How* far?"

"Just a mile up this road, back the way we came, jag right, then left."

Norman took the grocery sack and Ray took the baby, who stared at him with wide brown eyes. Emily stepped onto the bus where Molly met her with still-damp eyes. She raised a hand in greeting and Emily nodded, then hesitantly took a seat opposite Molly, so she was at the front of the bus sitting behind the same half-high silver partition wall Ray had banged into two nights ago.

Ray, arms outstretched, handed Christian back to his mother, and Norman started the bus. Ray sat in the seat behind Emily. No one spoke.

A mile later, then a jag right and left, they were in front of an AME church.

189

"Right here," said the girl.

"At the church?" asked Norman.

"You can turn around easily here, in the parking lot," Emily said. "I live next door. My father's the pastor." The lawn next door was freshly clipped. Azaleas grew across the porch in front of the house. A sidewalk traveled in a curve from the church to the parsonage.

"I get off here, too," said Ray.

"Wait!" said Molly.

"We've got people here who can get him home," said the girl with a smile. "Thank you for the ride."

Norman opened the door for them and stood up.

Ray followed Emily as she got off the bus with Christian. "I've got him," she said when Ray tried to take him. So he picked up the paper sack instead and saw that it held a bottle of milk.

"Good luck, man," said Norman, a catch in his throat. He stuck out his hand and Ray took it.

Molly's eyes filled with tears. "I hope . . . I hope you'll be all right over there," she said.

"You got the address of my company," said Ray. "You write, I'll write back."

"Okay." Molly sniffed. This would not do. Ray was not Barry. But Ray was . . . Ray. She knew someone who was going to Vietnam. It was heartbreaking.

She started to say something more, but Ray was gone as suddenly as he had come.

Norman watched him follow Emily to her porch, where a door opened and someone — someone who had been waiting there for Emily and Christian — ushered them all inside.

Norman thumped back into the driver's seat, grabbed the steering wheel, and rested his head between his hands. "The world is a scary place," he said.

Molly already knew this. She said nothing.

"Those white kids at school," continued Norman, lifting his head. "The ones fighting in the lunchroom . . ."

Molly wouldn't go into the lunchroom anymore, either. "What about them?" she asked finally.

Norman engaged the clutch and put the bus in gear. "They don't know anything."

TIME IS TIGHT

Written by Booker T. Jones, Al Jackson, Jr., Donald "Duck" Dunn, and Steve Cropper
Performed by Booker T. and the MGs
Recorded at Stax Records, Memphis, Tennessee, 1969
Drummer: Al Jackson, Jr.

It was a quick drive up the interstate highway into Memphis. They breezed past the state sign: WELCOME TO TENNESSEE!

"Finally!" said Molly. She used the local road map to find the address. "Can we just drop off these cymbals and go? Please?" She used her most plaintive voice. "We could get to Little Rock before dark. And we could eat somewhere. I'm starving."

"Sure," said Norman. He swung the bus onto McLemore and they saw the sign: STAX, in bright red letters above a theater marquee. And under that, SOULSVILLE, U.S.A.

"There's a record store!" said Molly.

They found a place to park the bus on the street, a block away. Windows up, doors locked, cymbals in their black case and in Norman's arms, Norman and Molly walked back toward the theater. The neighborhood looked abandoned, with vacant storefronts and weedy sidewalks. Two shirtless brown-skinned boys shrieked and sprayed each other with a hose in front of a house with metal awnings over the windows.

Norman and Molly reached Stax, and it took a moment for Norman to realize: "It's a theater! That's a marquee! There's a ticket window!"

The door was locked. When it finally opened to their insistent knocking, a woman with a bouffant hairdo poofed atop a pale face pancaked with makeup greeted them. She wore a sleeveless shirtwaist dress with large pockets, low heels, and red lipstick. A cigarette hung between her lips. She plucked it from her mouth with two fingers, turned her head, and blew smoke into the dark lobby.

"May I help you?"

"We're here to return these symbols to Al Jackson," said Norman. "Roger Hawkins sent us."

When the woman didn't register the name, Norman added, "From Muscle Shoals."

Immediately, the woman brightened. "Oh! Roger! Yes, of course! Well, come in! I'm Estelle. I own the place. Well, I own it with my brother Jim. You won't find Al here this early in the morning. We're lucky if he shows up before noon. But there's somebody back there, I'm sure . . ."

She began turning on lights. The carpet was lavender. The walls were purple. Estelle opened another door and said, "Follow me."

The carpet in the hallway was deep green. Before they reached the studio, it changed to a bright red. The studio itself was nothing like the one in Muscle Shoals. The floor sloped, for one thing. "That's because this used to be the Capitol Theater," said Estelle, when Molly remarked on it. "We renovated it ourselves!"

The control booth was on the stage where the movie would have been shown. It was empty and the lights were off. A line of bongos sat near the stage. Acoustical drapes hung on the walls, and folding chairs were scattered here and there. Microphones stood atop long silver poles like soldiers at attention. A Hammond M3 organ caught Norman's eye. "Wow!"

"It's a beauty," said Estelle. "Booker played 'Green Onions' on it."

"'Green Onions'!" said Norman, so surprised. "Booker T and the MGs! Far out!"

"Number three on the Weekly Top Forty," cooed Molly.

"And number one on the R&B chart," said Estelle.

Norman walked past the organ to the baffle walls that hid the drums, which sat on a platform built just for them. A Rogers kit. A 20" bass, three toms — 12", 16", and 13" — and a Powertone wood-shelled snare. The cymbals included a hi-hat, a crash, and a ride.

"He's already got cymbals," Norman pointed out.

"There are many kinds of cymbals, dear, as I'm sure you know," said Estelle.

"Yes'm," said Norman. "Should I just leave these on the drum stand?"

Estelle looked at Norman as if she were sizing him up. "Why don't you wait for him in here? I've got to get back to the record shop. We open in an hour."

"Yes, ma'am!" said Norman. Just to sit in a studio and soak it in, to stare at it all and try and understand how it worked. Bliss. He looked at Molly to see how badly she disapproved.

"The record shop!" said Molly. "May I come with you, Miss Estelle?"

"Folks call me Miz Axton," said Estelle. "Or Lady A. Take your pick."

"May I come with you, Lady A?"

"Of course!"

Molly left Norman worshipping Al Jackson's drum kit.

"Do you hear the groove?" Estelle asked Molly. "You can dance to it, if you want." Molly did not want, but she did want to keep listening to record after record forever.

"It's so good," she said, for the fifteenth time.

"Here's just one more," said Estelle. She put Eddie Floyd's "People, Get It Together" on the turntable, and Eddie began to sing and tell Molly she was outtasight, whether she was black or white, rich or poor, she'd better get it together.

"I can't believe all of these were recorded right here, on this spot," marveled Molly.

"Not all of them," said Estelle, "but that one was. Booker and Eddie wrote it." She changed the record once again. "And here's one of my favorites, also recorded right here. 'Soul Man' by Sam and Dave — do you know it?"

Molly clapped her hands. "Number two on the Weekly Top Forty!"

Estelle laughed. "You're good!"

"I know."

"Oh, I miss this," said Estelle, suddenly teary. She grabbed Molly's hand with both of hers. "You're just precious!"

Molly thought to say she was utterly not, just ask Norman, but she knew better. And something else she knew not to say: These records were good, but they were not the Association with their beautiful soaring melodies and complex harmonies.

Estelle stood up and lit a cigarette. She dabbed at the tear on her cheek with the back of her hand.

"When I first opened Satellite Records, it was the neighborhood hangout," she said. "Before Satellite was here, kids had to take the bus out to Sears to look at records — and Sears only had country music. So kids came from all over the neighborhood

195

to go through our records and listen all day long. I played record after record for them, just like I did for you. I told them, 'This is the hot new beat!' I even put a speaker outside to lure them in so they'd buy! Kids would dance on the sidewalk!"

"Really?"

"Really. I reported our weekly sales to *Billboard* magazine. They never knew we were this little record store attached to a recording studio — that's how many records we sold!"

"What happened?"

"Oh, lots of things. For one, we lost Otis in that plane crash. That really took the starch out of us."

"Otis Redding?"

"That's right. He was our big star. 'Sitting on the Dock of the Bay,'" Estelle sang. "Oh, that was a time, when we recorded that." She reached for her pocketbook on the counter and pulled out a packet of tissues. "We lost Otis in December '67. Then Martin King was murdered here in April, just four months later. It split this city apart."

Molly didn't know what to say. It was tragic. *And Bobby after that,* she thought. *And Barry after that.* She shook her head. Barry was still here. He wasn't lost to them. But Bobby and Martin were. A line from the song "Abraham, Martin, and John" floated into her head. *Didn't you love the things that they stood for?* It made her sad.

Estelle patted Molly's hand. "We never looked at color coming through the door at Stax — and we've got an integrated band! But after Dr. King was killed, it wasn't the same anymore. Most everyone in this neighborhood is black — all our singers are black — and I don't know, maybe we white people — me and Jim — look suspicious to folks around here now. We've had break-ins. We keep the doors locked. And now Al Bell is getting us back on our feet, but he wants this space for offices, so I think the record store's days are numbered."

"That's terrible," Molly said.

They sat in silence for a while, as the record player needle played into the empty bed at the back of the record. Estelle lifted the needle arm and placed it in its holder. She stubbed out her unsmoked cigarette. "Loss is hard."

It was Molly's turn to tear up. Estelle took a tissue for herself and handed Molly one as well. "Have you lost someone, dear girl?"

Molly nodded.

Estelle patted Molly's hand. "Time changes everything, doesn't it? That's why I want you to take these records, Molly."

"Oh, no. I couldn't."

Estelle gazed out the large record store windows at the neighborhood surrounding the store and said, "Music heals. I listen to 'Dock of the Bay' and think about how Otis smiled when he recorded it. It helps."

"Doesn't it make you sad?" Molly asked.

"It does," said Estelle, "but the sadness turns into gratitude, and that's what I want to remember. I'm grateful we had the time we had. One day, Stax won't be here, either, you know. All things pass. But I will have these records to listen to and remember the good times — and the not-so-good, because life is that way, isn't it? — and it will comfort me to remember."

A memory floated into Molly's heart and something shifted. "When I was nine," she said, "my brother, Barry — that's who is lost to me — took me to the movies in downtown Charleston. We got all dressed up. We went to see *A Hard Day's Night* starring the Beatles. Do you know it?"

"Oh, yes," said Estelle with a smile.

"It makes me sad to hear any of the songs from that movie now."

197

Estelle took a deep breath and let it out while Molly's sad feelings weaved around her like whispers.

"Tell me something about that day," said Estelle.

"We went straight to the music store after the movie, where Barry bought his first guitar. He learned all the songs on the album to *A Hard Day's Night*, and I sang along to every one of them while he played." Molly bit her bottom lip so she wouldn't cry.

"What a good time!" said Estelle. Molly nodded. "That's what to remember," Estelle went on. "None of us stays the same. Music reminds us of the journey, of where we came from, and it even shows us where we're going. You'll see."

"Yes, ma'am," said Molly. She didn't see.

"Listen to those songs again," said Estelle. "Let them bathe the sadness away so you can see the gifts it brings you."

"I will," said Molly, and as she said it, her sadness softened.

Estelle pulled a bag from behind the counter for the records she and Molly had listened to. "One day I'll be gone, too," she said. "One day, I hope, you'll play these records and remember this day, remember me. Let me send you on your way with a little bit of Stax."

Molly smiled at Estelle. "Thank you, Lady A."

Estelle handed Molly the bag. "You are so welcome, dear girl."

Al Jackson, Jr. moseyed into the studio at eleven. He wore a striped shirt, a goatee, and a kufi cap. He opened the cymbal case and pulled out two Zildjian ride cymbals.

"Ahhh, beautiful!" he told Norman. "But they ain't mine, man."

"No?"

"No way."

"Well, I . . . I don't know what to do with them now."

"You said you're going to California?"

"Yeah. Yessir."

"I know what you should do with them."

"What?"

Al pulled a small card out of a pocket inside the cymbal case.

"Take 'em to Hal Blaine. Capitol Records. Los Angeles. They're his."

SUSPICIOUS MINDS

Written by Mark James
Performed by Elvis Presley
Recorded at American Sound Studio, Memphis, Tennessee, 1969
Drummer: Gene Chrisman

"Who is Hal Blaine?" asked Molly.

"I don't know," said Norman. "Some drummer in California."

"How does Al know the cymbals belong to Hal Blaine?" asked Molly.

She and Norman had left south Memphis for the city proper and now sat in a turquoise-and-butter-yellow booth at the Arcade, the restaurant Estelle had recommended. It was full during the lunch rush and they'd been lucky to get a booth. Their table was littered with sugar packets and platters dotted with a half-eaten stack of pancakes, bacon and eggs, a cheeseburger and fries, a chocolate milkshake, glasses of orange juice, and two cups of very sweet coffee with glasses of milk half-emptied into them. They had feasted.

200

"There was a card," said Norman. "And they have these nicks on them, or cuts, or something, on the bottom, made with a rat file, where they hook to the cymbal stand, so they'll tilt the way he likes them."

"Well, we go through Los Angeles. But really, Norman, how many more musical stops do you need to make?"

Norman stirred the cold, milky concoction in front of him. He would never learn to drink coffee. "I don't know. Maybe none. But now I've got these cymbals . . ."

"The faster we get to San Francisco, the more time we have to look for Barry." She tried a tactful voice. She wasn't good at it. Her anxiety showed.

Norman finished his half of the cheeseburger they'd split. "I know," he said, his mouth full. "Believe me, I know. We should call my mom tonight, too, to see if I've got any mail from him."

Molly sat back on her side of the booth and sighed. "I'm so full it hurts. Everything looked good and I was so hungry."

"Me, too," said her cousin. "Maybe we can take some of this with us."

"What time is it? I left my watch on the bus."

"It's just one o'clock. We've got plenty of time to get to Little Rock — it's only three hours away."

"There's a campground there," Molly began, just as two girls banged into the restaurant. The tall one had a pony-tail, like Molly's, and was smartly dressed in a sleeveless blue button-down shirt and white shorts. The shorter one had wild straw-yellow hair and wore cutoff jeans as shorts. She looked around until she caught Norman's eye. He looked away quickly.

"Full up," a hostess called to them as she whizzed by, carry-ing an order.

"That's okay!" said the yellow-haired girl. "I see our friends!"

Before Molly could turn around to see who was talking, the girl sat next to her in her booth. She radiated heat from the day and her freckled face was beaded with sweat. The ponytailed

201

girl, cheeks red from heat or exertion or both, stood at the table and said, "Stop it, Birdie. Get up."

"Yes," said Molly, all nerves on alert. "Get up!" This girl was older than she was, and much rougher. Probably tougher, too.

Birdie helped herself to the other side of the cheeseburger Norman had cut in half. She took a giant bite. "Ummmm!"

Molly shot Norman a look: *Do something!* But Norman was all eyes on Birdie and the girl standing in front of him.

The waitress marched smartly to their table, her pad and pencil in hand.

Instinctively, Norman moved over and the ponytailed girl, who saw the waitress coming, sat gingerly beside him. She folded her hands in her lap and stared at them.

"What'll y'all have?" said the waitress, clearly irritated. Anyone could see, this table could be cleared for waiting customers who had written their names on the paper by the front door.

"Two Coca-Colas!" said Birdie in a cheery voice, as if she'd just invented the drink herself.

The waitress stalked away.

"Does that mean no?" Birdie asked.

"Who are you?" said Molly, wary but putting on her toughest voice.

"I'm sorry —" began the ponytailed girl.

"Oh, it's okay," Birdie interrupted. She picked up Molly's fork, pulled over her plate, and began to eat the leftover pancakes.

"No, it's not," said Molly, gathering courage by the minute. "Let me out!" She wanted to shove Birdie, but she didn't want to touch her.

"Listen," said Birdie as the waitress slapped two Cokes on the table and dropped two straws next to them. She also tore the lunch bill — to which she had added two sodas — from her pad and gave it to Norman, who took it wordlessly.

"Pay at the front," the waitress snapped.

Birdie squinted at the waitress's name tag. "Thank you, Dottie."
Dottie stormed away.

"Listen," Birdie repeated. "You drive a school bus, you're a
sitting duck. We just got off the Greyhound from Jackson — bus
station's right over there . . . a ways." She waved a hand in no
general direction. "We've been walking. Saw you get off your bus
and come in here. We waited to give you enough time for your
lunch, but you're taking forever to eat it, so I've come to help you!"

The ponytailed girl sat up straight and found her voice. "What
she means is, we're lost." She took a sip of her drink and made
a short, appreciative sound.

"This is Mags," said Birdie.

"Margaret," said the other girl. "I'm Margaret, and I'm out
here in the wilderness with a lunatic."

"This is a city," said Molly primly. This girl was older, too,
but not nearly as scary. "I've been in the wilderness and this is
not it."

Birdie drained her Coke in one long gulp while Norman and
Molly watched in amazement.

"Ahhhh! Better." Birdie belched. "We must have walked two
miles! We're also broke after that bus ride, but that's another
story. Are you going to eat the rest of those fries?"

"What do you want?" asked Norman. He sounded overwhelmed and unsure. Molly kicked him under the table and
opened her eyes wide as he looked at her. *Do something!*
Norman stared back with a look that said, *What do you want
me to do?*

"We want a ride to this address." Birdie reached into her
shorts pocket and pulled out a crumpled piece of paper on
which she had written *827 Thomas Street, Memphis.*

Margaret took two long, ladylike sips of her drink and said, in
a voice that indicated she was restored by the soda and the air-
conditioning, "I think we walked in the wrong direction. *Someone*

203

was sure this was the way. *Someone* wouldn't listen to reason. As usual."

"But now we've found a ride!" said Birdie. "We don't have to walk back the two miles, and we'll be going the right way!"

"This is not how I would have done it," sniffed Margaret.

"Well, you're not me," sassed Birdie.

"Thank the heavens." Margaret sipped at her drink again.

The waitress appeared at their table and began to clear dishes. "Y'all come back," she said in a flat, uninviting tone.

"You don't mean it, Dottie," Birdie replied.

Molly's face caught fire with embarrassment. *Let's see Birdie treat Mama Louise like that*, she thought.

Birdie grabbed the last piece of bacon from the plate in the waitress's hand. "Thank you, Dottie!"

Dottie stiffened. "We have customers waiting."

"Right," said Norman, his own embarrassment showing.

"Let me out!" Molly snapped.

"Whoa!" said Birdie, as she stood to let Molly by. "You and Mags would be great friends."

Molly managed to get out of the booth without touching Birdie, who she was convinced had something living in her hair. She snatched the paper out of her cousin's hand. "Give me the check, Norman. I'll pay it." She stalked to the register.

"I'll pay for the Cokes," said Margaret. "We're not that broke." She followed Molly to the register — but not before she said to Norman, "She's not always like this." Then she reconsidered. "Well, yes, she is."

"Lucky you," said Birdie. She trailed behind Margaret, calling back over her shoulder, "Don't just sit there, Norman!"

Molly and Norman argued on their double-time march to the bus. Birdie and Margaret held back.

"I promised Ray," whispered Norman. "I promised I'd pick up the bodies in need."

"They are not in need," Molly hissed. "They are in *want*."

"Same thing," Norman hissed back.

Molly raised her voice. "Not by a long shot, buddy boy."

"Hey!" said Birdie. "Lookee there! It's a protest!"

The four of them formed a little gaggle and stopped to look. Police cars idled in the block ahead, near a single-file line of people walking slowly with placards in their hands.

"That's the Lorraine Motel," said Birdie, like she was a tour guide. "Martin Luther King was killed there last year."

Molly shuddered at the remembrance. And her thoughts strayed to Ray as well. Maybe he'd be home by now.

Norman kept his eyes on the protestors as the four of them reached the bus. It felt strange to be this close to such a tragic place, a place they'd only heard about in the news.

"This is my sixth time in Memphis," said Birdie, interrupting everyone's thoughts. "I keep count."

"That's six too many," countered Margaret.

"Sez you," said Birdie.

"You visit the Lorraine Motel?" Molly felt the gravitas of the place envelop her. The clutch of protestors walked down the sidewalk in single file, with their signs, slowly and silently.

"Nah. I just know it," Birdie said. "I visit my father. He lives here in Memphis."

"He does not," said Margaret quietly. "And he is not your father."

"Close enough," said Birdie.

"Does he live at this address?" asked Norman. He looked at the crumpled paper again.

"He does today," said Birdie. "Will you take us?"

Norman looked at Molly for an opinion, but he also felt his promise to Ray still held.

205

"Gaaaaa!" Molly climbed into the bus. "Everybody stay here," she ordered. Norman raised an eyebrow but obeyed. "Give me the address, Norman."

She yanked the lever and closed the folding door on the rest of them, leaving them in the boiling midday sun. It was boiling in the bus as well. She opened her window and dropped into her navigating seat behind the driver. She consulted her road map. Then she reappeared at the door.

"It's three miles up the road, give or take. It's out of our way — we need to go the opposite direction. But —" here she sighed and looked first at Norman, then at Birdie "— a promise is a promise, and maybe I can stand you for three miles. But no more! We drop and go, understand? Please sit far away from me."

"Done!" crowed Birdie. "You see, Mags? I told you they'd be nice."

Three miles later, all windows down and a hot breeze blowing through the bus, they rolled in front of a large white building with AMERICAN SOUND STUDIO plastered across it in bright red letters.

Birdie screamed from the back of the bus. "That's it! Turn here!"

Margaret said, "Or just stop at the next red light and let us off, that's fine."

"Is that a recording studio?" Norman yelled back at Birdie.

"Oh, no you don't!" shouted Molly.

Norman made a right turn on a side street and began looking for a place to park the bus.

"Norman!" Molly called. "Drop and go!"

Birdie was already making her way up the aisle. "Stop first!" she hollered. "I will do a lot of things, but jumping off a moving bus is not one of them, although I did jump once from a moving train — ask Mags, so did she — but that was onto soft, cushy grass. You jump off a moving bus, even a bus traveling just ten miles per hour, you suffer cuts and contusions and possible broken bones, which require splints, casts, stitches, or at the very least rubbing alcohol to kill the germs, and at the very medium, a washing of the wounds with antiseptic to get out the gravel, and at the very worst, a tetanus shot. I hate shots."

Molly opened her mouth to speak, but Margaret beat her to it. "Just stop. Take a breath."

Norman found a place to park behind the building. He cut the engine and turned in his seat to talk to Birdie, who was almost on top of him and holding on to the stanchion like she might swing around the metal pole, into the stepwell, and fly off the bus. Norman opened the folding door.

Then he repeated himself. "Is this a recording studio?"

"It is," Birdie began. "And —"

Norman cut her off. "And your father is in there?"

"My almost father," replied Birdie impatiently.

"Really," said Norman. "Who's in there?"

Birdie closed her eyes like she was in church. "The one. The only. Elvis."

"*The* Elvis?" said Molly. She couldn't help herself.

Margaret answered with a sigh. "*The* Elvis. Yes."

"Elvis Presley?"

"Is there any other?" Birdie asked, then answered, "Elvis Aron Presley, The Mighty and Rightful King of Rock and Roll."

"I dispute that," said Margaret.

"Indisputable," sniffed Birdie. "Not to mention a real movie star."

"I beg to differ," said Margaret.

"Differ away," said Birdie. "In your heart you know it's true."

"How . . . ?" began Norman.

"It's a long story."

"We just gave you a ride. Spill it."

Birdie plopped herself in the seat with Margaret, who had already moved over. "Elvis and my mama had a thing, back in the day — I'm telling you, long story, Elvis was very young —"

207

"You don't know that it was a thing," corrected Margaret.

"I consider it a thing," said Birdie. "I have the letters. So I was convinced he was my father. My mother would not deny it, and she also would never tell me who my father was —"

"But now you know," said Margaret, like she was talking to a toddler.

"I came up here to prove it, three years ago, only Mags and I got into some trouble —"

"Surprise, surprise," said Margaret.

"— but it all worked out in the end, and Mama even wrote to Elvis and he wrote back. That could have started up everything for them again, making him my stepfather as well as my father —"

"Stop."

"But he is no longer available, of course, because of Priscilla. But he and my mama *are* friends again, and Priscilla's fine with it, and he invited me to come up anytime. I knew he'd be here today because he told Mama he would, so here I am."

"Again," added Margaret.

There was a sudden silence. No one spoke and no one moved.

Then Molly popped up and began going from seat to seat, shutting windows.

Wordlessly, everyone helped.

They locked up and made for American Sound Studio.

A LITTLE LESS CONVERSATION

Written by Mac Davis and Billy Strange
Performed by Elvis Presley
Recorded at Western Recorders, Hollywood, California, 1968
Drummer: Hal Blaine

"Biiird!" Elvis Presley's southern drawl came through the playback speakers and into the control booth. "You brought friends!"

"Here we go," said Margaret.

Norman and Molly were transfixed. In the studio beyond the control room stood a man in white bell-bottom pants and a midnight-blue velvet jacket with a white shirt riding under it and a neckerchief peeking out over the shirt.

He was tall.

He had a jet-black shock of floppy dark hair and sideburns to beat all sideburns.

He was Elvis Presley.

"Let's play it back, boys," he said. "Take five."

And like that, he was out of the studio and Birdie was in his arms.

"Been a long time, girl!" said Elvis.

"Too long!" said Birdie.

"Glad you caught me before I head to Vegas," said Elvis. "I've got a four-week run there coming up."

"Take me with you!" said Birdie.

Elvis laughed. "Can't do that, Bird, but I can take you and your friends — and Margaret, hey Margaret honey — home tonight for fried chicken. You want to see Priscilla and Lisa Marie, don't you?"

"Not really," said Birdie.

Elvis laughed. "Lisa Marie is walking everywhere now. She's a little beauty."

"I'm sure," said Birdie, sounding completely unsure.

"You *are* coming for supper, right?"

"Right!" said Birdie, brightening. "Can we spend the night?"

"Sure thing," said Elvis. "Do you have bus fare home?"

"Well . . . no."

"We'll take care of that," said Elvis.

"Playback on two," said an engineer in a hopeful voice.

Elvis ignored him. "How's your mama?"

"She's fine," said Birdie. "She's always fine."

"Who are your friends?"

Norman and Molly had not budged an inch.

"They gave us a ride," said Birdie. She gestured. "Norman and Molly."

"Pleased to meet you," said Elvis. He stuck out a large hand with many rings on the fingers, and Norman tried to shake it, but his knees were trembling, so he just laid his hand in Elvis's and Elvis shook hands for both of them.

"Good grip you got there."

"Yes," Norman said, after a small silence.

"Yes," repeated Molly.

"They don't talk much," said Birdie. "And Molly here, she's just like Mags."

"Margaret."

"Then she's a good friend," said Elvis, "just like Margaret is."

"We're cousins," said Birdie. "Nothing more."

"Agreed," said Margaret.

Elvis smiled. "I'm in the middle of something here. Do you want to stay and watch?"

"Oh, yes!" said Birdie.

"Right here." Elvis led them into the studio with his finger against his lips in a shush.

He indicated where they should sit.

"Playback on two!" Elvis drawled.

Two astonishing hours later, Norman, Molly, Birdie, and Margaret were in the spacious hull of a stretch limousine with Elvis Presley, waiting for his driver to reappear with six sacks full of Krystal hamburgers.

"I used to do this with Dewey Phillips," said Elvis as the driver handed the drinks through the window. "We'd order up a hundred Krystals and pick 'em up at midnight, go to his house, wolf 'em down with the gang, and play pool all night."

The burgers were small, square, and delicious. Molly was barely hungry, but Norman had a hollow leg and could eat anytime, and Birdie seemed to follow suit. Margaret no-thank-you'd herself out of the hamburger chow-down and quietly sipped on her Coke. Molly looked out the smoked windows of the limousine at the Peabody Hotel.

Elvis sat on one long seat by himself. Margaret and Birdie sat on the curve around the side, and Molly and Norman shared the other long seat. Sodas sat in holders. The tiny table in the middle of the compartment was littered with burger wrappers and fries. The air-conditioning hummed and the driver was invisible behind a darkened glassway. It was almost cozy. Elvis turned his attention to Norman and Molly.

211

"So. Traveling across this great country in an old school bus that Bird says is gonna break down any minute . . ."

"It wheezes!" Birdie choked, with her mouth full.

"It's fine," said Norman. He unwrapped another square burger. It was smaller than the palm of his hand.

"And your cousin — your brother — doesn't know he's been drafted."

"That's right," said Norman. He ate the burger in one bite.

"And you're going to get him and bring him home in time for his physical?"

"He's ordered to report," said Molly. Impulsively, she added, "He doesn't want to."

"Huh," said Elvis. "I remember being drafted. And being ordered to report."

"You were great in the army!" Birdie piped up.

"You were only five, Bird," said Margaret. "You don't even remember it."

"I keep up," Birdie said. "If you did, you'd know he was great."

"Well, I *was* great," said Elvis with a chuckle. "I was a sharp-shooter and a jeep driver and a reconnaissance scout. And of course I was in the army when I met my Priscilla."

Birdie humphed.

Molly wiped at the sides of her mouth with a napkin. "Did you go on furlough after basic training?" Norman nudged her with his knee.

"You'd better believe it," said Elvis. "You get two weeks to go home, and I did. The Colonel and Anita — that was my girlfriend at the time — picked me up in a Cadillac at the gates of Fort Hood at six a.m. and we hightailed it home to Memphis. Got there before midnight."

"Oh," said Molly. Not at all the same as Ray's journey, she thought.

"Vietnam is different," said Norman, out of nowhere. "You fight. In the jungle. It's dangerous."

"My uncle went to Vietnam," said Birdie. "Screwed him up. He hardly talks anymore. Just tends his bees and keeps to himself."

"He was always a gentle person," added Margaret.

"Well, son," said Elvis. He tapped the glass to signal the driver to return them to the studio. "Serving your country is always an honorable thing to do. I could have gotten the special treatment in the army, could have worked in an entertainment corps, but I wanted to be a real soldier. A soldier is one of this country's highest callings. To serve with pride is a mark of distinction and high moral character."

Norman raised his eyebrows at Molly, who shrugged her shoulders. She thought Elvis and her dad would get along just fine, except for the hair and the sideburns and the rock and roll. She couldn't remember: Did Barry like Elvis?

As they all left the limousine — Elvis, Margaret, and Birdie for the studio, and Molly and Norman for the bus — Elvis clapped Molly on the shoulder and added, "A soldier takes care of business and makes his country proud. Tell your brother I said so."

As they boarded the bus, Norman said to Molly, "Wait until I tell Barry he needs to enlist in the army because Elvis Presley told him to." He closed the folding door and started the engine.

Molly sat in the navigator's seat behind the driver, opened her road map, and whispered, to no one, "What if he's right?"

EVERYDAY PEOPLE

Written by Sylvester Stewart (Sly Stone)
Performed by Sly and the Family Stone
Recorded at Pacific High Recording Studios, San Francisco, California, 1969
Drummer: Greg Errico

Driving west in late afternoon meant the glare was blinding. Norman fished his sunglasses out of the box next to the driver's seat, pulled down the visor, and headed the bus across the mile-long cantilevered bridge high over the mighty Mississippi River. The sun blinked through each steel truss overhead, flashing its welcome to Arkansas.

The bus clattered over each deck plate beneath the tires. Molly craned her neck to see the spiderlike steelwork above them. It looked like something made with Barry's old Erector set. She felt lightheaded and curiously free as the hot summer air blew strands of hair out of her ponytail and across her face. She watched the sun wink-wink-wink, bright and shining, across the expanse of muddy water far below them.

She breathed deep and exhaled her troubles.

Up front, Norman began to sing enthusiastically with the

radio, weaving his head in time. "I . . . am everyday people!"

Molly joined in and both of them sang as loud as they could. "And so on and so on and scoobie doobie doobie!" They laughed at the same time Sly Stone screamed, *We got to live together!*

They had been so careful on this trip, so cautious, and so overwhelmed. It was thrilling to be swept up in happiness! The music was a better healer than any kind of talking could ever be. *Just like Lady A said it was*, thought Molly.

Norman turned the radio up as loud as it would go and together they sang out the unbelievable day. Days. The craziness of the road. The amazements of the journey. The gift it was to be alive on this day and driving across the Mississippi River, into Arkansas on a great adventure.

Molly bounced in her seat. She knew all the words, and Norman was astonished. Except for a few catchy licks, he hardly knew songs had words. He always listened so intently to the music.

"Listen to those toms!" he shouted. "That's a great drummer!" He matched the beat on his steering wheel with his hands and jounced in his seat as the bus rolled onto the other side of the bridge. Arkansas.

Molly consulted one of Aunt Pam's Triple A publications. "There are laundry facilities at the campground!" she called.

"Great!" said Norman, with fake excitement. "Pass me a Krystal!"

Elvis had given them two bags full of burgers and had insisted they take them. "You never know when you might get hungry. And you won't have to cook tonight!"

Molly opened a bag and pulled out a one-hundred-dollar bill.

"Oh my gosh! Norman!"

"I see him!" Norman crowed. He turned off the radio and flipped on his right turn signal.

215

A boy was hitchhiking on the side of the road, walking backward, facing them, arm held high, thumb out.

"No! Norman!"

"No what?" He sounded so happy. "We're picking up a body in need! That's what I promised Ray I'd do. And we've got hamburgers!"

He pulled the bus off on the shoulder as traffic whizzed by. He opened the folding door. The boy trotted toward them. Molly tucked the bill into her shorts pocket and hoped fervently she wouldn't lose it.

The boy had a fresh haircut, short and neat. He wore crisp khaki slacks like Norman's and a striped pullover shirt. He stood at the bottom of the stepwell, looked up at Molly and Norman, and blurted, "Thanks a lot!"

"Where to?" asked Norman in his most friendly voice.

"Little Rock, or as close as you get to Little Rock."

"That's where we're going," said Norman. "Hop in."

"Cool!" said the boy. He sat in the front passenger seat so recently vacated by Margaret and Birdie. He carried a knapsack like Ray's. He pulled a canteen from it and offered Norman and Molly a drink.

"Thanks," said Norman. He swigged from it and passed it to Molly. She shook her head. "No, thanks."

"Want a hamburger?" Norman asked.

Molly checked the bags for anything else Elvis might have left them before offering one to the boy. He took two Krystals and his canteen. "Thanks a lot!" he said again. "My name's Kyle. You?"

"Florsheim," said Norman, without thinking. Then he blushed.

"That's a shoe," said Kyle.

Molly was direct. "He's Norman, I'm Molly. Why are you hitchhiking?"

216

"I was visiting my dad in Memphis," said Kyle between bites of burger. "I wanted to go home."

"Can't he drive you?"

"Not today," said Kyle, and Molly left it at that.

Norman merged back onto the highway with a grinding of gears and a stutter of the engine.

"Sounds bad, Florsheim," said Kyle. "Want me to look at it?"

Norman checked his gauges. "It's finicky," he said. "I think it's all right."

They rode in silence. Little Rock was ninety-four miles away, sixty-six miles away, forty-two miles away, twenty-nine. The bill in Molly's pocket felt heavy, like the world's largest diamond or a sack of ball bearings.

As they rounded a curve and passed a sign that told them Little Rock was sixteen miles away, they heard a crunch-like pop from the front of the bus. Norman looked up into the student mirror and saw Molly gazing at him in worry. She turned to Kyle. "Are you a mechanic?"

"No, but I know a lot about engines," said Kyle. "It's a hobby. I've got a '64 Pontiac Tempest GTO Hardtop in my mom's garage in Little Rock."

"Wow," Norman said, hoping his lack of enthusiasm would stop Kyle from saying more, as Norman knew nothing about cars.

"Yep!" said Kyle, proud. "A Gran Turismo Omologato. First muscle car of its kind. Got a screamin' 389 V8 under the hood. And a four-speed manual transmission, probably similar to the one in this bus."

Norman doubted it. Kyle was boasting now.

"Why aren't you driving it?"

"I can't have it in Memphis. My dad won't let me drive there."

They drove fifteen more minutes and were closing in on Little Rock when, as if on cue, the engine began to smoke.

"Norman!" screamed Molly. "We're on fire!"

"We're not!" Norman yelled back. "Calm down!"

The smoke was white and billowy, rolling over the windshield and coming in through the open side windows.

"There's an exit ahead," said Kyle. "Pull off!"

An hour later, the bus still sitting on the shoulder of the exit ramp, Kyle gave up poking around in the engine and proclaimed they needed a tow. "It's something with the oil — if you keep having to add so much, you've got a leak." He looked up the ramp to where a gas station beckoned. "I wouldn't drive it. I'll call my mom, and she can send a tow truck."

"We've got Triple A," Molly answered. "I'll go call from a pay phone at the service station. Somebody has to stay with the bus."

"I'll do it," said Norman. "I'll call."

"No, I'll do it," said Molly. "I need to call home, too."

"Then I'll call Triple A."

The three of them walked to the service station to make their calls. They got drinks from the machine. They waited for a tow. The sun began to dip below the Arkansas pines. The campground was on the far side of Little Rock.

Molly and Norman sat on the curb while Kyle used the phone. They sighed at the same time, side by side. The river and the bridge and the song had been a gift. Now they were back to the grinding unknown.

"More meat loaf, Norman?" Kyle's mother, Phyllis, held the spatula over Norman's plate in anticipation of a yes.

"Yes, please," said Norman. "It's really good. Thanks."

"Well, good!" said Phyllis. "I am very glad I can provide a

hot meal while you two are on the road. You must stay here tonight, all right? We don't know how long that bus is going to be in the shop!"

"We have money for a hotel," said Molly. Her hundred-dollar bill carved a canyon in her pocket.

"I insist," said Phyllis. "The other kids are at their dad's, and there is plenty of room, even with Drew here." She smiled a benevolent smile at a boy sitting at the opposite end of the table. He wore glasses with thick black frames and had a very neat crew cut.

Drew said, "I do not take up much space. I am in Sylvester's room on the bottom bunk. Norman could take the top bunk, although Kyle usually sleeps there when he is not at his father's house in Memphis."

Kyle groaned, either at Drew kicking him out of his own room or at the mention of his father's house, Molly didn't know which.

"Exactly what I was thinking, Drew," said Phyllis. "Do you mind a top bunk, Norman?" She grimaced in her son's direction. "I'm sure Kyle won't mind the couch for a night or two."

"No, ma'am," said Norman. "I appreciate it." He cast a glance at Kyle, who shrugged.

"And, Molly, you can sleep in Felicia's room."

Molly tried a smile. "Thank you . . . very much."

"Thanks for the ride from the garage, too," said Norman.

"Yeah," echoed Kyle. "Really cool of you, Mom, all of it."

Phyllis gave her son a look that spelled trouble. "We will speak later, young man."

Kyle's face turned the color of the ketchup he'd used to smother his meat loaf.

Phyllis turned her attention back to Norman and Molly. "Shall I call your parents and let them know you're safe?"

"Oh, I called from the service station," Molly said.

"Yes, dear, but you should let them know where you are now! I'm sure your parents are worried — did you tell them you broke down?"

"Well . . . no," said Molly. "I kind of skipped that part."

"You know, Norman," said Phyllis, "it's unsafe to be out there on the road alone —"

"He's got me with him," Molly pointed out.

"You know what I mean, sweetheart," said Phyllis.

Molly wanted to tell Phyllis that she was not her sweetheart, but she kept her mouth shut.

"It's just too dangerous," Phyllis continued, "both of you out there on your own, so young. Who knows what could happen to you. It's scary."

Kyle poured more ketchup on his meat loaf. "Not as scary as the missiles out at the air force base."

Drew piped up. "ICBMs aren't scary when maintained properly, although a high-pressure line did rupture on August 8, 1965, killing fifty-three people who were working in the area."

"What?" Phyllis looked alarmed.

"Yes," said Drew in a matter-of-fact voice. "They suffocated when welding sparks ignited the hydraulic fluid from the high-pressure line, which instantaneously consumed all the available oxygen."

"My *heavens*," said Phyllis, her hand to her chest. "Is that what they teach you in Young Engineer's School?"

"They want us to be careful," Drew explained. "So we need to know the risks. And the history."

Molly spoke up. "I've heard of ICBMs. Intercontinental ballistic missiles. Aren't they supposed to be used to bomb the Russians if they try to invade us?"

220

No more Land of the Free, Home of the Brave, buddy boy. Don't you understand anything?

"That is possible," said Drew, "but I am not interested in

bombing the Russians. I am interested in space travel. When you send a man in a rocket into space, he has to come back without burning up on reentry. I am going to work on reentry systems one day."

"When you send an ICBM into space, the reentry vehicle comes down on your target, wearing a nuclear warhead," said Kyle. "There are nuclear warheads in those silos." He pushed back from the table.

Norman paused with his fork halfway to his mouth.

"That is correct," said Drew. "But only in war. I am not interested in war." He sneezed into his napkin and gently put it back in his lap. "Titans are used to launch space capsules as well. Or they were. They launched the Gemini capsules, and one day they will launch other payloads into space, maybe even a space station. Saturn rockets are launching Apollo space capsules, and will launch Neil Armstrong, Edwin Aldrin — nicknamed Buzz — and Michael Collins into space next month, on July 16, 1969. A reentry vehicle is attached to the capsule and will bring them home safely."

"He knows everything," snarked Kyle.

"Not everything," said Drew, unoffended.

Phyllis sighed and started clearing dishes from the table.

"But I know a lot about Titan II rockets," Drew continued. "There are fifty-four of them. Eighteen are at sites in Arkansas, supported by Little Rock Air Force Base, sitting in silos underground. So I cannot see them, but I know that each one is one hundred and three feet tall, ten feet in diameter, and weighs one hundred and fifty tons. That's three hundred thousand pounds."

Molly suddenly felt very small.

"They can be up and out of their silos in less than a minute after launch command. Each silo is at least seven miles from the next one — that's how powerful they are. They can travel at fifteen thousand miles per hour."

Silence followed Drew's monologue.

Finally, Norman spoke. "Groovy."

Phyllis ran soapy water in the sink. "Let me help," said Molly, remembering her manners.

"Well, I gotta go," said Kyle, on his feet.

"Oh, no you don't, young man," said Phyllis. She jammed dishes into the dishwasher as Molly held them out to her.

"Mom!" Kyle pleaded. "You know I can't stand it there!"

Phyllis grabbed a dish towel and dried her hands as she walked back to the table. Kyle took a step backward.

"You left your brother and sister there by themselves!" said Phyllis.

"They love it there!" Kyle protested.

"You hitchhiked home!"

"I'm alive!"

"You won't be when I'm through with you!"

"Mom."

"How long will it take to fix your bus?" asked Drew.

"Probably two days," said Norman, grateful to Drew for changing the subject. "They have to get a part."

"What is wrong with it?"

"Broken oil seal. And maybe a pinhole leak in the oil hose."

"I wish I could ride with you to California," said Drew. "And I could, if your repair takes longer than two days."

"You could?"

"I mean I would like to," said Drew. "You will have to drive through Flagstaff, Arizona, to get there."

"Yes!" said Molly, surprised.

"The Lowell Observatory is there," said Drew. "And the Clark Telescope. It has mapped the moon."

"It has?"

"Yes. When President John F. Kennedy said, 'We choose to

222

go to the moon!' in 1961, there was no map of the moon."

"There wasn't?"

"I would like to see the craters of the moon through the Clark Telescope. I would like to visit the meteor crater there, too. A meteor slammed into the earth fifty thousand years ago, and the good news is that the astronauts used the crater to learn how to drive their lunar roving vehicle, or LRV, on the moon. We will see them do this on television on July 20, 1969."

"Drew," said Phyllis as she stretched Saran Wrap over the left-over green beans, "I'm sure you will get to the crater and the telescope another day."

Drew didn't answer Phyllis. "When my school here is over, I will go to California to another one. It is at Vandenberg Air Force Base, where I will watch a Titan II test launch. I would come with you on your trip if I could."

Phyllis shut the refrigerator door too forcefully. "Drew! Even if it takes their bus three days — or four, or seven — to be repaired, it's too dangerous to ride across the country by yourselves. I know we are just your host family while you are at this school, but I'm telling you just the same, and I'm sure your own mother would, too, it's too dangerous."

"We're used to danger," said Molly.

"How so?" asked Phyllis.

Norman took over. "We hiked on the Appalachian Trail last year. No problem."

"By yourselves?"

"Might as well have." Norman offered no further explanation.

"I am here by myself," stated Drew.

Kyle brought his plate to the sink. "Mom, I was hitching home to you."

"I've told you a hundred times not to hitchhike!" said Phyllis, a slightly hysterical edge to her voice.

223

"Everyone does it," said Kyle.

"If everyone jumped off a bridge, would you?"

"I know," said Kyle. "I'm sorry. I didn't want to miss band practice."

A skitter fluttered across Norman's shoulders. "Band practice?"

WIPE OUT

Written by Bob Berryhill, Pat Connolly, Jim Fuller, and Ron Wilson
Performed by the Surfaris
Recorded at Pal Recording Studio, Cucamonga, California, 1962
Drummer: Ron Wilson

"And leave your laundry in this basket," instructed Phyllis, giving the last of her commands for an overnight stay that included not leaving the top off the toothpaste and not flushing in the middle of the night.

"You must need clean clothes, traveling all the way from Charleston, and you have a long way to go yet." She seemed resigned to Molly and Norman's fate. "I'm doing several loads of laundry tonight — I have to work tomorrow and need my uniform. Drew can help me fold."

She walked out of the bedroom and Drew followed her, blowing his nose into a napkin. "I might have a cold. Do you have Vicks VapoRub?"

Molly couldn't decide if she should put her underwear in the basket or not. It made her shy to think about anyone else seeing it. But if she didn't, she had a feeling Phyllis would ask her where they were. So she did.

Norman dumped his four oxford shirts, four T-shirts, four pair of white socks, and two pair of khaki slacks into the basket. No underwear. Molly took hers out of the basket just as Phyllis returned to the bedroom.

"Oh, for heaven's sake!" said Phyllis, hoisting the basket to her hip. "I'm a mother! You think I haven't seen underwear before?" Molly dutifully dropped her underwear back into the basket. Phyllis stared at Norman until he followed suit, and then she disappeared. Kyle appeared in the doorway and said, "C'mon, let's get out of here while we still can."

Norman left Hal Blaine's cymbals in their zippered case on the top bunk at Kyle's house. He stuffed his drums into the trunk and back seat of Kyle's car, wherever he could fit them. Molly had to sit on her cousin's lap. She held Kyle's guitar and rested her feet on his amplifier. She wore her shoulder bag with the strap across her chest.

"Why do you need a purse?" Norman said. "I can't fit you in here as it is!"

"Why do you need a snare drum?" Molly retorted. The hundred-dollar bill was now in her wallet, as she was afraid to leave it anywhere by itself. She needed it with her.

Norman turned his attention to Kyle. "You didn't say anything about band practice when I was taking my drums out of the bus!"

"It wasn't exactly the time to mention it when my mom had steam coming out her ears."

"Oh. Right."

"You're lucky we had a van to pick you up in. We may not have it much longer."

"Why not?"

Kyle rubbed his thumb back and forth against his index and middle finger. "Moola. My dad has it, we don't."

Of course. "I hear you, man," said Norman. "I know that story."

"Yeah," said Kyle. "I hope I don't have to sell my car."

They growled across town in Kyle's GTO and parked on the street in front of his bandmate Steve's house. It was an enormous two-story place with gas lampposts, a wide manicured lawn, and perfectly placed maple trees. "Steve's got the drums, so we meet here on Tuesday nights. And the neighbors are nice about it. Leave your kit in the car for now."

"Hey!" said Steve, waving a hand and walking down the long driveway to the car. "We didn't know if you were gonna make it."

Kyle introduced everyone. "Steve on drums. Dave on lead guitar. Matt on rhythm guitar, Dennis on keyboards, me on bass. Everybody sings but me."

"Big band," said Norman.

"We're good, too," said Steve. "Nice to meet you!" He had very neat hair and lots of very white teeth. Everyone had very neat hair and very white teeth. They were all very . . . white.

Dennis arched his eyebrows at Molly appreciatively. "Do you sing?" he asked. "We could use a girl singer."

Molly blushed. Dennis was cute. "No" was all she said.

"Norman here's a drummer," said Kyle.

"Yeah? Want to sit in?" Steve, clearly the leader, asked.

"I've got my kit in the car," said Norman.

"Set it up!" said Steve. "Show us what you got!"

"First we practice," said Kyle. "We've got a gig this weekend."

"A gig!" Norman sighed. Mr. Harter had probably found another band by now. It had only been four days but it felt like they'd been gone four months.

"Yep, we've got a gig at a club out at the air force base on Saturday night," said Steve in a perpetually cheery voice. "Some colonel's daughter is turning sweet sixteen and she asked for us!"

227

"She could have asked for the Coachmen — they've recorded their own songs," said Dave. "They have records."

"So have the Romans," said Matt, "and they show up in togas, with their equipment in a trailer painted to look like a chariot!"

They were all perpetually cheery, Molly decided.

"Who would want guys in togas playing their party?" scoffed Dennis.

"We don't have anything close to this scene in Charleston!" said Norman. He was now perpetually cheery as well. Molly rolled her eyes, spotted a folding chair near Dennis's electric piano, and said, "Can I sit here?"

"Wow, sure!" answered Dennis. "It's my lucky day!" He shot Molly a huge grin. Her cheeks burned and she looked anywhere but at Dennis.

The band played raucously through "Paint It Black," "Satisfaction," "Hang On Sloopy," "Gloria," "Wild Thing," "Day Tripper," "Dizzy," and "Hanky Panky." Every song they practiced had a great guitar lick for Dave or rhythm hook for Matt or bass line for Kyle or drum track for Steve, or some melodic drama for Dennis. They sang, they harmonized, they switched parts and started over, both with instruments and voices, as they tried to improve each performance.

They were good. Norman told them so. "Far out!" And Molly added, "Weekly Top Forty songs all!" She was smitten in spite of herself, especially with Dennis.

"We have to be good, to get the gigs," Dennis said. "And we have to play the hits. There's a lot of competition out there."

He smiled his toothy smile at Molly and once again she blushed. She crossed her legs and bounced her foot in time to the next song.

Neighborhood kids showed up enthusiastically as the hour went by.

"You've got groupies!" said Molly.

"Yeah," said Kyle. "It's fun."

Steve's mother brought out a pitcher of lemonade. "We've got a little meeting going on inside," she said. "You know how attorneys love to talk shop! But don't stop, we love it!"

Norman was in rock-and-roll-band heaven. He was hammering out the beat with his hands on a large red toolbox, using it like a pair of bongos.

A little boy brought some cookies from next door to share and the band took a break. Dennis wolfed down his snack and ruffled the hair of the big-eyed boy who brought it to him, drank a glass of lemonade in one gulp, wiped his mouth with the back of his hand, and then cast another smile at Molly, who finally couldn't help but smile back.

"No, thank you," she said primly when Dennis offered her a cookie. But inside, her mind buzzed. *Oh, this is nice! This attention. I like him.*

And she knew: This is what it would have been like for Barry, if he and Norman had started their band. Norman was a geek, but Barry was a god. He only had to smile. The girls would have been all over him.

Molly closed her eyes and wished Barry were here to see this, instead of wandering lost through San Francisco, sleeping under bridges or in parks, like Marvin Gardens had done. She sighed. How long before they could get back on the road to find her brother?

She opened her eyes to see Steve banging his sticks together and counting off. The band flew into "I Saw Her Standing There." Dennis pointed at her and sang: *Wooooo!*

Norman began to set up his kit as the band went right into "Secret Agent Man." The younger kids ran around on the driveway and *pew-pew-pew*ed each other, James Bond–style, and the little girls danced and twirled. Dennis smiled at Molly, who was still in her seat, foot waggling. She reddened and uncrossed her

229

legs, crossed them again in the opposite direction, and watched Norman as he set up. But she could feel Dennis's eyes on her.

She felt curiously moved by the thought of a one-hour boyfriend in Little Rock, Arkansas. Her heart, that unfeeling organ, beat a little harder, and her breath came a little faster, as she decided she would fall for Dennis. In Little Rock. For one hour.

Norman sat behind his drum kit and held up his sticks. "Ready for anything!" he said.

"Okay, you animals out there!" Steve called. "Here comes what you've been waiting for! Our signature number!"

The driveway kids screamed and came running. The musicians readied themselves in an instant.

"Keep up!" Steve yelled to Norman. He whooped in a high-pitched cackle that made Molly cover her ears. Then he yelled, "Wipe ouuut!" and there were drums.

"Whoa!" said Molly. She was on her feet with expectation, as was everyone else in the garage, in the driveway, or wandering by. Steve set the pace — fast — and Norman kept up. He'd played "Wipe Out" more times than he could count. At home, he'd stack his favorite 45s on the turntable so the records would drop, next by next, as each finished playing, like they were in a jukebox, and he could learn the drum parts by playing along.

The guitars set the tune in place, then gave it over to the drums. Norman instinctively stopped and let Steve have the floor. Steve played some measures and handed it back to Norman. A friendly competition ensued where they traded licks and saw who could make the most noise. The guitar players loved it and started trading off the bass line.

Dennis came out from behind his piano, as he didn't have a part to play in "Wipe Out," and stood next to Molly. He grabbed her hand and, before she could yank it away in surprise, he twirled her around with his arm over his head and began dancing with her. Her surprise turned to laughter as she began to dance with Dennis, her one-hour boyfriend. The kids clapped and danced, and Norman yelled, "Yeah!"

Whether that was for her, or for the thrill of the experience, she didn't know. She grabbed the hands of a couple of kids and twirled them around, and soon all the kids were twirling each other while the guitars played their 12-bar blues licks and the drums beat it out with each other.

Back and forth they went with the cymbals, from ride to crash and back again, waving the same arm right to left to right again, wildly, then with both hands to the toms, the snares, the cymbals again, their legs pumping the pedals for the bass drums and hi-hats. Rather like driving a school bus, it occurred to Molly as she caught Norman's performance out of the corner of her eye.

A kid with flaming red hair yelled, "Do the Funky Chicken!" and the groupies, boys and girls alike, obeyed. *Bwack-bwack-bwack!* Molly laughed so hard she doubled over, doing the Funky Chicken to "Wipe Out" with a pile of third graders.

"Wrapping it up!" shouted Steve. Norman and Steve played in tandem to the big finish, and as they all crash-landed on the same clamorous note, Norman leaped from his stool and raised both arms over his head like a football umpire holding drumsticks pointed to heaven and yelled, "Score!"

For one night, he was part of a real band and Molly was a real groupie.

Steve, laughing, grabbed a handful of clean cloths from the rag box next to a workbench. He threw one to Norman and they began mopping up. It was a hot June night, made hotter by the physical exertion.

"That's hard work!" said Norman, euphoric.

"That was great, Norman!" said Molly with true admiration.

Steve agreed. "Not bad," he told Norman. "Not bad at all. What did you say your name was again?"

"Florsheim."

231

They all laughed, and Norman laughed with them.

"I need a name," he confessed, drummer to drummer. "I don't like Norman."

"Norman Mailer," said Matt right away. "He's a writer — know him? He's a friend of my dad's. They served together in the Pacific in World War II. He just published a book about the war. My dad has a signed copy."

"World War II?"

"No, the war now," said Matt.

"That's a conflict," said Steve. "We haven't formally declared war on Vietnam."

"That's stupid!" said Matt, who grabbed one of Steve's rags and dried the sweat from his forehead. "We're at war! Soldiers are dying!"

"You're just arguing because you have to register for the draft in September," said Steve. "You're an old man now, Matt."

"You're right behind me in a couple of years, Steve, so get ready!"

"I can't even drive yet," said Dave, as if that might protect him.

"Robb is still missing," said Dennis in a quiet voice. He explained for Molly. "He went MIA six months ago, somewhere in a jungle 8,782 miles away." He sat back at his piano. He didn't smile.

"Robb?" said Norman, just as softly, and with hesitation.

"My older brother," said Dennis. He noodled a few notes with one hand on the piano and said, "Are we done for the night?"

Molly thought, *I should fall in love with Dennis for that.* But her heart knew better. It wasn't ready for boyfriends or love. Her heart had only one trajectory on the horizon right now and she had just been reminded of it. It beat in a steady rhythm: *Barry, Barry, Barry.*

27

The bus had a new oil line, shocks, brakes, and windshield wipers, all courtesy of Elvis Presley's hundred-dollar donation. But they had lost two days to repairs. In order to make enough room for spare oil, and for comfort, Norman had left four more seats with the mechanics, who were already sitting in them by the time he and Molly rumbled off the lot, with Kyle raising a hand in good-bye.

Kyle had borrowed Phyllis's van for an hour on Wednesday so he and Norman and Molly could go to the lumber store and buy a gallon of paint and some brushes, and more plywood. They had the lumber man cut the plywood to Molly's measurements and now the back of the bus was roomy enough for Molly's taste, and the CHARLESTON COUNTY SCHOOLS sign was completely obliterated by a fat white rectangle.

"You should paint something over it," Kyle had said, and so

Molly borrowed some paint cans from the mechanics on Thursday morning and painted a flower garden on each side of the bus.

"It's a hippie bus!" Kyle declared.

"Hardly," answered Norman.

"You should paint the whole thing!" said Kyle.

Molly liked the idea. But they had no time to waste now; they would have to press ahead like they were on fire. They'd been gone for almost a week. She took the paint cans back to the mechanics. "Keep 'em," they said. "Fair trade."

They entered Oklahoma and found only country music stations on the radio. Molly plugged into her transistor radio but had no better luck. She abandoned it for the bus radio. They listened to Johnny Cash sing "A Boy Named Sue."

"Who would really name a boy 'Sue'?" Molly said.

"Easiest drums ever," said Norman. "Bass-snare-hi-hat, same pattern, over and over. But then, country music is all about the guitars."

Interstate 40 was under construction so often and the traffic was so snarled, they got onto the less-traveled side roads that led them out of their way and into Muskogee. As they passed the sparkling new civic center, they saw posters:

MUSKOGEE CIVIC CENTER
IN PERSON TONIGHT
ONE SHOW ONLY 8 P.M.
COUNTRY SHINDIG NO. 3
MERLE HAGGARD AND THE STRANGERS
HEAR MERLE
SING HIS NEW
CAPITOL RECORD
— HIT —
OKIE FROM MUSKOGEE

"Another silly song," said Molly. "But I like it." She thought of band practice and its silliness. "Did you see those kids doing the funky chicken to 'Wipe Out'?"

"I saw you making funky chicken eyes at Dennis."

"I was not!"

"You were." Norman turned off the radio. "He's way too old for you, Molly."

"I'm fourteen! He's only sixteen. He told me he just got his driver's license."

"That's too old," said Norman. "I'm responsible for you out here, and I can't do my job if you're flirting with piano players!"

"He was flirting with me! And I'm responsible for myself, thank you."

"You don't understand, Molly. Guys that age . . ."

"You're that age," Molly reminded him.

"I'm a year older. And I'm different."

"I'll say."

They rode in silence toward Oklahoma City. Molly tried to decide if she'd hurt Norman's feelings. "You're a good drummer," she finally said.

"I'm not that good," Norman replied.

Neither of them turned on the radio while the miles melted away under the bus. "Have you ever had a girlfriend, Norman?"

Norman shifted into fifth gear and surprised Molly. "If you want to get a girlfriend — and this is something Dennis knows — you either have to be an athlete or a lifeguard or be in a band. That's one reason I wanted to be in a band this summer. Nobody wants to date a high school marching band geek named Norman."

"*That's* why?"

"And I like the music. Do we need gas?"

"Not yet. I don't think."

"Do the math. See if we can make it to Oklahoma City. Use eight miles per gallon for the bus, although that's ambitious. Use seven. We've got a sixty-gallon tank. We don't want to get below twenty gallons." The thought of Buddy and his midnight gas station gave Norman a shiver. "And I don't want to drive at night."

Molly figured with a pencil, a ruler, and Aunt Pam's poodled notepad. "We can make it," she said.

They found a Phillips 66 service station in Yukon, Oklahoma. Four American flags flew out front from various poles. A sign told them they were crossing the Chisholm Trail. "Yippee Ti Yi Yo!" sang Molly. Norman answered with "Git along, little dogies!" and they both laughed.

Norman's laughter was more a groan. Last summer, that was the theme song on the Appalachian Trail, a cry of encouragement led by Pam and echoed by Janice, and begrudgingly followed by Norman and Molly. They had learned every verse.

"And look, there's our first cowboy hat," said Molly.

As the attendant put close to forty gallons of gas in the tank, a brown-haired kid with a ten-gallon hat cocked back on his head sat on a bench outside, under the overhang apron, and picked on a guitar with three strings. It was almost as big as he was.

"Nice tune," Norman said.

"Thanks," said the kid, without looking up or stopping. "I'm workin' it up."

"Yeah? What's it called?"

"'Mama Tried.' It's a song by Merle Haggard. You know it?"

Norman shook his head. "Nope."

"Hey!" Molly appeared with a bag of ice in her arms. "We just saw he's playing in Muskogee tonight!"

"Yeah." The kid stopped playing and looked at them with bright blue eyes. "I can't go. Are you going?"

"We're going the opposite direction," said Norman. "You like country music?"

"It's the best!" said the kid. "And Merle's the best, too. Did you know, he's been to prison!"

"Not exactly my definition of the best," said Molly.

"That's what the song is about — listen! I'll sing it!"

"Not again!" said the attendant. He was cleaning the bus windshield, stretching to reach as much of it as he could. "Play something else!"

"Aw, Mr. Jackson! I've just about got it!"

"Fine, fine," said Mr. Jackson. He beat his squeegee against the bucket.

The kid had a new audience and he knew how to capture it. He sang "Mama Tried" to Molly and Norman — it was short — and they clapped wildly.

Molly picked up her ice. "That's a strange song," she said.

"You're good!" said Norman.

"Not as good as Merle," said the boy. "He lives in Bakersfield, California, where the best music is, and I'm going to go there one day and meet him. I'm gonna be a star, too!"

"You are?" said Norman. He smiled for the first time since they'd left Little Rock that morning.

"How old are you?" asked Molly.

"I'm seven," said the boy in a serious and commanding voice.

"All right, Troyal, Mr. Famous Star," said the attendant. "Run on home now. It's lunchtime."

"Yessir," said the boy. He lifted a hand to Molly and Norman. "See ya on stage!" He walked away with his guitar strap across his chest so the guitar rode his back.

The attendant took their money, studied Molly's artwork on the side of the bus, and looked at Norman sideways.

"Y'all ain't hippies, are ya?"

237

"Nossir," said Norman.

"Well, you don't dress like hippies," said the man, looking Norman up and down in his road uniform.

"We're not hippies," Norman assured him.

"I sell American flags," said the man, like this was a test. "I think you need one."

"We do!" said Molly in her brightest voice. They bought a flag.

"Good," said the man. "Those hippies are tearing up this country."

"Yessir," said Norman. His heart was beating harder than it needed to. "Thanks for the gas. Sir."

"Thanks for the business," said the man.

Molly dumped the ice into the ice chest, and they were on their way.

"We forgot the grocery store!" she realized.

"We're on Route 66," said Norman. "There will be plenty to eat. There's Rick's Donuts right over there, across from the bowling alley. Will that do for now?"

American flags flew from the donut shop, the bowling alley, and the auto parts store.

"Okay," said Molly. "But we need to stock up. It's over a thousand miles between here and Los Angeles and your Hal Blaine guy. Then we head north to San Francisco. That's another four hundred miles. We've been on the road for five days and we're only in Oklahoma."

"We're almost in Texas."

"So far, we have traveled one thousand two hundred and seventeen miles. If it takes us another week to go that many more miles, we're going to have to put Barry on a plane home. We'd better hurry."

"I thought you were going to tell him to run."

"I'm having second thoughts."

"Right," said Norman.

"It's his decision."

"Right."

"Right."

There was not plenty to eat on this particular stretch of Route 66. The roads were long and desolate across the top of the Texas panhandle, nothing but broad vistas of flat, open range dotted with scrub grass and sagebrush. Mounds of tumbleweeds plastered themselves against the post-and-barbed-wire fences, with one occasionally topping the fence and rolling toward the road in the brisk wind that buffeted the bus.

"Home, home on the range," said Molly. "Wow."

"You're not kidding," said Norman. The radio picked up nothing but static. Molly began closing windows to keep down the dust.

The day lasted forever. Norman became bleary-eyed staring at the road. They were rolling through the miles, but he wished he had listened to Molly and taken the time to find a grocery store. They left the construction on new Interstate 40 too soon in search of a better road, but what they found was heat and dust and hunger.

"It's so hot," Molly complained. "And flat as a pancake. There's nothing out here, not even trees! Maybe we should turn back."

"I don't want to waste time going in the opposite direction," said Norman. "Is there a way back to 66?"

"We've already passed a cutoff to Amarillo," said Molly. "We're almost in New Mexico. There aren't many roads out here." She mopped at her neck with the cloth that Norman had used after "Wipe Out" in Little Rock and passed it up to him so he could do the same. "I wish we could install air-conditioning."

They finished the box of Rick's Donuts and bought peanut butter crackers at one gas stop, pork rinds and potato chips at another. Molly repeatedly filled paper cups with water from the melting ice in the chest. She rubbed an ice cube on her arms and neck and used the melting cold water to wash her face. She wet the rag and put it on Norman's neck. They rode that way in silence for a long time.

The swirling dust gave them a spectacular sunset as they stopped for the night at a small mom-and-pop campground advertising itself as "The Gateway to New Mexico!" and "See the Grasslands!" with a pay phone for calling Janice and Pam, showers and toilets in crude bath houses, and a pole with one plug for electricity at their campsite, but no food in sight. No other campers, either.

They dug through Aunt Pam's many boxes and came up with a pair of jeans in Norman's size at the bottom of one box, along with a note from Pam: *I know you don't like dungarees, but these are Levi's and they are tough, like you, and you might need them on the road. Happy Trails!*

There was also a box of Pop-Tarts, a can of tuna, three apples, and some sweet potatoes, which they wrapped in foil and stuck in the coals of a small fire. Norman ran an extension cord from his record player on the picnic table and they played all the records that Estelle had given them at Stax, as well as Wilson Pickett's version of "Hey, Jude" from Rick at Muscle Shoals, and some records Norman had purchased at Moody's Melody Shop in Little Rock with Kyle.

When they had satisfied their hunger, they sat in lawn chairs and watched the night fold in around them. Softly, Molly began to sing the last verse of "Git Along, Little Dogies."

"Your mother was raised a-way down in Texas, where the jim-son weed and the sandburs grow. We'll fill you up on prickly pear and cholla until you are ready for Idaho!"

Norman listened quietly with his head tilted to the star-studded sky. "Mom would have loved this," he said in a homesick voice. He sang a few lines of "Don't Fence Me In," one of Pam's night-time around-the-fire anthems on last year's trip.

Molly watched him warble and felt great affection for the boy who had agreed to drive her across the country to find her brother. She licked her fingers and wished they had butter for the sweet potatoes. She tried to think of some way to tell Norman she liked him, that he was doing a great job.

"Your mom is much more adventurous than mine," she finally said. "Your mom *inspires* my mom."

"Yeah," said Norman. *She inspires me, too.* He couldn't say it. Boys didn't talk that way. They didn't say *You inspire me* or *I love you.* But he could see now, Pam's positivity was a good thing. He needed it. And, just maybe, he had needed this trip. It wasn't just the music. It was what the music did for him. It was growing him up. Something like that. Or maybe the driving and the landscape did that. Maybe having to put up with his cousin did that. He was too tired to figure it out, but he was different. He could tell.

Every bone in his body ached from the long driving day. He longed to put his head on his pillow. He got up to poke the fire. With the sun down, the temperature had dropped and it was chilly.

He tossed their paper plates in the fire. An insistent breeze tugged at them and clouds covered the stars. "I'm gonna lay out the sleeping bags," he said. "I'm beat. I'll bring you your sweat-shirt. It's getting cold."

"Take the record player," said Molly. "I'm right behind you."

As Norman made their beds ready in the bus and Molly consulted her maps with a flashlight by the fire, footsteps approached them in the dark.

"We heard your music," said a boy's voice.

Molly leaped to her feet with a small scream. Map pages scattered and the boy raced to catch them before they swirled into the fire.

Molly grabbed her Rand McNally Road Atlas and held it in front of her like a shield. "Who are you?"

"We come in peace!" the boy hurried to say. "I'm Ben!"

"I'm Carol!" said a girl.

He was black. She was white. She held up a brown-eyed baby with soft black curls. "This is Moonglow." As if she'd been coached, Moonglow leaned away from Carol and reached out both of her arms for Molly.

Thunder split the heavens over them and the sky opened up.

Inside the bus, Norman lit a lantern and hung it on a hook from the ceiling. It swayed wildly, casting ghostly shadows, while the rain and wind pounded the bus in a quick and sudden rage that gave way to a popping sound like a BB gun, its pellets banging the roof and hood like something was trying to get inside.

"What's that!" yelled Molly.

"It's hail!" shouted Ben.

The sound was so loud, Molly covered her ears and Moonglow began to cry. Carol nestled herself into the front passenger seat opposite Molly and pulled up her shirt to nurse her baby. Norman froze with the realization, sat down hard in the driver's seat, put a hand on each knee, and stared straight ahead, into the downpour.

Moonglow stopped crying and the hailstorm ended. The sounds of Moonglow's nursing seemed to fill the bus. Molly wanted to cover Carol with a sheet. She was red with embarrassment and couldn't imagine what Norman must be feeling. She stared out her window into the darkness.

Ben sat behind Carol and spoke in soft tones to the baby while he stroked Carol's hair. Molly couldn't help but steal glances their way. *We can't even go to school together peaceably in Charleston! This would cause a riot!* She walked to the back of the bus and stood on her sleeping bag while she pulled on her sweatshirt.

The storm left as abruptly as it had arrived, leaving an impressive lightning display in its wake, with thunder crackling in the distance. Moonglow finished her supper and was asleep at her mother's breast in the front passenger seat of the bus. Carol sang softly to her daughter and rocked in the seat as the rain moved on to the grasslands.

Norman grabbed a flashlight from the box by the driver's seat, lunged open the folding door, and dashed down the steps to survey the damage.

"It doesn't look too bad," he said to nobody. "We'll know more in the morning."

"It rains like this now and then," said Ben, who had followed Norman outside, with Molly close behind him. "Never lasts long. The rain feeds the tumbleweeds."

"I've *seen* the tumbleweeds," said Molly.

The air filled with the songs of frogs rejoicing over the rainwater. A coyote howled. Another took up its call and soon a band of coyotes bayed in noisy chorus at the moon sliding out from behind the clouds. Molly shivered.

Norman stepped around a giant puddle and played his flashlight into the woods.

243

"They won't hurt you," said Ben. "They're farther away than they sound."

Carol snapped down her window inside the bus and whispered, "She's asleep. I put her on a sleeping bag in the back." Norman glanced at Molly and breathed a long sigh through his lips. Carol and Moonglow. Emily and Christian. Ray and his promise.

He addressed Ben with a tired curiosity.

"What do you need?"

GOING UP THE COUNTRY

Written by Alan Wilson
Performed by Canned Heat
Recorded at ID Sound Recorders, Hollywood, California, 1968
Drummer: Aldolfo "Fito" De La Parra

The next morning, Molly read out loud from *An Adventurer's Guide to Travel across America* as they rode through a landscape of shinnery oaks and prickly pears, past the vast grasslands inhabited long ago by plentiful buffalo and bison herds, land tended by the Kiowa and other tribes before the Homestead Act of 1862 sent white settlers pouring into the territory.

"You mean before invaders brought cholera and chaos to Indian land," said Ben.

"It doesn't say that," said Molly.

"It wouldn't," said Ben.

Molly frowned. "Why wouldn't it?"

"Because 'the Kiowa and other tribes' didn't write that book," said Ben.

"This is an official guidebook," said Molly, looking in confusion at the cover.

"That's the problem," said Ben. "There's the official version of the past, and there's the real past."

"How do you know which version is real?" Molly asked, genuinely curious.

"Start paying attention to who's telling the story," said Carol. "The story changes depending on who's telling it."

Molly put the book away but not her questions.

They entered New Mexico at Texline. They stopped three times in the crossroads town of Clayton, once at a diner for a hearty breakfast, then at a grocery store for supplies, and finally for gas and ice. It felt good to be well stocked and ready for the long day ahead, although Norman's breakfast was sitting like a brick in the bottom of his stomach, and his eyelids were heavy with fatigue. He and Ben had slept on bus seats and he'd given Carol and Moonglow his space and sleeping bag on the foam rubber mattress in the back.

As they left the gas station, a skinny red dog boarded the bus with them.

"Hey!" said Norman. "Who do you belong to?"

"You," said the attendant.

"Nossir, he's not ours."

"We can't keep feeding him here," said the attendant, "and nobody will claim him. He's a stray. Been here a couple of weeks. Somebody on the way to Colorado or Texas or Oklahoma dumped him. A nuisance. Seems to like you, though."

He was the ugliest dog Norman had ever seen. Probably mangy, certainly flea-bitten. Absolutely filthy.

The dog trotted down the aisle of the bus and helped himself to Norman's sleeping bag.

"Here, boy!" Norman called, and the dog trotted back up the aisle. "Sit." The dog sat. He seemed to smile at Norman with huge brown eyes and a flappy snout. He offered a paw and Norman took it.

Did a dog qualify as a body in need?

Norman scratched the side of his face and asked the attendant, "Got any flea powder?"

Molly came around the corner from the bathrooms and the ice machine and saw her cousin with a garden hose, a bottle of shampoo, and something living, white with foamy suds.

"We've got a dog!" Norman called as he wrestled with the animal, who wanted dearly to be anywhere but where he currently was.

Molly stalked past Norman without a word and boarded the bus.

They had a dog.

They rumbled onto the highway, a sextet in the bus: two boys, two girls, one baby girl, and a boy dog. The dog immediately shook himself dry at the front of the bus, in the middle of the bus, and at the back, where he settled once again on Norman's sleeping bag.

"Here, boy! Here, Flam!" Norman called.

"That's his name? Flam?" Molly asked. "What kind of name is that?"

"It's a drum rudiment. A practice pattern. I miss practicing."

"Can he be another pattern?"

"Paradiddle?"

"Fine. Get in the back, Flam, you're wet!" The dog flopped at Molly's feet.

Norman had pointedly given Carol one of his white T-shirts to drape across her shoulder for Moonglow's meals. "For modesty," he explained.

"Do you mind if I stretch out for a few in the back?" asked Ben. "These seats aren't much for sleeping overnight."

"Tell me about it," said Norman. "Go ahead." Molly watched Ben as he kissed Carol on the top of her head and asked her if she'd rather take his place. Carol shook her head and smiled at Ben. She fed Moonglow and pointed to the New Mexico road map that Molly had folded open just so on her lap on top of the road atlas.

"There aren't many roads out here. The best way to get back to Route 66 is to drop us home, then travel two hours south to Santa Fe — maybe three with the bus — then two hours to Albuquerque, and then it's a straight shot on Route 66 to Los Angeles. You'll be there before you know it."

Molly had her ruler, pencil, and poodle pad ready. "This puts us at least two hours behind my schedule," she said, clearly annoyed. "Probably three."

"No problem, man," said Ben, in a sincere voice. "Let us off. We can hitch from here." Norman's and Molly's eyes met in the student mirror above Norman's head.

Molly went back to figuring. "We could still make it to Albuquerque in one day, if we just drop them off and keep going."

"Drop and go?" said Norman. He raised his eyebrows and gave Molly in the mirror a weary half smile.

She blushed at the remembrance. "Stop."

"Can we get there before dark?"

"If we don't mess around," Molly said. They had to shout because all the bus windows were down and the hot air buffeted them. Flam panted in the aisle, at Molly's feet. "You understand it's adding two or three hours to our time, to go north first, then down to Santa Fe."

"I get it," said Norman. "We'll . . . make up the time tomorrow." He didn't sound sure.

"We really appreciate it," said Ben.

"You should stay the night," said Carol. "We have beds

and plenty of room. And you look spent, Norman. Did you get enough sleep last night?"

"I got some," said Norman.

"And tomorrow's the summer solstice," said Carol. "The longest day of the year. We always do something special. You don't want to miss it."

"We won't miss it," said Molly. "We'll be driving right into it."

"Mol," said Norman, adjusting in his seat and sitting up straighter at the thought of a real bed. "Yesterday I drove over six hundred miles, do you know that?"

"I know that, *Norm*." Molly glanced at Carol, who suddenly seemed more thoughtful than Molly was. "I know it was a lot, Norman."

I'm beat. That's what he wanted to say. *I need to sleep for a week. I don't feel good.* He could hear Phyllis correcting him at Kyle's kitchen table — *Well, Norman! You don't feel well!* Then she would put a hand to his forehead. *Are you all right?*

He said nothing.

"We have plenty of room," Carol repeated. "And we can feed you a home-cooked meal."

Molly stifled a nasty retort. Instead, she said, "We can camp along the way if it starts to get dark. We have food."

"Whatever you want," said Norman. He was in no mood to argue. His head hurt.

He tried to concentrate on the road ahead. Everything but the hot-white sky was brown and ochre and red. They rode past mesas and jagged outcroppings reaching for the sky and a desert floor dotted with clumps of grasses and mesquite. There were tiny towns and enormous ranches and all the barbed-wire fencing in the world along a long lonesome road with a mountain range ahead in the distance. The sun spilled into the bus from all sides. The glare was impossible.

The wind was constant and the gusts were wild. Norman

249

struggled to keep the bus in his lane. Not that it mattered too much, as there were scant few cars on this road. Flam had positioned himself beside Norman, and Norman had given him a blanket from Aunt Pam's stash. Ben snored on Norman's sleeping bag. Moonglow snoozed on her mother. Molly plugged in her earphone and tried her transistor again, but got nothing. Carol stood up with Moonglow. "I think I'll go nap with Ben," she said, just as Molly looked ahead of them and saw something on the sandy desert floor racing like lightning, heading straight for the bus.

"Look out!"

It was the size of a buffalo. With ease it had rolled over its companions jammed against the barbed-wire fence and now it galloped toward them at a frightening pace. Norman swerved into the empty oncoming lane, but still it hit them and exploded on impact. It slammed into the grille of the bus and tumbleweed shards showered the windshield. The bus rocked wildly as Norman applied the brakes and tried to keep it steady. Thorny fragments of tumbleweed flew up and over the bus and in through the open windows. Flam yelped and slid into the stepwell, then scrambled to get to his feet.

The impact of the crash sent Moonglow airborne. She popped out of her mother's arms and vaulted across the bus aisle where Molly, heart in throat, caught her like she was a football.

No one had screamed. No one had spoken. It was over as quickly as it had begun.

Norman pulled the bus to the side of the road. "Everybody okay?"

Ben was on his feet. "What happened?"

"We hit a tumbleweed," said Norman. "Or it hit us."

He opened the bus door, and he and Ben followed Flam out into the sun.

Moonglow gurgled at Molly and reached for her face. Carol had tears in her eyes as she collected her baby. "Thank you so much!" and Molly felt moved by the exchange. "You're welcome" were the first kind words she'd spoken to Carol. She felt like crying. They were alive.

Outside, Norman and Ben squinted at the bus in the brilliant sunshine. A chunk of the grille was missing. Woody tumbleweed stems stuck out like long pins in a metal pincushion. The glass on the right front headlight was broken and the light was hanging from its socket. The hood was scratched like wild cats had been fighting there.

Norman got on his back and scooted a few inches under the bus. He came out and brushed off his hands as he stood up. He felt dizzy. "I can't tell if it hurt anything underneath. Nothing's leaking that I can see."

"Once you get into those mountains, you're almost to our place," said Ben. "We've got friends who know a lot about keeping engines running. It's only an hour away."

"Okay," Norman agreed. He rubbed at his temples. He was suddenly queasy. The brick that was his breakfast heaved up his gullet. He turned away from Ben and the bus and threw up.

29

WASN'T BORN TO FOLLOW

Written by Gerry Goffin and Carole King
Performed by the Byrds
Recorded at Columbia Studios, Hollywood, California, 1967
Drummer: Michael Clarke (concert)/Jim Gordon (studio)

When Norman opened his eyes, Molly was there beside him. There was worry in her voice. "Want some water?"

Norman half sat up and sipped cool water from a tin cup. He was in a real bed in a tiny adobe room with a fireplace that warmed the walls and everything within them. It was the coziest he'd felt since leaving Charleston.

"Where are we?" He vaguely remembered pulling into the yard and children crowding the bus, happy waiting arms taking Moonglow from Carol, and other, capable arms guiding him to a place to sleep.

"You're at New Buffalo," said a voice on the other side of the bed. Norman turned to look at a young woman with smoky brown eyes and corkscrew black curls spilling around a head scarf like a halo around her head. "My name is Sadie." Norman blinked and swallowed.

Sadie gestured *Shhh* to a girl who entered the adobe room

in a breathless rush. She had golden hair that tumbled over her shoulders, and bold blue eyes that shone like stars from a freshly scrubbed face. "This is Sweet Caroline," said Sadie. "She's been away this afternoon."

"And now here I am!" said Sweet Caroline, blinking her eyes at Norman. "Who are you?" Then she giggled like it was the silliest thing to even ask. Or like she was the cutest being on the planet and didn't Norman see that.

Molly answered for Norman. "I'm Eleanor Rigby," she said, annoyed at this new girl. "And this is my cousin Florsheim."

Sweet Caroline laughed with her mouth open in glee. Sadie put a hand on Sweet Caroline's leg and said, "I'm glad you're back. Let's check our patient."

Sweet Caroline opened her eyes wide, like she was about to impart state secrets, and whispered, "Sadie is the Loving Earth Mother. I'm observing."

"Observing what?" asked Molly.

Sadie placed the back of her hand gently on Norman's pale forehead. "Your fever has broken. It must have come from exhaustion. Or a bit of altitude sickness. We are almost seven thousand feet above sea level here. You've had quite a climb from the Texas panhandle, where you picked up Ben and Carol and Moonglow."

"And Flam," said Molly. "Let's not forget about Flam." She tried not to sound ugly, but they really didn't need a dog.

At the bottom of the bed, curled in a comfortable circle, Flam thumped his tail and looked at Norman through eyes half-hidden in his furry red legs.

"Sweet doggie!" chirped Sweet Caroline. Norman tried to sit up. His head hurt.

"There are a lot of people here," said Molly. "Some of them looked under the bus and said it's all right. They replaced the headlight, too — they have lots of car parts here and bunches of trucks they're trying to get running again."

253

"Are they sure it's all right?" Norman supported his weight on his elbows.

"Yes. The headlight doesn't exactly fit, but it's good enough for now. They spent a lot of time with gloves on, yanking tumbleweed pieces out of the grille, too. I thanked them. Profusely."

"I want to look at it." Norman swung his feet to the side of the bed, sat up, and realized he was still dizzy. He held on to the mattress with both hands and got very still.

"Uh-oh!" said Sweet Caroline.

"It's almost suppertime," said Sadie. Her skin shone a burnished brown in the firelight and her voice was smooth and soothing, like a body of cool, still water.

"Loving Earth Mother," said Norman. "Where have I heard that before?"

"Right here!" said Sweet Caroline. "I just told you!"

Sadie held up a hand to silence Sweet Caroline, and Sweet Caroline obeyed.

"I came in to see if you were hungry," Sadie said to Norman.

He groaned. "No."

"Well, I am," said Molly. Her voice was laced with relief. Her cousin was awake, had no fever, and was going to be all right, but not in time to get them to Albuquerque before nightfall. She had sat by his side while he slept and had come to terms with the fact that they wouldn't be leaving tonight. Now she tried to think of something comforting to say, but what came out was, "You've been sleeping for hours! Come out when you're ready." She gave him two swift, hesitant pats on the hand and walked out of the adobe.

"We've got peppermint tea for your stomach and plenty of rice and beans and tortillas," said Sadie. "And Barb made a lemon meringue pie." She put a warm hand over Norman's cool one. "Sleep more first. Drink water."

"I'll sit with him awhile," said Sweet Caroline.

254

Norman slid back under his blanket. Flam settled himself at his feet. They both sighed.

Outside, Molly walked across the grassy llano in time to watch the sun explode, its yellow orb turning into prisms of deepest purple and pink and red and orange as it slipped behind the mountains in the distance. Waves of green wheat danced in front of her, where a man leading a horse from the field to the barn cast long shadows.

Sadie came to her side. "Isn't it magnificent?"

"Yes," Molly said emphatically. "I never knew a sunset could color the whole sky. Where are we exactly? I know I'm at New Buffalo, in New Mexico . . ."

"That's the Sangre de Cristo mountain range over there," said Sadie. "It's the southernmost part of the Rockies. You're on a mesa; it's flat, like a tabletop, and it goes on for miles. On the west side, there's a sheer cliff drop at the gorge of the Rio Grande. It's our version of the Grand Canyon. You can watch storms develop here on the mesa from a great distance — and look, there's snow on top of the mountains way over there, even in June. See the sunset reflecting on the snow?"

Molly admitted it was beautiful, like nothing she'd ever seen in Charleston, where they lived almost in the sea, surrounded by water and the familiar smells of the mud and marshes.

"How did you all get here?" Molly asked.

"Different ways. We are seekers. We heard about this place one way or another. And there are others, you know, living in similar communities in Vermont, Tennessee, Oregon, California . . . but none of them has this." Sadie gestured around her to the scrub oaks, the juniper, the piñon, and the desert grasses fading into shadows. "Most of us here felt drawn to this place, as if we didn't have a choice. It's magical, don't you think?"

She did. "Where did you come from?" she asked Sadie.

"Everywhere," Sadie answered. "Paul is from New York City.

255

Sharon is from Chicago. David is from Virginia. George is from Ohio. I'm from California. I was in college. I dropped out a year ago. Three years was long enough."

Molly did the math in her head. Sadie was twenty, then. "Are you the oldest here?" she asked.

Sadie smiled. "Age isn't a number," she said. She put a finger to her forehead. "It's where you're at."

"Where is Sweet Caroline at?" Molly asked.

Sadie laughed. "She's new here. I don't know much about her yet. She'll settle in. Nobody is much over twenty-five or under eighteen, except the children, of course. These are my brothers and sisters now, my family. This is the New Buffalo commune. We're changing the world."

Molly looked at the young woman beside her. "How?"

"Come to supper," said Sadie. "We'll tell you about it. This way."

They walked through a beautiful arched adobe entryway with mallows growing around it into a courtyard and past a communal fire ringed with logs, where two boys thumped softly together in unison on homemade hand drums. A sunburned man carrying a sack of something on his shoulder walked past them, wearing jeans, boots, and no shirt. He dumped his sack on the ground and began to wash up beside a basin of water at an outdoor sink. A bearded man who had been chopping firewood joined him.

An old beat-up Wonder Bread truck with its circles turned into blue and red and gold Van Gogh–like suns and stars and swirls rattled into the parking area, and two young men began unloading piles of quilts into the waiting arms of those who met them, including Molly. "From the Lutheran church ladies," said the driver. "Enough to go around! Especially if we share."

"And we got egg money!" said another. "We traded it for chicken feed, a bale of hay, flour, and salt."

"*And* a little sugar and four lemons," said the driver. No one seemed to notice that Molly hadn't been there forever.

Molly and Sadie entered the pueblo and walked through a washroom, an enormous pantry room, and into the kitchen. "Sink's fixed!" said a man with hair longer than Molly's. It spilled across his shoulders. "You still have to tote water from the Hondo, but now it'll drain into the garden."

"Pea soup!" said a woman stirring a pot at the woodstove. She wore cowboy boots, a short white dress, and pigtails. "How many for supper tonight?"

"We're rich!" said the young man who drove the bread truck. He planted a kiss on the cheek of the woman at the woodstove. She turned and threw her arms around his neck and ardently kissed him back.

Soon they were all in the common room. Four earthen steps led down from the kitchen into the large circular room built into the earth, where a fire burned and smoke curled through a hole in the roof. Earthen benches lined the circular walls. Everyone stood together around the fire holding hands. Molly had no idea whose hands she was holding, and she didn't know what else to do, so she stood as still and quiet as everyone else and watched. The sunburned man began.

"We thank you for the food made here with loving hands. We thank you for the food from other hands. We ask your blessing on our efforts in the fields, in the community of man, and with one another. We ask for strength and wisdom and compassion in a world of materialism and greed and war. We pledge to use our gifts and talents for good. We will continue to strive to open our hearts and minds to the ultimate consciousness and light. May peace continue to grow. Amen."

Molly looked from face to face in the firelight as the sunburned man spoke. They were young and younger, poor and poorer but claiming they were rich. They were all shades of

257

black and white and brown. They were short and tall, skinny and skinnier, and all of them from somewhere else. Their faces were earnest and serious, determined and dedicated, worn and weary at the end of a long workday, and somehow shiny, too. Carol smiled at Molly. Molly smiled back.

She wondered if this place would feel like home to Lucy. She had a wild thought to write her a letter. She knew the address.

She remembered her nightly phone call, but there was no phone here and no way to call her mother. And for some reason, in this common room, holding hands with strangers, that thought was a good one. If Norman were not with her on this trip, no one she knew in the entire world would know where she was.

The thought was thrilling. She was surrounded by a sense of safety here that surprised her. She could live here, she thought. Maybe she would.

"Amen" went around the room, and Molly blinked out of her reverie. "Amen," she said. Amen and Amen.

PEOPLE GOT TO BE FREE

Written by Felix Cavaliere and Eddie Brigati
Performed by the Rascals
Recorded at Atlantic Studios, New York, New York, 1968
Drummer: Dino Danelli

After their communal supper, couples drifted to small campfires on the mesa or sat around the fire at the community gathering place with their homemade drums. Someone was always drumming. Someone else had a guitar. Someone produced a flute, and someone else a harmonica.

"Tomorrow's solstice!" said a young dancing boy wearing pants but no shirt or shoes. "We get to sleep in the meadow!"

"That's right," said a woman with long brown hair in a bedraggled ponytail. She scooped the child into her lap. It occurred to Molly that her own ponytail was sloppy, too, and that was fine with her.

Norman wandered out from the adobe building, blinking his eyes. He walked toward the flickering communal fire with its bodies softly talking, and saw smaller fires beyond that one, dotting the darkness, along with the black outlines of tall ponderosa pines. As he tried to make out what he was seeing, a body walked between the fire and something behind it. "A tipi!" he whispered. There were several.

The smell of supper had beckoned him from his adobe room near the common room. He was hungry after all. They made room for him on a log, and Sadie brought him a tin plate of pinto beans, brown rice, and a hunk of bread baked over the fire in a covered kettle.

"Thank you, Sadie," he said sincerely. He wanted to tell her how much her touch had meant to him earlier, and how it had helped him sleep, but he didn't dare.

He ate slowly and silently and listened as the children played near the fire and a German shepherd tried to make friends with Flam, who stuck close to Norman and was rewarded with Norman's bread.

Norman looked for Molly and caught her eye. She gave him a *You okay?* look and he nodded *I'm okay. You?* They shared their story with these new people and in turn heard about ideas that were new to them.

"We don't need things for the sake of having things," said a girl with freckles and glasses. "We don't need a lot of money. What we need is community and caring."

"Caring about one another?" asked Molly.

"Yes, and caring about the planet, caring about Mother Earth, Father Sky, and the possibility of an expanded consciousness. We are all one, you know."

Molly didn't know.

"We are trying to tend the land in such a way that it sustains us," said a young man with thick, unruly black hair and a bushy beard. "We want to be self-sufficient, not relying on the man to take care of us. We can supply what we need here, grow it or make it, and share what we have with one another without expecting anything in return. This is freedom."

Land of the Free. Home of the Brave.

"We call this place New Buffalo to honor the buffalo who sustained the Indian tribes here years ago." This from the sunburned man.

"The Taos Pueblo are still here," said a boy in a football jersey, with a shock of blond hair that kept falling in his face. He tucked it behind his ear. "They showed us how to make the adobe bricks to build this place. They lent us tools, and this is really their land. They were here first."

Facts that weren't expounded upon in *An Adventurer's Guide to Travel across America*, thought Molly. Ah. She understood.

"They helped us after the fire, too," said the jersey boy. "Last year we accidentally burned down part of the adobe. The Taos Pueblos were the first to show up afterwards with blankets and food."

"But they really don't want us here," said an older man with weathered skin and circles under his eyes. "They tolerate us."

"That's not true," said jersey boy. "They have the most loving and generous hearts. People like Little Joe Gomez, Joe Sunhawk, Frank Zamora, Henry Gomez. They know our hearts are in the right place."

"Love has nothing to do with it," said the weathered man. "If you want freedom, that's one thing. Don't expect the Pueblo to show you how to get it. Their spirituality and sacred practices and way of life belong to them, not us."

"It's not the Taos Pueblos or even the Hispanos that want us out," said the sunburned man. "It's the white people in Taos, the Taosenos. They think we're invaders."

"We *are* invaders," said the weathered man.

"They don't like longhairs," said jersey boy. "That's what they call us."

"They call us dirty hippies," said Ben, suddenly appearing and sitting next to Carol. "She's asleep," he told her.

261

Someone threw a log on the fire and everyone's face was illuminated.

"It's beautiful here," Molly said. "But you're in the middle of nowhere."

"That's the point," said Sadie. "We want out of the cities. Away from the noise and the materialism and crass commercialism of our parents' generation. We want to be free. This is our family now."

I like my family, Molly wanted to say. She felt the first pangs of homesickness as she realized Lucy might be suited to this life but she, Molly, wasn't. She wanted electricity and a grocery store and a record player. She wanted the beach. She'd grown up and lived around the rhythm of the tides all her life. Her family was in Charleston . . . wasn't it?

Norman put his empty plate at his feet and picked up one of the drums. He was still a little lightheaded, but now that he'd eaten, he felt fine. More than fine, next to this fire, with these people.

"What does freedom sound like?" he asked Sadie. He started a beat on the drum first with his fingers, then a little palm, back to the fingers, then both hands, trying to find a new rhythm, a new cadence, something to match the way he was feeling by the fire. Free.

"Sounds like that," said Sadie. She tossed a stick onto the fire and watched Norman settle into a groove with the beat. Soon more drums joined in and copied Norman's creation. Then a flute and a guitar tossed notes back and forth until together the little band birthed a sweet new tune that swirled around them all and floated up, over their heads, heading for the twinkling blanket of stars in the chilly night sky.

So many stars! thought Norman. *What a beautiful sky.*

Sweet Caroline danced lightly into the circle and joined them. She cupped Norman's ear as she danced past him and announced to everyone, "The veil between the worlds is very thin at solstice." Norman smiled. He didn't mind this at all.

Molly picked up a homemade tambourine, gave it a little

shake, and thought about Dennis, who now seemed so pale in comparison to the sunburned man or the weathered man or even Ben. She smiled to herself. Well, Dennis *was* pale, compared to Ben, who wrapped an arm around Carol and pulled her close to him. Carol laid her tousled head on his shoulder.

Molly thought of Barry then, of how often she had leaned her head on his shoulder, of how, when she was little and he scooped her up, she tucked her face into the crook of his neck to smell his particular Barry smell. In the summer, like right now, that smell would be suntan lotion and salt and sweat and the sea.

Barry always knew just what to do. She trusted him.

Come on, Molly! I won't let go! he'd say as he took her deeper into the ocean at Folly Beach and taught her how to ride the crests back to shore. And when a wave took them under, he never let go. She coughed and cried, and he pulled her close. *Come here, Polka Dot, let me count those freckles.*

Molly caught lightning bugs in a jar at night, and Barry released them before morning so they wouldn't die. He cut her the largest slice of his birthday cake. He listened to her when she fought with Mom and he always whispered, *I'm on your side*, even when she knew she was wrong.

Barry was steadiness. Barry was kindness. He was not the sort of person who would go to another country and kill anyone.

Molly's heart twisted into a tight little knot. She was homesick for her family in the days before the war came between them, before Walter Cronkite rattled off his statistics every night and gave her dad heartburn, before Barry fell in love with Hendrix and grew his hair longer than hers, and Uncle Lewis left the family and her dad got hard and angry, and Barry stayed away more and more and then everything erupted and Barry left home and stayed gone, and Dad didn't care and Mom didn't know what to do, and Molly was fourteen and sitting outside in a commune in New Mexico with Norman, who knew less what to do

263

than her mom did, and who was going to take care of them now? What was the plan?

The young man with a thick head of wild black hair and a bushy beard interrupted Molly's thoughts. "There are lots of us here," he said. "We're trying to create what we never had, or we're making room for whatever is coming, because something *is* coming, something *is* asking for expression."

"It's the Age of Aquarius," said Ben. "Harmony is coming."

"Struggle is coming," said the weathered man. He nodded to Norman and Molly. "Maybe you'll find what you seek here with us. We're all meeting tomorrow in the Aspen Meadow above Santa Fe for solstice. Come with us. Bring your bus. You can go on your way from there, if you want. But come see."

"We leave early in the morning," Molly said before Norman could answer.

"Too bad," said Sadie. She smiled at Norman, who blushed.

"Go in peace," said Ben.

31

BORN TO BE WILD

Written by Mars Bonfire
Performed by Steppenwolf
Recorded at American Recorders, Studio City, California, 1967
Drummer: Jerry Edmonton

Norman and Molly slept in the common room, which doubled as a hostel for travelers passing through. Four enormous tree trunks held up the ceiling of vigas — wooden beams made from smaller tree trunks that had been stripped of their bark and fitted together like a dome. Smoke from the fire in the center of the round room drifted lazily toward the hole in the ceiling and out into the brisk night air. The common room, tucked into the earth and waiting for them like a mother, was warm and snug and welcoming, and Molly realized, as she crawled into her sleeping bag, how exhausted she was, and how grateful, too, for a safe place to sleep. She was too tired to consult her maps. She could do it in the morning. She slept like the dead who had inhabited the mesa centuries ago. If the veil was as thin as Sweet Caroline said it was, she could feel their spirits in her sleep.

When morning came, a rooster crowed and a young woman

gave birth in one of the tipis. Her laboring cries could be heard across the community, which gathered near her. By the time Molly had emerged to find out what was happening, Norman was already standing at the edge of the crowd with a tin plate of oatmeal in his hands. Sadie stood next to him. She placed a hand lightly in the middle of his back, and Norman found he liked it. He settled into her touch with a sigh.

Molly saw this, and popped Norman on the shoulder. He jumped and Sadie moved her hand. He was wearing a T-shirt but no button-down oxford shirt over it, and the jeans Pam had tucked into the bus for him. Molly couldn't resist. "Norman, they look like they just came from the Penney's catalog counter and off your mom's ironing board!" He ignored her, but it embarrassed him.

The newborn baby cried and a cheer rose from the collective.

"Where's Sadie?" said one.

"Here!" Sadie took Norman's plate, handed it to Molly, grabbed Norman's hand, and said with great earnestness, "This is when I go to work. Can you help me?"

Norman didn't ask Molly's permission. Whatever Sadie needed, he would help. He gave no thought to the scene they were walking in on. They disappeared inside the tipi and closed the flap.

"I'll pack," Molly said with as much sarcasm as she could capture, although to think of a new baby coming into the world in a tent on top of a mesa in New Mexico . . . it was something she'd never imagined to be present for.

"It's a girl!" cried a young man with an enormous mound of brown curls falling into his eyes. He stepped out of the tipi long enough to let everyone know. "Her name is Summer! Born on the solstice!" He ducked back inside.

266

"Welcome, Summer!" was the cry then as people circled the tipi and sang a song about peace on earth.

"To the meadow!" shrieked a gaggle of kids running and threading themselves around the grown-ups.

"Molly, come look!" called Carol.

Norman's bus sat in the parking area, painted white. A group of painters young and old were spattered with their handiwork. Flam acted the role of inspector, walking around and around the bus as if his opinion on the paint job was the one that counted.

"Don't you love it!" exclaimed Carol. Moonglow sat at her mother's hip and clapped.

"How . . . ?" began Molly, shocked. Norman would be so upset.

"We wanted to say thank you for the ride yesterday," said Carol. "I saw that you'd started painting it already, so we just finished it for you."

"Here," said Ben, appearing at Carol's side with a paintbrush. "Your turn, Molly. We didn't touch your flowers. And there's lots of white to work with now."

"Let it dry," said Carol. "Then it'll be a canvas just waiting for you, and you can paint to your heart's content. We'll help you. It will be fun to do in the meadow."

There was no resisting them after that. Molly walked the perimeter of the bus with Flam and admired the paint job. These kids were obviously practiced at it. The bus looked great to Molly's eyes. It had completely lost its Charleston County Schools look, along with four seats.

"Norman told me we could take a few," said a young man named Charlie-O who was trying to grow a mustache. "I asked him last night while we were drumming. We could use them in the pueblo. We'll fix you up with some flooring we took from the old mining camp in the valley. We can do it —"

"— in the meadow," Molly finished with him.

"Yeah!"

267

She decided to intercept Norman and break it to him before he stumbled upon his unrecognizable precious bus on his own and accused her of sabotage.

She walked back to the site of the new birth in the community to find Norman and Sadie emerging from a different tipi from the one they'd entered. Norman wore no shirt or shoes. His chest was blindingly white. His jeans were crazily crisp. Sadie carried a blanket over her arm, a small bottle of something in her hands, and Norman's missing clothing.

Molly came to a full stop. She didn't even know how to begin. What could she say or do in this situation? She was embarrassed to be standing there, watching Norman take his T-shirt from Sadie. Then he did the most amazing thing Molly had ever seen him do. He hugged Sadie. He hugged a girl. He hugged her with the entirety of his long arms and tall body, he folded her right into his bare chest, slowly and fully and completely. And Sadie hugged him back.

Molly turned on the heel of her Keds and walked away as fast as she could.

They carried an extra tent with them in the bus as they left the mesa with everyone else and caravanned to the Aspen Meadow. Flam took to riding in a seat now with his snout hanging out a window. Summer and her parents stayed at New Buffalo along with the midwife and Sadie and a small home crew who would celebrate there.

Norman's spluttering at the paint job was all he managed before their bus filled with kids and they were on their noisy, singing way. Then they were in the meadow with the mallow and cacti and hundreds of white-trunked aspens in full green leaf. They were in the meadow with hundreds of kids from the communes around Taos; from Morningstar East with all its battered vehicles dotting the parking area like a crazy-quilt landscape; Five Star and its winning baseball team already organizing a game; Reality Construction with its Wild West vibe; the Family with their mounds of beads and scarves and rings and Las Vegas winnings, which meant hot dogs for everyone; and Lama, who brought a real life swami from India who had kids sitting cross-legged in front of a makeshift geodesic dome structure covered in a parachute, their eyes closed and fingers fixed in a supplicating position.

"What are they doing?" asked Molly.

"Meditating!" said Sweet Caroline.

"What's that?"

The mood was festive and made more so by the arrival of the psychedelically painted buses of the Hog Farm and their charioteer, Wavy Gravy. Kids spilled from the buses and into the meadow with great shouts of happiness and abandon. They had a hog with them, too, who promptly set to sunning himself. The kids set up an enormous black gong on a tripod of poles and rang it to bring everyone to order and begin the celebration.

There was little order to be had, however.

"Who brought the food!"

"Look in the Kitchen Bus!"

Norman, swept up in the moment, handed over their peanut butter, bread, jelly, a bag of cookies, and all their Kool-Aid packets and sugar, which was met with great acclimation. He wore a huge grin on his face. Even in his sputtering over his painted bus, the grin had not left him. *This place*, he thought. *These people. Constant improvisation. It's like jazz. And I fit in. This could be my life. Freedom. Improvisation. Jazz.*

"Let's go to the hot springs!" someone shouted. "Let's go swimming!"

269

Molly found herself swept into that group, thanks to Sweet Caroline, who grabbed Norman by the hand and asked him to drive. They left Flam with the Hog Farm kids — they had dogs, too. When they got to the springs, Molly was horrified to see sixteen kids peel off their clothes, drape them over the boulders, and climb, laughing and screaming and splashing one another, into the rock-rimmed, sandy-bottomed pools of warm water hidden only by the rushes and the river grasses that grew near the old stagecoach stop along the Rio Grande.

Norman peeled off his T-shirt. "Oh, no you don't!" said Molly. "You've already had enough fun for one day!"

"What are you talking about?"

"I know what you were doing in that tent with Sadie!"

Norman untied his Converse All Stars. "You don't know anything, Molly."

"I know she's too old for you, Norman. She's been to college!"

"Now look who's talking."

"I mean it, Norman. This is not right."

"Why not?" He peeled off his socks.

"Because!"

"Because why? Because it makes you uncomfortable?"

"Yes! For starters!"

"Then don't come. Stay here with the bus. I'm not going to miss my chance for a little bit of freedom because you don't want me to!"

"Norman! You're scaring me! What's happening to you?"

He took off his belt and tossed it onto his shoes and socks. "Was Sadie undressed?"

Molly thought about it. "No."

"That's right. She wasn't. It's not what you think. She gave me a back massage."

"What's a massage?"

He sighed, but he hadn't known what it was, either, until he'd watched Sadie massage the newborn Summer.

"I feel *great*," he declared with a conviction he didn't know he possessed, "and I'm going swimming."

"Norman —" Molly began, but Norman turned around, walked away from his cousin, and disappeared in the tall reeds.

MAGIC CARPET RIDE

Written by John Kay and Rushton Moreve
Performed by Steppenwolf
Recorded at American Recording Company, Studio City, 1968
Drummer: Jerry Edmonton

NORMAN

I drive back to the meadow singing "Wooly Bully" at deafening decibels with everyone in the bus. Everybody but Molly, who sits in the very back, bouncing in the last seat and scowling with her arms crossed. Her loss! Sweet Caroline sits in the navigator's seat behind me. She's a terrible singer, but I don't care. She's a *great* swimmer.

Nobody knows all the words to "Wooly Bully" but nobody cares. We *all* know the chorus. I want to drum out the beat on the steering wheel, but the road is too narrow and winding for that. Some kids dance in the aisles and I yell, "Sit down!" but I'm laughing. Sweet Caroline yells, "Yeah! Siddown!" And we laugh together, the two of us.

In the meadow, the Hog Farm Band is playing something awful and out of tune with beat-up instruments — a trumpet, a sax, some guitars, a recorder, a flute, and a cowbell. They're playing their crazy hearts out, mainly because Wavy is conducting them in a clown costume complete with rubber nose, big shoes, and a bowler hat. They have no drums.

"I can fix this!" I shout.

"Welcome, young prince!" Wavy bellows. "Come play!"

I start handing out my equipment. One snare, two toms, a bass drum, some cymbals — not Hal Blaine's — three sets of drumsticks and some tympani mallets. I want to shout: *My brothers! My sisters!* But I catch myself as willing hands reach for drums and sticks and keep right on playing.

"Attaboy!" shouts Wavy. "It's cosmic! We're the Cosmic Solstice Orchestra, the CSO!"

Sweet Caroline blows me a kiss — *Oh, thank you!* — and runs after Molly, who is stalking away from me. Two terrible tunes into the orchestra's performance, someone starts yelling from across the meadow, "Bus race!" The CSO disbands immediately and kids start running for six colorful buses that are lining up at an imaginary start line, engines revving.

The saxophone player for the CSO — the most pimply-faced kid I've ever seen — says, "You've got a bus. You in?"

"I'm in!" I say, but I'm not sure. "How does it work?"

"C'mon! I'll show you! My name's Red, what's yours?"

"Florsheim."

"Ha! Shoes!"

We climb on and make for the middle of the Aspen Meadow in my white bus. Kids are running pell-mell to the competing buses, climbing on them, slapping them like they're horses, calling *Giddyup!* crowding onto the roof racks. I rumble past them and Red points them out. "That's Road Hog. That's the Hospital Bus. the Kitchen Bus. That one's Blue Bayou. That one's Further — it's famous — don't know that other one. And oh, there's Queen of Sheba, my favorite."

They are all haphazardly rolled into place as if the starting line is just a suggestion. I trundle my bus into a gap-toothed opening between the Hospital Bus and the Kitchen Bus and put it into park. "Now what?" I ask. I hear barking outside and open the folding door. "Come on, boy!" I call to my dog, and Flam scrabbles on board.

Kids start climbing onto the roof of my bus and I panic. I yell back to Red. "Is this okay?"

"Oh, yeah, man!" shouts Red. "Let me out! I'll help."

Red gives kids a leg up onto the bumper, then they scramble in front of me onto the hood, then onto the roof where Barry installed a canoe carrier. It's not much to hold on to, so I run outside and yell up to them, "I don't think it's safe!" They ignore me, as more kids pile on. I look around helplessly and Red says, "It's cool, man. Nobody dies or goes to jail."

Wavy appears in front of the buses and yells, "Who's in charge?"

"Nobody!" comes a chorus from everyone.

"Well, somebody put a flag up at the other end, so we know where to turn around!" Wavy yells. White exhaust from the buses puffs around us like clouds. The noise from the engines is crazy-loud, but I can pick out Sweet Caroline's voice calling for Molly. I look for her but can't see her.

Wavy climbs onto the roof of the Kitchen Bus. "Let's run one at a time!' he yells. "Use a stopwatch! Fastest time's the winner!"

"That's for sissies!" yells the driver of the Hospital Bus.

"That's Ken," Red tells me. "Watch out for him. He's a terrible driver."

"Let's go!" yells Ken. "Once around the meadow, turn around at the flag and get back here first!"

The rest of the crowd surges onto the bus roofs. There are metal racks around the roofs of the other buses that function like porch railings. I swallow hard and look for Molly. Nothing. "Wait a minute," I start to say, but Ken's holler fills the meadow.

"Start your engines!" This despite the fact that all engines are revving and ready to go. "Wait!" comes the collective call. Kids change allegiances to buses like they're betting on a horse race. They climb off one and onto another as they get settled. The roof of my bus is swarming with bodies and it sounds like a stampede is going on. The whole bus rocks and I open my arms to catch a kid who slides down the front windshield with a squeal.

"Wait a minute!" I say again.

"Whose bus is this?" yells a girl in pigtails.

"Florsheim's!" yells Red.

"Well, come on, Florsheim! Floor it!"

I give up. I half smile and half wave and get back on my bus, nervous. Molly would tell me not to do this. Barry would do it in a heartbeat. What about me? My heart knocks at my rib cage with uncertainty as I dump myself in the driver's seat and put my feet on the pedals, my hands on the steering wheel. The bus continues to rock as kids settle themselves on the roof. Flam whines and I let him out the door. I peer at the buses next to me, parked at cockeyed angles.

Wavy gets on his knees from his perch atop the Kitchen Bus and points straight ahead with both arms. "The United States of America! And step on it!"

I close the door. Then I open it. I need to see as much as possible.

A barefoot kid in torn jeans takes off his red T-shirt and holds it in the air like a flag in front of the bulls. The buses are so much bigger than he is and they are making so much noise, puffing and pawing to be first out of the starting gate.

That's when I admit, it's exciting. It is. It's like waiting to take your solo and whale on the drums, or the guitar, or sing your

275

part. There is so much energy in it, even the air in the meadow is vibrating.

"This is great!" says Red. "Come on, Florsheim. Let's beat 'em all!"

And in that moment, I make a decision: I'll show them what I can do.

The shirtless boy waves his flag and the buses lurch, wheeze, rattle, and roar off the start line. Kids scream above me, around me. Exhaust envelops us like the morning fog over the Cooper River in Charleston. I can't see a thing.

But after so many days of constant driving, I know how to get this bus off the starting peg handily, and I take the lead. My passengers are a mass of shrieking banshees over my head. "Hold on!" I yell, even though I know they can't hear me. My heart pounds, my pulse races. All I can hear over the grinding of gears is a steady chant from the riders above me. "GO GO GO GO GO!"

MOLLY

It was bad enough I had to sit by myself in the puny shade of a gnarly old tree while they were all "swimming" at the hot springs, I had to suffer them all coming back in fits of stupid giggles and silly jokes and leaps and twirls, climbing on the bus, with one guy singing "Figaro, Figaro, Figaro!" over and over like he was at the opera. And worse, Norman with his hair dripping wet and his feet bare, paying no attention to me at all.

When we get to the meadow, Sweet Caroline wants to be my best friend. She runs after me off the bus, past the Wavy Gravy band, past the sunbathers and the kids tossing footballs.

"Molly!"

"I don't want to talk to you!"

"Molly!" she keeps calling and I keep walking.

But then the whole mood in the meadow changes. "Bus race!"

276

somebody shouts, and the buzz it creates is contagious. Suddenly, kids are everywhere, not much older than I am, not much older than Barry, and they swarm around me like they know me, *Come on!* and they run past me laughing and shouting *Come on!* and a girl I don't even know says, "Ride with me!" and grabs my hand, and we're running, me stumbling to keep up with her.

The bus is called Road Hog. There's a ladder on the back. "Up!" shouts the girl I don't know. A tall boy standing at the ladder grabs me at the waist and hoists me high enough on the ladder to grab hold. I grip the rungs and start climbing. Kids are above me, reaching down hands. Kids are below me, waiting for their turn. The tall boy hoists up another kid and I keep climbing. It's like being at recess in school when I was a kid, climbing up the side of the monkey bars so I can swing across, only at the top, there are kids and kids and kids, and one of them is Sweet Caroline, dangling over the roof edge, her yellow curls in her face and still damp from the hot springs.

"Come on, Molly!" she yells. The tall boy grabs my hand and pulls me all the way up and onto the roof of the bus, and in spite of myself, I laugh, partly because I didn't fall and kill myself, and partly because everyone is gleeful and it is breathtaking to be so high, on top of the world in a meadow surrounded by mountains of pine.

"The air smells different," I comment, lightheaded.

"That's the piñon trees!" says Sweet Caroline. "This way!" We thread our way to the front of Road Hog and some kids make room for us there. I thump next to Sweet Caroline and twine my arms around the roof rack so I won't slide off.

Kids are boarding the bus below me, still coming up to the roof behind me. The air splits with the sound of growling engines, their exhaust meets my nose, and suddenly we are moving, swaying, and kids are screaming, scattering on the ground below or falling into one another on the roof above, and the buses are

277

racing like lumbering monsters across the bumpy meadow grass and up the hill.

"Hold on!" screams Sweet Caroline. She is glowing with excitement. My heart — that slumbering organ in my chest — hammers so hard against my ribs it brings tears to my eyes. I lurch and slide along with the bus and open my mouth to scream along with everyone else, and that's when I see Norman — Norman! He's driving his bus! In the race!

"Norman!" I scream, but he can't hear me. "Norman!"

NORMAN

The Hospital Bus veers in front of me and I have to brake. It gets way ahead of us all, but conks out going up the hill. Its riders abandon ship and scurry out of the way like mice. That leaves me, Norman, in the lead.

"This is great!" says Red. "You can do it!" I slow to pass the Hospital Bus and manage to avoid flattening any riders. Some of them clamber onto my bus and grab seats inside — "Thanks, man!" — and we keep going, up and around the flag, and start back down toward the finish line.

MOLLY

Norman is in the lead! And we're right behind him. Road Hog wheezes to the right of the Hospital Bus, which appears to be dead.

"Watch out!" comes the screaming from the top of our bus. We're headed too far to the right, and there's the swami from India in a turban and a long white robe waving his arms at us while people sitting on the ground in front of a big tent start to scatter.

The bus lurches to the left to correct itself and almost bangs into the Kitchen Bus with Wavy Gravy on top screaming, "Be carefuuuuuul!"

A man jumps out of the Hospital Bus and claws his way onto Road Hog's wide fender, where he waves both arms in front of the windshield and screams, "Press on! Press on!" Then he slips off the bus and I watch him roll like a tumbleweed away from us.

NORMAN

We're all rumbling ahead now, almost bouncing down the hill, on the stretch back to the starting line. The engines are having a much easier time of it downhill and the race is close, although we're spread all over the wide course. "Floor it, Florsheim!" I shout, and I pull ahead of the pack until I see a little kid standing smack on the course in front of us, just standing there, frozen at the sight of all these buses barreling for him.

"It's a kid!" yells Red.

Wavy's on top the Kitchen Bus screaming, "Get the kid! Get the kid!" Someone on the ground grabs the kid and rolls out of the way with him. In my panic I have veered sharply to miss the kid and my bus begins to wobble like it wants to fall over. I work desperately to keep it from toppling. Riders slide off the roof.

"TENT!" yells Red. I see it — it's a pup tent — but I can't maneuver to miss it. My mind is wrinkling. I can't breathe.

I run over the tent and it flies into the air and lands on the windshield of the Queen of Sheba Bus.

"Nobody in the tent!" yells Red in the wildest voice I have ever heard.

I manage to get my bus back on the course as Road Hog begins to pass me.

"Norman!" I hear. "Gooooo, Norman!"

279

It's Molly's voice and it's everything I need right now. I smash the clutch, jam the bus into fifth gear, stomp the accelerator, pop the clutch, and jump ahead of Road Hog just far enough to nose the win. "Yes!" I shout. *Yes* never felt so good.

Kids at the finish line dodge the incoming buses and cheer. Riders begin boiling off the buses and onto the vibrating ground. I cut my engine and suddenly all the engine clangor stops and it's quiet enough to hear a baby crying nearby.

I leap from my seat onto the ground in one movement and whoop like a conquering barbarian, my arms raised and my fists pumping over my head. I am victorious! And . . . I am so relieved it's over.

Kids are tousling my hair, pounding me on the back, asking, "Who are you, man?"

"He's Florsheim!" spouts Red. He is so proud it makes me laugh.

Then Wavy appears. "It's a miracle nobody got killed!" he crows. "A miracle!" He claps me on the back. "What's the name of the bus, young prince?"

"It doesn't have a name," I tell him.

"Well, now it does," says Wavy. "Is it male or female?"

"Neither."

"Ahhhh," says Wavy. "'Do I contradict myself? Very well, then I contradict myself, I am large, I contain multitudes.' Thank you, Walter Whitman. I christen this bus Multitudes!"

The crowd cheers. "Long live Multitudes!"

"And the Silver Bell as your prize!" says Wavy. He hands me a bell to attach at the bus door. "May Multitudes wear it with pride. And may Road Hog win it back next year!"

A girl named Saffron drapes love beads around my neck. Then Sweet Caroline is right in front of me. She nudges Saffron aside and kisses me. Kisses me. *A girl kisses me.* I stagger backward in surprise, find my footing, and then do the only sensible thing. I kiss her back.

MOLLY

I see that kiss. I see everything. I see the way they make over Norman, the way he laps it up, the thrill on his face when he is kissed, the applause from the crowd. And I know I won't get him out of here today if Barry's life depends on it. And it might. I walk over to where the gong is ringing and a couple wearing love beads and meadow flowers is getting married.

"Let these be your desires," says a woman standing in front of them. "To wake at dawn with a winged heart and give thanks for another day of loving."

"The Prophet," says a girl next to me, watching. "Do you know it?"

I shake my head. I don't have a winged heart, and my days aren't full of loving. I try to picture Barry in San Francisco, but I can't. I picture him in the army, wearing a uniform, slogging through the jungle like the soldiers I saw on the news. I picture him coming home in a box. I picture us at his funeral, and I cringe. We need to get going. We are wasting time on this longest day.

NORMAN

The sound of drums is everywhere across the meadow, but for once I don't play. I sit at the bonfire with Sweet Caroline and my new friends as the daylight finally fades on this longest day and I wonder what the veil is that Sweet Caroline said is so thin on solstice. She squeezes my hand and asks me a question. "Are you a Virgo?"

I shake my head and answer her. "No. I'm a drummer."

She giggles. I love that giggle.

Kids walk in a circle around the bonfire and toss pebbles into it with their whispered wishes imprinted on them. Some of them cry. Wavy is there, too, and he tells us, "Being deeply loved gives you strength. Loving deeply gives you courage. Take care of one another."

Barry floats into my mind. *Come on, Norman. Come with me. I'll take care of you.* He was only sixteen, so I was fourteen, Molly's age now. He took me with him to Myrtle Beach, ninety-four miles up the coast, north of Charleston. I was so excited! We walked the boardwalk, rode the rides, listened to the beach bands, and he promised me we'd start a band together. *I'll be right back*, he said. *We'll get pizza.*

He disappeared for hours while I sat on a bench in front of the Skee-Ball place, watching the road as the boardwalk emptied for the night and I had nowhere to go, until there he was with the car, smiling that megawatt grin, shouting, *Hop in!* and telling me all about it, what happened, and telling me what to tell our parents. Which I did. And which, suddenly I realize, meant I took care of him.

I'm not that kid anymore. I'm somebody else. I have a dog. I have a girl. I have a bell. I've had a swim. The world is a strange place.

"What breaks your heart?" Wavy is saying as the sparks from the bonfire float into a mulberry sky. "That's where you will find your purpose. Don't follow your bliss! Follow your heartbreak. That's where you can work to change the world. Now, take in a deep breath and let it out for peace!"

"He's an emotion machine," says a kid near me.

"I should look for Molly," I say to Sweet Caroline.

"I saw her," Sweet Caroline replies. Her voice is soothing, enchanting. "She's safe, she's in the bus."

I close my eyes and sigh as Sweet Caroline rests her head on my shoulder.

MOLLY

I would spend the night on the bus, but kids have lanterns and are painting it, and no, I don't want to help, thank you, so I drag the small tent out of the back and find a place to set it up, unroll my sleeping bag, and decide to sleep in my clothes. I need a sweatshirt and a flashlight, though, so I troop back to the bus and rummage for what I need.

The flashlight isn't in my navigator's box or the box next to the driver's seat, so I feel around in the dark until I find a small metal box under the driver's seat. I pull it out, switch on the map lamp, and open the box.

There is the envelope with what's left of the money from Uncle Bruce. It doesn't look like much. There is Norman's tape from Muscle Shoals. And there is something else. Letters. A year's worth of letters, stacked on their sides like little soldiers, one after the other, and held together with a loop of string. Letters to Norman. From Barry.

Come here, Polka Dot. Let me count those freckles.

THE AGE OF AQUARIUS

From the musical *Hair*
Written by James Rado, Gerome Ragni, and Galt MacDermot
Performed by the Fifth Dimension
Recorded at Wally Heider Studios, Hollywood, California, 1969
Drummer: Hal Blaine

The morning sun washed over the bees in the meadow flowers as Norman found Molly in line for breakfast.

"You're not going to believe the bus!" he said, laughing. "It's wild!"

Sweet Caroline, her long yellow hair a coagulated mess, hung on to Norman like laundry on a clothesline. "It's groovy!" she chirped, which made Norman laugh again.

Molly reached for her breakfast in a paper cup.

"Wow, what is that?" asked Norman. "Gravel?"

"It's granola," said a young woman in the makeshift kitchen. She wore a bandana and a slip. She handed Molly an apple for her other hand.

"Thank you." Molly was starving. "I'm ready to go," she told Norman without looking at him. She had her hair in a neat ponytail once again. She had scrubbed her face and filled their coffee thermos with water from the creek.

"Where did you sleep last night?" Norman asked.

"Over there," she said simply, without gesturing. The granola was dry oats with raisins and sunflower seeds. She would need water to wash it down. "I'll meet you at the bus."

If Molly hadn't seen its transformation happening with her own eyes, she wouldn't have believed the bus was theirs. M U L T I T U D E S was painted in purples, blues, reds, and greens under her crude flower garden. Eyelids and lashes and brows were painted around the headlights so the bus was looking at her. She half expected it to blink. Swirls and splotches and stick figures and peace signs skipped across the white surface and flowers bloomed everywhere Molly looked. She walked all the way around and stopped at the open door. A bell hung outside. She rang it and entered.

"Breakfast!" she called in an irritated voice. She handed the granola to the first person who sat up, and kept the apple for later. "This bus is leaving in ten minutes!"

By the time she returned with her tent and sleeping bag, Norman had the bus idling and was checking the oil. "We'll stop for gas in Santa Fe," he said. "It's close."

Sweet Caroline cooed in the affirmative as if she was along for the ride. Molly didn't protest — what would be the point? They pulled out of the Aspen Meadow with Sweet Caroline aboard.

Molly kept quiet. She didn't even wrestle Sweet Caroline for the navigator's seat. Prying her out of it was going to be a battle. Sweet Caroline had claimed it before Molly got on the bus and now she kept her hand on Norman's shoulder, rubbing it just so, and said she knew how to get to the Plaza Café, where they could get the best breakfast in Santa Fe.

Norman's jeans looked the worse for wear after a day and night outside, which was a good thing. He'd completely given up his white oxford shirts and was wearing a Mickey Mouse T-shirt with *Disneyland* scrawled under Mickey's smiling face. It was too small for him. Molly could not help the look she gave him

285

when she saw him sitting in the driver's seat in a shirt that must have belonged to Sweet Caroline, his alabaster skin peeking out around the bottom and the flesh on his upper arms seeing daylight for the first time this year, if you didn't count the moment outside the tipi with Sadie. Or the moment at the hot springs.

Sweet Caroline saw Molly's look and said, "It's too big for me."

Sweet Caroline was wearing Norman's T-shirt, which barely managed to look like a dress on her. She had very long legs. Her hair was now neatly brushed and shining. She wore a wreath of meadow greenery and flowers. She giggled.

Molly kept her mouth shut and took her place in the front passenger seat behind the half-high silver wall by the stepwell. The seat where Birdie and Margaret had sat, where Emily and her baby had sat, where Ray sat after Emily left the bus. Where Kyle sat before the bus – Multitudes, if you please – had conked out on the road to Little Rock. The seat where Carol had nursed her baby. It was a famous seat. And now Molly was in it.

Once they reached the Square in Santa Fe, Molly searched through her suitcase for a pair of shorts for Sweet Caroline and found tucked into a side suitcase pocket the skirt and scarf that Lucy had bought her in Atlanta. "Oh!"

Molly unrolled the skirt and shook it out. Its beautiful, bright colors reminded her of the walk down the Strip, the music at the Twelfth Gate, the feelings that she had almost allowed into her life again. She hadn't realized until this moment how she had loved that night.

"So pretty!" exclaimed Sweet Caroline.

Molly handed it to her. "A loan," she said. She couldn't bear to part with it again. Sweet Caroline wrapped it around herself expertly, tied it handily, and twirled in the bus aisle.

"Now you're dressed to go out in public," said Molly.

They found the Plaza Café and had the best meal of the trip. Norman and his new space-alien persona could not ruin Molly's meal. Neither could Sweet Caroline, who talked and giggled incessantly. Molly cut herself off from listening or participating in the conversation and Norman didn't even notice. Molly worried about Flam running off, but he waited patiently on the sidewalk for them in the shade of the awnings. Passersby gave him a pat and he thumped his tail.

Molly had never heard of huevos rancheros but loved it. Norman got the green chili cheeseburger and moaned appreciatively at every hot bite. Then he ordered a second one. Sweet Caroline ate every syrupy bit of her blue corn pancakes except the bites she fed Norman from her own fork. Molly gritted her teeth and pretended she didn't notice.

Norman took his second burger and fries with him in a paper sack as they left the restaurant. He bought silver and turquoise bracelets for Janice and Pam from the local artists on the Square. Sweet Caroline pined for a silver hair clip and Norman bought it for her. When Sweet Caroline spied a silver ring and giggled, Norman bought that as well. In return, Sweet Caroline kissed him on the cheek.

Molly had had enough of the lovebirds. "I'll meet you at the bus," she said. She let them get ahead of her and watched them waltz past a young man wearing a dirty army jacket, baggy brown pants, and work boots with no laces, the tongues flapping out. He sat on a low adobe wall and stared into space. Molly made note of his tangled black hair and vacant expression.

As she came close to him, he spoke. "This used to be a fort. There were wars here. Many skirmishes."

She considered not stopping. Norman and Sweet Caroline were well ahead of her with Flam, Sweet Caroline weaving her jeweled hand into the bright morning sun like it was a cobra.

The young man still stared ahead at nothing. "It was a stock-ade before that. Full of cattle. On their way to be slaughtered. Like we were."

Molly's scalp prickled. She slowed her step but kept walking.

As she passed him, he said, "Always keep your enemy in sight."

She turned around then and faced the man.

He finally looked at her. "I am not he."

She licked her lips, took a breath, and asked, "Who are you?"

Ten minutes later, Molly bounded up the stepwell and onto the bus.

Sweet Caroline was sitting in Norman's lap in the driver's seat, pretending to drive. "Where were you! We almost had to leave without you, didn't we, Norman?"

Norman tried a laugh but Molly cut him off.

"This is Victor Martinez. He's coming with us."

Sweet Caroline got up. She swung into the seat behind Norman, put her hand on his shoulder, and giggled.

"Stop giggling," Molly ordered. "Norman, start driving."

Victor Martinez came quietly up the steps. He looked at no one. There were only four rows of seats left in the bus and Victor sat in the last row. He smelled like too many days in the same clothes without a shower. He smelled like the dumpsters behind the Plaza Café. He carried a large paper sack with him, well creased and rolled over at the top where he gripped it.

Molly stuck out her hand to Norman, palm up. "Give me your extra burger." She walked the sack to Victor and handed it to him. "We just ate," she said. "We're full." Victor took the sack wordlessly and turned to look out the window.

288

Norman turned the key in the ignition. Flam jumped into the famous front passenger seat.

Molly walked back up the aisle. "Caroline, I don't care where you sit, but you can't sit in that seat. The navigator sits there. I am the navigator —"

Sweet Caroline blinked and Molly finished.

"I am she."

WAR, CHILDREN, IT'S JUST A SHOT AWAY

From "Gimme Shelter" by The Rolling Stones

A U.S. Air Force flight nurse and a Red Cross nurse attend to the needs of American wounded prior to their aeromedical evacuation from Tan Son Nhut Air Base in South Vietnam. The wounded are aboard an Air Force C-141, which will take them on a direct flight from Vietnam to bases in the United States near specialized military medical facilities.

LETTERS HOME FROM VIETNAM:

"Hi, honey. I had a hell of a day yesterday."

"Actually, I'm writing because I have to, or I'll go out of my mind. You wouldn't believe . . ."

Army nurse Donna Hamilton holding a Vietnamese baby during her second tour of duty in the Vietnam War, Long Binh, Vietnam, 1968

"Mom, I appreciate all your letters. When I read them, for a while I'm a normal person. I'm not killing people or worried about being killed."

A nurse tends to a patient just out of surgery in the intensive care ward of the hospital ship USS *Repose*, October 1967.

A chaplain gives communion to U.S. soldiers of the First Infantry Division, standing in a trench during services at Bu Dop, Vietnam, Tuesday evening, December 5, 1967. The area was under constant threat of mortar and rocket attack, so services were held in the trench for protection from incoming rounds.

"We are all scared."

"At times I feel like I'll never come home."

U.S. infantrymen pray in the Vietnamese jungle, December 9, 1965, during memorial services for comrades killed in the battle of the Michelin rubber plantation, forty-five miles northwest of Saigon.

"The days are peaceful but the nights are hell. I look up at the stars and it's so hard to believe the same stars shine over you now."

"I was carrying that thing all the way back and I didn't call bombs on these people . . . I hate to put napalm on these women and children, so I just didn't do it."

"You should have seen my men fight, Mom. My brave men. It would have given you goose pimples."

The body of an American paratrooper killed in action in the jungle near the Cambodian border is raised up to an evacuation helicopter in War Zone C, Vietnam, May 14, 1966.

YOU LEAVE THE HOUSE AT SEVEN O'CLOCK

in the morning, and you're at Universal at nine till noon; now you're at Capitol Records at one, you just got time to get there, then you got a jingle at four, then we're on a date with somebody at eight, then the Beach Boys at midnight, and you do that five days a week . . . jeez, man, you get burned out.

Bill Pitman, guitarist and member of the Wrecking Crew studio musicians

The Capitol Records Building just north of the Hollywood and Vine intersection in Hollywood, Los Angeles, California

Carol Kaye played bass in over ten thousand recording sessions — hit records, commercial jingles, television theme songs, film scores — and broke ground for women working as studio musicians.

I can only say we played HARD, very intensive. Our lives and the lives of our kids and family all depended on that sound. We used to say it was the "hungry" sound . . . We had all the creativeness, especially the jazz rhythm section players, to CREATE instant arrangements with licks, patterns, all sorts of ideas bouncing back and forth from us, we knew where to put the quiet parts, the key changes, the breaks, the fills, and the mid-range monotonous hook lines, all sorts of things you do constantly in jazz, which is spontaneous constant improvisation.

Carol Kaye, bass guitarist and member of the Wrecking Crew

I STARTED WRITING A POEM ABOUT A SOLDIER IN VIETNAM, THIS IS EARLY VIETNAM. THIS IS THREE YEARS BEFORE THE TET OFFENSIVE. THE POEM IS ABOUT A KID WHO IS DYING IN A FAR-OFF LAND AND WHAT'S THE LAST THING HE SEES? WHAT'S THE LAST THING HE THINKS ABOUT?

Terry Kirkman of the Association talking about writing the Association song "Requiem for the Masses"

TERRY KIRKMAN

Antiwar demonstrators, April 1969, in San Francisco, California

THE WEIGHT

Written by Robbie Robertson
Performed by The Band
Recorded at A&R Recorders, New York, New York, 1968
Drummer: Levon Helm

They were four on the bus. From Santa Fe to Albuquerque, no one spoke. Then they picked up Route 66 and started west. "I want to make Flagstaff, Arizona, by dark," said Molly. "No stops."

"We need gas," Norman pointed out. "And we need to call home. We haven't called in two days and now we're near telephones and they'll be awake soon in Charleston." He almost sounded like himself. She knew her mother would be beside herself with worry.

They entered a brilliant red landscape — red mesas, red rocks, red roads, red sand — all under the brightest blue sky Molly had ever seen. She wished she had a pair of sunglasses. They pulled off the road onto the dirt parking lot at a gas station on the Laguna Pueblo reservation outside Albuquerque. A sign on the square adobe building said HANZIE'S. Under that, HUNTING LICENSES SOLD HERE.

Victor stayed on the bus, but everyone else exited. "We'll be right back," said Molly. Victor didn't acknowledge her. He took off his jacket and looked out the window at the basketball hoop nailed to a backboard against a telephone pole. It was missing its net.

Molly wanted to ask Norman how their money was holding out, but she didn't want to ask in front of Sweet Caroline. She called home from a pay phone near the only bathroom.

"We were ready to send out the National Guard!" said Janice with such relief in her voice Molly almost cried. That would not do.

"We're fine, Mom. We couldn't find pay phones in the mountains, but now we're about to drive across the Arizona desert and then we'll be in California. Almost there!"

"I'm going to call Pam right away," said Janice. "She's still in Atlanta with The Aunts. You know how positive she is, but even positive people worry."

"Is Lucy still there?" Molly asked.

"Oh, yes," said Janice. "But the boy who was there left."

This news made Molly sad.

"Everything is just fine here, Mom," Molly repeated. "Nothing to worry about. The bus runs great. We're eating and sleeping and seeing the country. Nothing to worry about."

"Call tonight if you can," said Janice. "Let us know where you land."

"We will," Molly promised. "Got to go, Mom. Norman's pulling out!"

Hanzie saw them off. "We don't get too many strangers through here, now that the interstate is taking over," he said. "Nice bus."

"Thanks," said Norman. "Thanks for everything." He climbed on board and saw that Victor was finishing his burger. He put his napkin and the burger wrapper neatly into the paper sack it came in, rolled the top down, and put it on the seat next to him.

He glanced at Norman, who nodded to him. Then he looked out the window.

Sweet Caroline came from the direction of the bathroom. "You know where we need to go, Norman," she said.

"Where's that?"

"Disneyland!" She giggled.

"I don't know," Norman began.

"I do," said Molly. "No." She had six bottles of Coca-Cola in a carrier. She opened the ice chest and began to wedge each bottle into the ice.

"I really, really want to go to Disneyland," said Sweet Caroline. She sat in the navigator's seat, remembered her orders, and moved across the aisle. "Please, Norman?"

"I knew she wanted something." Molly shoved the sodas into the ice, closed the ice chest, and shoved it between the seats.

"What are you talking about?" said Norman. "Stop that."

Sweet Caroline pouted.

Victor stared out the window at someone burning trash in a rusty barrel nearby. "Orange groves," he said. "Disneyland. Orange groves."

"Yeah?" said Norman.

"Disneyland was built on acres and acres of orange groves that were bulldozed to make the park," said Sweet Caroline. "I saw it on a television show!" She beamed at Victor. "Acres and acres of orange trees! Gone."

Victor blinked at Sweet Caroline as if he was connecting that fact to a memory. "I see orange when I dream," he finally said. "Clouds of orange fire. Then black."

No one, including Sweet Caroline, knew what to say to that, and Victor didn't seem to mind. He fell silent and looked back out the window.

They made good time across the Arizona desert on Route 66 and the new stretches of Interstate 40.

"Look!" chirped Sweet Caroline, cheered by every mile that brought them closer to California. "Watch for Elk!"

"Wow," said Norman. "Elk." Sweet Caroline smiled at him. He used the student mirror to keep a watch on Victor, but there was no need. Victor slept, his jacket under his head for a pillow, against the window.

Molly had read every one of Barry's letters by flashlight in her tent, then returned them to their box in Multitudes. She had searched them for any clue to Barry's whereabouts, but they held none. They were rants about their father, orations on the war, bombasts about music, but nothing about Barry's life or what he was doing or how he was feeling, where he lived, who he had met, when he might come home. They had made Molly sad. Barry hadn't asked about his sister, either. *He just needs to be reminded that his family loves him*, she thought. *We are getting close.*

The heat lulled her to sleep in her navigator's seat until she realized with a jerk that it might do the same to Norman. She opened the ice chest and passed out sodas and then cups of water from the melting ice. She dug out a camping bowl for Flam and poured him some water, too. Sweet Caroline, who had long ago removed Molly's skirt, made herself useful dipping one of Pam's washcloths in the cooler's ice water and dripping it dramatically around Norman's neck and shoulders.

"Stop that," said Molly.

"It helps," said Norman. He put the washcloth on top of his head. "Thanks." He really wanted to close his eyes, but he also wanted out of this desert. The radio and Molly's transistor played only static and no one felt like a sing-along. Molly packed the transistor away in her suitcase. It had been a bad idea to bring it along.

"Look!" Sweet Caroline became animated in her seat. "The Petrified Forest!"

"Perfect," said Norman. He pulled into the Visitors' Center parking lot.

"Far out!" said Sweet Caroline. "Not Disneyland, but still, petrified everything!"

"We're not stopping," said Molly.

"I just need a minute," Norman said. "It'll be air-conditioned."

It was. The building was modern and beautiful, with glass walls and shiny floors and people everywhere. Smiling families dressed in their vacation clothes. Mothers carrying purses. Fathers wearing sport shirts and slacks. Kids with haircuts and clean clothes. They looked nothing like the kids Molly had just left at the Aspen Meadow. She'd had to make Sweet Caroline put on her skirt. She'd coaxed Victor inside as well. They let Flam out to run.

They spent a restorative half hour refrigerating themselves, drinking from the water fountains, stretching their legs, looking at the exhibits, pretending they were going to spend the day there. Victor had a bench to himself as adults guided their children away from him. He never said a word until they got back to the bus. Then, as Norman wearily climbed on board and Molly began opening windows again with Sweet Caroline's help, he said, "I can drive."

Norman raised his eyebrows. "I don't think so, man."

"Yes," said Molly, making the decision for them instantly. "Thank you, Victor. I'll navigate. We're headed for a campground outside of Flagstaff. Norman, get some sleep. We're two and a half hours out."

Norman looked at Sweet Caroline. Sweet Caroline looked at Norman. Molly clapped her hands together once and got Norman's attention.

"Give Victor the keys," she said.

Victor shrugged. "I drove a tank in Nam. I can drive this bus."

Norman scrambled off the bus and stalked past some onlookers who were staring at Multitudes' portable canvas. Molly

305

followed him. When they were far enough away for comfort, Norman wheeled on his cousin.

"That guy's not even conscious!"

"Neither are you!"

"I've just driven halfway across the state of New Mexico, and halfway across Arizona! He slept the whole way!"

"So he's rested!"

"Why are you on my case? Yesterday at the hot spring, last night's disappearing act, and now this —"

"Because you're being an idiot!"

"Because I go swimming with a bunch of kids? Because I win a bus race? Because I have a dog? Because I have a girlfriend?"

"She wants something, Norman."

"She wants me." His voice caught on the words.

"She doesn't." Molly saw Norman's face begin to fall. She softened her tone. "I'm not trying to hurt your feelings, Norman, but she doesn't."

"You don't know anything."

"I know you're too tired to drive."

Norman rubbed his hands up and down on his face. He scratched his scalp vigorously with both hands, which made Sweet Caroline's ridiculously small T-shirt ride up and down on his soft belly.

"What's the story with this guy?"

Molly wasn't ready to tell. "Let's just say he's a body in need."

Norman sighed and looked at the bus. "Fine. You'd better know what you're doing, Molly."

"Somebody had better," she said.

They watched parents taking Polaroid pictures of their kids standing in front of Multitudes. The kids were dissolving in laughter, posing and making funny faces, raising two fingers in peace. "Sock it to me!" said one kid. "Veeery interesting!" said another.

306

"Wimps," said Norman. He wiped at his eyes. "They should have gone hiking on the Appalachian Trail."

Molly sighed, relief in her voice. "Yeah. They're squares."

"She likes me," said Norman.

"Let Victor drive," replied Molly.

Norman handed her the keys. They climbed into their chariot and raced across the high desert.

THE LETTER

Written by Wayne Carson
Performed by the Boxtops
Recorded at American Sound Studio, Memphis, Tennessee, 1967
Drummer: Danny Smythe

Thirty-five miles out of Flagstaff they passed Meteor Crater Road, and Molly thought of Drew finishing camp in Little Rock and flying to Vandenberg Air Force Base in California, earnest Drew missing the Meteor Crater and the Clark Telescope. She'd forgotten about them. UNITED STATES NAVAL OBSERVATORY FLAGSTAFF STATION said a sign. She watched it wink past them.

Norman had snored through the hours. He woke as they stopped in the high elevations surrounding Flagstaff with its snow-capped peaks in the distance, mountainous evergreens, and red soil. They replenished their supplies, bought real dog food for a happy Flam, and decided to keep going. Victor was a very good driver and easily threaded the on-and-off nature of driving both Route 66 and the freshly finished sections of the new Interstate 40. They finally stopped for the night in Kingman, Arizona.

Victor made the campfire while Norman set up the tent. Flam stuffed himself, wandered in and out of the campsite, sniffing and exploring, and finally flopped under the picnic table, spent. Sweet Caroline helped Molly fry bacon in a giant iron skillet, slice potatoes into the grease, fry them until they were golden brown, then drain the grease and add a dozen eggs to the mix until they were set like a pudding. "Fritatta!" she proclaimed triumphantly.

Molly decided to accept that this concoction was called *frittata*. They ate the entire skillet between the four of them and then quartered an apple pie. "Just needs ice cream," cooed Sweet Caroline.

They all took showers to wash off the dusty day — days. Norman took Flam into the showers with him, and the dog came out shaking and rolling in the pine needles. Molly washed two loads of laundry in the campground washers and Norman strung a clothesline between two trees. Their lawn chairs were by the fire, but they all sat at the picnic table with one of Aunt Pam's tablecloths covering it and a lantern to light as night fell.

Victor looked like a different person. He was tall and skinny, like Norman, and the khaki slacks Norman lent him almost fit. He had said little beyond what he'd told Molly on the Square in Santa Fe before he boarded the bus.

"Where are you from?" Norman asked as they let their supper settle.

It took him so long for Victor to answer, Molly thought he wasn't going to. He stared at his empty plate, then broke his silence. "I don't remember my life before."

"Before?"

"Before."

No one spoke.

"It's not important," said Victor.

"It is!" said Sweet Caroline. She had been sitting too close to Norman, who didn't mind, and now she reached her hand across the table for Victor's. He withdrew it before she could touch it.

Norman hesitated, then asked, "Was it . . . horrible?"

Molly opened her mouth to answer, *Of course it was horrible, you moron!* then shut it.

"You are all very nice," Victor finally said. "I shouldn't have come."

Molly tried to make her voice gentle. "Why not?"

Victor sighed. His wet hair had waves in it as it dried. It hadn't been cut in a long time. He must have had a razor in his paper sack, for he was freshly shaven. The food and the shower and maybe the company seemed to have revived his spirit some.

"I slept in an old car in Santa Fe," he said. "They towed it. But I had a bush to sleep under, too. And the side of a building off the Square. I knew those places. I had friends there. We shared whatever we found — food, blankets, medicine, cigarettes."

"We can be your friends, Victor," said Sweet Caroline without hesitation.

"I don't know this place!" Victor said with sudden alarm in his voice. "And I can't go home!"

Molly and Norman exchanged a glance.

Sweet Caroline looked stricken. "I can't go home, either," she said softly.

"Why not?" whispered Norman, almost to himself.

"I have bad dreams," Victor added. His voice cracked.

"You're safe here," Molly said. She was sitting next to Victor and wanted to put a hand on his arm, but didn't dare.

As if he knew it, Victor moved over to put a little more distance between them. Then he licked his lips as if he did want to talk but wasn't sure what or how much to say. He looked at his baggy pants and his jacket hanging on Norman's clothesline and said, "I had a future."

Sweet Caroline began to cry. Victor stood up and took two steps backward.

"I'm sorry," he said.

Sweet Caroline shook her head. "No, no, it's not you."

Victor began to walk away. He pulled a pack of cigarettes out of his slacks pocket.

"My cousin's being drafted," said Norman quickly. "We're trying to find him. We're on the way to San Francisco. You're welcome to ride with us as far as you want."

"We're stopping at Disneyland," said Sweet Caroline. She sniffed and wiped at her tears.

Molly rolled her eyes. "We are not."

"We must," said Sweet Caroline. She collected herself and seemed to make a decision. "That's why I'm here."

"What?" Norman stood up now.

"Is your cousin really being drafted?" asked Victor.

"Just a minute," Molly said. "I'll be right back." She brought Barry's letters out to the fire. "Please," she said to Victor, indicating a lawn chair. "Sit. You can smoke here."

"Where did you get those!" Norman spluttered.

"You know where I got them."

"They aren't yours!"

"They're written by my brother, and you didn't even tell me you had them on this bus!"

"You didn't ask!"

Victor covered his ears. "No more war!" It came out as a wail.

Immediately, Molly changed her tone of voice. "I'm sorry. I'm sorry, Victor. I'm so sorry."

"Yeah, man," said Norman. "I'm sorry." Then to Molly he said, "It's fine."

"I know it is," she snipped.

Sweet Caroline was next to Victor now. She touched his arm and he flinched. "Sit," she said in such a gentle yet insistent voice she could have been Victor's sister. "I'm going to comb this tangle of hair."

Molly held her breath. Norman stuck his hands in his pockets and watched. Victor looked Sweet Caroline in the face, and she smiled at him warmheartedly, openly, with no guile.

Victor hesitated but finally sat in a folding chair. Sweet Caroline got her comb off the picnic table and stood behind him. She began at the very tip of his long hair with tiny, careful strokes. Victor jerked at her touch but Sweet Caroline said, "Shhhhh . . . Shhhhh . . . " and little by little, Victor relaxed under her ministrations.

Norman was stunned. His hair was too short for Sweet Caroline to comb or even wrap her finger around, and he missed her touch already, even as Victor seemed comforted by it. He thumped into a lawn chair.

Molly remembered to breathe. She sat in a chair and began to read Barry's letters, beginning at the beginning. She had meant to keep them to herself, but maybe they would help Victor to know he wasn't alone.

I don't believe in the domino theory . . . We have no business in Vietnam . . . A bunch of old guys telling us young guys to go to some foreign country and kill people . . . Why? What have the Vietnamese people ever done to us?

Victor tensed and Sweet Caroline stopped combing. Molly didn't know whether or not to continue, but as Victor settled again, she did.

San Francisco was great, but it got too intense, so I came back to Atlanta for now. You've got to see this band, man. Here's a copy of "The Bird," read all about them. I'm worried about being drafted. If this war goes on for two more years, you're going to face this decision, too, cuz.

Molly fought tears as she read. *Barry, Barry, Barry.* She reached for Aunt Pam's tablecloth and blew her nose on the corner of it. Norman exhaled a heavy sigh and looked away.

Sweet Caroline tenderly combed Victor's hair. Molly found

her voice and read more. Norman put food away and tended the fire. There was no Wavy to tell them that compassion is a wonder drug, that "it feels good to be nice," that acts of kindness beget more kindness. They didn't need Wavy tonight. They had one another.

Sweet Caroline interrupted Molly's letter reading to list for Victor all the reasons he should come to Disneyland. Pirates of the Caribbean. The Magic Castle. Goofy. Cinderella. She sang "A Dream Is a Wish Your Heart Makes," and Victor closed his eyes and smiled. Norman was impressed — even with her terrible singing voice, the song was sweet because it was full of feeling.

"At Disneyland all your dreams can come true," she said.

"What are *your* dreams?" Norman asked her. Immediately, he wished upon the first star he saw. *Please let them include me.*

"I have bad dreams," said Victor.

"I'm sorry," said Caroline. She kept combing Victor's hair, in long strokes now, from his forehead, along his scalp, to the back of his head. Victor gave a soft moan as she began to massage his neck. Sweet Caroline did not giggle.

"I haven't been touched in a very long time," he whispered.

"Then it's about time," she whispered back.

Norman's face was on fire with embarrassment. It felt so intimate and so private and so like he should have been the one Sweet Caroline was whispering to. He was jealous. He felt sorry for himself. He was losing her; he could see it.

A log shifted on the fire and Victor stared at it. Molly quit reading the letters. Flam snored under the picnic table.

"I killed people," Victor said.

Norman's eyes sought Molly's although he did not turn his head.

Sweet Caroline put both hands on Victor's shoulders and held him that way, gently. "I know," she said.

Molly couldn't believe Sweet Caroline's composure.

"I want to die," Victor said.

Tears filled Molly's eyes as she heard once again what Victor had told her on the Square.

"We don't want you to leave us," said Sweet Caroline. "Do we, Molly?"

"No," said Molly. She was trembling, but Sweet Caroline seemed steady. "Do we, Norman?"

"No," said Norman. "No, man. We need you."

"Why?" Victor looked Norman in the eye for the first time since he'd met him.

Norman tried to think. "If anybody will know how to talk to Barry when we find him, it will be you."

Victor shook his head.

"Yes," said Molly. "I feel it." She did not. What she felt was dread.

"Come to Disneyland first," said Sweet Caroline. "That's where we'll find my mother. She'll take good care of all of us."

"Your mother!" Molly sat up straight.

It came out in a tumble. "Yes, my mother. I've been trying to get to her for such a long time, and I'm sorry, Norman, I thought you would take me, I thought I could talk you into it, but you didn't want to go and I didn't want to make you go. I do like you, I really do, but not the way you think I do. I shouldn't have led you on. What I really want is to go to Disneyland." She took a deep breath.

Norman couldn't speak. He stared at Sweet Caroline as his vision clouded with tears. It hurt.

"So what you really want is a ride," said Molly. "I knew it."

Victor covered his face and sobbed, once, then stopped himself, which brought them all back to him. "It doesn't matter!" he said. "Don't you see? None of this matters!"

"You're right," said Sweet Caroline. She squatted in front of Victor and pulled both his hands from his face, held them in hers. "You're right. It's not important, Victor."

"Why is your mother at Disneyland?" asked Norman when he could speak.

Sweet Caroline answered without taking her eyes off Victor. "My mother left us to find herself fifteen years ago. I was a baby. I grew up in foster homes. My mother came to California. She was the first Snow White at Disneyland when they opened. Then she went to Hollywood and acted in a million movies — she was an extra. I used to watch old movies on television to see if we could find her in them."

Sweet Caroline's eyes were full of glistening tears, but she was smiling at Victor, keeping him with her as she told the story.

"Over the years, she wrote letters to me and told me she would bring me out to be with her as soon as she had enough money saved, but she never did. The letters never had return addresses. I couldn't write to her, I couldn't call her. I never even knew her."

"How would you find her by going to Disneyland?" asked Molly. She closed the top on the box of letters.

"They'll have an address for her there. It's a place to start." She let go of Victor's hands. "Just a minute, I'll be right back. Don't go away."

She stood up and turned to Norman and Molly. "You two have everything and you don't even know it. Norman, you have a dog, a bus, a cousin — two cousins — and you have a quest. An important quest. You have family. A mother who loves you and will do anything for you — you told me so yourself. Your father loves you, too, even if he's insane right now. He's human. You're so lucky."

She returned to Victor, who was watching her with fascination and growing understanding. He stood up. She stood directly in front of him.

"I want someone to journey with who will love me and who needs me and who will let me help him and who will help me. I want you, Victor. Do you want me?"

Molly swallowed. This wasn't happening. She was dreaming.

"I am . . ." Victor began, trying to find a word. ". . . damaged." But something in him moved as he said it, Sweet Caroline could tell, and Molly could see it transform him. His face softened as if it was letting go of a burden.

"So am I," said Sweet Caroline. "I'll be your family, you be mine. You can never be like Barry, with the chance to make your decision again, and not go to Vietnam. I know that. I understand that. We can't undo what's been done. I can never be like Molly, who has a mother and a father and a house to grow up in with them, memories to make with them. But we can be family to each other and it can be good. Together we can have a future. I'm willing to try. Are you?"

Victor stood up. "I . . . I don't know what to do." The longing in his voice was unmistakable. So was hers.

Sweet Caroline reached up and touched Victor's face with both of her hands. "Neither do I. Let's take care of each other."

She wrapped her arms around his waist. She was short and he was tall. She tucked her head under his chin. He lifted his arms and slowly, slowly wrapped them around her. She sighed deeply. She transferred her affections so easily and truly, it took Norman's breath away. He sat with a thud on the picnic bench. Molly got to her feet. She couldn't think of one thing to say.

"We're going for a walk," said Sweet Caroline. She led Victor away by the hand. He stopped her and turned around to Molly.

"Thank you."

"For what?" she asked. Her throat filled with tears and her nose started to run.

"For noticing."

She sniffed and smiled crookedly at Victor. "You're welcome."

They disappeared in the dark, two souls who had chosen each other.

"We'll be back," said Sweet Caroline.

In the morning they were gone.

MARY, MARY

Written by Michael Nesmith
Performed by the Monkees
Recorded at Western Recorders, Hollywood, California, 1966
Drummer: Hal Blaine and Jim Gordon/the Wrecking Crew

Just before dawn, Norman poked at the fire's embers, added some foraged wood, and brewed coffee in the campfire pot they'd taken with them on the Appalachian Trail. He used their can opener to punch holes in a can of sweetened condensed milk and found the jar of sugar in Aunt Pam's box labeled *Staples*.

Molly braided her hair and liked how it felt. She tied her Keds and pulled on her sweatshirt. Norman, with his short hair and a slight stubble around his chin, wore his jeans and a YMCA T-shirt.

As Molly appeared for coffee, Norman said, "I'm sorry. For everything." Molly sighed, trying to think of what to say. She settled for "It's her loss," and then added, "Love is weird, isn't it?"

"Girls are weird," he said. He'd understood that Lucy hadn't loved him, but he'd tumbled for Sweet Caroline and now he felt foolish for ever believing a girl could love him back. He finished folding the laundry, a task Molly assigned him. Victor's clothes were gone, but Sweet Caroline had left Norman her Mickey Mouse T-shirt. He gave it to Molly.

"They're doomed," she said.

"Probably," Norman agreed.

Norman seemed to have a selection of T-shirts now. "Did you trade all your white T-shirts for these? Is that what you were doing in the Aspen Meadow?"

Norman shrugged. "It just happened. I still have some of mine. But I like these. Want one?"

"Well, I don't want to wear Mickey Mouse," Molly announced. But she was tired of her usual uniform. She picked a sleeveless pullover shirt in red and white stripes. She would wear it to California.

They packed the tent, broke camp, and climbed on board Multitudes. "We've got to get across the Mojave Desert before noon," said Molly. "The heat will boil the bus. I read it in *An Adventurer's Guide to Travel across America*, a book that is not always completely truthful, as we've seen, but I believe this much."

"I'm ready," said Norman. He turned the key in the ignition, Molly settled into the navigator's seat, and Flam, not quite ready for the day, trotted back to the sleeping bags and flopped down for a snooze. Daylight began to announce itself in shades of silver and gray as they trundled past the Mohave County Courthouse, a radiator repair shop, a Harley-Davidson dealer — *Barry!* — and pulled onto Route 66. The road was lonely and dotted with signs that declared

LAST GAS FOR 100 MILES

CHECK FOR DRINKING WATER AND COOLANT

IN CASE OF BREAKDOWN STAY WITH YOUR CAR

"You're sure you checked all the engine fluids?" Molly asked.

"Yes," said Norman. "Twice."

They began the descent into the basin of the Mojave. The Sierra Nevada mountains in the far distance created a rain

319

shadow on the desert floor, trapping the humid air from the Pacific Ocean and cooling it so it evaporated before it could water the desert. As a result, dust and sand danced on the dry winds, and plants captured what little moisture passed over the mountains and held it in their spines and thorns. Large desert tortoises dug deep burrows in the sand and sheltered under crevasses. The land was wild and silent.

"It's spooky in the dark," whispered Molly.

"It'll be daylight soon." Norman squinted into the distance. "What's that! Gaaaa!"

Molly jumped as the bus headlights illuminated what looked like ghostly monsters menacing them from either side of the empty highway.

Norman leaned forward in his seat and strained to see. "They're trees!" He laughed nervously. "Trees."

A grove of Joshua trees dotted the landscape, their thick trunks spreading and branching into many bristling arms that seemed to reach skyward for them like ominous ogres on the march.

"Still spooky," said Molly. Blinking blue lights zigzagged across the sky and were gone as suddenly as they had arrived.

"What's that!"

"It's a UFO," said Norman.

Molly reached over the silver partition and slapped Norman on the shoulder.

"It's probably some plane from some air base around here," said Norman. "Didn't that Drew kid say there were missile bases out here or something?"

"Telescopes," said Molly. "And you missed them when you slept through Flagstaff."

The sky lightened and so did their mood. The sun rose behind them in the east as they barreled west with the windows up against the cool desert night.

They crossed the Colorado River.

"Welcome to California!" said Molly with glee in her voice. Norman smiled at her in the student mirror. Finally, California.

The bright morning sun crested the Sierra Nevadas and immediately began to bake the bus. Molly walked past each window, opening it and letting the hot air circulate. Soon they were driving through the oven that was the daytime Mojave Desert.

"It's so much hotter than yesterday," said Molly. She got them some water in paper cups from the melting ice in the ice chest.

Norman's thoughts drifted to Sweet Caroline and her ministrations of ice water, giggles, and a cool washrag. He shook his head so he would think of something else. There were few other cars on the road, the occasional tractor-trailer truck, and so much brown everywhere. So much sand.

"Remember when that boy sank in the quicksand in *Lawrence of Arabia*?" Molly asked.

Norman didn't answer. *Lawrence of Arabia* was not one of Pam's more positive moves, although it had started out that way. When Lewis turned forty, Pam decided they would all celebrate with dinner at the Swamp Fox Room and *Lawrence of Arabia* at the Riviera Theater on King Street. They dressed in their very best clothes and polished their shoes. Uncle Bruce opted in for dinner, and out for the movie.

That left seven of them at the Riviera watching Lawrence yank off his head scarf and throw it, over and again, to the Arab boy, Daud, trying to save him as Daud sank under the sand in the Sinai Desert. Molly, who was barely ten, wailed so long and loud that her dad had to pick her up and take her into the lobby, where her sobs could still be heard throughout the theater.

Finally, Mitch took her outside — in December — and home. *You've just got lots of feelings and that's a good thing*, Barry told her later, when she remained inconsolable at home, fresh tears cascading down her cheeks whenever she thought about poor Daud. The incident was part of their shared family lore.

"I never did see the end of that movie," Molly said now. Flam thumped his tail from a blanket at Molly's feet.

They rode through oppressive heat and heavy silence across the vast Mojave with no radio signal strong enough to reach them. Dust swirled in front of their bus, came at them in puffs, and then, as the wind picked up, flew like a herd of gigantic Texas tumbleweeds rolling into one another, combining their stretch and strength until all Molly and Norman saw ahead of them was a blanket of dust, brown and thick with menace.

"Shut the windows!" shouted Norman. He slowed the bus to a crawl.

Molly jumped from her seat like she was back at the Riviera Theater, ten years old. Her heart raced, her pulse pounded, as her fingers frantically squeezed the metal pincers on the sides of each window, lifting each glass until it clicked in place, moving swiftly to the next one, dust coating her lips, swirling into her nose and eyes, making her cough as she ran from seat to seat, then gave up on the windows and ran to the back, where she tripped over the boxes and stepped crookedly onto the foam rubber mattresses, twisting her ankle and sliding into Norman's bass drum.

The dust invaded the bus and smothered her. Suddenly, she was Daud, buried under the earth, sand in her ears, her nose, her eyes, her mouth, unable to scream for help. She rolled herself into a ball, pulled her sleeping bag over her head, and pressed her face into the foam rubber mattress. She willed herself to be anywhere else.

Norman left the highway — Molly could feel it. She knew he would have to stop driving. She waited for him to stop the bus, but it seemed to go on for a long time, the crunch of a dirt road under the tires until the bus slowed and then stopped. She heard Norman coughing and closing the windows in the back near her.

Then she felt him beside her, with Flam. He pulled one of Pam's blankets over the three of them and they stayed that way for what seemed like a long time. It got very hot in the bus.

Are we going to die out here? She wanted to ask the question, but she would not open her mouth. She kept her eyes closed. Norman left their blanket fort and returned pulling the ice chest behind him.

"Here." He peeled off his YMCA T-shirt, dunked it in the icy water, and gave it to Molly. "Put it over your face. I've got one, too." He stripped the pillowcases from their pillows and soaked them as well. He laid one over Flam's head. The dog lay very still, as if he sensed the danger.

The wind blew so insistently it rang the bell outside their bus beside the door. Time slipped away from them. They slept. Then, finally, Flam began to sneeze and work his way out from the blanket. Molly opened her eyes. It was eerily quiet.

"It's over," she said.

"I think so," Norman agreed.

They opened every window and door, back and front. The seats were coated with a layer of dust in the way the tree pollen coated everything at home each spring.

"Where are we?" asked Molly.

"I don't know exactly," said Norman.

They opened the folding door and stepped outside, into the haze.

Molly had read in *An Adventurer's Guide to Travel across America* that people who didn't stick to the highways got lost in the desert and were never found. "What if we're stuck out here forever?"

"We won't be," said Norman, but he didn't sound sure. He tried to reconstruct their path. "I got off at the first road I could see and suddenly I was on this dirt road, and I don't think I made any turns on it, but I can't be sure. Now we're here, under these . . . trees."

The air was spangled a brilliant yellow gold with late-morning sun and dust. They were parked beside a small stand of cottonwood trees and clumps of mesquite.

"I didn't see the trees," Norman marveled. "I could have driven right into them."

"But you didn't," said a voice.

Molly yelped and grabbed Norman's arm.

"I won't hurt you," came the voice. It was a woman sitting at a table under the cottonwoods. A burro was standing next to the table, swishing its tail and looking at them placidly. Flam growled at the burro but stayed behind Norman.

"You're almost out of the desert now," said the woman.

"Where are we?" Norman asked. Molly could feel his pulse racing.

"You're in Daggett," said the woman. She wore a wide-brimmed hat and a long dress. She held a notebook in her hands and a camera hung from a strap around her neck. "You are one hundred miles from your destination."

"How —?"

"I saw you coming," said the woman. "I can lead you back to your wagon road when you are ready."

Molly gripped Norman harder, to steady herself. It gave Norman strength as well. "Who are you?"

"I'm Mary Beal," the woman said. "My friends called me Mamie. I've been here a long time. You are just passing through."

"Yes," said Molly, finally speaking.

"Your conveyance is colorful," said Mary Beal. She took a page from her notebook. On it she had sketched a ghost flower from the desert and a map. "That's a *Mohavea confertiflora*," she said. "I'm not much of an artist. I usually photograph my plants, but my camera doesn't seem to be working anymore. If you follow this map, you will find yourself at your destination in time for your appointment."

324

"Appointment?"

"They are waiting for you," said Mary Beal. "You impress them with your passion."

Molly opened her mouth, then shut it.

"Your conveyance will get you there with no problems," said Mary Beal. "It has rested from the heat, in this shade, and it is ready to take you."

Molly couldn't help it. She pictured Glinda, the Good Witch of the East, telling Dorothy that all she had to do was tap her Ruby Slippers together three times and they would take her home. She gave Norman's arm a slight tug.

But Norman had nothing to say to that, either. *It's not like Mary Beal is a mechanic down at the garage and has had a look under the hood. Or has she?* He dug his fingers into his palms to make sure he was awake. He was.

Mary Beal reached for the rope tied to her burro and tucked her notebook into the saddle pack it carried. Flam growled once again. "You don't have to worry about Rocky," she said to the dog. "He is a gentle soul."

Before she could walk away, Norman found his voice. "Do you live around here?" he asked impulsively.

Mary Beal turned to Norman. "I used to live in a tent house on the Van Dyke ranch. This town was quite a sight when Dix first arrived here. Cattle drives, brothels, shoot-outs, a silver mine, and frontier people who didn't understand the desert. I came here myself to get over a bout with tuberculosis. When I fell in love with the desert and decided to stay, Dix built me a cottage on his ranch."

A train whistled insistently in the distance.

Norman looked at the vista surrounding them but saw no ranch, no cottage. "Is it nearby?"

"I don't live there anymore," said Mary Beal. "You'll pass my new place on your way back to the highway. You'll know it when you see it."

325

She nodded to Molly and Norman, adjusted her hat, and walked away with her burro, her notebook, and her camera. She faded into the waving heat and brilliant sunshine until she seemed to have disappeared.

"Thank you!" called Norman with some desperation in his voice.

"Whoa," whispered Molly. Flam whined at her feet. "Let's get you some water, boy."

They drank their fill, poured water over their heads and shoulders, arms and backs to cool themselves and wash off the dust, and started on their way again, windows down once more, directions in Molly's hand. As they passed a tall iron entrance gate that spelled out DAGGETT PIONEER CEMETERY, Norman stopped the bus and looked at Molly. She nodded and he turned in.

It didn't take them long to find her.

MARY BEAL
1878 TO 1964
BOTANIST OF MOJAVE DESERT

Wordlessly, they each reached for the other's hand and took it. They stood together in front of Mary Beal's grave until they began to boil in the sun. Then they climbed into their conveyance and careened through Southern California, to Hollywood, to their appointment.

GOOD VIBRATIONS

Written by Brian Wilson and Mike Love

Performed by the Beach Boys

Recorded at Western Recorders, CBS Columbia Square, Gold Star, and Sunset Sound Recorders, Hollywood, California, 1966

Drummer: Dennis Wilson (concert)/Hal Blaine (studio)

The receptionist at Capitol Records did not know they had an appointment.

"Can I help you?" A cigarette dangled from her very red lips, and every red hair on her head was sprayed in place like it was part of a cranberry helmet. She turned her head, blew smoke toward the gold records hanging on the wall, and put her cigarette into a holder in a bright red ashtray. She raised her eyebrows and gave Molly and Norman an impatient, expectant look.

Norman once again wore his white oxford shirt and wing tip shoes. Molly was surprised at how different it suddenly made him look — he had changed so much on the road. He was sunburned and he had dressed up for Hollywood.

They had come to the building shaped like a stack of records with a needle at the top, the building with the name on it that was also on so many of their records, from the Beatles to the

327

Beach Boys, the records sporting that orange-and-yellow swirl on Molly's 45s, and a name she had never given a second thought to until they stood in the lobby of the building with the gold records decorating the marble walls.

Norman held the cymbals in their case under his arm. He cleared his throat.

"Is Hal Blaine here, please?"

"Who wants to know?"

Molly, who had just survived sure death in the desert, smirked at the receptionist and hoped she noticed. *Eleanor Rigby and her sidekick Florsheim.* No, she wouldn't say that. She waited to see how Norman would respond. She wore Sweet Caroline's red-and-white-striped shirt and her usual shorts and Keds. She was cold; the air-conditioning was freezing everything in the room.

"He's expecting us," Norman said.

"Really," said the receptionist sardonically. She looked Norman up and down like his bad mother. "Who sent you?"

"Mary Beal," Molly snapped.

"Who?"

Norman shot Molly a look. "Al Jackson, Jr., at Stax Records in Memphis, Tennessee," he said.

"Really."

"Also Roger Hawkins at FAME Studios in Muscle Shoals, Alabama."

"Uh-huh."

The receptionist's dismissiveness began to grate on Norman. He could have died in the desert, too. "Actually," he said, his voice gathering all the authority his seventeen years could summon, "Jai Johany Johansen of the Allman Brothers Band."

He stared as menacingly as he could, directly into the receptionist's eyes, and hoped she could hear his mental command. *Hal Blaine now! And step on it!*

The receptionist plucked her cigarette from its perch on the red ashtray. "Just a minute." She disappeared.

"Great," said Norman, deflated. "They aren't going to let us back there. Or up there. Or wherever."

"Patience," said Molly, surprising herself. "She's just one person and not very nice."

"Not very groovy," said Norman. He smiled at his own bad joke, which lessened his anxiety. "I don't even know who Hal Blaine is," he said.

The receptionist appeared with a business card in her hand. "Call this number."

Norman took the card from the receptionist's fingers. She had very long nails. They were also red. "Do you have a phone I can use?"

"No."

At Stan's Drive-In, they found burgers, bathrooms, and a pay phone.

Arlyn's Answering Service, the card said. Norman dialed the number and asked to see Hal Blaine.

"Mr. Blaine is completely booked through July, but I can schedule you for a date in early August. Which studio?"

"Which one does he play in?"

"Capitol, Gold Star, Columbia, Sunset, A&M, Western, RCA — are you a producer?"

"I just need to give him something," said Norman. "It's a piece of his equipment."

"He has a valet who does cartage for him," said Arlyn. "His name is Rick Faucher. I can give you his number."

"Cartage?" *Valet?*

"He takes Mr. Blaine's drum kits from studio to studio and sets them up, breaks them down, takes care of them. Are you a musician?"

Norman finished the call, then put another dime in the pay phone and dialed the number Arlyn had given him.

"Where are you?" Rick Faucher asked once Norman explained what was going on. "We've been looking for those cymbals!"

"Capitol Records," lied Norman.

"Holy —" began Rick and then stopped himself. "*Don't move. I'll meet you at Capitol in a half hour."

Thirty minutes later, they were tucked into the earth at the bottom of Capitol Records in the control room for Studio B. Rick said, "Don't mind that receptionist. She's from the service. Never seen her before. Linda would have told you Hal was here."

Now Molly wished she *had* told the smoky red receptionist that her name was Eleanor Rigby, but probably she wouldn't have known who that was.

Norman had completely forgotten about the receptionist. He was inside a subterranean spaceship with seven layers of wall for absolute silence, and floors that floated on cork to eliminate vibration, baffles to absorb sound floating from the ceiling and adjustable to any angle — the musicians at Stax and FAME would have been so jealous! — and Nat King Cole's Steinway in its own isolation booth.

The studio was full of musicians. They were deep in discussion. Hal Blaine gestured with a drumstick while he sat at his kit. It was the most impressive set of drums Norman had ever seen.

"What is it?" he asked Rick.

"You've never seen anything like it because there isn't anything like it," answered Rick. "We built it."

"It's a monster kit," marveled Norman.

"That's what we call it!" said Rick. "It's starts with a blue sparkle Ludwig kit — can you see it?"

Norman nodded. "It's a double bass set."

"That's right." If he'd been a peacock, Rick would have spread his colorful feathered fan. "We added two rolling racks of tom-toms, four on one side, with one rack, and three on a second rack. We can roll them right into the van and to the next gig. They're completely adjustable and each tom is a different size or sound, so Hal can do those rolling toms you hear in songs like 'Up Up and Away' and 'Good Vibrations,' most anything by the Monkees or the Association, like 'I'm a Believer' and 'Windy' —"

"What?" Molly joined the conversation. "He was the drummer on 'Windy'? I thought that was Ted, the cute one!"

"It's Ted Bluechel in concert," said Rick. "But it's Hal on the record. And that's what you want — you want the best. At concerts, people hear with their eyes. You teenagers will cut your idols some slack in concert, but not when you buy their records."

"Quiet, please," said an engineer in the booth. "Let's go again."

"Watch and learn," whispered Rick. "They'll break to listen to their takes, and I'll introduce you. It's the least I can do for a fellow who personally drove Hal's Zildjians across the country."

"I bought these cymbals when I was a kid!" Hal crowed a short time later. "I'm real attached to their sound, real sentimental about 'em. Thanks for the mission of mercy!"

They were in the studio and Norman was sitting behind the monster drum set, afraid to touch anything.

"Go on!" Hal said. "Have a whack at 'em!" He handed Norman a pair of drumsticks.

Hal was ebullient. "I thought they were lost forever! But now we're reunited! Rick swore they were in his van, and then they weren't, and they weren't anywhere else, either."

331

He'd been on the phone with Rick Hall at FAME, who'd put him on the phone with Roger Hawkins, who'd told him that Jaimoe had taken them by accident the last time he'd visited FAME. "But Roger hadn't known it until Florsheim brought them to him."

"I'm . . . Norman," said Norman. He surprised himself.

Hal barreled ahead. "That still doesn't explain how he got 'em, but who cares now! They're back!" He held them up to the light. "You see how I filed these babies? They fit just so on my old cymbals stand — of course, now you can buy stands that tilt, but back then . . ."

Molly wanted to interrupt, but there wasn't an opportunity. And Norman could have listened to Hal all day. Fortunately, Hal didn't have all day, and neither did they. Rick was trying to dismantle Hal's kit in order to cart it to the next studio gig. Musicians were putting away their instruments and heading out. One of them was a woman with an electric bass guitar. She nodded at Molly and Molly nodded back, then looked at her wristwatch. It was already three o'clock.

"You play rock and roll?" Hal asked Norman.

"Yessir."

"Call me Hal." He picked up his sticks and pulled a seat next to Norman. "Rock and roll is just a backbeat on two and four." He played the rhythm. "But you need to learn everything. Dance music, Latin music, waltzes, oom-pa-pas, all time signatures. Come on, do it with me."

Rick quit dismantling the equipment. "Hal . . ."

"Five minutes," said Hal. He looked at his watch. "We've got time." He handed Norman a second pair of sticks. Norman handed the first pair to Rick.

For the next five minutes, Norman copied Hal as best he could and Hal kept a one-sided dialogue running. "Listen to all music, get training, know how to read music. Practice. Develop a good ear. Replicate what you hear. The Big Banders and orchestra guys — even the jazzers — laughed at us, this crew of session musicians, these kids off the street wearing our Levis and addicted to coffee and Coca-Colas, when we started doing rock and roll instead of easy listening. It was beneath them. They said we were wrecking the music business —"

"That's why they call them the Wrecking Crew," Rick interjected.

"Right," said Hal. "And that's a badge of honor!" He took Norman's sticks and handed them to Rick. "Good work." Norman had no idea what he'd played, if anything.

Hal tapped his hi-hat with both of his sticks in one hand. "Look at this. I invented a tambourine that attaches to my hi-hat on the drum. I've got a cowbell holder on top of my hi-hat so I can play eighth notes on the hi-hat and do the Latin *tic-tic-tic* in between the eighth notes. Like this." He demonstrated. "Do you read music?"

"Yessir!"

"Good. Are you in a high school band?"

"Yessir."

"Yeah is fine," said Hal. "I was in drum and bugle corps." He handed his sticks to Rick. "And after the army, I went to music school in Chicago. These guys who don't bother to learn how to read music will never be session musicians —"

"Unless they're Glen Campbell," Rick interrupted. He put the sticks away. He took the cymbals off their stands. He packed them into cases next to the recovered Zildjians.

"Glen Campbell!" Molly interjected. "'Wichita Lineman'!"

"That's right," said Hal. "I played on that tune. Glen's part of the Wrecking Crew, but he's famous now, so we don't see him so much. Talk about an ear. That man's got one. But he's an exception to the rule. Learn how to read music."

Norman started to tell Hal that Roger Hawkins didn't read music, but he thought better of it.

Rick began to move the first rack of toms. "You're all set up at Sunset Sound with the second kit," he said. "You start at four."

"On my way," said Hal. Rick headed in one direction with the drums. Hal motioned to Norman to follow him in another. "Being a studio musician, that's the highest echelon, in my opinion. You don't have to do the road, you can go home at night, and you can do everything! Television, movies, jingles, soundtracks, commercials, records, I've done them all. You're not the star when you're a studio man. You're the accompanist. You make them sound good."

Molly couldn't stand it any longer. "Who did you make sound good?"

Hal smiled as the elevator doors opened and the three of them walked past the red receptionist who glowered at them. "The Beach Boys, the Grass Roots, Frank Sinatra, Simon and Garfunkel, Elvis Presley —"

"Really?" Norman and Molly laughed.

"Really." Hal looked puzzled. "He's great, you know."

"I know!" Norman said. "We met him in Memphis!"

"Right," said Hal. He shook his head.

"The Association!" said Molly.

"Yep, the Association. They've got a pretty good drummer, actually, Ted something; I just saw him, he's in town."

"He is?" Molly's heart began to race.

"He's going to the hoot at the Troubadour tonight. I told him I might stop in. They've been on tour and they haven't been to the Troubadour since they made it big. Or maybe they're just satisfying their obligation — Doug Weston makes all the bands that get their start there come back."

"Tonight?" Molly felt swimmy-headed. The Association. At the Troubadour. Tonight. *What's the Troubadour? Who cares?* "What time?"

"Mol —" Norman began, but she cut him off.

"What time?!"

They stepped outside and into the afternoon sun. The Hollywood sign shimmered in the heat, high on Mount Lee, as if it was waving to them. "I don't know," Hal answered. "Eight o'clock? They've got a show every night. Neil Young's been there this week, Poco is there tomorrow — look." A poster was stuck on the telephone pole by the bus. "Every Monday night is hoot night. Is that your bus? Wow."

"That's it," said Norman. "And this is our dog." Flam had waited patiently in the shade of the sheet-metal awnings by the front door.

Molly tore the poster off the telephone pole.

Hal gave the dog a pat. "Remember what I said," he told Norman. "A song is a story. Listen to the singer sing it. Listen to how the lyrics are phrased, figure out where the drama is. Then add your beat, your sound, your snap. That's your chapter in the story."

Molly scanned the poster but couldn't find an address. "Where is the Troubadour?" *Drop and go*, that's what she thought they'd do in Los Angeles, just drop the cymbals and go. But they still had time to get to Barry, and to get home. Every day she sat in the navigator's seat and worked out their timing. They had time.

"And stay clean," said Hal, gazing at Multitudes and raising his eyebrows. "We are a bunch of professional musicians who are clean guys doing good work. Producers know we're sober. They know we're straight. They know we can play just about anything. Word gets around, and producers get in touch."

He stuck out his hand to Norman. "Good luck."

"Thanks so much," said Norman.

"Thanks for the return of my cymbals."

Molly's toes were tingling. Mary Beal had been right.

They *did* have an appointment.

"All right! All right!" She waved the poster and fairly exploded. "Where's the Troubadour?"

ENTER THE YOUNG

Written by Terry Kirkman
Performed by The Association
Recorded at Columbia Studios (voices) and G.S.P. Studios
(instruments), Los Angeles, California, 1966
Drummer: Ted Bluechel, Jr. (concert)/Hal Blaine (studio)

MOLLY

The address is on the poster, hidden in the swirls of artwork, along with the telephone number, which I have to call because I don't have a city street map. Los Angeles is gigantic. It goes on forever, spreading out like butter on toast, and we get lost because of all the one-way streets, or maybe because I'm so anxious to find the place and get in the long line Hal Blaine told us we'd be in.

"Performers start lining up hours early to get on the list," he said, "vying for a chance to perform and be heard by the record producers who sit at the bar in the back, hoping to discover the next big hit. You just get in line with them."

Finally, we find it, and sure enough, there's the line, snaking out the door and around the corner. "This is gonna take a while," says Norman. "I'm bringing Flam." He doesn't complain and he doesn't say we need to get on the road. I appreciate it and should probably say so, but I don't. I'm just too nervous.

336

The late-afternoon sun blazes all over us and everybody sweats. We listen to the talk in line, all about gigs and bands and best places to play around town, who's playing at the Whisky, the Paladium, or the Ash Grove. Nobody seems to know that the Association is going to be at the hoot tonight. I'm not about to brag that I have inside knowledge. I just want in the door.

"Why don't all these rock and rollers have to go to Vietnam?" says a woman with long red hair. "My brother's got to go."

I turn my body so I can hear the conversation.

"Barry McGuire was a Green Beret," replies a bearded man with the red-haired woman.

"He's not a rock and roller," says the red-haired woman. "Not really."

A man wearing a hat and carrying a guitar case says, "I happen to know one of 'em's a fortunate son."

"What's that?" says the red-haired woman.

"His dad's got money. Or influence. Or both. Listen to the song."

"It ain't me," says the bearded man, which makes the man in the hat laugh.

A couple standing in front of us in line is listening, too. The short man says, "Tell your brother to do what Gregg Allman did. He shot himself in the foot."

Norman pretends to lean down and pet Flam, but he really just wants to hear this. So do I.

"What?!" says the red-haired woman, and the short man explains.

"Yeah, a couple years ago, I think, when he was trying to make it big out here. Gregg got his notice to report for his physical, so he flew home to Florida and shot himself in the foot so he wouldn't pass his physical exam."

Molly took a deep breath.

"Yeah!" said the girl with the short man. "We read about it. They made a party out of it, drew a target on Gregg's moccasin,

337

between his foot bones, and everything. He showed up for his physical the next day all bandaged up and bleeding, limping with a cane, and the military goons let him go. He didn't have to go to Vietnam."

It made me shudder. I whispered to Norman that I was adding a foot-shooting party to my list of possibilities for Barry, but Norman just shook his head. "Crazy," he said. "He shot himself in the foot. On purpose."

"That band's going to be big," says another man in line. "I've heard them play. Mark my words." I tug on his white oxford shirt and Norman smiles at me.

Finally, the line moves and I pray silently we'll get in. When we get to the door, Norman asks if we can tie Flam outside for a little while, says we're from out of town, we've come a long way, no we don't want to get on the hoot list, we just want to listen, here's our money, and the bouncer at the door starts to say no until another bouncer in a Troubadour T-shirt says, "Hey! I used to have a red dog just like that. His name was —"

"Let me guess. Red," says the first bouncer.

"Yeah! You can leave him with me, kid," the second bouncer says.

I know my heart has made an appearance because it begins to bump in my chest. We might stumble across the Association any second.

But this is taking forever. I suffer through act after fifteen-minute act on the hoot list. A ventriloquist, two terrible singers, a folk trio, a guy named Steve who makes balloon animals and plays the banjo. Norman loves that guy.

"You have no taste," I tell him.

"I'm going to get something to drink," he says. "I'll be back."

The place has a balcony, but I'm standing as close to the stage as I can get. There are only a few tables anyway. It's hard to see because of the smoke and the low lights and the dark paneling everywhere. So I just stay put while a man named Doug, who says he owns the place, recites "The Love Song of J. Alfred Prufrock" and people jeer and boo and tell him to stop.

So he stops and says, "Enough for now! I'll come back to it later. I have some announcements . . ." and there is more booing.

Maybe the Association isn't coming! I want to cry. I came all this way. All this way. We have eight days left to get to San Francisco, find Barry, and get home before he has to report for his physical. Coming to the Troubadour was a mistake.

"We should go," I turn to tell Norman, but then remember, he is gone for his drink.

At that exact same moment, Doug finishes his announcements. "And now!" he says. "A surprise for all you freaks! Here's some hometown boys we put on the map at the Troub! You knew them as half of the Men, and before that some of 'em were the ever-evolving and revolving band the Inner Tubes. Give it up for our old house band, and notice — all of you out there who hope to make it big! — they are honoring their commitment to come back when they become famous! The Association!"

Cheering! Applause! Surprise! I have actual goose bumps. I am short of breath. The Association! In this very room! With *me*!

The band runs onto the stage, picks up their instruments, and launches into a song without even a hello. The music I know so well comes to life right in front of my eyes and ears and I think, *I can't stand it! I'm going to faint!*

It's "Windy" and I am Windy, tripping down the streets of the city, smiling at everybody I see, Windy with stormy eyes, hating the sound of lies, with wings to fly above the clouds. Me. Molly. I am she.

I . . . feel . . . everything.

There is cute Ted on the drums. There is Larry playing the guitar. And there is Terry — my Terry, who, I can now see, looks nothing like Barry, even with his crooked smile and the gap between his two front teeth.

339

The Association is almost close enough for me to reach out and touch. They sing "Enter the Young," and the music is no longer about just me, it's about all of us in this room, and I can feel that each of us knows it, we know they are singing about how we've learned to think and care and do daring things — which I have done! which Norman has done! — and how we are going to do these things together, laughing or crying, even if we stumble and make mistakes, and whether we live or die, we are going to do wonders, because we are stardust, we are magic.

That's what I hear, that we are young and we are demanding recognition, and we are going to change the world.

People behind me are dancing and cheering and laughing and I am standing at the stage, watching them play these notes and sing these words, and I am close to crying, because I know it is hard. It is hard to be young and afraid and stumbling and stardust. It is hard to feel. It is hard to be alive in the world when the world hurts.

And when the band — my beautiful band — starts singing "Cherish," a song about loving someone who doesn't love you back the way you love them, that song hits me in the heart like a hammer. I hear its truth.

Barry is my brother and he said he loves me, but he didn't trust me enough to write me, to let me know he's all right, to ask my forgiveness for leaving me so cruelly, and to assure me he'll see me again.

He just left.

He left me alone with Mom and Dad, their broken hearts, *my* broken heart, to fend for myself. How daring was that?

I stand very still at edge of the stage, my eyes fixed on the Association, as I allow their music — melody, harmony, energy, lyrics — to spill over me, feel for me, and wrap me in its gospel. I hardly notice I'm crying a silent stream of slow-moving tears that make their way, one drop at a time, down my windburned cheeks, to a point at my chin, and onto Sweet Caroline's red-and-white-striped shirt.

I take a breath to steady myself as the Association finishes their beautiful song and bows and each of them — Larry, Ted, Russ, Brian, Jim, Jules, and my favorite, sweet Terry, run past me and leave the stage, waving, to thundering applause. Doug comes back to the microphone with "How about that!" and the cheers continue.

Norman has threaded his way to my side. "I brought somebody who used to play with your band," he says.

The man, whose name is John, smiles at me and says, "Your cousin told me how much you love these guys. Would you like to meet them? I sang with them in the Inner Tubes. I can introduce you . . ."

Doug is reciting more "Prufrock." Something about measuring out life in teaspoons.

> And would it have been worth it, after all,
> Would it have been worth while,
> After the sunsets and the dooryards and the sprinkled streets,
> After the novels, after the teacups, after the skirts that trail along the floor —
> And this, and so much more? —
> It is impossible to say just what I mean!

I wipe at my nose and return John's smile, which makes the shine of tears brimming at my eyes spill in a tiny cascade down my cheeks. It is impossible to say just what I mean. I swipe at my cheeks.

"No, thank you," I finally say. "I want to go home."

SPACE COWBOY

Written by Steve Miller and Ben Sidran
Performed by the Steve Miller Band
Recorded at Sound Recorders, Hollywood, California, 1969
Drummer: Tim Davis

NORMAN

The hoot is still going strong when we leave with Flam and climb back on the bus. I turn on the interior lights while Molly unfolds a map.

"There's a park near here, or at least it's a bunch of green on the map; maybe we can park there for the night," she says. "I know you're beat. We crossed a desert today."

"Wasn't that last week?" I say. My joke doesn't work; she says nothing. No joke: I can hardly keep my eyes open.

"You okay?" I ask.

Her response is automatic and flat. "I'm okay. You?"

"No, you're not," I say. "Why didn't you want to meet the band?"

She fiddles with her pencil. "I'm sad," she finally says. Then she adds, with some wonder in her voice, "It's a feeling."

I don't know how to talk to girls about their feelings. I can't even talk about my own feelings.

"I don't know," Molly continues. "I started thinking about Barry. We're doing this crazy thing because of him, for him, but he doesn't even know we're coming. And even if he did . . ." She trails off. "I don't know," she finishes. "Maybe we're doing it for my mom. Maybe we're doing it for me. I don't know anymore why we're doing it."

I can't follow this loopy line of thinking. I have my own thoughts about Barry. But I'm too tired to have this conversation. I scratch the sides of my head with both hands, scrubbing my scalp, to wake myself up enough to think. "Let's eat something," I say. "That will make you feel better. I want a chocolate milk-shake. You?"

Molly smiles. "Good idea."

A half hour later, bellies full, we are on a narrow road that twists like a corkscrew through the trees as it climbs higher and higher into the park. I have to shift gears constantly and watch for cars coming at me down the hilly road in the dark, our head-lights blinding each other.

"Let's turn around," says Molly in a worried voice. "This isn't a good idea."

I'm worried, too, but I'm vigilant. "It's got to end somewhere," I tell her. "The cars coming from the other direction have to be up here for a reason."

Two nail-biting minutes later, we top the last rise and we're suddenly in a clearing on top of the world. Straight ahead is a huge space-age building with flying-saucer domes bathed in brilliant white lights.

"Bus parking here for the late-night observation! How many?" shouts a man in a colored vest. He eyeballs Multitudes suspiciously but asks the question anyway.

I pull into the parking area. "A bus full!" I shout in a commanding voice, in case he makes us leave when he finds out we're only two.

343

The man scribbles something on a clipboard, shakes his head, and waves us into bus parking, right up close. "Bunch of hippies!"

"Wow," says Molly. "What is this place?"

"Can you believe it?" I answer. Suddenly, I am wide awake.

Molly is off the bus with Flam and into the pools of light reflecting off the building and lighting the grass and the wide sidewalks, the obelisk in the middle of the grass, and the people everywhere. There is a sign above the massive gold doors on the main building:

GRIFFITH OBSERVATORY

People pour into and out of the double doors, swarm on the sidewalks, and snake around the observation decks with the huge binoculars on metal stands. Little kids run around on the grass, laughing and chasing one another. Parents call them to look into the giant binoculars. A cool breeze pushes me along, and I don't even bother to close the bus windows or lock up. There is no need, says the breeze, and then I laugh at myself. I'm listening to breezes.

Molly and I stand at the observation deck and stare across the valley below, where the lights of Los Angeles twinkle and race away from us for miles before they meet the darkness. A kid gives up his binoculars and I grab them to take a look. The first thing I see is the lighted HOLLYWOOD sign. Another kid yells, "The Pacific Ocean! I can see a Ferris wheel!"

I offer the binoculars to Molly. She wraps her hands around the turning levers, presses her face to the metal frame, and says, "I wonder, if I wished, if I could see all the way to Charleston, to the Atlantic Ocean, and home?"

She gives the binoculars to a little girl waiting behind her and says to me, "I want to go home, Norman."

344

"I know," I tell her. "But we've come too far, now. And we're so close, Molly. Really close."

"Compared to what? Being in Charleston?"

Frustration scratches at me. "It drives me crazy for you to push me to come on this trip, and then, when we are almost there, tell me you want to go home!" I say. "I wanted to stay in Charleston, you'll remember. I could have had a gig!"

"You didn't have a band!"

"Thanks to you, I still don't!" I rub my forehead with my fingers. "I'm sorry," I say. "I'm tired. Let's go, okay? We've got to find a place to stop for the night."

As we walk back to the bus, Molly says, as if she's trying to be conciliatory, "How *are* we going to find Barry? Where do we even start?"

"Now you're asking the right questions!" I say. I whistle for Flam. "I told you Barry could take care of himself. I told you it would be hard to find him. I'm not even sure I want to find him."

Molly slows down. "Really?"

"I don't know, Molly. I . . . don't know. What's going on with you?"

She sighs. "I've been thinking about it," she says. "Barry wrote you, but he never wrote me. I didn't know if he was alive or dead for a year, and you did, and, yeah, I know why you didn't tell me, but that doesn't make it right. And it's not right, what Barry did, leaving us, leaving me, not letting me know he was okay."

I think about how to answer this. How much to say. "Maybe he was protecting you," I reason.

"From what?"

I see Flam waiting for us at the bus door. "I don't know, Molly," I say. But maybe I do. I run my hands over my face. I haven't shaved in ten days. I hardly shave anyway, but I can feel the scratchiness of my whiskers. I looked in the bathroom mirror at the Troubadour and saw raccoon circles under my eyes. I'm turning into an old man on this trip. I feel ancient.

A bunch of kids runs from the observatory across the grass

345

and onto a large waiting bus that says CHARTER on the signboard. And under that, a handwritten sign: *Young Engineer's School.*

Flam laps water from a bowl, while we watch the kids board the bus.

"Enter the young," says Molly.

"What?"

"Nothing," she says. "I'm tired, too."

"Hello, Molly. Hello, Norman."

I blink and there stands a kid with a crew cut and black-framed glasses.

"Drew!" says Molly. "Norman, it's Drew!"

"You are correct," says Drew. "I am surprised to see you here."

"*You're* surprised!" says Molly. "Norman! It's Drew!"

I start to laugh. It's so good to see someone we know. "What are you doing here?" I ask Drew. "I thought you were going to some air force base."

"I am going to Vandenberg Air Force Base tomorrow," says Drew. "But tonight we are at the Griffith Observatory in Los Angeles."

"So I see!"

"I thought you were going to San Francisco," says Drew.

"We are," says Norman. "We are on the way."

"The Apollo astronauts trained here," said Drew. "They learned how to identify the thirty-seven navigational stars that their guidance computer uses. This is in case of equipment failure. Inside the observatory, there is a Zeiss refracting telescope in the east dome, so you can see the stars."

Molly looks like she wants to hug Drew, she is so delighted to see him, but she settles for "Good for you, Drew."

Drew pushes his glasses up on his nose and asks me, "Are you still called Florsheim?"

"How did you know about that?"

"Kyle told me. He said you are a good drummer."

"Drew! Hop to!" shouts a man in shorts, a baseball cap, and a jacket.

Drew waves at the man and says, "I have to stay with my group."

"Right," I tell him. "See ya, Drew."

Drew says, "My sister Jo Ellen is an attorney-at-law in San Francisco. If you need legal services, she is someone to call. Jo Ellen Chapman. Just in case."

"Thank you, Drew," I say.

"You're welcome," Drew replies. "What happened to your bus?"

"Oh. It got painted," says Molly, almost jovially. She is suddenly so happy.

"You have a dog," says Drew.

"This is Flam," I tell him. Flam looks at Drew with shiny dog eyes but doesn't move.

"Drew!" The man in the jacket starts to walk toward us.

"I have to stay with my group," Drew repeats.

"Are you spending the night here?" asks Molly in a hopeful voice.

What a good idea to ask about a place to stay. I should have thought of that.

"There is a campground in the park," says Drew. "We have reserved spots. I do not think it is against the rules for you to follow us there."

So we do. They give us a parking space. We climb into our sleeping bags. And finally, *finally*, we sleep.

GOIN' UP TO THE

THE VAST LONELINESS
IS AWE-INSPIRING
AND IT MAKES YOU
REALIZE JUST WHAT
YOU HAVE BACK
THERE ON EARTH.

Apollo 8 Command Module Pilot Jim Lovell

SPIRIT IN THE SKY

From "Spirit in the Sky" by Norman Greenbaum

"Earthrise." Apollo 8, the first manned mission to the moon, entered lunar orbit on December 24, 1968. That evening, the astronauts — Commander Frank Borman, Command Module Pilot Jim Lovell, and Lunar Module Pilot William Anders — held a live broadcast from lunar orbit, in which they showed pictures of Earth and the moon as seen from their spacecraft, and read Bible passages from Genesis.

The deck edge operator on the USS *Intrepid* receives the signal to "tension" an A-4 Skyhawk attack plane on the starboard catapult during flight operations in the Gulf of Tonkin in September 1968.

A Douglas A-4F Skyhawk attack plane is brought to the launching position on a steam catapult aboard the USS *Intrepid*.

Flying low over the jungle, an A-1 Skyraider drops five-hundred-pound bombs on a Vietcong position below as smoke rises from a previous pass at the target, on December 26, 1964.

POLICE SEIZE PARK; SHOOT AT LEAST 35

MARCH TRIGGERS AVE. GASSING; BYSTANDERS, STUDENTS WOUNDED; EMERGENCY, CURFEW ENFORCED

Students at the University of California, Berkeley, looking for a place to rally that was not as controlled by campus authorities as Sproul Plaza, took over a derelict plot of land owned by the college on the outskirts of campus, and called it People's Park. Residents and businesses in Berkeley donated funds and materials to make the park a reality and open to all, but the university soon announced plans to reclaim the park, at which students protested.

On May 15, 1969, Governor Ronald Reagan, who called UC Berkeley "a haven for communist sympathizers," sent the National Guard to campus, where their helicopters sprayed tear gas on students and soldiers came in with shotguns, bayonets, and full riot gear. The protests spilled into the streets of Berkeley, with soldiers firing tear gas canisters and buckshot into the crowd.

One student was killed, one was permanently blinded, and over 150 were wounded. Dozens were arrested. A state of emergency was declared in Berkeley and the unrest went on for weeks.

A National Guard helicopter flies by the Campanile on the University of California, Berkeley campus, spraying tear gas on demonstrators in Sproul Plaza on May 20, 1969.

WHEN SOMETHING DIES IS THE GREATEST TEACHING.

Shunryu Suzuki, founder of the San Francisco Zen Center, from his book *Zen Mind, Beginner's Mind: Informal Talks on Zen Meditation and Practice*

Flag-draped coffins of some of the American servicemen who were killed in attacks on U.S. military installations in South Vietnam on February 7, 1965, are placed in a transport plane at Saigon, February 9, 1965, for return flight to the United States. Funeral services wereheld at the Saigon airport with U.S. Ambassador Maxwell D. Taylor and Vietnamese officials attending.

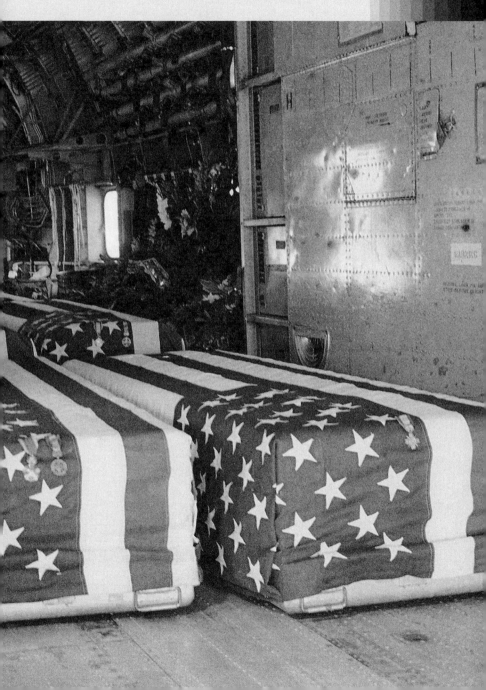

Protesters marching as part of an Asian Americans for Peace rally
in Little Tokyo, Los Angeles, California, January 17, 1970.

ALL ALONG THE WATCHTOWER

Written by Bob Dylan
Performed by Bob Dylan
Recorded at Columbia Studios, Nashville, Tennessee, 1967
Drummer: Kenny Buttrey

Performed by the Jimi Hendrix Experience
Recorded at Olympic Studio, London, England, and
Record Plant, New York, New York, 1968
Drummer: Mitch Mitchell

They traveled all day Tuesday until Norman could drive no more. "My arms and legs are rubber. I need to get off this bus."

They had chosen the coast road for part of the journey, as the new Interstate 5 route to San Francisco was not complete. Furthermore, Molly told Norman, she'd slept on it and had decided she was done worrying about Barry if he couldn't worry about her, so he could just go do whatever he wanted to do, and yes, she would go to San Francisco if Norman insisted, but she would not wring her hands and cry over Barry.

"Right" was Norman's comment. Molly, the emotion machine. He didn't have the luxury of all those feelings.

"You don't believe me," Molly said. "Watch and see. I'm going to wear flowers in my hair, because that's what normal people do when they go to San Francisco."

361

"You can't fit flowers in your hair," said Norman. "Your hair's like a helmet."

"Sez you!" Molly pulled the rubber band out of her hair and let it fly around her face. Norman watched her in the student mirror over the driver's seat and wondered how long she could keep it up.

They stopped for gas, for groceries, and again for supper. In searching for a campground, they stumbled on a freshly painted sign: THE COTTAGES AT AVILA BEACH.

"I want real beds for a night," said Norman. "Want to try this?"

"Yes!" Molly said immediately. Windblown and weary, Molly was more than ready for a bed. She had stoically let her hair fly around her so wildly it looked like a bird's nest. The bus bumped down the sandy lane to a bungalow with a sign out front: OFFICE.

"Great bus!" a sandy-bearded, barefoot man in overalls, no shirt, and a porkpie hat greeted them. He sat on the porch next to a record player that blasted a Jefferson Airplane album, playing it to the empty beach. "I know they've got newer albums out," he told Norman, "but *Surrealistic Pillow* is my favorite. Where you headed?"

"San Francisco," said Norman.

"From South Carolina," said the man, looking at Multitudes' license plate. He shook Norman's hand and introduced himself as Eddie. "Long way from home," he observed.

"Yessir."

"Eddie is fine. Hey, doggie."

"That's Flam," said Norman.

"Good dog."

"Embryonic Journey" began to play on the record player.

"Man, I love this tune," said Eddie. "Listened to it over and over again in the South China Sea. Wish I could play guitar like that. This guy — Jorma Kaukonen — he's a virtuoso."

"I know this one!" said Molly. "My brother played it for me. He's a guitar player."

"Yeah?" said Eddie. "He's got good taste."

Despite her previous declaration, Molly suddenly found herself warming to the idea of finding her brother in San Francisco ... maybe, she told herself, because they were now so close. Maybe because the music soothed her bruised feelings. She shook the thought from her head. She was angry with her brother. That's right.

"His name is Barry," she continued. "We're looking for him in San Francisco. Against my will." She gave Norman a *See! I meant what I said! I want to go home!* look.

"Molly," said Norman. He braced himself for anything.

"Really!" said Eddie, ignoring the look between Molly and Norman. "Is he lost?"

"Who knows?" said Molly. "He doesn't say."

Norman groaned.

Molly felt emboldened now and asked Eddie, "Why were you in the South China Sea?"

"I was on an aircraft carrier, the USS *Intrepid*. I didn't see land for nine months. The army couldn't do what they do in Vietnam without navy pilots and their aircraft crews to keep them flying," said Eddie. There was pride in his voice.

Molly's resolve to not care about Barry's future once again wavered. It was like riding a seesaw. She took a seat on a wooden chair. *Get it together, Molly*, she told herself.

"Vietnam?" asked Norman. He sat on the chair next to Molly. He had his own seesaw to consider.

Eddie took Norman's question as an invitation. He lifted the needle from the record and settled into a porch rocker. He stroked his beard with forefinger and thumb as he talked.

"I was a plane handler. Me, Eddie Mullin, aviation machinist mate, hydraulics, sixth-class. I went to boot camp at NAS Atlanta, to aircraft carrier school at NAS Pensacola, and to hydraulics school at NAS Memphis. Then they shipped me out to the South China Sea through NAS San Diego."

363

"Naval air station," said Norman. "We've got one in Charleston, too."

"That's right."

"And an air force base," said Molly. "So you didn't have to fight in the jungles?"

"It's a different fight," said Eddie. "You work seventeen hours a day, seven days a week. Your job is to keep those fighters flying. You live with over two thousand people on your ship, and sleep in bunks stacked six high. You take care of your aircraft so the pilots can complete their missions successfully. You hope they return. You live in a twilight zone in the middle of nowhere, and eat a lot of powdered hamburger."

"How did you get there?" asked Norman.

"They take you there! Let me tell you, it's a weird feeling when you're on an airplane and you're surrounded by only sea to the horizon everywhere you look, and then, suddenly, you see this *speck* down below, and that's where you're supposed to land. You start dropping like a rock. And when your plane hits that deck, you *feel* like a rock. You hope the handler is gonna grab the arresting wire on the first try and you're not going to end up in the ocean!"

"Wow!" said Norman, clearly impressed.

Molly felt herself changing her mind about San Francisco. She pulled her rubber band off her wrist and began to gather back her hair.

"It was the biggest experience of my life," said Eddie. "A nineteen-year-old kid joining the navy to see the world." He laughed.

"You're nineteen?" asked Molly. He looked so much older.

"I'm twenty-three now," said Eddie. "I flunked out of college my first semester — I didn't want to go to college anyway — and enlisted in the navy because I knew the draft, which is always the army, would come for me. And, sure enough, they did. I got my notice to report for my army physical when I was two weeks into navy boot camp. But I was already spoken for. That's how disorganized the army is."

Norman pulled at his earlobe as he listened.

Eddie placed the needle back on the record, at the beginning of "Embryonic Journey." "I sure do like this tune. There's just something about music that connects us to something larger than ourselves. Very Buddha-nature."

"What's . . . Buddha-nature?" asked Molly.

Eddie stroked his beard, smiled at Molly, and said, "It's a luminous expression of awareness."

"Oh," said Molly. "I see." She didn't. She petted Flam, who shoved his nose under her hand, and she said, "My brother has been ordered to report for a physical in Charleston."

Eddie breathed out through puffed lips. "And you're the rescue posse."

"Sort of," said Norman. He wasn't sure what they were anymore.

"Well, Uncle Sam's got him now . . ." said Eddie.

They fell silent. Then Eddie slapped at his overalls, turned off the record player, and said, "Did you stop for conversation, or would you like to take a load off and rent a cottage overnight? Want to be our first guests?"

"Yessir!" said Norman. He felt like saluting, which made him feel ridiculous.

"Yes, please!" said Molly. The sounds of the sea had been calling to her since the moment they'd rolled up to the cottages. She couldn't wait to walk barefoot on sand, stand at the edge of the earth, and let the salt water cover her feet. She took the rubber band out of her hair once again. She wouldn't think about Barry one more minute.

Eddie opened the bungalow screen door and waved them inside. He handed Norman the key to cottage number four

365

just as a clean-shaven, bare-breasted man in bell-bottom jeans appeared with a plate of brownies.

"This is Flo," said Eddie. "We're trying this experiment, now that I'm back from Nam and had a little inheritance drop into my lap. We're gonna live on the beach for the rest of our lives."

"Really!" said Norman.

"Have a brownie," said Flo. "Take a load off." He smiled, which made hundreds of freckles spread across his pale face in a grin. "Sweet puppy!"

Suddenly, magically, they had real beds to sleep in, a real shower, a real room of their own with real towels. And a real beach.

They hauled their suitcases into the small cabin. Molly dumped dog food into a bowl for Flam and he happily began to crunch. Norman sat on the edge of his bed and stared at the floor.

"You okay?" Molly asked automatically.

"I'm okay. You?" he answered. But he wasn't. He put his elbows on his knees and his head in his hands. A bleak silence filled the room.

"Norman?"

Flam finished his supper and trotted to Norman. Norman ignored him. The sound of the surf rolled through their open windows.

"We're almost there, Norman." He was not okay. The old anxiety crept into Molly's heart, all the sadness in the world. "Just one more night, Norman," she added gently.

He lifted his head and sighed heavily. "This is an impossible trip," he said. "We should have gone home in Los Angeles. I should have listened to you."

She dearly wanted to say, *I know. I'm always right.* Instead, she shifted her thinking about Barry once more. "It's a good idea to keep going," she told Norman, "and to find him."

When Norman didn't respond, Molly continued. "Maybe he can join the navy. We might find him tomorrow, and he could go to the navy recruiter's office and the army would never know, and by the time his physical date rolls around, he'd already be at boot camp. He wouldn't have to fight in the jungle, he wouldn't have to die, he wouldn't have to end up like Victor."

Norman put his head back in his hands.

"My dad would be so happy, too," added Molly. "It would fix things for our family. We should go to San Francisco. We should find Barry. And you know what, Norman?" She was sure now what they needed to do. "We should do what Mom wants. We should bring him home."

Norman began to cry. Molly reached out a hand, pulled it back, reached it out again, but Norman flinched when she touched him. So she let him cry. She sat in a chair near the door and watched him for a long time. Her heart twisted in on itself. She didn't know what to do next.

Finally, Norman lifted his head and said quietly, "I thought you didn't care what Barry did." He sniffed and wiped his face. "I don't understand you, Molly. Make up your mind!"

Molly wrapped her arms around herself and stared at her cousin.

"We don't know where he is," Norman continued. "We have eight days to find him and get him home. That's impossible. The whole thing was impossible from the beginning. We have no idea what to do next. We really don't. I am no hero. And guess what. Neither is Barry! You think it will fix things to bring him home?"

Molly's mind began to race. She looked around their room. They were so far from home. The surf crashed onto the sand. Seagulls called beyond their door. The most important thing to do right now, she decided, the only thing she knew to do, was to answer them. So she set her jaw.

"I'm going swimming," she announced.

Norman lifted his eyes to his cousin's. "Now?"

"Now. Let's go. You know how the ocean works, Norman, you've been around it all your life! You put on your suit and you run in. C'mon, I'll race you!"

She tugged him off the bed and he unfolded himself, hesitant and yet compliant. She opened his suitcase, threw his Boy Scout shirt on the bed with a laugh, and tossed him his suit. She ran into the bathroom with hers. "Go!"

For a little while, they were kids again. They raced each other to the water, Flam at their heels, barking. The beach was a half-moon of toasted sand hugging San Luis Obispo Bay. It horseshoed to a pier and ended with the San Luis Lighthouse at the point. It curved around them like an embrace.

The tide was coming in and they had the place to themselves. Tiny plovers scooted along the wet sand near the water's edge, making footprints that the surf washed away. Flam would not go into the water. He ran back and forth on the beach and chased the seabirds.

Molly and Norman screamed into the sky as they hit the surf and dove under the salt water. They washed away the past ten days of unbelievable life and tried to find their former selves. They twisted and turned somersaults and came up gasping for air, waves slapping them in the face. It was glorious.

When they had yelled their throats raw, they left the water and walked to their cabin. The tide line was thick with sand dollars and shells, a feather, strings of kelp, and pocks of tiny holes where the sand crabs fished and burrowed into the wave wash. All of this life was sprayed artfully across the wet sand like a tiny galaxy. "Look," said Molly, pointing to it. "A Milky Way."

"It's a big world," said Norman.

"It's an infinite universe," said Molly. "Or that's what my science teacher said. You think men will really walk on the moon?"

"If Drew has anything to say about it, they will," said Norman.

Blue butterflies danced around white blossoms in the buckwheat plants by their cabin. The sunset would soon be gone and the purple night sky begun. The Point San Luis Light blinked *safe here, safe here, safe here.*

"You never see this in Charleston," said Molly with a sigh. "The sun rises on the water there."

Norman stopped beside Multitudes' door and tapped his prize bell softly. "We've been from sea to shining sea," he said. He looked at Molly in a kind of astonishment.

Molly thought about how to answer her cousin and settled on one word.

"Groovy."

Norman laughed and then a sob heaved out of his chest. Just one.

"Norman?"

He waved her away. "I'm okay." He sniffed and wiped at his nose with his salty arm. "I'm fine." He was. He would drive to San Francisco. And then? Then he would drive home.

They got showers with plenty of hot water and lathery soap and scented shampoo and clean towels and plunged into their beds, onto cool crisp sheets. Norman fell asleep mid-sentence, trying to tell Molly about the first time he picked up a pair of drumsticks.

Molly was already dreaming.

I-FEEL-LIKE-I'M-FIXIN'-TO-DIE RAG

Written by Joe McDonald
Performed by Country Joe and the Fish
Recorded at Vanguard Studios, New York, New York, 1967
Drummer: Gary "Chicken" Hirsh

The next morning, Molly showed up at Flo and Eddie's wearing the skirt Lucy had given her.

"Girl!" said Flo. "Let me see!"

Molly twirled and Flo insisted on making them all breakfast. Eggs, sausage, toast, and the coffee they had learned to drink on the road. Eddie squeezed oranges. "From our little grove out back," he said.

Norman thought of Victor. *Orange groves. I see orange when I dream. Clouds of orange fire. Then black.* "You don't have to make us breakfast," he said.

"I'm a very good cook," said Flo, spatula in hand, apron looped over his head and across his shirtless chest.

"Thank you, doll," said Eddie.

Flo gave Flam some eggs. "You should leave this puppy with me," he said. "He loves me!"

"He loves me, too," said Norman.

Molly wasn't sure Flam loved anybody, really. He was a largely expressionless dog who—in her opinion — lacked any discernable personality. No wonder he'd been abandoned in New Mexico.

Flam wagged his tail and ate enthusiastically, and Molly felt bad for thinking such mean thoughts about him. He loved food. That's what Flam loved. She could live with that.

After breakfast, they all walked over to Multitudes for a tour. Flo surveyed the bus with a critical eye. "I think you could use some housekeeping in this traveling caravan. What have you got for curtains?"

"Flo is a Renaissance man," said Eddie.

Within minutes, Flo was back at the bus carrying wooden dowels, hooks, a drill, and an armful of green fabric. He had exchanged his apron for a tool belt. He was still shirtless. He climbed on board Multitudes and began to eyeball the windows.

"What are you doing?" Molly stood with the broom at the open back door of the bus and watched Flo shake out his fabric. He pulled a measuring tape out of his tool belt. "Honey, you just need a little curtain for the blasting heat, for privacy, and for hominess. You can pull this fabric over the curtain rod at night and put it away in the morning if you want."

"Is that a parachute?"

"Forgot my scissors," said Flo. He jumped out the back door of Multitudes onto the sandy ground and looked back at Molly. "Yes. You don't think I wasn't in Vietnam, too? Sergeant First Class Florian Finelli, at your service, Sky Soldier with the One Hundred Seventy-Third Airborne Brigade, Operation Junction City 1967, the only combat airborne mission of the war so far, and proud of it."

"You are?"

"Of course I am. I lost a lot of buddies over there. You don't think I'm going to say their courage wasn't worth it, do you?"

"What?" Norman asked as he and Flam joined them. Flo repeated himself. "Our objective was to destroy the Viet Cong's

371

headquarters on the border of Cambodia in Vietnam. We used canopies to drop heavy equipment — jeeps, trucks, howitzers, supplies. And men. Eight hundred forty-five of us flew under the silks that day, in two twenty-six-second drop zones — that's all the time we had.

"Let me tell you, you stand in the doorway of a C-130 aircraft fifteen hundred feet in the air and leap into the turbulence of the propeller wash at one hundred and thirty knots — your heart flies right out of your body. You have to jump out the door so you can catch it."

The pride in Flo's voice touched Molly in a patriotic way. "That's amazing," she said. Norman agreed.

"I always wanted to be a paratrooper," said Flo. "Broke my leg when I was twelve, jumping off our barn roof with an umbrella so I could fly."

Eddie appeared with a bucket of paint. "Flo's a hero," he said. "Got the bronze star."

Flo waved off Eddie's praise. "I liked the uniforms. You shoulda seen me. Sharp." Flo winked and Molly laughed.

Then she remembered: "I need to make a phone call," she said. "We forgot last night."

"Go ahead, doll," said Flo. "I'll fix you up in here."

"I'll start loading," said Norman.

"I'll be right back to help," Molly told him.

"Thank goodness!" said Janice once Molly got through. "Where are you?"

"Two hundred miles from San Francisco," said Molly. "Almost there."

"I have an address for you," said Janice. Her voice shook. Molly heard Aunt Pam in the background, saying, "Let me talk to her!"

Molly's breakfast bunched in her stomach. "What? Norman! Wait, Mom, I need a pencil and paper. What happened?"

"Barry sent another letter. Aunt Pam has it. It has a return address embossed on it. Here she is."

"Let me find some paper!"

After some frantic jostling on both ends of the phone, Aunt Pam spoke. "Molly, is Norman there?" She did not sound positive.

"Yes, ma'am. But he's outside loading the bus."

"Then I'll tell you," said Aunt Pam. "Got a pencil?"

"I'm ready."

Aunt Pam read off the return address. Molly stared at it.

"I don't understand," she said. "What is this?"

"It's just what it looks like, Molly," said Aunt Pam. "Barry is in jail."

Norman banged through the screen door. "What?"

Molly held out the phone. She opened her mouth, but no words came out.

"Mom?"

"I'm sorry for opening the letter, Norman. You know I value your privacy, but when we saw where it was from . . . the mailman just delivered it, minutes ago . . ."

A letter. "It's okay, Mom. Please, just read it."

Pam cleared her throat.

Norm —

They won't let me make a long-distance phone call. I only get one piece of paper, one stamp, and one envelope. I hope you pick this up before your mom sees it. I got arrested, bro, on a trumped-up charge. It's brutal out here. Do you still have the money you were saving for that new drum set? If you can get me some bail money, send it to the address on the envelope. I wrote the inmate number on it. I gotta get outta this place, man!

Barry

373

Norman forced himself to have no reaction. "What's the post-mark date, Mom?"

"Three days ago," Pam said. "It came airmail. Just now."

"We're on the way," said Norman. "We're a few hours out, but we don't have a lot of money left."

"We called the jail," said Pam. "The bail is one hundred fifty dollars. We don't have it right now, but we're working on it. Janice is going to have to tell Mitch. Maybe he can fly out there."

Norman rubbed two fingers up and down his forehead. What a disaster. "We can be there this afternoon," he said to his mother. "Nobody needs to come until we know more, okay? I'll call you as soon as I can."

"Thanks, sweetie," said Pam. "We'll hold tight and wait to hear from you. Call soon. Are you okay?"

"I'm fine. We're both fine."

He hung up the phone and looked at Molly.

"We're not fine," Molly said.

"I know."

Molly stalked back to the bus just as Eddie was finishing painting his name by a symbol near the door. She hadn't known what it was until Eddie explained it yesterday while admiring Multitudes. "It looks like a fancy number thirty," she'd told him. "It's an Om," he'd replied. "It's a sacred spiritual incantation. You say it like this: Aum." Molly had heard it in the Aspen Meadow.

"It creates a feeling of oneness, of connectedness, of peacefulness," Eddie had said.

Molly shook her head. There would be no peace today.

Flo finished tacking a curtain rod above the windows of Multitudes.

"We've got to go," Molly said. She told them both about Barry's letter.

"Whoa," said Eddie.

"What are the charges?" asked Flo.

"I don't know," said Molly.

"What's the bail?"

"One hundred fifty dollars."

Flo whistled. "It must be murder." Molly looked stricken. "I'm kidding, doll," said Flo. "Kidding."

Molly watched Norman stride toward them from the office. Eddie and Flo exchanged a long look as Norman said, "We've got to go."

"Do you want us to go with you?" asked Eddie.

"Yes," said Norman. Emphatically.

"Really?" said Molly.

"Strength in numbers," said Eddie.

"We need an adult," said Norman. "We're not even eighteen and we're dealing with the police now."

Flo looked at Molly. "You need all the help you can get right now, Miss Molly. War is hell, honey."

DARK STAR

Written by Robert Hunter and Jerry Garcia
Performed by the Grateful Dead
Recorded Live at Fillmore West, San Francisco,
California, 1969
Drummer: Mickey Hart

Eddie wore a shirt under his overalls. Flo put on a shirt and shoes. Norman drove, Molly sat in the navigator's seat, Flam rode in the famous front passenger seat, and four hours later they were all at the San Francisco city jail.

"It's high noon," said Flo, looking at his watch. "In more ways than one."

"Button your shirt," said Eddie.

Barry's jailers would not let them see him. "Come back at visiting hours! Can't you read?"

"We need a lawyer," said Eddie.

"We've got one," said Molly. "Where's a phone booth?"

She used the phone book to look up the name Drew had given them: Jo Ellen Chapman. The phone was answered on the first ring.

"Hello?"

"Oh! Hello. Jo Ellen Chapman?"

"Yes. Who's calling?" The voice was not unfriendly.

"My name is Molly. I'm a friend of your brother's. Drew."

Jo Ellen was concerned. "Is everything all right?"

"With Drew, yes. With us, no."

Molly described their dilemma while Jo Ellen listened.

"I just happened to stop home to pick up some files," she said. "Can you come to my office? I'm in the Castro. Do you have a pencil for the address?"

They were sitting in the waiting room when Jo Ellen returned. She ushered them into a small office, barely big enough for the five of them. Stacks of file folders lined the desk and more stacks on the floor threatened to topple over.

"I'm new here," she said. "This is my first job out of law school. I'm not sure I can help you. We do civil rights litigation, mostly violations of the First, Fourth, Eighth, and Fourteenth Amendments."

"They've all been violated," said Flo.

"Excuse me, who are you?"

"We're the veterans. Moral support," said Flo.

"We're the adults," said Eddie.

Jo Ellen raised an eyebrow and continued, speaking directly to Molly. "I called the jail. Your brother is being held on charges of trespassing, unlawful assembly, failure to disperse, disturbing the peace, and resisting arrest. He evidently was part of a demonstration in the Haight."

"An antiwar demonstration?"

"No, just a demonstration. I think more of a disturbance. Another man attached to this case says he might press charges, says he was assaulted."

Assaulted. The word hit Molly so hard she leaned against the desk. It catapulted her back to her living room a year ago and the argument, her dad coming for Barry, Barry stumbling backward, Barry walking out. Gentle Barry.

"That can't be right," Molly said.

Norman bit his bottom lip.

Jo Ellen curled a sheet of yellow paper behind its pad and picked up a pen. "Let me get some details from you. My boss, Cassandra Harris, is in court right now, but she'll be back and then I'll know more about what we can do. Do you have bail?"

"No," said Norman. "But I can get it."

"You'll need it if the judge decides not to dismiss the case."

"I'll get it," Norman repeated.

Cassandra came in as Jo Ellen was gathering information. "We've got a full plate right now, with our People's Park defendants," she said after Jo Ellen filled her in. "We really can't wedge in one more case."

Molly suddenly had a tight ball full of tears in her throat. She gargled her feelings. "You have to! We've come so far! We're from Charleston, South Carolina! We drove all the way across the country to get him! And there is no way he did . . . what they say he did."

Jo Ellen looked at Cassandra. Cassandra looked at the posters on Jo Ellen's wall.

ONE MAN, ONE VOTE

The Women of Vietnam Are Our Sisters!

War is not healthy for children and other living things

LOVE IS ALL YOU NEED

Cassandra sighed, removed her suit jacket, and hung it on a hanger behind Jo Ellen's door. Her skin was deep brown. She wore her hair natural, in waves of pin curls, and she had a watch on one wrist, a silver bracelet on the other. "We can probably get this dismissed if the other man doesn't press assault charges," she said. "Jo Ellen, you'll talk to him. Find out what happened, see if it is assault, and see what he wants to do."

"Got it," said Jo Ellen as she made a note. "Right away."

"How much is bail?" Cassandra asked. Jo Ellen told her and Cassandra whistled. "Have you got it?" she asked Norman.

"I'll get it," he answered. He needed to think. Aunt Janice wouldn't have that kind of money. Neither would Pam.

Cassandra continued. "I know the prosecutor. He hates these . . . disturbances . . . and so does the judge. The judge hikes up bail until the defendants want to go home so badly they'll promise to leave town as a condition of dropped charges. But there's always a fine to pay. Let me make a call. What do you want as your outcome?"

"We want him to come home to South Carolina with us," said Molly, tears at the edges of her eyes. "He's been ordered to report for a physical exam."

"You mean he's been drafted," said Cassandra.

"Pretty much," said Eddie. He stroked his beard in thought. His golden hair stuck out around his porkpie hat and his shirt was faded under his overalls.

"Who are you?"

"I'm —"

"We're not twenty-one," said Norman. "Neither is Barry. I thought we needed an adult."

"Good thinking," said Cassandra. She pointed at Flo with his clean-shaven freckled face. "You stand in as a brother if we need you in court."

Flo straightened up. "Well, I *am* the eldest," he said. "Twenty-four next week."

"Happy birthday to you," said Cassandra, with more than a hint of sarcasm in her voice.

"Thank you very much," said Flo sarcastically back.

"Get the bail money," said Cassandra. "If we can't get into court today, you'll at least be able to get him out of jail. You'll need money for the fine and court costs, and money to pay us as well — whatever you've got. We need to keep the lights on."

"Yes, ma'am," said Norman.

Cassandra pointed a finger with a polished nail at Flo. "Jo Ellen, get him a tie."

"Right away," said Jo Ellen. "I'll walk them out."

"Thanks a lot," said Norman as they were ushered out of the cramped office.

"Where can we reach you?" asked Jo Ellen.

"We'll be at the Zen Center," said Eddie.

Molly blinked. "We will?"

"Page and Laguna Streets."

"I know it," said Cassandra. She gave Eddie an appraising look. "Good."

Jo Ellen walked them to the door. "So you're from Charleston."

"That's right," said Norman.

"My dad's a pilot and is stationed at the air force base in Charleston. My family is moving there this summer."

"Really!" said Molly. "Drew will be in Charleston?"

"That's right," said Jo Ellen with a smile. "He's a trip, isn't he?"

"He really is."

"My sister, Franny, calls him Saint Drew." Jo Ellen looked at Norman and said, "She's graduating high school next year. Maybe you'll be in the same school, Norman."

Norman colored at the mention of another girl for him to think about.

Flo had been unusually quiet since being picked to represent the family in court. Now he spoke up as they trooped down the stairs and spilled onto the street, where Flam waited for them. "Could we get something to eat before we go visit the monks?"

"Why are we visiting the monks?" asked Molly.

"Eddie spent a lot of time with them when he got back from Nam," said Flo.

"I wanted quiet," said Eddie. "Nine months on an aircraft carrier with constant noise — you'd want quiet, too."

"It's nice there," said Flo. "They know us. They'll come get us when the phone call comes in."

43

EVIL WAYS

Written by Clarence "Sonny" Henry
Performed by Santana
Recorded at Pacific Recording Studios,
San Mateo, California, 1969
Drummer: Mike Shrieve

NORMAN

I drop them off at the Zen Center, and they take Flam with them.

"Come on, puppy!" calls Flo.

"You can't keep him," I tell him.

"What's a zen center?" asks Molly.

"We'll show you," says Eddie. "The sun may be hidden by clouds, but it is always there."

Molly gives me her *help me!* look.

"I'll call home," I tell her. "I'll take care of the money." Then I turn the corner and drive up Haight Street. Within a few blocks, Multitudes is getting stares from the hippies that are everywhere, hanging on street corners, sitting on the sidewalks with their backs against buildings and smoking, wearing love beads and sandals and headbands and blousy tops and bell-bottoms like Flo's. The place is thick with the smell of them.

They don't look like the Atlanta hippies. Those hippies now seem like a bunch of kids playacting. These Haight hippies don't look like the hippies at New Buffalo, either. Those kids worked all the time. Their hands were callused and their muscles were sore. These are leisure hippies watching me drive by. The world is falling apart around us and they look unaffected by anything. I stop at the light at Ashbury and we stare at one another.

It's the middle of the day on a Wednesday and they have nothing to do. I envy them. I could be practicing with my band for my Shakey's gig. I could be working — it could even be at Biff Burger — and earning money for more equipment, or records, or bus parts. I could be writing my cadences for band, or tinkering on the bus in the backyard. My friend Max would come over after supper and I'd say, "Come look! I put in the radio!" I'd crank up the sound and we'd sit there with Cream's "Sunshine of Your Love" blasting the backyard crickets into silence.

Instead, I'm looking for a pawn shop. Turns out, they're easy to find.

"What can I do you for?" asks the owner, whose name is Wilson. His shop windows are plastered with concert posters for all the bands playing in town.

A half hour later, I no longer own a drum set. Barry no longer owns a guitar. I've pawned it all. The drums, the guitar, the amps, the 6,435 extension cords, all of it. Barry's Stratocaster brought the most money. "Sweet!" said Wilson as I handed it across the counter and he took it in his hands.

What I pocketed should be enough to pay Barry's bail, the court costs, a fine, and get us home. Maybe. Who knows? I don't know what these things cost. Wilson offered to buy Multitudes, too. "You could buy plane tickets home for everybody!" But I said no. I'm not going to part with my bus.

I call Pam, who has the gift of being serious, positive, and smart at the same time. I tell her the charges and she sucks in her breath. They haven't told Uncle Mitch yet. After years of being Barry's sidekick, I am suddenly the one in charge.

"We might be able to get into court this afternoon," I tell Pam. "Hold tight. I'll let you know as soon as I know more. Tell Aunt Janice not to worry. We've got a good lawyer, and we've got some reliable adults with us. And," I say, finally, "we've got the money."

There is a short silence on the other end of the phone, then Pam says quietly, "You sold your drums."

"It's okay, Mom."

"Mom," she repeats.

"Yeah," I say.

The operator comes on the line and asks for more money to continue the long-distance call. "I'll call again soon!" I say and Pam calls out, "Be careful!" and we are disconnected.

I stare at the graffiti in the phone booth. *It's only stuff*, I tell myself about my drums, but I miss them. One day I will have drums again, I tell myself, and I know this is true. But right now, I know we don't have money lying around. I know Lewis is spending it all on the floozie. I know Aunt Janice will have to ask Uncle Mitch for the money, and I know if he comes to San Francisco, it will only be worse for Barry, which means it will be worse for all of us. Because it has always been like this. *Why?* I ask myself. *Why?*

Barry's letter sticks in my craw like a swallowed chicken bone I can't dislodge. I might choke on it. His tone is so *cavalier*, just like he always is. He expects me to say *How high?* every time he says *Jump*. All my life, I looked up to Barry. I wanted to be like him. I would do — and did — anything for him.

But when I wanted him to help me recruit members for my band, he was too busy. When I wanted him to put together a band and put me in it, he forgot about his promise and said he wasn't interested in a band. When he wanted me to keep quiet about his whereabouts, or even the fact that he was alive, I did it. Molly is right: I should have told her. I helped break her heart by not telling her he was safe. Barry left her without a good-bye. Because that's what Barry does. He does as he pleases. Has, all his life. Why do we let him get away with that?

Because he gives us all just enough back to keep fooling us. Because Barry has always been the best and the brightest kid in our family, the athlete, the leader, the future. The energy. Mr. Everything to Everybody. Bow down to Barry! He is the prince who was promised, like in the fairy tales, the one who will lead us mere mortal kids out of the darkness of childhood and into some kind of enlightened life.

I didn't realize he was trying to get away from us, but now it's clear to me. He wanted out. If it hadn't been Vietnam, it would have been something else that gave him a way. When the arguments started at family gatherings and Uncle Mitch got unreasonable and Lewis left us for the floozie and the bleakness began to gather, we all supported Barry, our king.

We championed him, like he might save us. We treated him better than we treated ourselves. We gave him the piece of cake with the most icing on it. We made up stories to cover for his absences without knowing where he'd been. We told ourselves he was going through phases. We made excuses for his behaviors. We gave him everything and let him take it.

Here, take more.

But something in me knew.

Barry can take care of himself. That's what I told Molly when she first came up with this harebrained idea to come get him. She knows it's true, too. We both know it, Aunt Janice knows it, Pam knows it, and yet we came, me and Molly, to take care of Barry.

And now we need money. For Barry. Because he got in a fight and he's in jail. All hands on deck for Barry. Well, I've got money now, and I'm here.

I make a purchase for myself. "Thanks, Wilson." Then I stride out the door and back onto my bus.

Let's get this over with.

MOLLY

There is a sign at the door: ALL ARE WELCOME. Another says MAY ALL BEINGS REALIZE THEIR TRUE NATURE. Eddie points to a large Om and smiles at me. He is happy to be here. His friends are happy to see him. They make tea for us. They smile.

We are in the courtyard waiting for the phone to ring somewhere. Silent monks in long robes and with clasped hands walk past us in a line, a fountain burbles, green plants sway. More tea is served. The smell of incense surrounds us. Somewhere a tiny bell rings once, softly. Everything about this place says *calm*.

But I am going crazy with worry. Eddie thinks he's comforting me when he says, "Sit quietly. Your don't-know mind will become clear. You may even get in touch with your Buddha-nature."

Flam sticks close to Flo, who pets him and asks me, "Do you want to go sit in the meditation room?"

I shake my head. I try to relax. I take my first deep breath in San Francisco when a quiet, smiling monk in a long robe comes to tell us we have a phone call.

44

DAZED AND CONFUSED

Written by Jake Holmes
Performed by Led Zeppelin
Recorded at Olympic Studios, London, England, 1968
Drummer: John Bonham

MOLLY

"All of you, say nothing," says Cassandra as we walk together through the echoing rotunda of City Hall to the courtroom. "The man who was threatening to press charges has declined to do so, I don't know why. I would have, but that's another story. As it stands, we may have a good chance for dismissal here. How long has it been since you've seen your brother?"

"Over a year," I say, stepping faster, trying to keep up with Cassandra's fast clip.

"Say nothing when you see him," says Cassandra. "This is a courtroom, not a family reunion picnic."

"Yes, ma'am."

"Where's Flam?" asks Norman.

"We left him at the Zen Center," I tell him.

Cassandra opens the door with one hand and removes Eddie's hat with the other. She takes a closer look at Flo as he passes

387

her into the courtroom. "Come here." She straightens his tie. Flo wears sandals, bell-bottoms, one of Norman's white oxford shirts, and a tie Jo Ellen gave him.

Eddie takes my hand and leads me to the row behind the defendant's table. I let him do it. He's a nice guy — I know it, and so does he. Norman sits next to Eddie and me, and Flo sits at the end of the row. So Eddie and Flo flank us, like sandwich bread.

"I'll be back." Cassandra disappears under a sign that says JUDGE'S CHAMBERS. She shuts a door.

My heart bangs against my rib cage. I have a hard time breathing. Now Norman takes my hand and squeezes it. I squeeze back. We wait an eternity. I wonder where Jo Ellen is. Where is Barry? Is he behind that door? Are all welcome *there*? I say nothing. I do as I'm told.

A policeman walks up the aisle, opens the small gate, walks across the courtroom and through the JUDGE'S CHAMBERS doorway. A man dressed in a three-piece suit does the same. He has a tall young man with him. Everyone disappears.

Soon a court reporter leaves the judge's chambers and sits in a box by the judge's bench. I've seen them do this on TV. She is followed by the policeman, the judge, and everyone who just trooped through the courtroom, and then — my brother.

Tears flood my eyes. There he is. Barry. He looks so much older. My heart!

Barry is your heart. That's why it's breaking.

NORMAN

When he finally walks into the room with Cassandra, he's strutting. Strutting! Smiling at no one — at his own good fortune, maybe — and strutting until he's in view of the judge, who is sitting higher than we are and looking out at us. We are the only other people in the courtroom, but Barry doesn't even look at us. He doesn't come to the defendant's table. He stands in front of the judge and next to Cassandra.

It goes quickly. Gavel down, a repeat of what was decided in chambers, dropping all charges, an agreement on damages from Barry's attorney Cassandra, an okay from the district attorney. Then a promise from Barry to pay specified damages, court costs, and a fine. Then a question from the judge to Cassandra. "Who can vouch for this man, counselor?"

Cassandra walks briskly to where we are all seated and pulls Flo to his feet, almost drags him through the small gate, and shoves him in front of the judge. Barry still does not look at us.

"I vouch for my brother," says Flo. "He is a lost soul. We have come to take him home." He puts his heart into it. He sounds like he's auditioning for a play. Barry stares at Flo but says nothing.

"Is this your wish, young man?" the judge asks Barry.

"Yessir," says Barry, as if he's known Flo all his life.

"How far away is home?" asks the judge.

"Very far," says Flo in a Julius Caesar voice. "Across the continent."

Cassandra clears her throat.

"Charleston, South Carolina," says Flo, more humble.

"So ordered," says the judge. Barry turns and begins to hot-foot it away, but the judge stops him. "Just a minute, young man." Barry turns back. The judge folds his hands on the judge's bench in front of him and speaks directly to Barry.

"Young man, you are lucky. Lucky you are not going to jail tonight and awaiting trial. Lucky you have this woman for an attorney. Luckier still in the district attorney. But luckiest of all that the young man you pushed down the stairs at the Castro Theater is not pressing charges. He has cracked ribs, a broken arm, and a black eye. You won't be lucky next time. You come back into my jurisdiction, the criminal justice system will be happy to put

389

you away — for years." He beats his gavel again. "Get out of my courtroom."

The judge leaves the bench and swishes his robes behind him, back to his chambers. Cassandra stalks away from Barry as he wheels around, turns on his megawatt smile, and lets us have it.

Cassandra stops at our row. "He's not worth it," she says to me.

Barry catches Cassandra's arm. "Hey. Thanks a lot," he says, still smiling.

"I didn't do it for you," says Cassandra. She's furious. "I did it for your sister. She's fourteen years old and has crossed this country to find you. You can thank her."

"I will!" says Barry. He claps me on the shoulder and moves me out of the way, grabs Molly, and pulls her to him. "Polka Dot, come here!"

Molly is sobbing. *Sobbing*. I race to catch Cassandra before she leaves the courtroom.

"Thank you!" I call to her. She stops. "I want to pay you," I say. "I have money."

"Give it to Jo Ellen," she says. "And see the clerk of the court to pay fines and court costs before you leave here today. I have to be in Berkeley in thirty minutes."

She begins to open the courtroom door, thinks better of it, and turns back to me. "I want to tell you something," she says. "We buried a Berkeley student last month, Jim Rector. Another man was blinded. Hundreds more were hurt during the People's Park protest. Governor Reagan called out the National Guard and things got bloody. We're still dealing with the aftermath and try-ing to keep students out of jail, expunge possible criminal records. The Guard is still on campus. These kids may be misguided, they may not be, but what I know is they are exercising their First Amendment rights and they are not throwing people weaker than they are down staircases and laughing in the faces of those try-ing to help them."

*You gotta go after the bullies. I would do it again. I would go
after the bullies.*

Cassandra puts a hand back on the courtroom door. "That's
all I wanted to say." She pushes open the door and is gone.

MOLLY

I don't want to let Barry go. I cling to him like he's a lifeguard and
I'm drowning, and he laughs and laughs, so happy to see me, or so
happy to be free, or both, who knows, but he laughs and I am in
his arms, and life is so good, so good, so good. I say that to myself
as I cling to him. I think about Mom pulling me to her. *Find him,
Molly. Find your brother. Norman will help you. Bring him home.*

My brother hugs me back with those strong arms and lifts
me off my feet and brings me to the aisle where he swings me
around. I start laughing through my tears.

When he puts me down, I start crying again. Barry squats in
front of me, pulls his shirttail out of his jeans, and wipes at my
eyes.

"You don't know what we've been through to find you!" I say,
choking on my tears.

"Shhhh," says my brother. "You found me. I'm here."

But I can't stop talking to him; it's been too long. And I need
to know something. I almost whisper it.

"Did you push that man down the stairs, Barry? Did you?"

Barry's smile dims, but not much. "It's complicated, Polka
Dot. I didn't mean it. Things got out of hand." His voice carries
that same assurance it always has, that *I'm going to tell you the
way it is* voice. "You believe me, don't you?" he asks, but it's not
really a question.

I nod. But I don't know if I do.

"He's got a broken arm," I say, searching for words.
"He's . . . hurt." Eddie hands me a handkerchief and I blow my nose.

391

"I know, and I feel *terrible*," says Barry. "But look, Molly —" He claps the palms of his hands on his chest. "It's over!"

It's over doesn't make it feel all right. I wipe at my runny nose.

"We have to clear the courtroom," says Eddie, pointing to someone trying to move us out.

"This is Eddie —" I start to say as Barry grabs my hand and pulls me through the doors and into the rotunda, where we find Norman standing with Jo Ellen and a well-dressed man wearing black slacks, a blue oxford button-down shirt, and brown dress shoes.

"Norman!" says Barry. He hugs Norman like he has been in solitary confinement for decades. "Thanks, man! Thanks for coming out here to get me! Thanks for springing me!"

Norman lets Barry hug him, but he hardly hugs him back. Barry doesn't notice, but I do. Everything feels off.

"You must be Barry," Jo Ellen says. She shakes his hand. "Congratulations, you're a free man." Even Jo Ellen sounds off.

Flo catches up with us. "How'd I do?"

I hug him madly and tell him he's my honorary big brother. Barry shakes his hand and gives him another one of his big smiles. "Thanks, man."

Eddie sits on a bench and watches us. He gives me a half wave when I notice him and a look that says *I'm fine here.*

Jo Ellen introduces the well-dressed man in the crew cut. "This is my dad," she says. "Lieutenant Colonel Phil Chapman, USAF." She makes introductions, then says, "I'm sorry I missed the courtroom; I was picking up Dad at the airport after I talked to the man who decided not to press charges —"

"Good man, that Parnell!" interrupts Barry, grinning.

"Is . . . is he all right?" I stammer.

Jo Ellen smiles at me. "He will be," she says. She glances at Barry and adds, "It's good of you to ask, Molly."

She turns to Norman and says, "My dad and I are driving

to Vandenberg tomorrow to meet Drew and then they fly home together to Charleston."

"You'll get to see a Titan missile launch!" I say.

"How did you know that?" asks Colonel Chapman. His eyes smile at me.

"We met Drew in Los Angeles," I say. "At the Griffith Observatory!"

"Ahhh," says Colonel Chapman. "He's a talker."

"He told us about the missile launch when we were in Little Rock," says Norman.

"Oh?" says Colonel Chapman.

"I know," I say. "It's unbelievable."

Flo shakes Colonel Chapman's hand with great vigor. "Some of you Fly Boys dropped some of us Sky Soldiers at Tai Ninh in '67. Never got a chance to say thank you. Maybe you'll accept my thanks for them."

Colonel Chapman shakes Flo's hand and smiles at him. "That's great to hear," he says. "I'll pass it on. Good to meet you, Flo. I'm flying C-141s over Nam now, with MAC, Military Air Command, strictly cargo and troops."

Barry interrupts the conversation. "Who's hungry? Can we eat?"

"I just wanted to say good-bye," says Jo Ellen. "I'm glad everything turned out well for you."

I hug her. "Thank you for helping us."

She hugs me back with such a warm embrace. "My pleasure."

"Yeah, thanks, Joanna," says Barry. "Let's eat! Come with us!"

NORMAN

So we all end up eating together in Chinatown, at Sam Wo on Washington Street, a place Flo rightfully declares the King of Noodles.

393

"It's also the skinniest building in the world," says Eddie. We are crammed together, seven of us, in a space by the kitchen. A sign says NO BOOZE, NO B.S., NO JIVE, NO COFFEE, MILK, SOFT DRINKS, FORTUNE COOKIES.

"This is how you know a Chinese restaurant is good," says Flo. "The locals eat here." He orders rice noodle rolls for all of us. I've only been to a Chinese restaurant once, I tell Flo. Flo orders chow mein, fried rice, and wonton soup for everyone. He and Colonel Chapman talk military shop, while Eddie sits and quietly listens.

"Families, eating together," says Molly as she looks around at the diners. She's so happy her face shines. "Generations of families. I'll bet they come here all the time."

"I've lived without family for over a year," says Barry. He stabs a noodle roll. "It's not so bad."

Molly looks stricken. "You don't mean it."

"It was pretty bad for us," I say.

"I don't care if I never go back home," says Barry. I can feel Molly steel herself across the table.

After a leaden pause, Jo Ellen asks Barry, "Did your attorney tell you about your draft notice?"

"Who's being drafted?" asked Colonel Chapman.

"I am, evidently," says Barry. "Yeah, she told me."

"Your physical date is July second," I say.

"I don't plan to report," says Barry.

Molly has taken a sip of her soup. She chokes on it.

"It was Mom's idea to bring you home," she says, coughing. "She said we would figure out what to do as a family."

"No way am I going home to let Dad scream at me again!"

Colonel Chapman leans his elbows on the table. "I personally know young men — or knew them — who would be happy to have their parents scream at them again, if they could be here, on this planet, alive."

"He disowned me!" Barry's charming veneer cracks for a moment, but only I can see it. It's in the way he blinks and swallows. I know him well. He takes a breath and is back in the game. "The war is stupid."

The chow mein is delivered and no one seems ready to eat it. The hush at the table makes everyone uncomfortable.

Colonel Chapman laces his fingers together over his plate. He clears his throat. "What do you plan to do about your induction notice?"

"Nothing," says Barry.

"You'll be arrested!" says Molly.

"No, I won't. I won't be here."

"Where are you going?" Molly asks.

"I don't know," says Barry. "I have a hankering to see the world. Just not Southeast Asia!"

"I see," says Colonel Chapman.

Finally, Eddie speaks up. "Does it mean anything to you that your mother wants you to come home?"

I see Barry's wavering again, and again I watch his recovery. "Nope."

"Really?"

"Really."

Molly puts down her soup spoon and stares at her bowl.

"You told the judge you'd go home," I say.

Barry shrugs.

No one speaks for a moment, and then Molly says, "I thought you should run, too, at first. Then I thought you should join the navy, or the air force, anything to keep you out of the army. But Flo is so proud of being in the army, so I don't know, because we made a friend who is so messed up after being in the army, and I don't know what you should do. It should be your decision — that's what I thought in the end. Or maybe you could just shoot yourself in the foot."

The entire table recoils at this thought.

Molly continues. "Whatever you do, you should at least talk to Mom. She hasn't heard from you in over a year. Her heart is broken."

I am so proud of you. I want to say that to my cousin, but boys don't talk like that, and Molly's voice is shaking so much I'm sure she'd cry if I said one word.

Flo saves the day when he says, "I'm proud of my outfit, I miss my buddies who died, and I'm grateful to be alive, but I wish we'd never had to go to Vietnam. So many are dead. And not just Americans."

"And for what?" says Barry.

"When your country calls, you go," Colonel Chapman answers. "I don't always agree with command. But I signed up to do a job. I'm morally and ethically bound to do it."

"I didn't sign up," says Barry. "It's not my war. My country is wrong. I refuse to go."

"Then don't go to war," says Eddie. "Go home and see your mother."

Colonel Chapman looks at Jo Ellen before he speaks to Barry. "Let me tell you what I do now, in the air force. I fly supplies over to Vietnam and bodies back. Hundreds and hundreds of bodies, in body bags, labeled, heading home to their grieving families —"

Jo Ellen interrupts. "My dad and I don't see eye to eye about the war. I agree with you, Barry. The war needs to stop. Millions of people in this country agree with you. There are kids out there in this country dying for a cause, in Vietnam, yes, but also across the Bay in People's Park at the University of California, all across the South for their civil rights, and protesting everywhere, standing up for what they feel is right. Not just young people — all people. But we especially need the young people. This is the way we change things. So here is where I land in this argument: It's not enough to sit there and say 'not fair!' What are you doing about it?"

Barry opens his mouth to speak, then thinks better of it. Instead, he drinks some water, then smiles at me and says, "Well, Norm . . . how are we going to get out of this one?"

I feel the gaze of every person at the table. An ache starts in my chest.

"Well, Barry," I answer my cousin, "*we* aren't. Not anymore."

PIECE OF MY HEART

Written by Jerry Ragovoy and Bert Berns
Performed by Janis Joplin/Big Brother and the Holding Company
Recorded at Columbia Studios, Los Angeles, California, and
New York, New York, 1968
Drummer: Dave Getz

Multitudes was at the Zen Center along with Flam, so they all walked to Grant Street after dinner, where taxicabs took them in different directions. Jo Ellen and her father hailed one.

"Good luck," said Colonel Chapman.

Jo Ellen smiled at them. "Maybe I'll see you in Charleston one day."

Flo gave Jo Ellen his tie as Eddie hailed the next cab. "See you at the Zen Center," Eddie told Molly and Norman. "We've got rooms for the night."

"I'll take care of the puppy," said Flo.

Norman thought to tell him he couldn't have Flam, but he didn't have the heart.

That left Barry standing in the gathering dusk with his sister and his cousin.

398

"Where do you live?" asked Molly. Her heart hurt. She had hoped for too much.

"Nowhere now," said Barry. "I was subletting an apartment in the Castro from the guy . . . some guy," he finished.

"Parnell?"

"That's the one."

They were awkward with one another. Norman shoved his hands in his pockets. No one knew what to do next. "I've got a girl I can stay with," said Barry. "She's not happy with me right now, but I can stay there."

"You sure?" Molly asked. *I'm sad; it's a feeling*, she told herself. But there was something more.

"Yeah," said Barry. "Isabella — she's my old lady, or was. She'll take me back. I left her once already, when I went to Atlanta. That's why I was there when the Allman Brothers Band came through in May. But I came back and she took me back. You should have heard that band, Norman."

"I did."

Barry looked authentically surprised. "You did?"

"Yeah. Thanks for that."

Barry brightened. "Far out, Norman! See? You need me!"

Norman pulled at his earlobe. "I thought I did," he answered. Then he posed a question. "Why did you write me?"

Barry licked his lips as if he needed to think about this. "I wasn't sure I wanted to leave," he finally said. "But the longer I stayed away, the easier it was."

Norman nodded. "It wasn't about me. Or any of us."

Barry pursed his lips. "I was figuring it out."

Molly swallowed to keep tears at bay and again tried to reach for something she was feeling but not quite able to touch. "Couldn't you ride home with us and figure it out?" she asked her brother.

Barry smiled that indulgent smile that Molly remembered. "Let me sleep on it. How's that?"

Hope washed over Molly like a salty ocean wave. "That would be so good, Barry!"

"Don't worry about me, Polka Dot."

"We have to go," said Norman. "Molly and I have plans."

"We do?"

"Yes. We do."

Panic rose in Molly's throat. She looked Barry square in the face. "Will I see you again?"

"Of course you will!" said Barry. "Norman, do you have any money?"

"I spent it all on you already," said Norman, sounding angrier than he wanted to. "And I need enough to get us home."

"How's the bus running?"

"Runs great."

"We painted it," said Molly.

"Yeah? I'd like to see it."

"Not a good idea, if you're not coming back with us," said Norman. "Look, we've got to go."

"Norman . . ." Molly began.

"How about," said Barry, looking pointedly at Norman, "after I sleep on it, I meet you tomorrow morning at the Zen Center? I know where it is." He turned his gaze to his sister. "Would you like that, Mols?"

Molly looked at Norman. He couldn't stand that look, the pleading in her eyes, the knowledge behind them that she couldn't have what she wanted. It was enough to break his heart.

"Fine," said Norman. He stepped off the curb and waved at a taxi like he'd seen Eddie do. "We leave at eight."

"See you tomorrow, Polka Dot," Barry said. He did not embrace her. Molly nodded, mute. From relief, from pain, from confusion, from something she couldn't name. *So many feelings.* The cab pulled to the curb.

Norman opened the car door for Molly and she climbed in without a word. Barry put a hand on Norman's arm and said, "I'm sorry. I know you came a long way." Norman stared at Barry's hand on his arm and then looked him in the eye. "You have no idea," he said. Then he climbed in the cab after Molly and shut the door.

Molly glanced at Norman. "Where are we going?"

"Fillmore West," Norman told the driver. "Corner of Market and South Van Ness."

"What's happening?" Molly asked.

Norman rummaged in his pocket. "I bought these today," he said, "at a pawn shop. The poster was in the window."

Molly snatched the tickets from his hand. "Iron Butterfly! You love them!"

Norman almost laughed. Someone excited for him. It was a good feeling.

"Barry would love this," said Molly. "Turn around!" she told the driver impulsively. "Norman, you should take Barry!"

"Never mind," Norman told the driver. "To the Fillmore, please."

"Norman, really," said Molly. "You two should do this together. I can go back to the Zen Center. I'm tired —"

"No." Norman gritted his teeth. "I don't want to do anything with Barry right now. Maybe never."

The driver weaved in and out of traffic. Molly swayed with the taxi's movement and said, "Why? Because he doesn't want to go back home? You may never see him again!"

He wanted to explain it to her, but how? "I want to take *you*," said Norman. "I'll see you a lot, and for a long time to come. We'll have this to talk about for years and years."

401

"We've already got a lot to talk about. *A lot.* For years and years."

"I want this, too. One day I might have to go to war. If I'm drafted, I will go. And I don't want to sit over there thinking about how I could have taken you to see Iron Butterfly in San Francisco but instead I took Barry, who didn't care two hoots about me, who didn't stick by me, who didn't stick by my family, who can't even bother to call his mother and tell her he's sorry he can't come home."

"He's mixed up," said Molly in a tiny, unsure voice.

"He's selfish," said Norman, sure of himself. "I appreciate you, Molly. Come to the concert with me."

There were other acts on the bill, but the wait was worth it. When the Butterfly came on stage, the dance floor swarmed with kids who tried to get as close as Molly had gotten to the Association at the Troubadour.

Bill Graham stepped to the microphone. "Doug Ingle, Ron Bushy, Lee Dorman, Erik Braunn — Iron Butterfly!"

Doug Ingle called out, "We love you, San Francisco!"

"In-A-Gadda-Da-Vida!" screamed the audience.

Doug laughed. "We save that for last!"

"In-A-Gadda-Da-Vida!" they screamed.

"This one?" said Doug. He played the opening organ lick. The crowd cheered and called out for "In-A-Gadda-Da-Vida."

The band complied with a forty-minute version of the song.

Doug started them off on his Vox organ, Erik played the signature guitar riff, Lee kept the bass line steady, and yet Norman only had eyes for Ron, the drummer. His drum kit was clear acrylic. You could see every move he made and how the light show above them played off the acrylic every time Ron's sticks hit the drum heads. He played with a matched grip, like Ringo Starr did. Norman played with a traditional grip on his sticks. Like Roger Hawkins did.

Norman's spirits ballooned like a man whose heart had just been started again.

Music heals — that's what Estelle had told Molly at Stax, and she could see it happening right before her eyes.

She had little interest in "In-A-Gadda-Da-Vida" as a song. You couldn't sing to it. There was no harmony. It was a seventeen-minute commitment, one whole album side. She could listen to five Weekly Top Forty songs in seventeen minutes, maybe six.

But there was something mesmerizing about live music and the energy in the room that surrounded it. She tried to pay attention, tried to share the song with Norman.

Ron Bushy, with his swinging mop of dark brown hair, goatee, and ridiculous faces, looked like he was being tortured and Molly said so. "He's not like the Association's drummer at all!" Cute Ted Bluechel, who looked like he was having the world's most scintillating conversation with you every minute he was *oh-by-the-way* drumming.

"That's acting!" shouted Norm. "Ron is *playing*."

"Ted played!"

"The Association plays pop."

"They do not!"

"So what if they do?" shouted Norman. "It's good pop."

"The organ player looks like Prince Valiant. How can he see? Get a haircut!" She made herself laugh, even though part of her cringed at the remembrance. "He plays that organ like we're in church."

"We *are* in church," said Norman.

Kids danced under the psychedelic light show. They moved like brilliant flashes of light in fragmented moments, which was

403

all they had, frozen in time. Norman grabbed Molly's hand and weaved through the pulsating energy until he found a wedge of space at a corner of the low stage nearest the drums.

The kid standing next to Norman shouted, "I can dig it!" and promptly slid to the floor. His friends helped him up and out as Norman moved Molly into his spot.

"Here it comes!" he shouted. First the guitar faded, then the organ, then the bass, leaving only Ron and his drums. There was just the bass drum and a steadily tapping hi-hat, until the toms joined in and the hi-hat faded. Every kid in the room turned into a drummer.

Some had brought their drumsticks. Some used their index fingers or open palms. They were drumming on every surface, just as Norman had for an entire year. Ron's tortured face broke into an agonized smile. "Yeah!" said Doug at all the volunteer drummers.

Norman laughed with a little kid's delight. He began the drum solo using his hands on the stage, as if the stage was his giant conga drum.

Then, "Here!" Ron Bushy kept his bass drum pumping as he tossed his drumsticks to Norman, one by one, who caught them with his heart in his throat. Doug handed Ron another pair of sticks so smoothly, Ron didn't miss a beat.

"Norman!" Molly made room and so did the kids around them. Norman began drumming the solo he knew so well, using the edge of the stage as his kit. "Yeah!" shouted Ron. The rest of the drummers in the room faded as Norman and Ron took center stage, playing back and forth with each other, call and response.

Norman didn't have to think about what he was doing — he let the rhythm take him. He shook his head from side to side and made faces like Ron's. Molly stood near him and was filled with admiration. *He's doing it.*

Doug's organ crept into Ron and Norman's solo, then the bass, then the guitar. Norman kept playing. He played out the day, he played out his anger and his hurt, and he played out the realization that they would be going home empty-handed.

The song ended with drums crashing to the finish in a cacophony of sound. Ron jumped up from his drum kit, sweat running down his face, and ran to Norman at the edge of the stage. "Great!" he shouted. Norman handed him the drumsticks. Ron grabbed them with a huge smile — no longer tortured — and said, "What's your name, man?"

He didn't hesitate. "Norman."

"Good name," said Ron. "Very groovy." He dashed back to his kit.

Molly laughed and laughed.

Norman, breathless, smiled at her.

"Let's go home," he said.

BEGINNINGS

Written by Robert Lamm
Performed by Chicago Transit Authority
Recorded at Columbia Recording Studios, New York,
New York, 1969
Drummer: Danny Seraphine

Flo wore an apron over his gift — Norman's Boy Scout shirt and sash with all its badges — and cooked breakfast for the monks. Oatmeal, apples, raisins, bananas, cheesy scrambled eggs ("my specialty!"), and buttered toast. Molly helped. She was dressed for the road: shorts, shirt, Keds, soft ponytail. She smiled at the smiling monks. They were easy to be with. They didn't ask questions, not even when Molly screeched at Norman, "You sold your drums? What!"

Flo dished up eggs for Flam. Eddie wore his porkpie hat and yesterday's overalls under a red cardigan sweater. He helped organize the living space in the back of Multitudes.

"And the amps! And the 6,435 extension cords!" said Molly.

"Six thousand four hundred thirty-four," said Norman. He wore Sweet Caroline's ridiculously small Mickey Mouse T-shirt, an unzipped sweatshirt, his jeans, and his Converse sneakers.

"Very funny." Molly looked under the seats. "And Barry's

guitar!" As they worked, she kept checking, watching up and down the street as she waited for Barry to appear. Eight o'clock came and went. She sat on the curb and let sadness wash over her.

Eddie brought out a box of food from the kitchen. "You all right, doll?"

Molly sighed. "I can't figure it out, Eddie. When Barry left us a year ago, I decided to stop feeling everything, because it was safer. It didn't hurt so much. But all I do now is hurt. And feel things. I can't figure out how not to hurt."

Eddie put down the box and sat next to Molly on the curb. He stroked his beard and finally said, "You will hurt for a long time. And then you won't. The challenge is to live the hurt and not let it swallow you. Pain is a teacher."

"I don't want to learn," said Molly. She brushed an ant away from her sneaker. "I will miss you," she whispered to Eddie.

"And I you," said Eddie. "I'm glad you happened on our little villa. We'll head back there today, Flo and I, and see if we can stand the solitude." He laughed.

"I'm glad you were there," said Molly. She stood up, smiled at Eddie, and pulled him to his feet.

Flo appeared with Flam and another box. "Snacks!" he crowed. "Stop and get some ice for that cooler and something to drink."

"Ice!" Molly laughed in spite of how low she felt. Ice.

Norman slammed the hood of the bus. "Ready to roll," he said.

Around the corner came a girl toting a fat cotton laundry bag. She was wearing sandals and a flowered dress, and her hair was a curtain of long brown hair that framed her face. She stopped at their bus. Flam came to her immediately, tail wagging, eyes shining, wiggling to be petted.

Molly's skin prickled. She knew who this was. "Isabella?"

The girl's face reddened. "Yes. Molly?"

Norman came from the front of the bus. "Hi."

407

Molly's heart fell. "Barry's not coming. Not even to say good-bye."

Isabella dropped her laundry bag and shook her head. "He's not coming. But I am . . . if you'll have me." Flam licked her hand. Isabella squatted and petted Flam. "Sweet doggie!" she whispered. Flam kissed her face and Isabella laughed.

Molly blinked. This was the most animated she'd seen that dog.

"Uh-oh," said Flo.

Norman raised his eyebrows. "Where are you headed?"

"Wherever you're going," said Isabella. She stood up. "I want family." She put a hand on her belly. "We want family."

Norman's face colored and a tingle ran up his spine. He had no idea what to say, but Flo did. "Nobody move. I'll pack some crackers. You know, for car sickness. Sometimes, when . . . I mean, delicate constitutions . . . no, I mean, it's just that they calm the stomach in case of nausea, and —" Flo interrupted himself and changed course. "Get the crackers, Flo." He disappeared.

"Really?" said Molly.

Isabella nodded. "If you don't want to take me with you, I'll understand. I thought I'd ask. I'd like to come."

"Girl!" said Eddie. He opened his arms. Isabella came into them, with surprise and relief. "Willing to go on a journey into the unknown. Now *that's* courage," Eddie said. He turned to Molly. "That's what you did, you know. Now go home. Hug your mother. Congratulate her. She's going to be a grandmother."

"We can't leave Barry," Molly said in a rush. She knew she sounded desperate but she didn't care. "I know him better than anyone! He's not some kind of monster. He's just mixed up. He's afraid. Dad threw him out. It was a horrible fight. He's lost, that's all. We have to save him! I won't leave San Francisco without him. I can't bear it!"

Isabella's eyes filled with tears.

"Give him time," said Eddie, to both Molly and Isabella. "Only Barry can walk his path. No one saves us but ourselves."

"And the music," said Norman. "It connects us. It gives us a family."

"Music is music," Molly countered. "I love music! But it is *not* my family. My family has fallen apart!"

Isabella sat on her overstuffed laundry bag and crisscrossed her legs on the sidewalk. Flam lay next to her, put his snout in her lap, and sighed. Isabella scratched behind his ears. Cars rolled past them on the quiet street. The morning was bright and cool. The fog was burning off. It would be a good day for a journey.

"Music is the rhythm of our humanity," said Eddie. "It's the soundtrack of struggle and peace, birth and death, love and war, joy and pain. Music is the heart you open and the family you choose."

No one spoke. Molly lifted her chin to the sky, took a deep breath, and exhaled it into the morning air. Norman, who had been watching his cousin carefully, now caught her eye. "You okay?" he asked.

Molly looked at the circles under his eyes, at his scruff of beard, his shock of unruly hair. He had suffered, too. "I'm okay," she said. "You?"

"I'm okay," said Norman.

A look passed between them and instantly she understood what she had been trying for so long to touch.

"Can you do this?" Norman asked.

She could.

With a calm she hadn't known she possessed, she answered him, clear-eyed and steady, with one word. "Yes."

Norman nodded. Then, like it was suddenly the most natural thing in the world to express, he said simply, "I love you." Just like that.

Molly's face softened in surprise. "I love you, too," she said. She smiled, and as she did, she opened her heart to the brokenness of the world.

Flam scrambled aboard Multitudes. Flo appeared with a lighted stick of incense in one hand, "to wave you on your way!" and an entire box of saltine crackers in the other. He handed the box to Norman, who took it and offered it to Isabella.

"So," he said, by way of invitation. "Are you on the bus, or are you off the bus?"

AMERICA
Written by Paul Simon Performed by Simon and Garfunkel Recorded at Columbia Studios, New York, New York, 1968 Drummer: Hal Blaine

And so they journeyed home together.

Norman taught Isabella how to drive Multitudes and they took turns eating up the miles. Norman wrote his cadences for band and Molly slept and Isabella drank in the sights from Multitudes' windows.

The route they chose home journeyed through Twentynine Palms, California; skirted Phoenix, Arizona; sped across lower New Mexico and through the deep heart of Texas; laced the tip of Louisiana; breathed deeply through Greenwood, Mississippi; exhaled past Alabama; looped south of Macon, Georgia; and sailed into Charleston, South Carolina, five days later.

They drove into a summer when men would walk on the moon and kids would throng to a farm in Woodstock, New York, and Wavy would be there on a stage telling them, "What we have in mind is breakfast in bed for four hundred thousand!" and people

411

of all shapes and colors and identities would march against injustice of all kinds, in an effort to bring down the established old order and redefine the ideals of liberty and justice, equality and opportunity, safety and kindness for all.

The future of America drove home. They were nineteen, seventeen, fourteen, and not yet born. They had their work cut out for them.

Has it not always been so?

MARE
IBRIUM

APOLLO 15
JULY 30, 1971

APOLLO 17
DEC. 11, 1972

APOLLO 11
JULY 20, 1969

APOLLO 14
FEB. 5, 1971

APOLLO 12
NOV. 14, 1969

APOLLO 16
APRIL 20, 1972

TYCHO
CRATER

"THAT'S ONE SMALL STEP FOR MAN, ONE GIANT LEAP FOR MANKIND."

Apollo 11 astronaut Neil Armstrong as he becomes the first human being to step onto the moon's surface, July 20, 1969

WE ARE STARDUST, WE ARE GOLDEN

From "Woodstock" by Joni Mitchell

A hip and hairy crowd of 250,000 youths converted
this farm area into a pop music mecca today. In the process,
they created the largest traffic jam in the history of the Catskills.

*State police were forced to close Exit 104 of the New York State Thruway,
leading to Route 17B, because of the heavy influx of youthful travelers.*

**The New York Daily News, reporting on
the Woodstock Music and Art Fair, August 16, 1969**

Wavy Gravy and eighty-five members of the Hog Farm arrive at LaGuardia Airport in New York from their commune in New Mexico on their way to Woodstock, where they had been hired to provide a free kitchen — and security.

Reporter: Oh, the Hog Farm,
you guys are the security.

Wavy: Oh my God,
they've made us the cops!

Reporter: What are you
going to use for security?

Wavy: Cream pies and seltzer bottles.

Reporter: How is that going to work?

Wavy: Well . . . do you feel secure?

Reporter: Well, sure.

Wavy: See? It's working already!

VILLAGE RAID STIRS MELEE

A police raid in the Stonewall Inn, a tavern frequented by homosexuals at 53 Christopher St., just east of Sheridan Square in Greenwich Village, triggered a near riot early today. As persons seized in the raid were driven away by police, hundreds of passersby shouting "Gay Power" and "We Want Freedom" laid siege to the tavern with an improvised battering ram, garbage cans, bottles and beer cans in a project demonstration.

The New York Post, June 29, 1969

The gay people have discovered their potential strength and gained a new pride.

Michael Kotis, president of the Mattachine Society, speaking about the first gay pride march and rally in *The New York Times* on June 29, 1970

We have to come out into the open and stop being ashamed, or else people will go on treating us as freaks.

Michael Brown, 29, a founder of the Gay Liberation Front, quoted in *The New York Times* on June 29, 1970

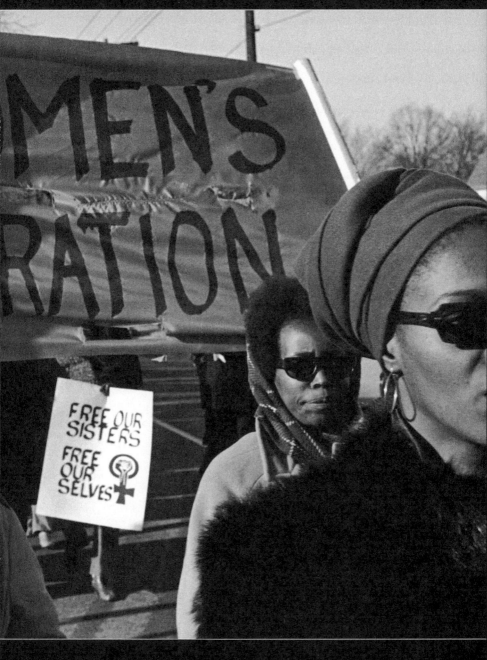

Women's liberation group marches in protest in support of the
Black Panther Party, New Haven, Connecticut, November 1969

Outside the Time Life Building during the Moratorium to End the War in Vietnam demonstration, New York City, October 15, 1969

A vast throng of Americans, predominantly youthful and constituting the largest mass march in the nation's capital, demonstrated peacefully in the heart of the city today, demanding a rapid withdrawal of United States troops from Vietnam.

The New York Times,
November 15, 1969

Under an altered sign, Native Americans who have taken over Alcatraz Island unload supplies from a boat, San Francisco, California, December 1969. For almost nineteen months, a group of Native Americans, under the name "Indians of All Tribes," occupied the island, which at the time was out of service as a federal prison. The occupation was based on their interpretation of the 1868 Treaty of Fort Laramie, which they believed granted them the right to reclaim any land originally theirs sold to and subsequently abandoned by the U.S. government.

THE ROCK.

Richard Oakes (Mohawk), who led the nineteen-month
occupation of Alcatraz Island by the Tribes of All Nations

To the Great White Father and All His People:

We, the native Americans, re-claim the land known as Alcatraz Island in the name of all American Indians by right of discovery. We wish to be fair and honorable in our dealings with the Caucasian inhabitants of this land, and hereby offer the following treaty: We will purchase said Alcatraz Island for 24 dollars in glass beads and red cloth, a precedent set by the white man's purchase of a similar island about 300 years ago. We know that $24 in trade goods for these sixteen acres is more than was paid when Manhattan Island was sold, but we know that land values have risen over the years. Our offer of $1.24 per acre is greater than the 47 cents per acre the white men are now paying the California Indians for their land. We will give to the inhabitants of this land a portion of that land for their own, to be held in trust by the American Indian Government for as long as the sun shall rise and the rivers go down to the sea -- to be administered by the Bureau of Caucasian Affairs (BCA). We will further guide the inhabitants in the proper way of living. We will offer them our religion, our education, our life-ways, in order to help them achieve our level of civilization and thus raise them and all their white brothers up from their savage and unhappy state. We offer this treaty in good faith and wish to be fair and honorable in our dealings with all white men.

We feel that this so-called Alcatraz Island is more than suitable as an Indian Reservation, as determined by the white man's own standards. By this we mean that this place resembles most Indian reservations, in that:

1. It is isolated from modern facilities, and without adequate means of transportation.
2. It has no fresh running water.
3. The sanitation facilities are inadequate.
4. There are no oil or mineral rights.
5. There is no industry and so unemployment is very great.
6. There are no health care facilities.
7. The soil is rocky and non-productive and the land does not support game.
8. There are no educational facilities.
9. The population has always been held as prisoners and kept dependent upon others.

Further, it would be fitting and symbolic that ships from all over the world, entering the Golden Gate, would first see Indian land, and thus be reminded of the true history of this nation. This tiny island would be a symbol of the great lands once ruled by free and noble Indians.

The proclamation of the Indians of All Tribes who occupied Alcatraz from November 1969 to June 1971

Chief Tim Williams of the Klamath River Hurok Indians of California addresses a crowd prior to the Indian takeover of Alcatraz Island.

ACROSS THE COUNTRY ON COLLEGE CAMPUSES, STUDENTS PROTEST THE U.S. BOMBING ON CAMBODIA AND PRESIDENT NIXON'S WIDENING OF THE VIETNAM WAR.

CAMBODIA — a small country of seven million people — has been a neutral nation since the Geneva Agreement of 1954 . . . North Vietnam, however, has not respected that neutrality . . . this is the decision I have made. In cooperation with the armed forces of South Vietnam, attacks are being launched this week to clean out major enemy sanctuaries on the Cambodian-Vietnam border . . . This is not an invasion of Cambodia.

Richard Nixon televised address, April 30, 1970, announcing the U.S. invasion of Cambodia

Protesting students at Kent State University in Kent, Ohio, disperse as National Guardsmen fire tear gas into the crowd minutes before their gunfire kills four students and wounds nine more, May 4, 1970.

Antiwar protesters, some Vietnam veterans in wheelchairs, marching toward the Capitol in the Vietnam Veterans Against the War march

The right of citizens of the United States, who are eighteen years of age or older, to vote shall not be denied or abridged by the United States or by any State on account of age.

Section 1 of the Twenty-Sixth Amendment to the U.S. Constitution, passed by Congress March 23, 1971 and ratified July 1, 1971, lowering the voting age from twenty-one to eighteen and giving all young people who could be drafted the right to vote.

The 25 million new voters from 18 to 24 years old, have the political potential to change almost the entire make-up of Congress in the next year's election.

***The New York Times*, September 20, 1971**

After a year of intense organizing by young people at colleges around the country, new academic departments begin to appear that support the demands of cultural causes: Africana Studies, Chicana and Chicano Studies, Native American Studies, and Women's Studies. The first Women's Studies program in the United States begins at San Diego State College in fall 1970.

We're back in the world. No more heat or red dust or sodden patties. No more incoming to spatter you around like paint, no more snipers. No more silent jungles or quiet dead, no more clattering choppers or friends moaning and you too busy to help. No more barracks-room boredom with thumbed letters and magazines you know backwards . . . No more dawns over mountains that scare you. Most of all, better believe it, no more Vietnam. We're out.

Life magazine, April 16, 1971

VIETNAM ACCORD IS REACHED; CEASE-FIRE BEGINS SATURDAY; P.O.W.'S TO BE FREE IN 60 DAYS

The New York Times, **January 24, 1973**

Last year some half-million GIs came home from Vietnam. This year another 200,000 are expected to return. The lucky ones come back with two arms, two legs, genitalia intact, alive. But that's it, no more parades . . . The Calley case sealed America's dismay over Vietnam. Even before they got back they knew the rule; don't talk about it. Don't volunteer to a pretty girl that you served in Vietnam. Don't expect anybody to give you a job just because you are a vet . . . You survived, so forget it.

Life **Magazine, April 16, 1971**

Released prisoner of war Lt. Col. Robert L. Stirm is greeted by his family at Travis Air Force Base in Fairfield, California, as he returns home from the Vietnam War, March 17, 1973.

The Interior Department announced today a change in regulations to lower the voting age of Indians in tribal elections to 18. Marvin L. Franklin, assistant for Indian affairs, said the regulations had been amended to conform with the 26th Amendment to the Constitution, ratified June 30, 1971, which lowered the national voting age to 18.

The New York Times, May 2, 1973

Only a free and unrestrained press can effectively expose deception in government. And paramount among the responsibilities of a free press is the duty to prevent any part of the government from deceiving the people and sending them off to distant lands to die of foreign fevers and foreign shot and shell . . .

From Supreme Court Justice Hugo Black's 1971 concurring opinion on *The New York Times*'s and *The Washington Post*'s publication of excerpts of the Pentagon Papers, revealing the government's early knowledge that the Vietnam War could not be won

The central question at this point is simply put: What did the president know and when did he know it?

Senator Howard Baker questioning White House counsel John Dean during the Watergate hearings, June 28, 1973

I have never been a quitter. To leave office before my term is completed is abhorrent to every instinct in my body. But as president, I must put the interest of America first . . . Therefore, I shall resign the presidency effective at noon tomorrow. Vice President Ford will be sworn in as president at that hour in this office.

Richard Nixon, announcing his resignation as president of the United States, August 8, 1974

A North Vietnamese Communist tank drives through the main gate of the Presidential Palace of the U.S.-backed South Vietnam regime as the city falls into the hands of Communist troops, April 30, 1975

SAIGON FALLS
APRIL 30, 1975

A CIA employee (probably O. B. Harnage) helps Vietnamese and American evacuees onto an Air America helicopter from the top of 22 Gia Long Street, a half mile from the U.S. Embassy.

At Tan Son Nhut military airport, an empty C-141 aircraft lands to transport Vietnamese refugees every thirty minutes.

Operation Frequent Wind: A South Vietnamese helicopter pilot and his family, safely aboard the USS *Hancock*, are escorted by a marine security guard to the refugee area during an evacuation, Saigon, Vietnam, April 29, 1975.

In twenty years of American involvement in Vietnam, 58,220 American soldiers died, along with an estimated one million North Vietnamese and Vietcong troops and a quarter of a million South Vietnamese soldiers, over the course of the war. Estimates range from hundreds of thousands to four million civilians killed in Vietnam, Laos, and Cambodia.

2,709,918 Americans served in Vietnam. This number represents 9.7 percent of their generation. 304,000 were wounded. 75,000 were severely disabled.

In 1965 half the population of the western world was under the age of twenty-five. You have an evolution and a revolution in consciousness when you have a situation like that.

Gail Zappa

It's not the size of the ship; it's the size of the waves.

Little Richard

A NOTE
ABOUT
ANTHEM
AND 1969

While I was researching the many varied threads for this book, my friend Steve Farrell sent me a quote about the sixties by Hunter S. Thompson, from his book *Fear and Loathing in Las Vegas:*

History is hard to know . . . but even without being sure of "history" it seems entirely reasonable to think that every now and then the energy of a whole generation comes to a head in a long fine flash, for reasons that nobody really understands at the time — and which never explain, in retrospect, what actually happened.

This sentiment seems true of any cataclysmic or momentous period in history, and especially of a decade as divisive and at the same time as coalescent as the 1960s.

In 1969, thunderheads formed on every American horizon, and storms broke over families and institutions, often splitting them apart and forever changing the lives of individuals who were clinging to the established, customary norm, as well as those trying hard to break away from it.

Music soothed the transition. The music of the sixties saturated, permeated, buoyed, and informed Everything — politics, passion, fashion, movements, changing cultural and social mores. So much was being born, and music gave a voice to it: to war, to peace, to life and death.

Debate and protest over the Vietnam War cleaved the country. You'll find those who went to war within these pages, as well as those left behind and the counterculture that rose from the careful, ordered, material days of the post–World War II 1950s. Also in these pages are those who did not benefit from the boom of those post-war years and instead struggled mightily for their civil rights and freedoms.

America's push to the moon takes the stage here, as well as America's love affair with the open road, and seeing this country with fresh eyes from new interstate highways.

Anthem also explores the idea of who gets to tell the story of America. The only story my many characters can tell is the one they are living and learning about, and they have only the lens they can see through at that particular time.

So, for instance, the young people trying to create a utopia on the mesas in New Mexico in the late sixties are largely ignorant of how their actions can be seen as disrespectful of or unwelcome to native cultures, although some may be beginning to understand. Some characters' views are overly determined by their idealism, age, and lack of awareness. Some are deeply affected — and afflicted — by their own damage, or blinded by their privilege.

Taken together, they represent some of the stories of 1969. There are as many stories, places of entry, and points of view as there are people and cultures to tell them. We will collect them forever. We need all American voices to make up the whole of who we were, in order to make sense of who we've become, and to chart an indivisible course to who we will be, with liberty and justice for all.

I was sixteen years old in 1969. I lived in Charleston, South Carolina, where teenagers drove school buses and public schools were just beginning a challenging integration. Boys were sent home if their hair touched their shirt collars, and girls' dress lengths were measured from the wearer's kneecap to the dress hem by homeroom teachers at St. Andrew's Parish High School. I knew the lyrics to every Top Forty song on the radio and was in love with the boy who played the sousaphone in the marching band.

Listed below are some timeline notes. I offer them here for purists, or completists, like my friend Charlie Young, who will know that the then-unknown Allman Brothers Band played free concerts in Piedmont Park in Atlanta, Georgia, in May 1969, but I have them there again in June, for my story's purposes. Also, a few songs listed at chapter heads have release dates after June 1969 but were recorded before then.

We reeled from catastrophe to catastrophe in the sixties. I stood in line for hours with my family, freezing in November's dark wind, to walk past John F. Kennedy's casket in the Capitol Rotunda in 1963. I sat in stunned silence with my family watching the news coverage about the Reverend Martin Luther King Jr.'s assassination in Memphis, Tennessee, in April 1968. I sat up all night two months later to see if Robert Kennedy had survived being shot in the Ambassador Hotel in Los Angeles, having just declared his victory in the California Democratic presidential primary. I was fifteen years old and afraid for my country, afraid for my future.

Then I watched, in July 1969, late into the night, a grainy black-and-white image of a man walking on the moon and felt some of the exhilaration of the space age and the limitless future and possibility ahead.

There was a sense in the sixties, held by so many young people, that there was a psychic shift happening, that the Age of Aquarius was coming through, that harmony and understanding were indeed on the horizon, that we might throw off the bondage of the old social norms and embrace a truly egalitarian future full of common human hopes and dreams and sensual, cultural, sexual, gender, and racial freedom, and the abolishment of hate and bigotry.

My friend Steve, who was for a time a student of Maharishi Mahesh Yogi, summed it up when he wrote me, "It was an amazingly beautiful reality that materialized, lasted briefly, and then disappeared into the past — and, tragically in my mind, ninety-nine percent of the people had absolutely no idea of what had happened and what was lost. And, it's something that was very subtle and difficult to communicate, even if someone is interested in understanding."

I hope you are interested in understanding. I hope this story can convey some of how it felt to be alive in 1969, on the cusp of the beginning of Everything.

SOME
TIMELINE
NOTES

— Members of the newly-formed Allman Brothers Band moved from Florida to Macon, Georgia, in spring 1969. They played free concerts in Macon's Central City Park and in Piedmont Park in Atlanta before recording their first album. "Mountain Jam" was recorded at Fillmore East in 1971, but there is a recording of it in Central City Park in 1969 and it was played that summer in both Atlanta and Macon.

— "Mama" Louise Hudson owned the H&H Restaurant in Macon, Georgia, with her cousin, Inez Hill. One day two members of what would become the Allman Brothers Band came in to eat with money enough for just one plate of food. Mama Louise, who called most everyone "baby" or "darlin'," began feeding the band for free until they had the money to pay her.

— The Strip was an area about eight blocks in length along Peachtree Street in Atlanta, concentrated between Tenth and Fourteenth Streets, a derelict and decaying part of town in the late 1960s that the area hippies took over for its cheap rent and proximity to Piedmont Park. It provided a gathering place for like minds until redevelopment took over in the early 1970s. Today, steel and concrete buildings pack the skyline, and what was once the Strip is the epicenter of business in Midtown Atlanta.

— The Catacombs, on the Strip in Atlanta, closed in 1968.

— The Twelfth Gate, on Tenth Street in Atlanta, just off the Strip, became more than a coffeehouse in 1970 when Joe Roman turned it into a jazz and blues club as well. I'm debuting jazz one year earlier.

— Cannonball Adderley never played the Twelfth Gate, but he did play Paris in March 1969. Bill Evans, McCoy Tyner, Mose Allison, Weather Report, and Little Feat did play the Twelfth Gate.

— Wilson Pickett recorded "Hey, Jude" at FAME Studios in Muscle Shoals, Alabama, on January 4, 1969. Duane Allman accompanied him. He also accompanied Clarence Carter in "The Road of Love," and for a short time he lived in a cabin on Wilson Lake in Muscle Shoals.

— The Muscle Shoals Rhythm Section split with Rick Hall at FAME Studios sometime in 1969 and started Muscle Shoals Sound Studio. They got their name, the Swampers, from Leon Russell's producer, Denny Cordell. They are mentioned in Lynyrd Skynyrd's "Sweet Home Alabama" lyrics, "Now Muscle Shoals has got the Swampers . . ."

— Estelle Axton of Stax Records closed her record store in late 1968/early 1969 and moved it across the street when new Stax owner Al Bell wanted her space for offices. It quickly went out of business.

— The debate continues over which Hammond organ — the B-3 or the M-3 — Booker T. Jones used when he recorded "Green Onions." Booker T. himself says it was an M-3.

— Elvis Presley did record at American Sound Studio, and did play Las Vegas from late July to late August 1969.

— Titan missiles were occasionally test launched from Vandenberg Air Force Base in the sixties.

— Merle Haggard recorded the album *Okie From Muskogee* at the Muskogee Civic Center in October 1969. It was released in December 1969. The single was recorded and released earlier, and charted the same week as the concert.

— "Do the Funky Chicken" was released in November 1969 performed by Rufus Thomas, recorded at Stax Records in Memphis, Tennessee.

— Mary Beal was a real person, a self-taught, pioneering botanist who moved to the dry climate of the Mojave Desert in the early 1900s to relieve a respiratory condition. She fell in love with the solitude and strength of the land, and wandered the desert with her camera, seeking out rare plant species, documenting them, and writing about them for *Desert Magazine* for many years.

— Hal Blaine was one of the most prolific drummers in rock and roll history. As a studio/session musician, he wasn't as widely known to teenagers who listened to their favorite bands' records, but he probably played on most of them, including forty number-one singles.

— The Association formed as a band in 1965 and got their start (as part of The Inner Tubes and then The Men) at the Troubadour. They were touring in March and July 1969. I bring them to the hoot at the Troubadour in June.

— JoAnn Dean Killingsworth was the first Snow White at Disneyland. She left home at fifteen to join a skating troupe and ended up in Los Angeles, but she did not leave behind a young daughter. Sweet Caroline's mother is fictional.

— New Buffalo was a commune in New Mexico above Taos from 1967 to about 1979.

— The Great Bus Race in the Aspen Meadow on the summer solstice 1969 was a real event. Peace activist Wavy Gravy is a real person, still living, as of this 2019 writing, and still living in community at the Hog Farm, which is now located in Berkeley, California.

— In 1958 Estella Wheatley Dooley was admitted to the American Bar Association, one of three black women at that time. In 1963 she was admitted to the California Bar. In 1966, after having been in private practice in Los Angeles and San Francisco, Ms. Dooley became the first black woman lawyer in the San Francisco Public Defender's Office. Cassandra is modeled on her.

— Iron Butterfly did play Fillmore West on June 24–26, 1969.

— Bill Graham moved the Fillmore from its original San Francisco location at the corner of Fillmore and Geary to the corner of Market Street and South Van Ness Avenue in 1968 and dubbed it Fillmore West.

ACKNOWLEDGMENTS

I wish I could introduce readers to every person who helped make this book a reality, who helped shape it (and me) and interpret it and temper it and trim it and give it structure and heft and meaning and truth.

They are legion, their influence goes back decades, and I am grateful for their time, talent, willingness, expertise, patience, and heart. Not to mention their senses of humor. Here are some of them:

— Betsy Partridge and Tom Ratcliff for the generous loan of their home in Berkeley while I was researching in the San Francisco area.

— Walter Mayes for his San-Francisco-in-the-Sixties knowledge and expertise.

— Kate Harrison for sharing her father's eloquent, persuasive 1966 letter to the draft board.

— Virginia Butler for sharing the heartfelt letters she wrote home while her husband was on a tour of duty in Vietnam.

— Charlie Young for his musical expertise and edification, and for teaching me to love the Allman Brothers Band.

— Tommy Archibald for his extensive knowledge of rock and roll and in particular the Beatles.

— Jerry Brunner, Woodstock alumnus, for his remembrances of the Strip and the Twelfth Gate.

— Laurie Findlay, who lived in community in New Mexico, and who offered an unerring, ever-present sense of belonging to me as I wrote this book.

— Gary Kemper for his memories of living in Los Angeles in the sixties and the monks at the Hollywood Temple of the Ramakrishna Vedanta Society of Southern California.

— Zachary Wiles for his indefatigable spirit and chauffeur services, toting me all over Los Angeles for research, including Griffith Observatory at night, Laurel Canyon and the Country Store by day, Capitol Records, the Sunset Strip, and a raucous evening at the Troubadour.

— Cathy Archibald, Cyndi Craven, Janice Johnson, Ron Hipp, and Steve Farrell for love and sustenance and sixties stories galore.

— Billy Short, whose memories of the Strip and the Allman Brothers Band in Piedmont Park in 1969 were essential.

— Drummer Paul Fallat, who let me watch him work — and take photos of him at work — and for his "trash can" cymbals.

— Fred Hughes, for his memories of marching in the St. Andrews Parish High School marching band in Charleston, South Carolina, in 1969.

— Terry Kirkman, for his memories of playing at the Troubadour with the Association, and details about the music industry then and now.

— The Georgia State University digital archives and The Strip Project online for sharing back issues of *The Great Speckled Bird* as well as photos and memories of Atlanta in the late sixties, the political underground sensibilities, and the counterculture.

— Chris Bishop and his work at the website Garage Hangover, for the wealth of primary source archival material on Little Rock, Arkansas, garage bands in the sixties.

— The contributors at the *School Bus Fleet* Magazine Forum online for their smarts and generosity in educating me on the many makes and models of school buses in the 1960s, including how they were configured, how they worked, how to drive them, how to repair them, and how to deal with tumbling tumbleweeds.

— The contributors at the Steve Hoffman Music Forums online who could energetically argue with one another over which drummer played on what track of which recording of what record in what year — in which session, with what band — but were generous with their expertise and their knowledge of rock and roll in a way that taught me so much about the evolution of American music.

— John Mullin, U.S. Navy aviation machinist mate, hydraulics, sixth-class in the South China Sea, 1967, for generously sharing his life and work as a plane handler aboard the USS *Intrepid* during the Vietnam War.

— Lisa Law, who lived at New Buffalo in the sixties, for her many amazing photographs, particularly of commune life, and for her documentary *Flashing on the Sixties*, which provided footage and primary source material about New Buffalo in particular.

— Art Kopecky for his journals and books about life in the New Buffalo commune, an invaluable resource.

— Documentarian Jonathan Ray, enrolled member of the Laguna Pueblo nation, for sharing his family memories, for reading this book so carefully in manuscript form, and for his thoughtful and insightful comments and contributions.

— Cree artist, writer, and educator Alfred Young Man, or Kiyugimah (Eagle Chief), an enrolled member of the Chippewa-Cree tribe, student at the Institute of American Indian Arts (AIAI) in Santa Fe, New Mexico, in 1969, and one of the founding members of the house band The Jaggers, for his expertise in reading this book in manuscript and his contributions to its final form.

— David "Sticks" Levithan, who said, "Make him a drummer," which opened new vistas for me and for the story. This book is elevated by Sticks's many contributions to its plot, clarity, rhythm, and flow.

— Phil Falco for design wizardry. Also an elevator.

— Els Rijper, without whom we would have no scrapbooks.

— Melissa Schirmer, who believes in the power of books to change lives and who waited for me.

— The audacious, stout-hearted, intrepid Scholastic team, both Trade and Fairs, that shepherds my books into readers' hands, including Maya Marlette, Tracy van Straaten, Lizette Serrano, Robin Hoffman, Emily Heddleson, Amy Goppert, Danielle Yadao, and Lauren Donovan

— Steven Malk, who shepherds me.

— Jim Pearce, jazzman extraordinaire and St. Andrews Parish marching band alumnus, who lived 1969 with me. I'd do it again.

— My far-out, crazy quilt of a family, the kind I dreamed of making in the sixties and that I got lucky enough to create, discover, fall into, and be surrounded by. You are all, to a person, the grooviest humans I know.

A BEGINNING BIBLIOGRAPHY

While there are scores of excellent resources documenting the late sixties, and I used more than I can handily list, here are some I turned to over and again while writing *Anthem*. I list them in part, too, because they are easily accessible to the reader and can serve as companions to the story, when read with an adult reader or teacher as your guide.

You'll find more resources on my Pinterest boards, at pinterest.com/debbiewiles/boards/, where I archived primary source material for years as I researched *Anthem*. The playlist of all songs in *Anthem* is included on Pinterest, too, and can also be found at my website, deborahwiles. com, on *Anthem*'s dedicated page.

WORKS CITED

American Experience, season 3, episodes 2–4, "Nixon," directed by David Espar. Boston: WBGH, 1990. DVD.

American Experience, season 4, episodes 1–2, "LBJ," directed by David Grubin. Boston: WBGH, 1991. DVD.

Anderson, Terry. *The Movement and The Sixties: Protest in America from Greenboro to Wounded Knee.* New York: Oxford University Press, 1996.

Bingham, Clara. *Witness to the Revolution: Radicals, Resisters, Vets, Hippies, and the Year America Lost Its Mind and Found Its Soul.* New York: Random House, 2016.

Blaine, Hal, and David Goggin. *Hal Blaine and the Wrecking Crew: The Story of the World's Most Recorded Musician*, 3rd ed. Alma, MI: Rebeats Press, 2003.

Bloom, Alexander, and Wini Breines. *Takin' It to the Streets: A Sixties Reader.* New York: Oxford University Press, 2010.

Brand, Stewart. "History — Some of What Happened Around Here for the Last Three Years." *Whole Earth Catalog*, June 1971.

Burns, Olive Ann. "A Church for Turned-On Types." *Atlanta Constitution Magazine*, June 1968.

Cianci, Bob. *Great Rock Drummers of The Sixties.*
Milwaukee: Hal Leonard, 2006.

Davis, David, dir., and Stephen Talbot, dir. *The Sixties: The
Years that Shaped a Generation.* PBS Paramount, 2005.

Edelman, Bernard, ed. *Dear America: Letters Home from
Vietnam.* New York: W.W. Norton & Company, 2002.

Francis, Miller. "The Allman Brothers Band." *The Great
Speckled Bird,* May 1969.

Gitlin, Todd. *The Sixties: Years of Hope, Days of Rage.*
New York: Bantam Books, 1993.

Goodman, Paul. *Growing Up Absurd: Problems of Youth
in the Organized Society.* New York: Random House,
1970.

Graham, Bill. *Bill Graham Presents: My Life Inside Rock
and Out.* Cambridge: Da Capo Press, 2004.

Guralnick, Peter. *Last Train to Memphis: The Rise of Elvis
Presley.* Boston: Little, Brown & Company, 1994.

Guralnick, Peter. *Careless Love: The Unmaking of Elvis
Presley.* Boston: Little, Brown & Company, 1999.

Hopper, Dennis, dir. *Easy Rider.* 1969. New York:
Criterion Collection DVD, 2016.

Kaiser, Charles. *1968 in America: Music, Politics, Chaos, Counterculture, and the Shaping of a Generation.* New York: Grove/Atlantic, 2018.

Keltz, Iris. *Scrapbook of a Taos Hippie.* El Paso, TX: Cinco Puntos Press, 2000.

Kesey, Ken. "The Great Bus Race." *Whole Earth Catalog,* May 1974.

Kirkpatrick, Rob. *1969: The Year Everything Changed.* New York: Skyhorse Publishing, 2009.

Kopecki, Arthur. *Leaving New Buffalo Commune.* Albuquerque: University of New Mexico Press, 2006.

Kopecky, Arthur. *New Buffalo: Journals from a Taos Commune.* Albuquerque: University of New Mexico Press, 2004.

Kurlansky, Mark. *1968: The Year that Rocked the World.* New York: Ballantine Books, 2004.

Law, Lisa, dir. *Flashing on the Sixties.* Flashback Productions, 2004. DVD.

Levy, David W. *The Debate over Vietnam.* Baltimore: Johns Hopkins University Press, 1995.

Makower, Joel. *Woodstock: The Oral History.* New York: Doubleday, 1989.

O'Brien, Tim. *The Things They Carried*. Boston: Houghton Mifflin, 1990.

Paul, Alan. *One Way Out: The Inside History of the Allman Brothers Band*. New York: St. Martin's Press, 2014.

Perlstein, Rick. *Nixonland: The Rise of a President and the Fracturing of America*. New York: Scribner, 2008.

Price, Roberta. *Across the Great Divide: A Photo Chronicle of the Counterculture*. Albuquerque: University of New Mexico Press, 2010.

Price, Roberta. *Huerfano: A Memoir of Life in the Counterculture*. Amherst: University of Massachusetts Press, 2006.

Roszak, Theodore. *The Making of a Counter Culture: Reflections on the Technocratic Society and Its Youthful Opposition*. Berkeley: University of California Press, 1995.

Esrick, Michelle, dir. *Saint Misbehavin': The Wavy Gravy Movie*. New York: Docurama, 2011. DVD.

Tick, Edward. *War and the Soul: Healing our Nation's Veterans from Post-Traumatic Stress Disorder*. Wheaton, IL: Quest Books, 2005.

von Hoffman, Nicholas. *We Are the People Our Parents Warned Us Against*. Greenwich, CT: Fawcett, 1969.

Wolfe, Tom. *The Electric Kool-Aid Acid Test*. New York: Farrar, Straus & Giroux, 1968.

WEBSITES

"1969" at The Allman Brothers Band, hosted by the Big House Museum, accessed 2018, https://www.thebighousemuseum.com/the-band/.

"A History of Griffith Observatory" at Griffith Observatory, hosted by Friends of Griffith Observatory, accessed 2019, http://www.griffithobservatory.org/about/griffithobservatory.html.

"Art Kopecky" about living in New Buffalo commune in the late sixties and early seventies with photographs and journal entries from that time, hosted by Art Kopecky, accessed 2019, http://www.arthurkopecky.com/.

"Garage Bands" in The Encyclopedia of Arkansas History & Culture, hosted by The Central Arkansas Library System, accessed 2018, http://www.encyclopediaofarkansas.net/encyclopedia/entry-detail.aspx?entryID=2591.

"Great Speckled Bird" at the Georgia State University Library, with all back issues of the underground newspaper *The Great Speckled Bird*, hosted by GSU Library digital collections, accessed 2018, http://digitalcollections.library.gsu.edu/cdm/landingpage/collection/GSB.

"In Bloom: Mary Beal's Mojave" at The Mohave Project, with photos and biography of Mary Beal, hosted by Kim Stringfellow, accessed 2018, http://mojaveproject.org/dispatches-item/in-bloom-mary-beals-mojave/.

"Lisa Law Flashing on the Sixties" about living in community in the sixties with photographs and articles, hosted by Lisa Law, accessed 2018, https://www.flashingonthesixties.com/.

"The Strip Project" about the hippie scene along Peachtree Street in Midtown Atlanta in the late sixties, with oral histories and primary source materials from that time, hosted by Patrick Edmonson, accessed 2018, http://www.thestripproject.com/.

"Whole Earth Catalog" back issues hosted by New Whole Earth LLC, accessed 2018, http://www.wholeearth.com/index.php.

PHOTOS CREDITS

Photos copyrighted ©

DUST JACKET

Jacket photos ©: background: Premyuda Yospim/iStockphoto

BOOK

Page 5: NASA; 6–7: Horst Faas/AP Images; 8–9 top: Horst Faas/AP Images; 8–9 bottom: Fred W. McDarrah/Getty Images; 10: Wally McNamee/Getty Images; 12–13: NASA; 15: Jim McMahon/Mapman ®; 16–17: Hulton Archive/Getty Images; 18–19: Paul Slade/Getty Images; 20 left: George Brich/AP Images; 20 right, 21: Hulton Archive/Getty Images; 22–23: Robert Altman/The Image Works; 24 top: Neal Boenzi/Getty Images; 24 bottom: Paul Slade/Getty Images; 25: Paul Slade/Getty Images; 26–27: Rolls Press/Getty Images; 29: Art Greenspon/AP Images; 30–31 top: Dang Van Phuoc/AP Images; 30–31 bottom: Art Greenspon/AP Images; 32: LBJ Library photo by Jack Kightlinger; 33 top, 33 bottom, 34–35, 36–37: Bettmann/Getty Images; 39: Charles H. Phillips/Getty Images; 40: Lee Balterman/Getty Images; 41: APA/Getty Images; 42, 43 left: Hulton Archive/Getty Images; 43 right: Bettmann/Getty Images; 44–45: David Fenton/Getty Images; 46–47: Hugh Van Es/AP Images; 49: Jack Sheahan/Getty Images; 50–51: Bernie Boston/Getty Images; 53: Ted Streshinsky/Getty Images;

Page 146: House Of Fame LLC/Getty Images; 148: Keystone/Getty Images; 150 left, 150 right, 151: Lisa Law; 153: John Brandi; 154–155: Steve Schapiro/Getty Images;

Page 290–291: VA061418, George H. Kelling Collection, The Vietnam Center and Archive, Texas Tech University; 292: John Olson/Getty Images; 293: PhotoQuest/Getty Images; 294 top and bottom: Horst Faas/AP Images; 295: Henri Huet/AP Images; 296: USC Libraries, California Historical Society Collection; 297: GAB Archive/Getty Images; 298: Michael Ochs Archives/Getty Images; 299: Robert Altman/Getty Images;

Page 348–349: NASA; 350: PHCS K. Shrader/U.S. Navy; 351 top: National Archives and Records Administration; 351 bottom: U.S. Navy; 352-353: Horst Faas/AP Images; 355: Lonnie Wilson/Bay Area News Group Archive. Used with permission of Mercury News Copyright © 2019. All rights reserved.; 356–357: Associated Press/AP Images; 358–359: Robert A. Nakamura/Visual Communications Photographic Archive;

ABOUT THE AUTHOR

DEBORAH WILES was born in Alabama, grew up around the world in a military family, and spent her summers in a small Mississippi town. Her books include the picture book *Freedom Summer*, and the novels *Love, Ruby Lavender*; *The Aurora County All-Stars*; *Each Little Bird that Sings*, a National Book Award finalist; and *A Long Line of Cakes*. The first book in The Sixties Trilogy, *Countdown*, received five starred reviews upon its publication and has appeared on many state award lists. The second, *Revolution*, was a National Book Award finalist.

Deborah lives in Atlanta, Georgia. You can visit her on the web at deborahwiles.com.

This book was edited by David Levithan and designed by Phil Falco. Its documentary features were coordinated by Maya Marlette and Els Rijper. The text was set in Futura, a typeface designed by Paul Renner between 1924 and 1926. The display type was set in FF Identification 04S, designed by Rian Hughes in 1993. The book was typeset at Jouve North America and printed and bound at LSC Communications in Crawfordsville, Indiana. The production was supervised by Melissa Schirmer. The manufacturing was supervised by Angelique Browne.